DYLAN BYFORD wa... ᴵ
Northumberland. He h...
now lives in the foot of t ..... ιαιιιιy.
A prolific playwright in his early writing career, Dylan has since turned to science fiction. *Calderdale* is his second cyberpunk novel, part of the Cyberdales series of crime thrillers set in a near-future northern England, riven with corruption, social unrest and urban decay.

Follow Dylan on X/Twitter @dylan_byford

CALDERDALE

DYLAN BYFORD

Northodox Press Ltd
Maiden Greve, Malton,
North Yorkshire, YO17 7BE

This edition 2024

1
First published in Great Britain by
Northodox Press Ltd 2024

ISBN: 978-1-915179-23-4

This book is set in Caslon Pro Std

To my family

CHAPTER ONE

I'd just finished stitching on the left eye of the latest face for my project and was admiring my thread selection of cornflower blue and ash grey, when the call came through from Mr Shin, telling me somebody was trying to murder him. At least, Mr Shin was the alias he used. His indistinct voice sounded a little metallic, as if rerouted through anonymous relays a few too many times. By that time in the evening, I'd already downed a few too many ethanolies and my memory had become altogether muddled.

'What?'

'There are people coming here tonight…to the facility. Well, you know… I believe they're here to murder me.'

I sighed. Why'd I have to handle this kind of shit? This wasn't my area. I was Justice. We didn't do rapid response. Didn't do rapid much. 'Is this an emergency, sir?'

'Yes. Yes. It is urgent.'

'Why've you come through to me?' I yawned, picking up the right eye from the pile. 'Algorithms should've taken this, right?'

'I called for a human handler.'

The accent was difficult to place, somewhere South Asian, possibly south-east Asian. This guy was clearly old-school, as he didn't have visuals. Then again, an anonymous relay would shred that shit.

'Then you need an Enforcement handler.'

'Are you not Enforcement?' He was almost shrieking.

'No, I'm Justice.'

There was a pause. 'You'll do.'

'Really?' I said, stabbing myself in the finger with the needle. 'Better wait for Enforcement, I'd say.'

'They'll be too late.'

I sighed. 'You want to tell me where you are? I'll see if I can get somebody.'

'Yes, yes… do you have your screen ready?'

'Course.' I was already twirling my bleeding finger in the air to bring up the Enforcement codes for the area where he was calling. Fellside Recycling Auxiliary Facility, placed somewhere called Withens, bang in the Buckle of the Great Northern Belt. It was yawningly familiar; my sister lived near there. When we'd cleared out her house, we'd taken some of her shit to the recycling site. At least, whatever I'd not nabbed for myself.

'You're at the recycling site?' I said. 'Up around the Buckle?'

'Fourth Sector,' he said. 'You see me?'

'You sound like you're running through an anonymised relay. Care to explain? Seem pretty happy to give out your location, though–'

'Yes, yes,' he snapped. 'I'm trying to avoid them listening… it doesn't matter. Just find me help, OK?'

'Listen, sorry, Mr Shin,' I repeated, blinking hard. 'This isn't my fucking job, you know? I'm a forensic analyst. Carrie Tarmell. I work in the Airedale Justice Division. I'm not your sector's Enforcement handler. Not sure why some comedian decided to–'

'I just need somebody from the police,' Shin interrupted. 'Listen Ms Tarmell–' He must've dropped the device because all I heard was a crack and the sound of distant whirring, like old servos being put through the mill. There followed a high-pitched whine and chuntering before the line cut out.

I recognised the sound. I'd heard it enough in my job. The sound of a circular saw hitting meat.

The head-up display flickered across my retina from my nose bead, the Fourth Sector Enforcement teams flashing up like little sweeties. I punched the crew closest to the recycling facility, left them a terse message, and took a deep breath. After a moment, the response arrived. They were being diverted to deal with another luxury tower invasion in Aitch Bee, but would hopefully stop by the unit on their return.

The line of ethanolies mocked me in their sad, crumpled cardboard containers from their perch on the arm of the sofa. Or were they crying for me? For Mr Shin? Their synthetic sweetness begged me to wash out my mouth. Either that or the burn of the renatured fuel distillate I'd injected into them before dropping them into my freezer. I stood, a little woozy, and stepped into the flat's kitchen, bypassing the gradually emptying bags and boxes from my shopping trip three days prior. A glass of cold water helped quell the sick feeling. But I kept playing the conversation around in my head. Trying to work out some way, any way, where I'd not come across as a complete piece of shit.

Though I'd whinged that I was Airedale and Fourth Sector wasn't my patch, the call coming through hadn't been a surprise to me. Airedale shared comms with Fourth Sector Commission now. One neighbour helping another. Around three weeks ago, a good seventy percent of their Justice team, from the commissioning Servant, down through the Chief Inspector and their DIs, were placed on mandatory leave. Their comms frozen with strict instructions not to contact anyone outside their division. All coinciding with a national investigation across their patch; fraud or corruption or something was all I'd been told. Disappointingly, I'd never got the juicy details, because I liked an old-fashioned case of insider dealing. Made me feel like I worked with proper wrong 'uns, folk who knew what they were doing; unless it left you with too much work.

In the end, I took myself to bed, the cocktails having their desired effect on my system, too tired to worry about this crap.

Next day, I had to unpick the full row of stitching of my drunken handicraft. I'd forgotten about the call as I returned to work, chalking it up to the usual list of nutters or loners seeking human contact and sharing their insane stories with somebody, anybody. Anyway, it was Enforcement's problem now. Justice analysts like me weren't there to stop people hurting each other, like Prevention. And we definitely weren't there to do Reconciliation's job, to make the reformed proper honest members of society again, rather than the lifelong wrong 'uns we knew they'd always be. No, Justice was just there to gather facts and to spin up a narrative coherent enough to get our conviction.

I had hoped the weird late-night call would disappear from my life completely and I could get back to putting mid to low-level offenders in prison. At least, until after the weekend. But it was four days later when Louie Daine called out of the blue.

'Hiya, boss.'

'Carrie,' he said, eyes redder than usual. I spotted this kind of crap, liked to think it was my keen forensic analyst eyes. My sister would've told me it was because I was a girl. But she only said this kind of thing to get me and mum into a fight.

'How're you, Louie?' I asked, because it was the right thing to do at this moment and I didn't feel like making his morning easy.

'Sending you to the Buckle today. Fourth Sector, you know? Fax Central, H Tower, down there somewhere.'

Louie Daine had made DI. Proper speedy promotion, but unsurprising, after Winters got caught doing the thing. When you were caught doing the thing, they acted fast, and nobody talked about it. So Louie wandered into work one morning as a digital analyst subcontractor, musing about whether he'd get work next week, and left a fully employed, permanent member of the Airedale Justice Commission. His startled face peering out from our message boards with the affectionate grip of our Chief Inspector, Ibrahim Al-Yahmeni, on his shoulder, making sure he didn't bolt.

'You know they're different places, right?'

'What?'

He was still getting used to covering the Buckle and Airedale. I had to help him out a little. He liked it when I corrected him.

'Fax Central and H Tower are in different places, Louie.'

'All in the Belt, though, right?'

I sighed. 'Why there?'

'They've asked for you specifically, that's why.'

'But I've got the Kai Reed case. And there's the old domestic up Saltaire, that file Ibrahim wanted us to…'

'I know that. It can wait. But this can't.'

'What's the urgency?'

'Possible murder.'

'Possible.'

'They need forensics down there. And apparently, one of their analysts asked for you directly. Community analyst. Reconciliation, I'm guessing.'

'Ah, shit.'

'Said you'd taken an escalated call.'

I felt sick. 'Yeah?'

'Yeah. Somebody called Mr Shin.'

CHAPTER TWO

An hour later, I was in a Fourth Sector autocar, working my way through the heaving urban sprawl of the Buckle. The car they'd sent less spruce than the pool cars we had up in Airedale. Though this was like saying an IED is less spruce than a Molotov. Still, at least in one of our cars, I could breathe without worrying about what viral load I was accumulating. When you're a forensic analyst, you have an intuition of what's covering any nearby surface. I'd swept cars like this in the past, memories of little pie charts showing percentages of blood, shit and semen smeared over dashboards and seat belts. I was sweating, despite the frosty February morning, and I had a window down the entire way to air out the piece of crap. And I wasn't touching that seatbelt. At least, not without latex protection.

The car took me directly to the community analyst's residence. Deborah Goolagong-Maloney. It traversed one of the stacked ring roads circling the hollow bowl of Fax Central, propped precariously on struts poking out into nothing. I was normally unfazed by heights, but this stretch of the journey always made me retch. I concentrated on breathing deeply. Eyes averted from the billowing steam rising from the Centre, I focused on the horizon, to the phalanx of matching towers marching away to the south-west and across toward Huddersfield. The H district.

Deborah wasn't waiting for me in the little subterranean parking zone, so I patched up to her flat. A flustered face appeared on my bead display, thick curly hair taking up most of the screen's real estate, but beneath this I could make out crusty eyes and a beaming smile.

'Hey, partner!'

'Deborah?' I asked, before cough-swallowing tricky phlegm. 'Sorry.'

'You must be Carrie, yeah? Carrie Tarmell? My new partner?'

'That's right,' I muttered. 'You need ten minutes to get ready?' I checked my watch. I was on time. Maybe a bit late.

'Oh, no, no,' she said. 'I'm ready. Ready as I'll ever be, ha! Be right down.'

I nodded and grunted then cut the call. If she wanted to leave her flat looking like that, it was her prerogative. Nothing to do with me.

To pass the time, I counted the cars coming in and going out of the underpass. Some were picking up people going off to work, bead light flickering data across their eyeballs, or bringing back young 'uns from night clubs and bars, their lurid outfits shimmering with ever-changing patterns, flowing from feathers to scales to galaxies and waves. This was a nice location to get out to a party. If you caught the fast train, you could be in the middle of York or Liverpool within half an hour. Not that I'd ever been to a nightclub in either district. I'd rather cut my eyelids off with a sharp piece of vintage A4.

The passenger door opened and a force of ylang ylang burst into my personal space with the aggressiveness of a wolverine. I turned to nod, but a hand shot out of the bundle of coat, scarf, and hat and grabbed me tightly.

'Call me Debso, yeah?'

'Debso,' I said. 'Right.' She spoke with an accent that I would have called Australian. But then that wasn't always the right thing to say, not these days, and I'd come off badly a few months ago with somebody I was chatting to online. I slid down in my seat and tried to keep my mouth shut.

'We going to the Dump then?' Deborah said, wriggling herself into her seat with a certain satisfaction.

'What?' I said.

'The Dump. Up Withens way. It's where the Fellside Facility is?'

'Yeah, that's right.'

'Let's go then!'

I tapped the dash, and the car set off. Deborah pulled on her seat belt, unnerving me a little. She saw my glance and nodded as she clipped in the double straps.

'I'd recommend it, Carrie,' she said meaningfully. 'These cars are proper rubbish. Enforcement keeps the best ones, obviously. Justice get... well, this.' She stroked the dashboard in front of her. Without her glove. That was about fifteen percent semen right there.

I swallowed a little retch.

Deborah didn't notice, looking out the window, a little sadly. 'Last week, one crashed. Killed one of our apprentices. He was only sixteen.'

We climbed the ramp from the loading area to join the now busy main east-west conduit. I begrudgingly, decided to use the seatbelt, grabbing the shoulder strap and clipping them in the middle. The pressure against my stomach only made things worse. The ylang ylang mixed with the tang of hot metal, busy motors, and the general organic major city pong didn't help either. I calmed my breathing, determined not to throw up with a member of another force in the car.

We travelled around Fax Central in silence, avoiding most commuter traffic, and started the climb out of the city.

I'd worked with Airedale's community analyst once or twice before – *the commie*, as they called him. Gerry was a hard thinker, with a habit of sucking and blowing air through the gap in his incisors before delivering an answer to any question. Even when processing mundane information like a choice between tea or coffee. But he always seemed to have the right answers. Our old DI, Ibrahim Al-Yahmeni, had tried to explain it all to me once, as part of a team-building workshop. *The commie* had the inside track to Airedale's subcultures down to the cellular social dynamic. Or some such shit. Reconciliation had never made much sense to me.

'You have a lot of work up at the Dump?' I asked.

'Up Withens? Oh, yeah, this is my commute most days. Though it's not the municipal units I spend time on. They look after themselves. No, further on up, there're a couple of camps spread around the old reservoir there. Camps full of very interesting groups... I guess you might call them gangs, but we prefer to call them *communities*.' I noticed how she enunciated and held the emphasis on when pronouncing 'communities'. It made me want to grind my teeth. 'Up on the Pikeside and on Withens Hill itself.' She continued. 'A number of very interesting, unique people. You heard of DaveDaveDave?'

'ThreeDave?' Every analyst knew the name. King wrong 'un was ThreeDave. 'He's up there, is he?'

'He prefers to be called DaveDaveDave,' Deborah said solemnly.

'Bet he does. Bet he makes 'em say it, and all, at the end of a big stick.'

'He loves his people: the BoTies, that is.'

I had nothing to say to that, so fell silent, imagining the scene, before realising what reservoir she was talking about. 'Shit! That's the Withens Reservoir? The poisoned-as-fuck one?'

'That's the one,' said Deborah. 'I try not to get too close, of course.'

Internationals had been called in on that one, about ten years ago. The contaminant had killed nearly ten percent of the South Leeds Sprawl before anybody realised what was going on. Toxic spore breeders had been using the reservoir on the sly, but also the really stupid ones had been dumping in it as well. Given the whole area a bad name.

Deborah reached down to her bag and produced a squat plastic flask. She unscrewed the top. 'I've not had my breakfast yet. Do you mind if I eat in the car? It's only porridge... I mean, it's a little more than that. It's got a bit of honey and some berries and...'

I turned to her and grimaced, rubbing my stomach.

'Of course,' she said, hastily, dropping the flask back into her bag. 'I'll have it later.'

'Thanks,' I said. There was an awkward silence, so I threw in a question I'd been meaning to ask her from the start. 'So, what's up with the rest of your Justice Division?'

Deborah wrinkled her nose. 'Not sure I want to talk about it. Probably some legal gagging clause or something.'

'No bother.' I shrugged.

'Still, I suppose you need to know.'

I shrugged. 'Yeah. Why not?'

'Fraud. Dirty, yeah... the lot of them. Can't believe I worked alongside the buggers. Dal Thomas, Rupe Reader, Carmel Rindi – she would've been your DI – all their own crews as well. Support staff. Back office. The lot. They were our DI and his analytical team. Working for the enemy. Good job Louie is still around to help us out. Do you know Louie Daine? Of course you do. He's your DI now, isn't he? Took over from that Al-Yahmeni fella. Good for Louie. I love him.'

'Everybody loves Louie,' I said.

'What I wouldn't do to him,' said Deborah, nodding to herself, 'if he'd let me. Which he wouldn't, of course? Am I right?'

My stomach did a little lurch. I gripped the door. 'Not for me, Debs, no.'

'Call me Debso.'

'Right.'

'Still, he's a lifesaver for the division down here, helping us out.'

'That's right.'

Deborah looked out of the passenger window, at a cyclist grimly elbowing his way through the autocars' anti-collision algorithms. 'Enforcement left you the same message, I'm guessing.'

'I guess,' I said, a little warily. I was still replaying Mr Shin's conversation in my head. 'Well, no, not really. Not after the first call. What did they tell you?'

'Said they'd had an emergency call put in during the night.

Somebody in distress up at the facility. They dropped by and found it empty.'

'Empty?'

'Yeah, that's weird, isn't it?'

'Recycling never sleeps.'

'That's the motto.'

'Shit.'

'But, seemed it'd been on that night.' She nodded to herself and looked across at me. 'What did he say?'

'Hmm?'

'Mr Shin? When he called you?'

'Mr Shin?'

'Yeah, what did this Mr Shin have to say?'

'Eh?'

'When you got the call?' said Deborah, slowly. 'What did he say?'

I shrugged. 'Just that somebody was trying to murder him.'

'Oh,' Deborah paused for a moment, scratching her chin. 'You said that as if it wasn't an issue.'

'Normally isn't.'

'You didn't think that was suspicious?'

I snorted. 'I worked in forensics. It's pretty standard. Thankfully, Prevention deal with most of that shit before it gets to Justice.'

She turned around to me and gave an appraising look. 'You worked up at Airedale long?'

'Since I started work, yeah.'

'How old are you?'

'Old enough,' I said. I hoped I'd said it forcefully enough to get her to shut up.

It didn't work.

'I'd say you were about thirty. Am I right?'

'Bout that,' I muttered.

'Long time looking at bodies.' She wasn't looking at me directly. But it felt like she was staring into my fucking soul.

'Yeah,' I muttered again. I flicked my fingers in front of my face. 'Going to check on some messages, OK?'

'Sure.' Deborah dug into her bag – an incongruous camo-pouch – and pulled out a battered old slab.

'What's that?' I muttered, grinning. 'You a collector?'

'This?' said Deborah. 'No, I can't do the beads, mate. Messes with my vision. I have to do it the old way.'

Wondered how she could watch proper porn on that thing.

'Sorry to hear that,' I said. 'Still, at least you can strike up a friendly conversation with your digital analyst.'

She shook her head and wrinkled her nose. 'Not really. Have you met Lemmy? He's not really… well, it's just that he and I don't share much. Language, you know? You know how the digitals are?'

'No,' I said, a little defensively. Airedale's resident digital analyst had just recently taken a career break from the team. Long earned, in my opinion. But I was missing him.

CHAPTER THREE

The car climbed the sprawling low-rise districts of High Sowerby and entered a different landscape. As the Great Northern Belt had grown over the decades, connecting up conurbations from east and west, they'd met here, in the Pennine ridge, in the high moors and the steep, river-cut slopes. Instead of building into the ravines, they'd simply dropped piles and girders and built across the gaps, leaving the old houses, and the odd railway conduit or road beneath. Sometimes you could see down into the past. We called these the Valleys. But we didn't go there.

We neared the top of the moor and entered acres of faux-stone printed houses assembled in their millions and cemented onto plastic breeze blocks with algae adhesive. The stuff stank, especially in warm weather. But everybody had to have their own little fortress, with their little private garden, and just enough space for an overgrown shrub to kill everything else around it. The rooms in my cramped flat were bigger than most of these houses with more life in a square of carpet. I guess, if you couldn't afford the cliff-wrought villas of Aitch Bee or the red stone mansions of the old town, this was the place to live but I wouldn't be caught dead pissing in a place like this, let alone fucking and bringing up children.

She lived here n'all, but thankfully, the car wasn't going anywhere near. I'd been avoiding the visit, cringeworthy peace-making, hugs, and pretending we cared about her shitty little job talking to computers and her shitty little place and her shitty little dreams of a better life somewhere out of here.

Thankfully, as we passed her flat, there were no faces at the window. Just a neat little pattern of handmade stars slung in a row.

We continued on, through the endless housing estates of High Sowerby, until we came to the rising walls of optimistically zoned industrial park. The park surrounded the hill in concentric circles of old-fashioned corrugated iron and modern bamboo composite, looking like the inside of an unwashed bath. I'd seen the hill and park from afar, but had never ventured beyond. The town planners had commissioned a scenic strip of woodland between, but it was never built. Sold to private parties, with a hefty bribe, no doubt. It must've properly pissed off the residents who'd sunk their credit into a little toy town terrace next door to a factory that farted out vat-grown animal protein. Bet it properly shafted their insurance, and all.

The place was a jumbled heap of unwanted refuse from an era when the world loved making unwanted shit. Only to make money by taking it all apart again.

'Your patch runs all the way up here?' I asked.

'That's right,' Deborah said, face inches from her screen.

'Not much of a community to analyse.'

Deborah looked up, squinting to focus on the surroundings. 'Oh, you'd be surprised where people live, you know. Over there, I know a family that's making a home out of an old attack chopper.'

'Attack chopper,' I sniggered.

'Yeah, a proper old helicopter. They used to bring them in for scrap from the coast. Hull or somewhere like that, right up here, for decommissioning. Whole place used to work in decommissioning old tech. The family name's Carpenter, I think. Made a lovely house, they have. Grow pot plants on the tail fins.'

I grunted.

'You can't see it,' said Deborah, as if reading my mind, 'but it's up there.'

'Whatever,' I said. 'Explains why they called it the Dump.'

We both fell silent for a while and Deborah turned back to her tablet. I half shut my eyes and continued to watch the passing debris.

'So, what's your latest case? You working on any murders?'

I looked at her in silence for a moment. 'I'm forensics.'

'Yeah,' muttered Deborah, embarrassed, 'of course, you are. So, anything exciting?'

At that moment, I was dealing with a domestic stabbing in Saltaire. The suspect's fingerprints were on the knife and neighbours confirmed it was him. He'd confessed. Case closed. I'd also finishing wrapping a double murder up in Keighley, where a young courier – Kai Reed – had strayed into somebody else's business, and had been ambushed by their foot soldiers, only for them to be jumped by the courier's gang in turn, resulting in a shoot-out along the railway. Five witnesses, corroborating evidence, trajectories and exit wounds aligned. Case closed as well. Except that they'd run off with bits of the fucking corpse, the little beggars. Not only that, turned out the gang hadn't been too keen my working on it, on having put their leaders in prison. And had discovered my address. Thankfully, the DI had pulled a few strings and ordered a security drone for protection.

'Search Kai Reed,' I said. 'That one made the news.'

Deborah made an excited cooing noise and tap-tapped away at her tablet. After a few minutes she made another noise, this time not so eager.

'That's the Anima, right? You put away their leadership?'

'The Anima?' I said.

'The name of gang up there,' she said. 'Also known as the–'

'– the Beasties,' I interrupted. 'Or the Little Beasties, to their rivals. And, yeah, I put away their leaders, whatever they call them.'

'Oh,' Deborah gasped.

'That a bad thing?' I snapped.

'When a gang loses its head,' Deborah said, very serious, 'then it becomes chaotic. Very dangerous time. They need a leader. Have they been behaving erratically recently?'

I took a deep breath about to launch into a long tirade but let this one go, instead. 'No, not so much.'

'Oh,' Deborah grunted. 'Surprising.'

'We are now arriving at your destination,' the car announced. We were making our way along an old high street, trying to gentrify the place with vintage shops, bookstores, and retro bakeries. The car slowed and pulled in through a pair of ornate automatic gates. I half-expected them to be built from recycled car parts and scrap machinery but they were standard reinforced alloy.

We were met by a young woman with deep black eyes and a solemn expression in the small car park beyond the gates. She was wrapped in a bulbous blue balaclava and a jumpsuit which must've once been lime green but now looked like an abstract painting.

She waved uncertainly and sidled over to the car as we climbed out. 'Hiya,' she greeted us.

'Hiya,' I said with a nod and contemplated whether I needed my additional biohazard kit. Probably be all right. 'And you are?'

'Katta. Katta Jenkins. Second journeyman on the site. Si, I mean, Simon West, is also here somewhere. Back there.'

'Carrie Tarmell, forensics,' I said, pulling on my duffel a little tighter and hoisting the hood over my bobble hat. I turned expectantly to Deborah, but she'd already wandered over to a stack of containers and was peering in the door.

'That's Deborah Goolagong-Maloney, the community analyst.'

'Uh huh,' Katta said, eyes following Deborah's progress as she walked from one container to the next. 'What's a community analyst do?'

'Fucked if I know… hey, Debs, what're you looking for?'

She paused her search and turned, a little guilty. 'Just having a look around… that's what we're doing here, isn't it?'

Resisting the urge to tell her, 'Yeah, that's all I do', I instead cleared my throat with what I hoped was some authority. 'Plenty of time for that,' I said, waving her back to me.

'If you're looking for Mr Shin,' said Katta, 'I've already done a thorough search. Can't find any… well, I can't find him anywhere.' She swallowed.

'OK. Can you take us on a little tour? Just to let you know–' I clicked my fingers up near my nose bead 'I'm now recording this conversation under the IG protocols of East Pennine–'

'Belt, Fourth Sector,' interrupted Deborah, close to my ear, trying to whisper.

'Oh, yeah, under Fourth Sector protocols – they're pretty much the same – so you have a right to say no and fuck off and that kind of thing.'

'No,' said Katta, 'I'm good. Just want to help find the old man.'

'Yeah. Then let's start. You take us around the site and tell us a little about Mr Shin and what he did here.'

'Then you'll find him?' she asked.

'Yeah,' I said, sadly, 'then I'll find him.'

'OK, follow me,' she said and set off deeper into the facility. The recycling yard was a warren of paths through a mountain of stacked containers, some rusting and others brand new. Most container doors were open, and inside heaps of electronic circuitry or bottle caps or shreds of textiles or tyres or neat stacks of chemical batteries spilled out. In and among the containers, larger heaps of industrial items sat. Beyond, they sorted vast pale mountains of translucent polymers into their component categories. Above it all, we could hear the hum of loaders bumping around the mounds, their LEDs flashing brightly in the pale morning light.

As we walked, Katta kept up a little monologue about her boss.

'Mr Shin was a master. A formally trained master recycler. You don't get many of them. He knew everything there was to know about PCP, T-PEX, IRTX, the lot. He'd learned what made up nearly anything – that flask she's drinking from, that's composed of four different polymers, some of which can't recycle.'

I turned around to catch Deborah mid-chew of her porridge. She swallowed and avoided eye contact.

'What was he like as a person?'

'Quiet, never told us about his past. We didn't even know where he lived. Si thinks he actually slept here, in the facility somewhere.'

'How would you reach him?'

'He had a bead. We just called him on that.'

'There's no answer on his bead, I'm guessing?'

Katta nodded. 'Nothing.'

'I'm thinking he wasn't the kind of fella to turn up late, was he?'

'Always here before us and always last to leave. Even worked the weekends. Sometimes had trips across the country on recycling business. But never took a holiday.'

'Recycling business?' I asked.

She shrugged. 'I guess. He didn't tell us much about it.'

'Can you remember the last time he made one of these?'

She shook her head. 'Possibly a month ago.'

'See if you can remember,' I said.

We reached the middle of the facility. Here there were a variety of vehicles parked and some trundling automated loaders with their crane arms hanging limply by their sides. There was something about the place that set my nerves on edge. Couldn't decide what it was. So I thought I'd blame the bots. We'd been to a factory massacre a few months ago, south of the Ilkley Moor Reservation. Bots hadn't been properly patched and someone or something had got into their controls. It was a real mess.

'These got updated software?' I asked, nervously.

'What?' said Katta. 'The bots. Yeah, they're all updated. We only get a virus about once a month. Though we had one about a week ago, I think. Si's pretty good at looking after them and patching them up. Ah, there he is.'

A young man, barely a teenager, scurried across the yard. He was about a foot taller than me but held himself in a crouched position, as though he'd spent a lifetime being told he was too large.

'Si West,' he said, waving. He was wearing filthy looking gloves over tattered overalls. The smell of rot came off him. I could hear Deborah quietly screwing the lid back on her flask of her porridge behind me.

'Are you the other journeyman?'

'Yes, that's me,' he said.

He was a sombre man, very matter of fact. I thought I'd get some good data from him. I let him know the IG situation and then cast my eyes around the yard.

'Katta says you think Mr Shin slept here. You want to show me where?'

'OK,' said Si, turning on his heel and walked over to a low building, about to duck inside.

'Wait,' I said. 'Anybody else been in today?'

'Sure,' he said. 'That's the office. I was in there this morning, looking for him.'

I poked my head in the door and sniffed. 'Yeah.'

Deborah was looking in over my shoulder. 'What you found? Blood?'

I stepped back and looked at her. 'No. There's no blood Debs, it's an office.'

There was a table and three chairs, all recycled, in their own way.

'Should we not go in?' asked Katta, whispering now.

'Don't know if it's a crime scene or not,' I said. It was weird to feel like the only one who knew what they were talking about. I was quite enjoying it. Until I remembered this was probably the cabin from where a terrified man had possibly made his last call. 'Once we can establish a formal crime scene, I'll call RapidRez, and they come in to secure the place. There're acres of legals to work out, and I'll do some proper work.'

'How do we know if it's a crime scene or not?' asked Katta.

'Gotta find a crime,' I said. 'How about a body?'

Si slowly shook his head. 'I've looked. Searched the whole yard. So has Katta, haven't you? Nothing picked up on the autoloader sensors, either.'

'This lot?' I said, nodding to the bots behind us.

'That's right,' said Si. 'They cover the whole site.'

'I'll need access to their logs. You have any cameras?'

He shook his head. 'Not working. We had a rig set up all over the yard, and via the drones, but we got a virus about a week ago. Knocked the whole site out.'

'You've not had security for a week?' I made a face. Then turned to Deborah, nodding in the direction of the reservoir. 'What about that lot, the gang, from over the hill?'

'The community,' murmured Deborah.

'We've not had much trouble from them,' said Katta, a little too quickly.

'Sure,' I said, turning to Si. 'But you're seriously telling me you've not got round to fixing your security rig for a week?'

'Sorry,' he said. 'I kept meaning to, you know, and now… we're going to find Mr Shin, aren't we? That's what you can do, isn't it?'

'Enforcement told you about the message, did they?' asked Deborah, before I could shush her.

Katta shook her head. 'We just came and opened up. Then saw the message on our beads. They'd dropped a location beacon by the gate. Something about an emergency call. They wanted us to report in with any news…' She blinked and fell silent.

'So, you waited two full working days before you made the call?'

Katta's eyes were welling up while Si stared closely at his boots.

'We thought he'd gone on one of his trips,' Katta replied. 'He hates to be a bother, does Mr Shin. He would hate to think we called in something urgent if it was just a trip.'

'He could still be on one of his trips, yes?'

I shrugged. 'Could be. Doesn't feel like it though. I'm here because there is a suspicion of murder.'

The two journeymen stared at me, frozen.

'You didn't know?' asked Deborah.

Si shook his head. Katta turned away, face crumpling. Deborah put an arm on her shoulder and walked her away a short way, and then returned to Si and gave him a squeeze on the arm.

When she came back, she was also in tears. 'They're… they're quite upset.'

I shrugged. 'Yeah?'

'Yes,' said Deborah. 'Nobody properly communicates anymore, do they?' She stared at my motionless face before blowing her nose on a handkerchief. 'Still, not much we can do, can we?'

'Let's get this done and fuck off out of here,' I said. 'Time to find a body… if there is one.'

'They just said they couldn't find anything,' said Deborah. 'How do you know there's one here?'

I sniffed deeply. A dull familiarity, doubtless connected to the source of my rattled nerves.

'There's definitely a body. I've a… fuck it, I just know, OK?'

'You got some tools, yeah?' asked Deborah. 'I've read about the gecko. And somebody told me you guys get something called a sniffer. You got a sniffer?'

I patted my top pocket. 'Yeah, handheld. Doesn't work though.'

'Oh,' she said, a little disappointed. 'What's a sniffer, exactly?'

'Picks up odour trails,' I said, reaching into the pocket. 'This one's handheld. You sweep it over shit and it tells you… well, it tells you it's shit.'

'Right.'

'Got another micro-drone that flies,' I said. 'Does the same, but with lower accuracy. It hovers about and picks up odour trails. Not as good as a dog. But it's getting there.'

The two workers had wiped their tears and came back over to stand near us.

'You think we need a dog here to sniff out Mr Shin?' asked Deborah, eyes wide. 'Heard about that from a force in Finland.'

I shook my head. 'I don't have a dog, no.'

'But you're going to do forensics, right?' asked Si. 'Something to help find Mr Shin?'

'I just need to do what I've done before. Been in this kind of situation a few times.' I tapped my nose. 'This is always a good place to start.'

'Secrets?' asked Katta.

'My nose,' I snarled.

'Oh.'

'You got an incinerator here?' I said, inhaling deeply. 'Smells like you've got one. Where is it?'

Katta and Si both, wordlessly, pointed across the yard to a small alley between a container and stack of old domestic units. Just beyond the container I could see a little wisp of something like smoke, coming from a squat black cube of metal.

'You use that much?' I asked.

'Hardly ever,' said Katta, squinting now.

'Been on recently, I'd say.'

'Yeah.'

We all trooped along the alley and around the corner, clustering around the front of the machine. It had a short chute attached to the front and, at the base of this, an opening into the bowels, protected by a partially closed hatch. I took a picture with the gecko and, protecting my hands with a bit of duffel coat, slid back the hatch. Inside was the still smoking heap of green waste and polymer crates, with something else beyond it, out of sight, concealed in the darkness.

I grabbed a metal pole, leaned up against a nearby wall, and rummaged around the ashes and half-charred muck towards the back of the chamber. After a few minutes of scraping and poking, I managed to pull aside a long branch of some unidentified tree. There, in the corner, was an unmistakable shape: a half-charred torso. All the skin was blackened and contracted back down onto the bones, some of which stuck through. It was clear that the head and all four limbs had been removed.

'*Bingo*,' I said. But I didn't mean it.

CHAPTER FOUR

The majority of the cases I'd worked since contracting with Airedale Justice weren't mysteries. Nobody pissed off enough to club someone to death with a vintage redbrick has the inclination for planning and scrubbing their tracks or setting up solid alibis. They were mainly run-of-the-mill cretins, low-status gang members told to push a rival lieutenant under an autobus, or shoot them in the face on the doorstep in the middle of the night. If you ask neighbours or family members to point fingers, they'll let you know immediately, sometimes provide a bit of primary digital evidence, plenty of circumstantial supplementary evidence, and some of it will even match up. The street cameras will have picked them out in an ill-fitting hat or an oversized hood but identifiable in court by their distinctive gait. All that was needed then was to build a case, spin a sensible narrative over the top, and deliver to the prosecution lawyers with a big fucking bow attached. We had tools which automated the shit out of that part, then my job was, pretty much, to press '*GO*' on my bead's app.

It was also supposedly my job to wrangle the gecko and sweep the sniffer around the place, maybe set off a few crawlers to get the mess off the floor. Then I would fire up an analytical service like Bladester or DidNotArrive to do the forensics stuff as per my contract. The DI was there to do the actual casework, consider the options, interview the suspects, create a virtual wall of wrong 'uns, and play a dark game of connect-the-dots. But a DI's time was tight; they're busy people. They had politics to play, personalities to soothe, coffees to buy, and backs to rub. Which didn't leave time for the real detective work. Plus, the tools made things so much easier. Besides, the crimes we dealt with up in Airedale or down here in the Belt, were so clear-cut and the tools so accurate, that we could rubber-stamp a fat bundle of cases and still get convictions. Our productivity stats, when compared to the previous decade, were through the frigging roof. So, the dead and the bodies rolled through my tools, and came out the other end in the language of an internationally recognised C-File standard. Day after day, week after week, month after month, year after year. And I just got my head down, worked the clock, punched in PO after PO and diligently submitted my invoices every Friday. There were no mysteries. We all knew who'd done it. And if we didn't get a conviction, we could always ask Enforcement to drop by and give them a-serious-chat. Because Enforcement operatives enjoyed that part of their job.

Except this time, *this* felt like a proper bloody mystery. To land something like this, an actual head-scratcher, which made you stand back and say '*what the fuck*'. It made my pulse pound like I'd dropped a whole can of Hombre, when alone at home, and I'd just heard a laugh in the darkness of my room.

Any opportunity to get out of Airedale and sniff a proper mystery. A bit of mental athletics to feed my brain something more challenging than: '*It was X who shot them, wasn't it? Yes?*' was something of a thrill. Plus, it was one of the few times I'd be able to formally designate a facility a crime scene. I had delegation for this shit, which was kind of thrilling, but dead scary at the same time. Delegation meant something.

'Right,' I said, stepping back, clicking my fingers to bring up my bead display. 'Nobody touch anything, OK?' I had to squint to read. I pinched my fingers and brought them closer to my eyes. '*Under paragraphs three and four of section forty-eight of the Justice Bill 2031, I'm hereby declaring this facility – and all known points of access – to be a formal crime scene within the jurisdiction of the Fourth Sector of the Great Northern Belt. This designation requires immediate Justice Division oversight and sealing for scanning.'*

'What does that mean?' Katta asked, looking at the charred remains and back to me, uncertain whether to cry or upchuck. I worried she might do both. That would really screw up the sniffer. Once I'd got it fully charged, that is.

'It means you both get to clock off. At least, for now.' I shrugged my satchel from my shoulder and stuck a hand in, searching for a crawler. There were a couple in there, alongside my gloves and a packet of crisps. I pulled the first out and gave its mechanisms a bit of a blow. You were supposed to sterilize the things on a regular basis and keep them in airtight containers, but I'd got convictions before with this mess. I just got the DidNotArrive app to filter out my DNA.

'What's that?' asked Deborah.

'Crawler. It'll cover the ground, pick up material, textile shred, micro-polymers, seeds, that kind of thing.'

Si had already stepped a few paces back, breathing deeply, back towards the incinerator.

'We just go?' Katta asked.

'Yeah, watch your feet.'

'No more work?' said Katta, looking nervously back to the charred torso. 'What did they do to him?'

I tried to step in front of her. 'Please move away from the area.'

'They've cut off his fucking head, haven't they? Why would they do that?'

'Debs,' I muttered. 'A little help, yeah?'

Deborah, also staring at the body, mesmerised, broke from her thoughts and nodded, walking briskly up to Katta. 'Let's get you a cup of tea, or chocolate, or coffee, or something like that, OK?'

'I'll call RapidRez,' I said to her departing back. 'Oh, take him as well, will you?' I pointed to Si's shaking body.

Deborah scooped up Si's elbow as she went. I was thinking I should've probably run the sniffer over both of them before they went, but it would be a waste of time as the odds were they would've both been drowning in Mr Shin's DNA. I needed somewhere to plug the piece-of-crap in anyway.

'Don't go in the office,' I shouted to Deborah. 'In fact, don't go anywhere you don't need to. Nobody even takes a piss without me knowing about it, right?'

Everything I looked at was now suspicious. It was strange how a formal designation could change your perspective on the world. If I'd arrived at the facility knowing full well it was a scene, then I would've already been treating it differently. But I'd been lazy. Or possibly too shit scared to properly consider it. It was only when I'd reached the middle yard, and smelt that smell, that I realised I'd fucked up. I had properly fucked up. Somebody was dead and it was all on me.

And I'd just been happily trampling through dust tracks and odour trails. All the while, shedding my cells and letting Deborah drop bits of her porridge wherever she liked. And then poking through his things without gloves and kicking shit over. This scene was already massively compromised. Too fucking lazy! Turn up with an uncharged sniffer and a community analyst who knew shit all. All because I wasn't prepared to take a call from a man clearly in distress.

I knew I shouldn't be doing this job.

I turned back to the incinerator – frustrated that my thoughts had started to produce a small bank of tears. I lifted the gecko from my duffel coat pocket. Thankfully it was in full working order and not too messed up alongside the other crap I kept in there. Placing it carefully on the chute, I stepped back and fired it up from my bead. Its LEDs flashed momentarily, running through the boot-up routine, before scampering into the hole, camera flashing as it went.

I twiddled my hands and brought up my display. The gecko's lights flashed in the cavernous opening, illuminating the hazy image beyond the sharp app icons and scrolling text which floated across my bead's interface. Unsure how I was going to go about this, I tried the usual route of going via a friend. I found his number and gave it a ring.

'Jonah?'

'Carrie?' Jonah answered, his big broad face projecting onto screen. It was clipping his background. The noise suggested he was at home.

'You got a minute?'

'Yeah, sure. Sorry, just doing the playtime, thing, you know?'

'Not really. I mean, yeah, I understand. Not that I've got kids, but, you know, I understand.'

'Sure.' There was a pause. 'What's up?'

Jonah was a friend of a friend, in Enforcement up in Airedale. Normally he'd be tooled up and pushing wrong 'un's faces in with his gloved fists. It was disconcerting to have to talk to him surrounded by shrieking kids.

'I need to track down a human-handler call, made to Fourth Sector Enforcement.'

'That's not me,' he said, immediately. 'I'm Airedale. Don't get access to that.'

'I know, I know,' I said. Sometimes you had to spell it out for Enforcement. Their operatives took a while to catch up. 'Listen, I don't want you to find it for me, I just need to know something – who would I get a copy of that call from?'

'Don't know,' said Jonah. 'Sorry. Each division has its own contract. There'll be the auto-service hosted somewhere, probably got a recording of the first call. You said it was passed to a human handler?'

'Yeah, they escalated it?'

'Probably same place. The call handling servers will have it. Hang on, I know a couple of people down in the Tower. I'll drop you their names. Oi, Jem, will you pack that in!'

'Thanks. Sorry, for bothering you and all, Jonah…'

'No bother… oh Jem! Hey, you little… sorry, Carrie, got to go.'

'Thanks. Bye.'

I stood there for a few minutes more, contemplating the flashes of the gecko from inside the incinerator. I was resisting the urge to get the metal prod and have another go in the muck at the back myself. See if I couldn't rustle up a head and a few limbs. Make it a set. But RapidRez would do that, when they picked up the body. Then I'd come back later. Or maybe somebody else would be put on this case and maybe they already had. The minute I'd called in the designation protocols, a clean, efficient young lady from Bark Island, H District, dressed in a chic, silver-fluted jumpsuit with an avant-garde rainbow stripe would have been placed on the job. Perhaps she was already on her way up here, having worked out the case from the backseat of her high-end pool car?

After a few minutes, the gecko emerged and crawled over the machine, focusing on the panel containing the manual controls and the physical bot authentications. I switched off its commands via my bead. No point doing the whole yard just yet. I'd run out of battery. But I would need to do that office and find his personal items.

The sound of Deborah's feet scrunching over the icy muck of the yard caught my attention.

'They're getting their things. Should we keep them out of the office?'

'Did you not hear me?'

'Eh?'

'It doesn't matter.' I sighed.

She took a breath, as though to ask another question but must've thought better of it, clamped her mouth shut and swallowed. I got that from people a lot.

'Why didn't they finish the job?' she asked, nodding towards the remains of the body. 'Should've kept firing that little beggar until it was just ash, shouldn't they?'

'Fucked if I know,' I said but I'd been asking myself as well. 'Maybe they were disturbed? Or assumed it would sort it out itself – don't know how these things work, myself?'

'Maybe we were supposed to find it?' A gleam of excitement in her eyes, which couldn't help wandering back to the incinerator's dark opening.

'Maybe. Whatever?'

'So… what happens now?'

'RapidRez'll get here to seal the gates and bag up this mess. Anything I find I like the look of, ship it down to H Tower – you got a nice freezer down in basement down there?'

'I don't know. Do you think they keep the bodies in the Tower?'

'Doesn't matter. Anyway, body'll go where it needs to go and that's that.'

'That's it?' asked Deborah.

'Well, that's the job. I go home.'

'You go home?'

'I've not got a PO for a murder case.'

'No?'

'No,' I said, shaking my head. 'I'm just down here for a missing-person. Found him.' *Maybe.*

'But you should be on the case?' said Deborah. 'It should be yours, shouldn't it? Now that you've called it in. You're collecting evidence…' she waved at the gecko cradled in my hand.

I grunted. She was right. I wanted it. It was a mystery and it would get me out of Airedale for a bit.

'So, let's assume you do,' said Deborah. 'I'll put in a good word for you. What happens now?'

'Well, I'll try to figure this shit out.'

'How about we?' said Deborah, face falling a little.

'It's a forensics thing.'

'Right. Murder?'

I was about to nod but hesitated. Better do this properly. 'Not necessarily. We don't know that.'

'Right.'

'Who's your digital?'

'Hmm?'

'Your digital analyst? What was his name again?'

'Lem,' she said, screwing up her eyes for a moment, before looking directly at me. 'It's Lem Kawinski.'

I twirled my forefinger in the air in front of me, moving through the contact lists for H Tower's team. I dropped him a message. Wanted to know why the cameras had gone down a week ago. Seemed suspicious.

I checked for messages from Jonah. Nothing through yet. Fucker had already forgot. You can't trust a parent to remember shit.

CHAPTER FIVE

Once RapidRez had arrived, I managed to get Deborah out of my hair. Sent her home in a separate car and told her I'd be in touch if I needed her, before following the key evidence back to the Tower. On the way, I put in a call for Louie to meet me there later. Now that the scene had been declared, I was keen to get the paperwork on the case sorted and manifest myself a PO. But I still had an hour or so of searching what constituted Mr Shin's bedroom, and hopefully build a case. His room consisted of a sleeping bag – with pictures of unicorns on it – and a pillow in the shape of a Christmas pudding. Stuck deep in a packing container, there was a small pot of cutlery, a couple of toothbrushes, a razor, , and few items of clothing.

Spending an hour processing the human detritus inside his sad pile of recycled crap through DidNotArrive had been less than fruitful. So, when the time was up and Louie pinged, I made my way to the Justice floor with a bad feeling about the request.

As the lift doors slid back, I gathered I wasn't going be bothered by other people. Place looked like a ghost town. Empty desks from window to window, some with discarded cups and personal effects on them. The whole Justice floor had been eerily abandoned.

I found Louie over by the east window, clutching an empty coffee cup, staring out at the lengthening shadows of the towers around us. He gave me a weak smile.

'Welcome to the Buckle HQ,' he said, looking around. 'Nice, isn't it?'

'Never been here before. Lively, in't it?'

'Where've you been?'

'Trying to identify the victim.'

'Missing a head,' said Louie, grimacing. 'Makes it harder, yeah?'

'Wasn't the body. I'm going up to the hospital tomorrow to meet the pathologist and talk about that. This were just his sleeping bag, toothbrush, and that.'

'Oh?' he said. He turned and looked at me, like he knew something I didn't. He seemed particularly interested in my answer. 'Got anything?'

'All recycled. Few too many times. No use as evidence; just noise.'

'Noise, yeah?' said Louie, again with that funny look on his face.

'We gonna stand here watching Bradford all afternoon?' I said, looking around for somewhere to sit.

'Sure,' said Louie, turning.

We wandered over to a meeting room booth and grabbed a chair. He slumped down, short legs swinging like a toddler. Normally Louie was the beating heart of the party, moving through all he met and leaving them laughing with filthy jokes and unexpected, yet often very welcome compliments. But it had become clear that, only a few months after he'd got the Airedale DI position, and started to commute across the Pennines from his place in Manchester, he'd been booted out of his house. I didn't know Louie's previous partner, Barry, that well but I'd been told they were all getting set for a proper wedding, with hundreds of guests and that. Until it all fell apart. And nobody really knew why. Least of all Louie, who'd spent the recent months scratching his short black hair and increasingly long stubble, lost in thought.

Some in the team were starting to whisper that perhaps he wasn't up to the job after all, that Ibrahim had made a mistake promoting him, that we needed somebody with more experience and someone a little less full of bullshit. They kept coming back to the fact that Louie Daine always said he was part Chinese. When we all knew he was part Kazakh. And those people kept on talking. Kept saying he was full of shit.

I didn't care about any of that. He was still kind of a friend. And I wanted that PO.

'This is better, in't it?' I said, relaxing into the seat.

'So, nothing from the personal effects?' said Louie, still intent on my answer. 'No DNA match? No identity?'

'No.'

Louie checked his bead display. 'How'd you know he's called Mr Shin?'

'Workers up at the site told me,' I said, too quickly. I could've mentioned the late-night call, but didn't. Didn't seem the right moment. 'So, when do I get the case? Pop me a PO? Add to my stack of murders?'

Louie regarded my grin for a long, sombre moment.

'The algorithm wasn't having it,' said Louie.

'Eh?'

'You logged it as a formal scene, yeah?' said Louie, twiddling his empty coffee cup in his hand. 'You selected A11. Algo wasn't having it?'

A11 was the European standardised code for homicide.

'It's a fucking body, Louie. Course it's murder.'

He shrugged. 'Could be other narratives in court. Anyway, I'm not the algorithm.'

'I have a body.'

'You have a…' He checked his display. 'A torso, Carrie. At least what looks like one, last time I checked.'

'Yeah,' I said, mentally forcing myself not to make a quip.

Louie continued. 'So, could be… could be a wet parts service gone wrong?'

'Could be. Vat-growing human parts is still a crime, right? Least in this country?'

'Yeah, but it's not murder. Plus, there's no correlating DNA match, am I right?'

'If you get me international access, I can find it.'

'You'll never get international. You know that. You're lucky to get Scotland.'

'You can put in a request though, can't you?'

'I can ask Ibrahim,' said Louie, but I could tell he was lying. You needed a good story to back up a request to the Chief Inspector. My story was weak. Even I could see that.

'Do that,' I said, followed by a hasty, 'please.'

'Anyway, something might turn up. For reference, it's been allocated a B3.'

'Missing persons?' I said, voice echoing across the whole floor.

'Yeah, look, I don't write the algos.'

'But you can override them. So, override that!'

'I need solid justification, not just you yelling at me.'

I took a breath. I hadn't wanted to tell him about this. But I had to now.

'I spoke to him.'

'You what?'

'The person who… I mean, I think it must be. The person who used to own that torso that were found in the incinerator.'

'You spoke to him?'

I told Louie the story of being woken in the middle of the night by an emergency call escalation. About the Enforcement team sent to help, how'd they let me know.

'Right,' said Louie. 'Why didn't you tell me this before?'

I shrugged and looked away. 'Didn't seem important.'

'You sure it was human?'

I frowned. 'What do you mean?'

'I get rung up by bots all the time. They're quite chatty.'

'Block 'em. That's what I do.'

'I don't know,' said Louie, wistfully, 'it's nice to have somebody to chat to, isn't it?'

I wasn't going to get drawn into his personal life. 'This one wasn't trying to sell me a weekend break on the fucking moon, Louie. Somebody were trying to kill him and he were shit scared.'

'You'll be amazed what they can do with AI vocals these days. Doesn't your sister do this kind of thing? Talk to her.'

I dead-eyed him for a moment.

'Just saying, that her company… can't remember the name, they could do this kind of thing. Create a chat bot, make it pretend to have a crisis. They do that shit all the time.'

'But why? What's the point?'

'Testing it? Perhaps it worked?' He smiled.

'I've got a man calling me in the middle of the night, scared summat's going to kill him and a few days later I've got a body, partially-incinerated, at the same site. That's a fucking murder, Louie! Can't you see that?'

Louie winced. 'I know, I know. It looks that's way. But until you identify who this person is, until they're on the register. There's not much I can do.'

'Coroner would call it murder.'

'Not got to the coroner service, yet.'

'Eh?'

'We don't have a body, we don't have a name, we don't even have a registered missing person.' Louie put down his coffee cup. A little forcefully, at least, for Louie. 'Possibly, they were off-grid, but the algos hate it when you're off-grid, messes up their systems.'

'If he were off-grid, he wouldn't be making bloody good money as a master recycler at the Belt's Fellside Facility. He'd be camped out in the hills shooting feral cows for his tea.'

Louie made a face. 'I'm trying to help, Carrie.'

I sighed. 'Post me the fucking missing persons PO, alright?'

'Yeah,' said Louie, hands twirling in the air.

'I'll get statements from the two employees. They'll confirm there was a Mr Shin working up at the yard.'

'That'll help your case, yeah. But they need to be formal.'

I nodded. The new PO pulsed in the corner of my screen. Normally they were a deep blood-orange, denoting the A11s. This one was beige. B-fucking-3.

'Ta,' I said, flashing a brief smile.

'You're to prioritise the real murders, right?' said Louie.

'Course.'

'You're going to be busy, covering Airedale and down here.'

I felt like he was building up to something and I wasn't wrong.

'I've been thinking,' said Louie, 'that you could do with some help.'

'A digital analyst would be nice.'

Louie ignored me. 'Just been speaking to that analyst, Deborah Goolagong is it?'

'Debs?'

'Yeah.' He grinned. 'She's a keener, isn't she?'

'Why're you speaking to her?'

'She spoke to me.'

'Why though? She's community. Works up…'

'Up above the Dump. Near the recycling centre? I think she's got some good ideas.'

I groaned inwardly. 'Has she?'

'Yeah, I think she could help you. Might be something in those camps, something of interest. You'll follow that up right? Perhaps she could take the formal statements for you?'

There was a long pause while I let Louie consider his suggestion.

'Yeah, I'll follow up on that.' I stood and made my way towards the lifts.

'There's another problem,' said Louie.

'What's that? What problem?'

'Enforcement want their drone back.'

'What?'

'This security drone, the one I got for you, after this bit of trouble with the double murder up in Keighley. Enforcement want it back.'

'That piece of shit,' I muttered. This wasn't good. It was a piece of crap, but the little bastards who killed Kai Reed – and who wanted me dead, and all – didn't know that, and it was keeping them from my front door at the moment.

'I know, I know,' said Louie. 'I'd worked hard to get that for you. But… they've got some trouble down in Bingley, something about that chemical spill from a couple of weeks ago, people are kicking off. They needed all their drones and had spotted the inventory was missing one. Spoke to Carhill and he had to come clean and so… they want their drone back.'

'But they can't fucking have it!' I realised I was shrieking a little bit.

'I'm sorry,' said Louie, stepping off his stool. 'I know. I know. You'll be fine.'

'I won't be fine, I'll be fucking dead, is what I'll be.'

'Can you find somewhere else to stay?'

'No, not really.'

'How about down here?' said Louie, waving a hand vaguely. 'You've got your sister down in the Buckle, haven't you? Lives up in near the Valleys… placed called Lovely?'

'Friendly,' I growled.

'That's it. You stay with her for a bit? Until we can get this drone back? It makes sense, doesn't it, if you're on this case?'

'Are you suggesting I stay with my sister?' I asked, placing enough menace in the question. But Louie's radar wasn't firing at all today.

'Yeah. Sure.'

'No. Fucking. Way.'

CHAPTER SIX

I liked to think that Ronnie and I had been together for at least two years. From that time we kissed at a club down in Bradford until the moment I sent him a quiet little voice message, before last Christmas, telling him it was over. But things had been complicated all that time, so to say whether we'd genuinely been together was spurious. We hadn't achieved a critical mass of meetups, of flowers, candle-lit dinners, or sex, to claim that we'd ever been boyfriend and girlfriend. Nobody ever calculated that shit, but you could generally tell whether something was a '*thing*' and not an '*I'm not sure, really*'. Because that '*I'm not sure, really*' was also only a critical mass moment away from a proper break-up. At what point did not returning messages promptly, failing to send flowers on Valentine's Day, not wanting to visit your mother on New Year's Day, and repeated '*I can't do this weekend, love*' coalesce into a nice, cleanly-packaged, easily-understood, easily broadcastable separation? So, he had to go. I could only live with so much ambiguity.

I didn't really have friends I could talk to about Ronnie. I'd left school friends behind years ago; they'd got married, or had kids, and I wasn't about to expose myself to the snot and saliva of somebody else's kid unless it was invoiceable. No, outside of those I knew at work – and they were a fucking useless bunch, to be fair – I had nobody else to talk to about breaking up. Except for my sister. And I'd rather rip my fingernails off with my teeth and dip my bloody finger in freshly-squeezed lemon juice than dial up her number on my bead. She'd never seen anything in

Ronnie; something she would repeatedly tell me, at every available opportunity. And if my mother were around, she would inevitably point out that sometimes women need to travel through life alone and that if a man wasn't there for me now, he wouldn't be there for me tomorrow. He would never be there when I needed him.

So it was, when I saw the three figures waiting for me at the entrance to my flat, that I internally cursed my mother's advice. A little voice told me, that if I'd still been with Ronnie, these three figures would've disappeared, sank into the background. He may have been an ambiguous boyfriend, but he was also unambiguously huge. And that would've made these shits – they were kids really – scatter. Then I was furious for having thought of this. I could already see the sneer on my mother's lips, about to launch into a new speech, about to talk of constructed identities and socially-narrated roles. She would bemoan the state of education that had allowed her daughter to reduce her self-agency to victimhood. And she would press another book on me, its little tome icon adding to the stack on my to-be-read list – the one I'd never looked at on my bead. I didn't see her as much as I should these days. Because it was tiring to sit and hear her tell me how much I should be doing better.

But I was tired now. Too tired to face up to these three wrong 'uns.

The autocar accelerated away from the weak LED lights outside my flat, its recorded boy-racer effects disappearing into the evening, leaving the usual background hum of sirens and thumping music. I lived in a block of flats stapled into the steep, stony slopes of Shipley, just below the southern ridge. It meant that the February fog – toxic steam from vat growers and emissions from dense residential blocks from the basin – would often float up the roads and snake their way around the side of the faux-sandstone cladding.

And the three figures had used this fog to make their entrance, stepping around the corner of the building as I reached the door. Dressed in their gang uniform – oversize bulky coats, shorts and fur-lined boots –faces were covered by toy masks of different woodland creatures. There was a fox, a badger, and a squirrel. They weren't bothered that this kind of costume would've sparked off the algorithms. Their ratios were already all over the databases. They didn't give a shit. They were going to disappear back into the stairwells and lifts and fire escapes and flood tunnels if there was any Enforcement action. They had proximity buzzers ready to alert them to any divisional activity. If I'd called up somebody they would just go. And, if I'd still had the security drone patrolling up and down my street, I knew they wouldn't be hanging about like this. Just making an entrance.

Fuck Enforcement. Fuck their drones.

I wanted Ronnie there. I even wanted my mother there. She'd been in the forces as well. She would scare the shit out of them. I was tired, and I wasn't feeling the independence strongly this evening.

'Fuck off,' I murmured into the mists.

They said nothing. I flicked them the Vs and pushed at the door. It'd noted my bead codes and opened upon my command. I kicked it closed behind me and headed up the stairs. Though the lift was working this week, somebody had been letting their pets shit in it. Those iguanas from the eighth floor, probably. I hated the fact that I'd ended up in a housing conglomerate who had collectively decided that it was acceptable to keep pets.

My flat was on the fourth floor. This was a shitty floor to be on. Just far enough to make climbing the stairs a bit of a tiresome task. But too low to justify the lift – bad smells or otherwise. Though we didn't get public health vigilantes coming in and disabling it, I did often see their stickers beside numbers one through to six: '*Are you sure? Just walk the floor*' and '*Lift to level 3? You lardarse.*' These people were supposedly secretive members of the public, organising themselves online and releasing their activism through these little stunts and messages. What they did was technically illegal. But we were never sure if they were actually just a deep-state team for the health ministries, possibly even a global department, intent on steering humanity back from the brink of self-induced destruction. By using the cover of individual protest groups, they could deploy ill manners without retribution. We, the long-suffering public, were used to being abused like this now. I didn't even like to think about what the vegans called us these days.

I pushed my way into my flat and immediately smelled something off. Probably from those bags of shopping I'd left on the floor earlier in the week. There must've been something that needed to go in the fridge. I kicked at the bags as I went by, curious but conscious that my nasal receptors would be dulled to the scent soon. The one benefit of being a forensic analyst. Smell ceases to be the issue it once was. I could see the culprit; it was a fermented cheese and coleslaw mix whose pot had cracked and spilt its content over loose lychees.

Assuming I could deal with it later, I stumped into the living room. My project was draped over the back of the sofa. I didn't want to disturb the latest set of carefully placed pins, so I sat myself down in the only comfy chair that wasn't being used as clothes storage and flicked on my wall screen. Though I didn't mind the nosebead, sometimes the retina shine made me weary, and I liked to rest my eyes.

Nibbling at a re-heated blue-cheese and bean burrito, I hit the info banks for anything on master recyclers. I already knew Mr Shin wouldn't be on anything, but I wanted something on his life. Most of the names that came back weren't in this country. There were plenty in China, Indian sub-continent, a few from the southern states of what used to be America, and some from Indonesia. A multitude of names and faces flashed by on the screen. I was looking at the faces a little, just in case I might accidentally find him, his previous life, a new name and an assumed life in the Leeds-Manchester Belt. But there was nothing I recognised.

What became most apparent was the lifestyle these people

lived. I saw yachts and mansions and fast cars. So, this was what life was like as a master recycler. Was this what Si and Katta had been saying, when they were saying we were lucky to have one in the area? They didn't normally live in an industrial cabin, tucked up in a secondhand unicorn-print sleeping bag with a Christmas pudding pillow.

'Just who are you?' I said, spitting out bits of burrito onto my legs.

Somebody must've been his boss. I dug around the files and found the servant responsible for commissioning the recycling facility for the Fourth Sector. It was somebody called Bridget Negussie. There was a little flash card, for her publicity, of her twirling in the snow somewhere dead posh, dressed to the nines and her braided hair flying. Looked like Aitch Bee.

Aitch Bee was the executive centre of the Belt, where the Servant-Mayor worked. The bit in the middle. A cluster of soaring towers and covered bridges and walkways, set around the valley of the old village, which lurked beneath, now in such darkness from shadows of the building above, that it had to be artificially lit, and artificially peopled by actors wandering around in vintage clothes and talking in funny accents. The tourists fucking loved it. Most other people avoided it. Unless you wanted to get on in the mayoral office, in which case you probably loved it as well.

I dropped Negussie a message saying I wanted to talk as soon as possible. Within seconds, an automated response popped back into my inbox, with her disembodied head appearing on the wall, telling me, in condescending terms, that my message was noted and I wasn't to worry because a member of her team was going to deal with as soon as they were back in the office.

There wasn't much more I could do. The little icon letting me know the latest results for my project was bobbing on my screen. My fingers were already twitching. I was about to give up resisting and head over to the sofa when a new message popped up. It was from Deborah Goolagong-Maloney. I sniffed and grimaced but opened it anyway. A little vid of her head appeared on the screen. 'Hi … is this on? Yeah, oh, hi, it's Debso. I heard you'd got the gig, I mean the case. That's great. Just wanted to say, really looking forward to working with you.'

I didn't reply, not wanting her to see me stuffing my face. I just sent her an ambiguous retro emoji of a face doing raised eyebrows and a half-smile. I used it for most of my responses. I liked to think it fucked people over.

Then I dropped the half-eaten burrito onto the floor, wiped my fingers on my trousers, and headed over to the sofa. There were faces to stitch.

In the middle of the night, over the increasing sound of the wintry wind, I heard a light tapping at the window of my bedroom. Though there were two lines of tall poplars, which had been planted to replace now redundant street parking along both sides of the street, there weren't any trees that could reach up to the fourth floor. Also, this didn't sound like a branch. If anything, it sounded lighter, much weaker, like a bird trying to get in. Although I attempted to snuggle further down under the covers, it was now in my head, and I knew I'd never be able to drift off again without dealing with it.

I groggily got out of bed and went to the window. Fumbling with the controls embedded into the sill, I found the one that switched the occlusion rating and dragged it down to zero. The pleasing grey and green geometric patterns disappeared and the darkness of the night appeared, letting in the ambient light from the city beyond. And there, right in front of my eyes, forcing me to refocus sharply and painfully, was the blinking red LED of a bee-drone. It flew away and then back into the window, making the same tapping noise.

At first, I was just confused. These were illegal, of course, unless you have the right paperwork and, because they were licensed-to-fuck, very few people had them, bar the military. And wrong 'uns.

I looked down towards the road. Stood directly beneath my window was a figure. This one had a hawk mask on. Its head was tilted, staring right at my window. I shivered. Looking around the street, the others had clearly sloped off to their beds, leaving this single one as a sentry.

'Fuck you,' I muttered.

I opened the window, pulling it back towards me and tried to reach out and grab the bee-drone. But its controller was wise to this move and the drone simply retreated a metre, out of reach. The cold air flooded into the room, chilling me. It also had the effect of making me wake up a little more. I wasn't letting this bastard get away with this. I ran back through the bedroom along the short entrance hallway to the living room. The half-empty bags in the hall tripped me up. Scattering groceries everywhere, I felt the wet stickiness of the cracked pot of fermented cheese coleslaw. Grabbing it, I ran back to the window of the bedroom. Evidently happy that they had done their duty, the hawk-faced youth had retrieved their bee-drone and was strolling across the road to take up their lone vigil under the poplars on the other side.

With a pleasingly accurate throw, I heaved the pot of fermented cheese towards the departing back. It fell short but as it landed on the road, its contents exploded forward out of the pot and covered the back of the left leg of the youth. Then I could hear distant swearing. It was enough to make me smile.

'I'm calling Enforcement on you now, you prick,' I shouted out the window and slammed it shut.

The hawk-faced one wasn't listening to me, trying to rub the smear off their exposed ankle. But they still weren't running. I guessed they'd have instructions to stay put until the last moment. They'd heard me say exactly the same thing, every night for a couple of weeks now. So had Enforcement. I'd called them too many times now and the algorithm had written my story up as a serial offender, not exactly blocked, but definitely pushed into the slow lane of emergency calls. I would have to do something that would require a certain amount of grovelling tomorrow but then the Enforcement bastards had taken away my sentry drone, so fuck them. Time to be inventive.

Trying to drag on trousers while also making the necessary hand movements to call up a display of all local Enforcement teams was a challenge but I managed it. Picking the nearest team, I recorded a terse audio.

'This is a Justice call-in. Screams heard at number forty-four, Kings Crescent.' I dropped in my authorisation codes and sent it. When a member of Justice Division – or any of the others, like Prevention or Reconciliation – called in an incident, it was escalated and prioritised. I knew that the vehicle with that team was already coming. Gratifyingly, I could see its position start to change.

'Got you,' I said to the darkness of the hallway, patting one pocket of my coat. The machine was now fully charged. I patted the other. 'Got you as well.'

Then I slipped out of the door and headed for the stairs. Making as little noise as I could, I went down four floors and made my way towards the back entrance of the block. This led to a small alley between the block and the retaining wall that kept bits of cliff from falling on us. It was lit by an automated LED and was full of stinking bins and a few loaders. I'd thought the LED had broken months ago but they seemed to have fixed it: it flicked on as soon as I stepped out. I hurried down the alley, keeping my head low in my coat, and slipped around the corner. The flashing lights of the Enforcement car was reflected in the windows of the street ahead of me. As I hurried towards the junction, I saw the figure making a run for it in the opposite direction, weaving in and out of the trunks of the poplars.

After crossing the road, I took the diagonal to get closer to the fleeing figure and dug the tracer drone out of my pocket. I needed to initiate its tracking routines, so I gave it a swipe across the stinking mess left on the fingers of my right hand then cast it up into the air. Larger than a bee-drone, it was nonetheless small enough to be hidden in the blackness and its quiet whine to be lost amid all the other noises of those things that fly at night.

I reached the main road. Coming along it, behind me now, was the flashing blue of the Enforcement team. I drifted into the cover of a tree just as they evacuated their car and stormed up to the building opposite my block of flats. I felt sorry for Mr Johnson, who was living there at the moment, but the absolute truth was he was a massive twat. And I was sure he did beat up the few women he ever managed to lure back into his hovel.

With the coast clear, I set off again. Unsurprisingly, the gang member had disappeared now but this wasn't a problem. I pulled up my bead and switched on the app that tracked the progress of my tracer drone. Worried that it might be too effective in its pursuit, I reset its parameters to stay at least ten metres away from human targets. Then set off down the road.

The path the hawk-faced one had followed took me down a few more streets in the district, before dropping down a snicket and onto one of the paths along the canal. Apart from a few brazen – and actual – foxes, I saw nobody else as I made my way across from one side of Shipley to the other. Up on the Heaton Heights, the path took a right-hand turn. This was dense housing, the odd tower in and among packed terraces, most of it rotting. Keep my hood over my head, we walked into 24-hour shops, bars, and cafes. People still drunk, staggering home with a salty mockery of some international dish clasped in their hands. I stepped over scatterings of deep-fried locusts and the remains of a dropped hāngī, its false gravy glinting greasily in the neon lights around me.

This wasn't the roughest area of the city. But it wasn't Shipley anymore. We were on the fringes on the Bradford section of the belt. And I wasn't convinced my senses would alert me to the real dangers. I kept my head down and moved fast. Then the trail took me off to the right, away from the lights and noise, back into sleeping neighbourhoods of newer builds. I'd been hoping we would emerge in the courtyard of a nasty little block and I would see the little shit scurry up some steps to his mother's place and walk in, all apologetic for being so late.

But instead, we turned yet another corner. Down the end of this street, surrounded on both sides by fences and overgrown hedges stood a large gate, hung with razor wire. Numerous electronic tags floated into my display, telling me it was private property, that it had planning permission pending, that there had been fifty-five complaints raised against intruders and that a Mr Rehman would press any charges if you tried to break and enter.

As I stood at the end of the street, I could see that I'd caught up with my watcher. The hawk mask had long gone, but the hood was drawn so tightly up over their face I couldn't see much else. They drifted into the shadows at the right hand of the gate and then disappeared.

Trying to look as nonchalant as possible, I strode down the short street towards the gates. As I approached, I was able to see and read the physical signage replicating the virtual tags. Beneath a large mass of black ivy, I made out the words: 'Golf Course'. Whatever the fuck that was.

There was a small squeeze space created on the right-hand side of the gate, where somebody – or a few people – had lifted the gate off its ancient hinges and pushed it forward a little. The tracer had followed their target through the gap; I could see them progressing down a driveway on the other side. Worried about drawing too much attention, I waved my hands in the air and lifted the drone a few dozen metres into the air.

'We do the hunting around here, buddy,' said a voice.

I whirled around. There were five of them behind me. Hoods were all up but these ones didn't wear any kid's masks. They just wore scarves across the lower half of their faces.

'Don't mind me,' I said, laughing. 'Just got lost, that's all.'

I waved my hand and sent my tracer drone the command to return to its normal charging point. In the distance, beyond the gate, there was a high-pitched whine as it accelerated away.

'Drone's gone,' said one of the gang. A girl, by the sound of it.

'That were yours?' asked another member. He had a deeper voice than the other kids. Still sounded like he should be in college.

'Eh?' I said, laughing. 'Listen, I should really…'

They rushed at me, together with a few others from behind, who I hadn't noticed. Though I'd been given some training when I'd signed up – and was supposed to go on the refresher courses – I wasn't able to hold off a dozen of them.

'We don't care for what you did.'

Three of them held me down. Then a third drew out a shockstick. Probably dropped by a patrol during the last round of riots.

'Take this as a first warning.'

It was when the stick discharged the first of the pain-charges directly into my throat and the second just above my left tit – and just before I passed out – that I decided maybe staying with my sister's for a few days was probably going to be OK.

CHAPTER SEVEN

'Of course, I'd love that.' My sister, Grace, had been an actress until the deep fakes took over, so I mistrusted everything that came out of her mouth. Not that I was averse to a bit of virtual fakery, especially this morning. I'd flicked the appropriate filters on my display before calling her. Wasn't going to let her see the state my face was really in, though it really wasn't that bad. I'd been patched up at the minor injuries place around from my flat shortly after I hobbled my way home from High Heaton and then slept long into the morning, riding painkillers and tranq. To be fair to the gang, they clearly knew there was a threshold of fucking-people-up beyond which they didn't stray. A careful optimal assessment of pain applied versus risk of escalation. Perfectly calibrated. Although I'd suffered – they bloody well made sure of that – I didn't have the level of evidence sufficient to waltz into Shipley centre and lodge a case. These days, you'd get laughed at and told to add your name to the bottom of the list. Then you sit back on your arse for about three years, while the temps and work experience go through your case and decide that it's not worth progressing, because of lack of evidence, no means of identifying the assailants, and so on. Process followed: productivity achieved.

I smiled. 'It's been a while, I know. I'm sorry. Been so busy.'

'Like me. Really busy.'

I gently pushed a rib, neatly sliced through with the surgical saw to reveal its blackened marrow, back onto the middle of the table. 'So, I'll be down there later today, right?'

'So soon?'

'Well, this case means I … you know.'

'Right. Aye.' She laughed. 'I'll have to tidy up.'

'Oh, don't worry about that,' I said. 'You know my place. Always a mess. Don't tidy up on my account.'

'I like it proper neat though, don't I? You know that.'

'I know that.' Outside of her eye line, my hands were clasped tight, nails digging into the palm, doing the wincing that my face was forbidden.

'You got much stuff with you?' she asked. By the look of the floating head I could see in front of me, she'd just got out of the shower. Rosy-cheeked and wet hair.

'I still need to go home and pack,' I lied, trying to avoid glancing at the holdall dumped in the corner of the lab. 'It won't be much. You know I travel light, me.'

'I do that,' she said. 'And the rest.'

I smiled, queasily. An icon popped up telling me I had another call coming in. 'Sorry, Grace, have to go now. I'll see you later, yeah?'

'See you later, Carrie! Bye!'

'Bye.'

I flicked my fingers from one call to the other. The large face and small, hooded eyes of the duty pathologist filled my screen, his snow-white whiskers predominant.

'Excuse me, again,' said Doctor Hausman. 'But, when you gotta go, you gotta go. And it takes longer, too.'

'No problem.' I lied. 'Just catching up with my sister… half-sister, I mean.'

'Oh, right,' said Hausman. 'You ready to continue?'

'What about the others?' I asked. Before the doctor had skated off to take his shit, the autopsy room had been busy with a couple of – rather too jovial, in my opinion – assistants, who were wrangling the robotic arm and camera apparatus that took up most of my table. Apart from the fucking body, that it. They were very matter-of-fact about it all. When I'd arrived, they'd given my injured face a professional sucking of teeth before both deciding that, though it was worth an expression of dismay, my wounds didn't need anything more doing to them. I was somebody else's problem now. Their real job was to stick cameras over corpses.

There was a grunt. 'Oh, have they gone? Well, probably don't need them for now…'

The assistants had explained to me that Dr Hausman – one of the senior pathologists on the team – had not appeared in the hospital grounds for at least ten years now. He did all his work remotely. The rumours were it was from a luxury cruiser powering its way – via vast, elegant fixed-sails – across the warmer oceans of the African and Indian coasts. The shorter of the jovial assistants had insisted the ship was called the Eternal Raft. The other that it was called the Big Jessie. I'd read about a few of these monumental ships. No longer full of retirees, they had started to cater for the nearly-retired. Though, looking at Dr Hausman, I'd say he'd gone beyond retirement age a little too far. And was enjoying the buffet a little too much as well. Maybe he wouldn't make it back to whichever drowned port on the Eastern Seaboard he hailed from.

'You want to hear the details?'

'Yeah,' I said. 'If you don't mind?'

He grunted and blinked. 'You're one of the forensics from up at Airedale, yes?'

'That's right.'

'Thought so,' he drawled.

'You heard of me?' I asked, rolling my shoulders a little. The bruises left by the shocksticks hadn't yet been completely deadened by the painkillers I necked upon getting up in the morning.

'I have heard there was a forensic analyst who required delicate handling.'

'Fucking what?' I snarled. I knew people talked about behind my back. But I'd never had one admit to my face.

He burped. 'I'm sorry. I like sharing facts.'

'Who told you that shit?'

'And that she was also a little rude.'

'Listen,' I said, knowing my cheeks were reddening, 'I've had a shitty night, I'm in here early so that I can talk to you, this place stinks and you're eating buffet. Can we just get on with this?'

'I can assure you,' he said, 'that I'm not being paid by the hour, if that is your concern. My contract with the Fourth Sector Justice team is on a case-by-case basis.'

I took a breath. 'What happened to the body?'

'Incinerated, I believe. You concur?'

In my peripheral vision, I could see the robot spring into life, its delicate sensors and tweezered fingers moving with the faintest whirr of servos. One of the mechanical arms darted straight to the lower end of the torso and gripped an edge of charred skin.

'Yeah,' I said. 'They pay you a lot for this?'

'Always worth establishing absolute fact,' said Dr Hausman. 'That statement, however, does not provide much additional evidence of what occurred previously. Much could have happened prior to the moment of incineration. Who is to say that perhaps this unfortunate soul was not simply dumped into the fire, as part of some elaborate barbecue?'

'Barbecue?' I said, queasily.

The face on my screen grinned, a little unpleasantly. 'There are specialist services available, I believe, if that's your recreation.'

'That's disgusting.' Although I believed him. There were enough people in the world, ten billion strong, to allow some of them to consider this as a possibility. The new meat-growing vat technology allowed anything to happen. There had been rumours of human flesh. It still made me feel a little sick. And I didn't feel sick easily. I swallowed back and took a swig of water from my flask.

'That's not what I'm following up here,' I said.

'Of course,' he said. 'That was only me musing, you understand? I am interested in the facts alone. There is one fact. See here.'

The screen was replaced by the view from one of the mechanical arm's cameras. It was a close-up of a lifted flap of skin. I rolled my chair across the floor and positioned myself so I could see the actual flesh with my eyes as well as the head up display's image. A couple of hand-drawn circles appeared on the screen, highlighting some sections of the skin.

'See here,' said Hausman, 'and here. You see something interesting?'

'It's a clean cut,' I said.

'Run it through your app, what do you use over there? BullBus?'

'No,' I said. 'We retired BullBus. We're all supposed to be running Bladester now.'

'Oh, Bladester, right? That is one sweet application.' He took the opportunity to disappear from view. When he returned, he was stuffing his mouth with an egg. An actual fucking boiled egg. This guy was unbelievable.

I took a hi-res image with my bead and called up Bladester. He was correct. It was much better than BullBus for this kind of work, though it liked to pretend it was posher than it really was. 'Where are you anyway?'

'My cabin.'

'You share it?'

'Sadly not,' he said. 'Though there is a rather fine lady who I have recently been–'

'That's all I need to know,' I said, quickly. Bladester's ridiculous chrome icons popped into view. I created a new project and uploaded the image of the skin. 'I was thinking more about which part of the world.'

He looked away briefly, as if checking out the porthole. 'You know, I actually have no idea. One part of the ocean looks much like another, yes?'

'Roughly?'

'Indian Ocean. I believe we stopped off at the Seychelles a few weeks ago. And I'm told we are heading south. Towards the sun.' He took a swig of something. 'How's your app doing?'

'It's getting there … ah, here we go.'

'You have a match? I'm interested in knowing where there is correspondence across our different systems.'

'Yes,' I said. 'I've got a seventy-three percent match.

'Against what? You have a blade?'

'It's saying it's a GoFo Circular Saw, version number 3.45.2, one millimetre.'

'Indeed. Interesting, yes?'

'Yeah,' I said, my fingers moving in the air. I dropped the make of blade into the public files and got an instant match. This was an industrial blade, used mainly for medical devices but also some food processing systems. It could be applied to meat factories but it was generally used in battlefield units, ruggedized pieces of kit needed for emergency amputations. But they were also used in hospitals. Probably had a few around here. Unfortunately, it was a generic. Dead end.

'You want to know something else interesting?' said Dr Hausman, running his tongue around the gap between his teeth and his cheeks, hoovering up every last fucking piece of egg.

'Yes,' I said. No wonder he did this remotely from cruises. If he'd been in the room, I'd have decked the fucker with a chair.

'The other leg was also removed. Similar blade.'

'That's not that interesting,' I said. 'Pretty predictable, really.'

'Aha,' he crowed. 'But that wasn't the interesting bit!'

I closed my mouth and stretched my neck a little. 'Right. You want to tell me the interesting bit?'

'His arms and his head were also removed, yes?'

'Yeah,' I said. 'I noticed.'

'Well,' said Dr Hausman, pausing for dramatic effect, 'it's the same blade, I'm certain of that, but used in very different circumstances. The cut on the legs was controlled, neat, but the arms were ragged, with snags and uneven lines. Then again, part of the neck. Until he died, of course.'

'Like he was … wriggling or summat?'

'I'd say more than wriggling,' said Dr Hausman, darkly.

I turned back to the torso, stepping up towards the top end of the torso. 'Show me.'

The camera and mechanical arm moved up also and drew a close-up image of the protruding shoulder blade nearest to me. Even without amplification, I could see that it was true. The edges, which had not been totally destroyed by the fire, showed a cut that was ragged, like the blade had gone in a few times.

'Give me all the images,' I muttered. 'I need to build it in Bladester.'

'I can send them all over, of course.'

As I worked through all the images, the scenario screen on Bladester built the model of death: a three-dimensional view of the body at points in time, constructed from the torso outwards, where all the hi-def detail was, but the model also plugged in grey generic legs and arms, then hands and feet and, finally, the head. The featureless face hung in the space before my eyes. No data. No face. Yet.

So, he was chopped up. Had he been alive at the time? There was something niggling at my subconscious about this but I couldn't quite remember why it was important.

'You're wanting to know whether this took place before or after death?'

'Um … yeah, whatever,' I muttered, coming back to the room.

'It's fifty-fifty, really. So I can't answer you.' He popped the last of the egg into his mouth and chewed it noisily.

'Helpful.'

'I am here to establish the facts.'

I thought hard. At this point in a case, we analysts were advised to keep a journal and record our notes and progress. This had been our third lesson of the first term of the course. Run by Big Man Vickers: Keep a journal. Keep a journal. Keep a journal, you lazy pricks. It was supposed to be used if there was ever an audit of your work. I stopped doing it from the second case I was put on. I'm not sure many of us ever did this – even Jizzi Rey, and he was a massive twat, so you'd expect it of him. But I tried to use my brain and my memories. I'd nearly managed to convince myself that it was because I had supernatural abilities of deduction and recall. But this was all bullshit. It was because I was lazy as fuck. Always had been.

So I had moments where I really needed to work methodically through this.

'He was dismembered,' I said, slowly, then thought of something, taking a look, 'I mean, I say "he" but are we … oh, yeah, OK, we're pretty sure it's a "he", at least, in the old-school biological sense.' I averted my eyes from the mess and got back to my thinking hard. 'We are not certain whether he was alive or dead during this process. At least, before they got the head. Guessing he died when the head came off, yeah?'

'Well, I guess so,' said Dr Hausman, before burping a little. 'Only, removing a head doesn't make somebody technically dead.'

'What?'

'Just saying, that's all. They do amazing things with monkeys these days.'

'That's too complicated,' I said. 'I'm not worried about monkeys, am I?'

'Suit yourself.'

'So, that's it?'

'One more thing you need. Time of death.'

'Yeah?'

'Difficult to tell, obviously, because of the fire damage. But the blood models suggest it was shortly after he was dismembered that the torso was cast into the incinerator and started burning. As we know, the incinerator switched itself off before the final remains were destroyed, for whatever reason. The flesh cooled down over that time, which I estimate to be approximately–'

'Six days,' I said, interrupting him, fighting the wave of sickness again.

'Yes,' he said, surprised. 'Was that a guess?'

'Corroborated by other evidence,' I muttered. 'So he died six days ago?'

'Yes.'

'And then he was burned in an incinerator.'

'The torso, you mean, not him.'

'Eh?'

'I'm saying, what you're looking at there, is no longer your Mr Shin.'

'Is that not him, you think?'

'That's part of a man,' said Dr Hausman. 'But that ain't a man. It's missing his head, for starters. Oh, a few limbs, but philosophically, they're neither here nor there, as I'm sure a few veterans would tell you.'

'I'm sure they wouldn't,' I said, thinking of Ronnie. He had, thankfully, not lost anything physical during service. But he had friends who had.

'I meant,' he said, more carefully, 'that the absence of a leg doesn't stop them being who they are.'

'Right,' I said. 'But it does, a little.'

'Identity is a troublesome concept, Carrie Tarmell.'

I tried to suppress a groan. Had he been reading my file? 'Is it really?'

'You know the building you are standing in?' asked Dr Hausman.

'No,' I said.

'It's called the Calderdale. You know where Calderdale is?'

'No, never heard of it.'

'I know,' said Dr Hausman. 'That's a sorrowful fact. When I was first employed by the hospital there, commissioned by the Justice department, I did a bit of research. I was interested in the name, you see. Though I'm from old Massachusetts stock, I still carry an appetite for the old country, whatever that means these days. I like to learn about places, you see? So, I went and researched the name "Calderdale". It was a place, a few decades ago, a council boundary, a geography linked by a waterway, if by nothing else. But nowadays, nobody really knows where Calderdale is. The Fourth Sector designation swallowed it long ago and so the name faded into the past. Leaving a few reminders, like the name of the hospital you stand in. We draw boundaries around a thing and give it a name. If we use that name enough, it becomes the thing. But sometimes the pieces just come apart. And then what are you left with?'

'Not actually bothered,' I said.

'No longer a thing,' he said, ploughing on.

'Perhaps the area just got renamed? Perhaps it just needed to change its name?'

'Perhaps it did.' He yawned. 'Now, if you'll excuse me, I need to go and have a swim.'

'Yeah, you do that.'

He cut the call, the mechanical arm and associated cameras drooped a little, as though the life had been sucked from them. I was now alone in the room with the body. If it was a body. Like the man said, a torso doesn't constitute a person. What if it was just a head? Would that have counted? I doubted it. Nobody calls a single head a body. It needs to be at least a torso and head combined, preferably with a few limbs as well. Bit discriminatory to make limbs mandatory. You can live without. But you're not a person without a head and a torso.

Why was I thinking about this shit?

I stood and headed for the door. My hand was on the handle before I remembered the real reason I'd come in person. It wasn't the preserve of the pathologist to worry about this kind of shit. This was forensics.

I returned to the remains and pulled out a small handheld cellular probe – resembling a bulky antique fountain pen – and ran it over the rib cage, nearest to the flesh which had avoided too much of the burning. It still wasn't getting much of a reading, so I extracted the probe, still a bit mucky from the last time I'd used it – probably on that blood up in Saltaire – so I tracked down some disinfectant wipes in the corner of the room and gave it a good old clean. Happy there was no longer a reading which would lead to awkward questions in a courtroom, I jammed the little chrome finger into the marrow of the sliced rib bone. It was harder than it looked. They were thin little fuckers. It took a minute, as by now it was mostly carbon, but there was something in there, in deep. I managed to get a sample on the probe and checked it against the databases on DidNotArrive.

Nothing.

Worried that I'd not got a clean reading, I tried again up near the shoulder. It returned a new reading this time. Swearing under my breath, I dropped it into DidNotArrive and waited a few minutes. It found the match. Local.

I stared at the result for a few minutes. Two different sets of DNA on the same body.

Of course, as soon as Deborah saw me in my post-punch up state, she immediately descended into Deep Fuss. And stayed there for a while It took a while for me to convince her I was OK and I managed to steer the conversation back to work.

'You've just been in the autopsy room, haven't you?' said Deborah. 'Dr Hausman, right?'

'Yeah, Hausman.' I winced as she moved my shoulder forward, in order to see the back of my neck.

'Didn't he say anything?' She waved vaguely at my face. 'About that? He not a proper doctor, or what?'

'I used filters, of course,' I said, as though this would be obvious. Nowadays, because beads had been around for a while, some people's floating avatar faces reflected themselves a great deal younger than they actually were. Or they were cats. A lot of people like being cats, for some reason.

'Ah, yeah. Jesus. What did they use on you?'

'Enforcement shocksticks, I think.'

Deborah whistled. 'Nasty. Who was it?'

'The ones I told you about… you know, the Anima, the Beasties.'

Deborah nodded, sagely. 'Like I said, they're behaving erratically and-'

I gave her the look and she shut up, suddenly interested in her massive tablet.

I stared out the window while she did this. We had grabbed a tea in a small cafeteria section of the Justice Division, on the eighth floor of the H Tower. The window looked out towards the east, so was in the shade by this time of day. It was a clear February day though, and you could see the towers of Leeds centre in the distance and, a little further on, the arcing, glittering hoops of the recent York Tech show.

'Look, it doesn't matter,' I said, turning back to Deborah, who was squinting at the screen. 'I survived, I'm here. I'm going to stay away from home for a bit. Hopefully they'll get bored intimidating me and go find somebody else.'

Deborah pulled a face that said: *Dream on, girl.*

'Anyway,' I said. 'Seems we have proper case, now. Louie's put you on it and all, right? You had a chat with him?'

'Sure. What's next?'

I told her about the pathologist's report and the limbs. Her eyes widened a little at the gorier details but didn't flinch. There were still many leads to follow up. There was more work to do up at the Dump, some basic sweeping, poking around. The two kids who worked up there needed to be properly interviewed and shaken down for more details. That servant who'd commissioned Shin in the first place was somebody I wanted to talk to. Plus the fucking digital analyst still hadn't responded.

'Does this Lem guy ever return his calls?' I asked Deborah.

'The digital? No. Not often.'

'Where can I find him?'

'Oh, he works out of… you know, I'm not sure.' She paused. 'We could ask Louie? Do you think he'd send one down from Airedale?'

I shook my head. 'That's a gap at the moment as well.'

'Oh well, I guess we keep chasing.'

'Yeah,' I said, edgily, wanting to get out of here. Keep moving.

Felt like I was on the clock now.

'You think we can find these other limbs?'

'Probably not,' I said. 'Either they were burned as well and we can't make it out from carbon or they've been dumped somewhere.

'How do we do that?'

'I'm working on it,' I snapped. I was still thinking about the DidNotArrive result.

'OK,' she said. 'What do you want me to do?'

'Do what you do,' I said. I smiled at last, having worked out the right way to get her out of my line-of-sight. 'Put in some queries with your contacts, yeah? Up at Withens? See if you can hear anything suspicious that happened that night.'

'I could start looking for the other limbs as well?' She seemed remarkably eager. Guess we all hate our real job at some points.

'Whatever. But if you do, you'd better start with landfill. Professional meat disposal, that kind of thing.' I reached into my pocket and gave her a handheld probe. 'Here, take this. Just prod it into likely holes.'

She laughed. 'Sounds like one of my old boyfriends!'

'Really? Jesus Christ!'

Her face fell. Too fast. 'No. Not really. I was just joking.'

We stared at each for a minute, not wanting to follow this up any further. I just wanted her out of my sight. Her coat, all greys and pinks, seemed to fill my entire view, in its rippled veins like a plug of day-old vat-grown pork.

'Best crack on then.'

'You coming along as well?'

I shook my head. 'No, I need to check out the facility again. Talk to Si.'

She nodded and turned to go, before stopping and turning. 'Oh, wait on Cazza! Don't I need to know the DNA signature? Make sure it's the right one?'

'It's Carrie,' I said.

'What?'

'Don't ever call me Cazza.'

'What..? Oh right, sure.'

I stared at her for a moment. 'If you find a human leg in landfill, Debs, you don't need to check. You can safely assume it's suspicious. Get a reading on the probe and bring it in.'

She giggled. 'Yeah, I can see that. I'm sorry. Guess that's why I'm not a forensics.'

'It's not really forensics, Debs,' I said, nastily. But it didn't seem to matter, because she was still as excited a puppy with a fucking bone.

'Right. Get a reading.'

'Then we can run checks.'

'But the DNA? Didn't you get the DNA from body? I mean, it would still be there, uncharred, wouldn't it?'

I stared at her for a moment. Then sniffed. 'It were inconclusive.'

'Oh.' There was a pause, as though she were waiting for me to continue. 'Right, I'll get getting on to these sites then.'

'Yeah,' I said, unsmiling. 'Best to.'

As she left, I looked back out of the window to the view, now becoming obscured by cold clouds coming in from the southeast. The towers of Leeds and arcs of York no longer visible. I took a nervous swig of water from my flask and breathed deeply through my nose. I wasn't sure why I hadn't wanted to tell Deborah the DidNotArrive results. Perhaps I was still processing it myself and didn't want to look a complete prat? Or that I was using damaged and contaminated equipment? The result was confusing and had made me question everything; not least of all, whether I'd done the right thing so far.

DidNotArrive had returned one name: Stan Davi. He lived on the coast, somewhere south of Bridlington. So far, this was standard. Except that he'd died in a yachting accident two years ago. The coroner's report showed a blue body laid out on the Estuary Division's facility in New Hull.

Two torsos.

CHAPTER EIGHT

My sister was waiting for me on the doorstep when the autocar rolled up. She had the third floor flat of a retrofit nightmare, pasted together from ancient Victorian head-duckers and modernist steel and glass. To be fair, it was a fucking awful mess. I liked to live in a place that didn't scream: '*Look at me, please look at me!*' But I guess it suited my sister to a fucking T.

Of course she was wearing her jogging shorts and a loose blouse. Despite it being after lunch, in February, and with snow still on the ground. Grace always kept her heating turned up to '*Advanced Sauna*' most of the day. Her hair was tied up in a loose bundle, meant to signify a hastily thrown together mess, but I knew her routine. I'd grown up knowing how long she took to make herself look half-decent. It was rarely short of half an hour. That 'do looked like a fifty-minuter at least. Like me, she liked the empty end of a dye-bottle, so I was never sure what was natural. At the moment, she was playing the part of a curly and abundant strawberry-blonde. Or raspberry squashed into straw. Or something. At least I didn't pretend my hair's bright purple dye job was anything natural. And anybody who didn't like it could fuck off.

'Come on up,' she puffed, hugging me, and placing a wet kiss on my cheek. 'I've been waiting ages.'

'Hiya, Grace,'

'You got all your bags?' she said, eyeing the small holdall I'd dumped on the floor. 'Any more in the boot?' She concluded almost wistfully.

'No,' I said and hoisted it onto my shoulders. As the strap hit the front of my chest, I had to hide the wince.

If she'd seen it, she didn't say anything. 'I don't know how you do it!'

'Going to steal your clothes, yeah?'

'Right, you can try, and that,' she said. 'But I'll rip your fingers off.'

'Yeah,' I laughed. 'You would.'

'I would not!' She chuckled again, staring a little hard at my face. 'What?'

'You been in a fight? Looks like a black eye coming up?'

'Every night, me. I love a scrap.'

'I know that,' she said, still staring at my eyes and cheeks. 'But normally you win.'

'Who said I didn't win this time?'

Grace looked me up and down. 'This why you've come to stay here for a bit?'

'Like I said, I needed to be closer to the case.'

'What aren't you telling us, Carrie?'

'Mum been talking?'

'Mum's always talking.'

'Know that. What she say?'

'Nowt.'

'Well then.'

Still staring hard at my holdall, she eventually turned her inquisitive eyes back to me. 'You never pack much, Carrie. I know that. But don't normally travel so light, that's all.'

'That all?'

'Yeah. That's all.'

Grace walked on and I followed her upstairs and along a few open walkways and glass-fronted stairwells until we arrived at her flat. It was always immaculate and today was nothing different. I deliberately dropped my bag on the rug in the middle of the sitting room. She immediately scooped it up – gratifyingly grunting a little as she did so – and floated it away to the spare room. I had a quick poke around her kitchen while she was gone, looking for something to eat. There was some rustic loaf which looked Ukrainian, by the seeds. I started to gleefully hack into it with a knife.

'You not eaten?' she said, coming back into the kitchenette area. 'I could rustle up something cooked if you'd like?'

I shook my head, spitting crumbs of the Ukrainian bread onto her floor. 'Don't have time. Got to be up at the Dump in about fifteen minutes.'

'The Dump?' The phrase uttered with a faint quaver of revulsion in the voice.

'Yeah.' I swallowed a little painfully on the rustic crust. 'Body in an incinerator up there. Not reached our comms teams yet, though, so don't tell nobody, right?'

'Bloody hell.'

Grace was paid for her voice. And so, I was more alert to her vowel sounds than most. Somebody in the Aberystwyth Joint University had run a mass survey of accents and come up with the old Halifax town accent as being the most trustworthy and friendly in the entirety of the English-speaking world – close second to the Otago Peninsula, but nobody lived there anymore, except penguin pushers. Unfortunately, old Halifax town was now Fax Central, and the accents had gone, along with the skyline and the wide, open moors. That didn't mean that the brand could still stick, however, and there were a few businesses in the town – in truth, distant nodes of larger conglomerates – who tried to leverage the customer-optimal authentic voice. Even if people had to be trained actors, like Grace, to deliver them. I had once told her she could do the same job sat in a boat off the coast of Thessaloniki, but she'd just smiled at me, like she did, and said that it wouldn't be true to her craft.

'You not going to work yourself?' I asked.

'Course, yeah. I've been on calls most of the morning. I were just waiting for you. And getting ready.'

'Getting ready?'

'Doing a late one today. Got an American meeting. So I have to go in and sit with the team.'

I looked her up and down. 'You going in that?'

A dark frown fell over her face. I felt like the bad older sister. But I didn't care that much.

She sniffed. 'No.'

'You could though, couldn't you?' I said hastily trying to make amends, but not sure if it was going to.

'You know what I do, don't you?'

I did. 'Yeah. You talk to processors all day.'

'I train machines in how to speak,' she said primly.

'Yeah, so you could wear what the fuck you like.'

'No. It's not–'

'I were joking,' I said, trying to smile.

'I were about to get ready,' she muttered before scurrying off to her room.

Feeling the heat myself, I was just about to peel off my own coat and make myself a tea, when a message pinged in my ear. I pulled up my display and snapped at the bobbing icon of an envelope. It was from somebody in the commissioning Servant's team, telling me their boss was available to talk, if I had time now.

'I'm off now,' I shouted after her, pulling my duffel coat back on. 'Gotta go, yeah? I'll see you later.'

'See you,' said Grace, from behind her closed door.

The return to the front entrance of the residential block was confusing but I'd made the journey a few times – and sober more than not – such that I wouldn't get lost. As I walked, I pulled up my contacts, and found the one for the Servant.

'Hiya, is that Bridget Negussie?'

'Hello,' said a welcoming voice. It also sounded a little slurred. The view shivered before me and then I could see her face. She was sitting in a posh train seat with proper armrests and a drinks holder, like I'd only ever seen on immersives. Behind her head the occasional tree flashed by, set against a clear blue sky.

'Ms Negussie is patched into a shared comms,' came another voice. This one sounded like they came from the New Leeds area, decadently accented. 'So that we can all assist.'

'All?' I said, sighing a little. It was usually like this when I spoke to a Servant. You always had to manage the lackeys as well.

The view swung around and I could see two other faces, one male, one female. They were the usual, hard-shaven, hard-bodied bright young things that attached themselves to Servants like ticks. Ticks with cutting-edge satcomms and chic pads on the moon.

'That's OK, isn't it?' said Negussie. The camera swung back to her to face and adjusted the focus so that she wasn't so blurry. She'd definitely been drinking.

'No worries,' I said. 'Just a routine call.' I rattled off the usual IG bollocks and she nodded and waved her hands in all the right places through the affirmation section.

'So, what's this about?' she asked.

'You haven't seen my messages?' I asked. 'I'm contracted to the Fourth Sector Justice Division at the moment. I've left you a few queries.'

Bridget Negussie lifted her head and looked away from the camera to one of the sharp-boned assistants. The audio feed cut out momentarily, as someone hit mute. The Servant's face became heavy with a frown but then she pulled a smile directly at me, showing her perfect white teeth. I felt bathed in that smile. I could see why some people make better Servants than others. I would never be able to smile like that, not even on a wedding day. Even on *my* fucking wedding day, not that this was ever going to happen.

'I'm so, so sorry… Carrie, is it? It seems your messages got a little lost under everything else coming in at the moment. I really can only apologise.'

'That's fine,' I lied. 'So, do you know anything about Mr Shin, about your dealings with him, and what may have happened to him?'

The smile never twitched. 'I'm afraid you'll have to repeat the request, Carrie.'

I took a breath. 'OK. Right, there's an investigation initiated in the Fourth Sector, up at the Fellside Auxiliary Facility. Murder case, at least, that's what we've submitted. The victim… I mean, suspected victim, is a Mr Shin. He was the master recycler up at the facility.'

The eyes in my view, previously woozy with booze, now sharpened. She'd been alert enough to notice the key area of weakness. 'Suspected?'

'That's factually correct,' I said, trying to make it sound routine. 'We still need to confirm samples with forensics.'

'Aren't you forensics, Carrie?'

I couldn't remember at what point I'd said who I was. But I was pretty sure I'd never explained my job title. Never play games with Servants. They remember everything. They'll have you.

I laughed. 'Yeah, you're right. But we're still waiting for results. That's not the point, though. I would really like to understand how Mr Shin became to be subcontracted to local government… way I see it, you are technically, his boss, Ms Negussie.'

She paused, just for a second, then looked up at her assistants. She looked back at me and widened the smile. 'We're just checking our files. My remit spans a great deal, you see. As well as municipal functions, like recycling, I also help promote local businesses and encourage European trade.'

'Is that right?' That where you are now?'

'Correct,' she said, and looked out at the dark mass of trees as they passed the window. 'We're heading south through the wonderful French nation. On our way to… oh, I don't know. I forget.'

The fuck had she forgotten. I also noted the way she'd said, 'recycling function', like even saying the word made her want to squirt some sanitiser on her white front teeth.

'I just need to know some more information about him, that's all,' I said. This whole conversation was making me a little uncomfortable.

'Do you have a first name?' asked Bridget Negussie, still

smiling, but now looking a bit more concerned at the task I had taken on.

'I'm afraid not.'

'That's tricky, isn't it?'

'Yeah.'

'Ah, it seems we have something,' she said, looking away to her colleagues again. 'So, the contract for the recycling function was commissioned by myself, three years ago now, but I never dealt with the master recycler himself at the time. We just dealt with their admin.'

'OK,' I said. 'You never negotiated directly with anybody?'

Bridget Negussie laughed. 'We were commissioning a recycling facility.'

'I'm sorry,' I said, feeling stubborn. 'I don't understand.'

'Well, there are some commissions you just… I don't know, they're just rollovers.'

'OK.'

She looked at me like I was a child. 'We've commissioned that same facility for the last twenty years. It's paperwork.'

'And you've never met the master recycler once in that time.'

'No,' she said. 'I've never met him, this Mr Shin.'

I took a breath. 'OK. Who did you work with then? Who was the admin who signed off at the site?'

Another brief pause. 'I've got the name… yes, it's Simon West. He's dealt with us the last couple of times.'

'Thank you,' I lied. 'I'll follow that up. If you have anything with any details relating to Shin – addresses, numbers, signatures etc – you'll send them over please, will you?'

'Of course,' said the Servant. She leaned in close to the camera and gave me the biggest, warmest smile. 'Good luck, Carrie. All the best. Bye.'

Still on the way to the Fellside Facility – after I'd finished the phone call with Bridget Negussie – I tracked down Si West's number and called him up at home. He looked a little edgy, but seemed to be expecting my call. I asked him to meet me up at the gates and to bring everything we might need to dig through the camera workings and the bots.

When the car pulled up, he was there, more nervous now than he had been on the day before, his lanky frame shivering in the cold. Up here, the wind was stronger, and the afternoon was getting darker. It was an easterly, blowing across from the continent and the North Sea, promising another frost tonight.

He greeted me quietly and stepped back to allow me to drop my codes into the RapidRez locks. I could see him check out my bruises with a concerned frown, but he said nothing. Perhaps he thought this was standard issue if you worked for Justice.

We stepped through and I turned to him. 'Let's go find some of the servers. But touch nothing, yeah?'

'Sure.'

I pointed out the cameras above the gate. 'So, they're all offline, now, are they?'

'That's right.'

'How long ago did it happen?'

'What? The cameras going down?'

'Yeah.'

'I discovered it on a Monday. Can't have been last week, because that would've been when…' he fell silent for a moment. I waited. 'So, it must've been the week before. What date is that?'

'The second,' I said. 'So you've been without security for two weeks now?'

'That's right. I tried to get the engineers to come out, but everybody was busy. Didn't get much help from Aitch Bee either. Right, here we are.'

Following a circuitous route, we arrived at a low building, newer than the rest. It'd been bought brand new, rather than recycled and repurposed. The hub for the loaders and drones. In one corner stood a large – and elaborately electronically-locked – cabinet. Si stepped carefully between the wheels and blades of the machinery and approached the cabinet.

'Do they help you out?' I asked, following him in. The LEDs glowed above our head, recognising our movement. We were losing the light now.

'Hmm?'

'Aitch-Bee? You said you phoned them.' From my conversation with Negussie from earlier, I'd already guessed the answer, but wanted to be sure.

'Not really,' he grunted. 'They don't help with much. But they're supposed to.'

'What are they supposed to do for you?'

'They've got call-offs we can use. You know, certified this and that. We get them to unblock the sewers now and then. But we never took their security package, so they're not bothered half the time.' He'd reached the cabinet. It had a large palm ID section in the middle. 'Um. Am I OK to touch this?'

'Wait a sec,' I muttered, fishing around in my pocket. I retrieved the gecko and held its head up towards the screen. But this was mainly for show. Just at a glance, it was fair to describe the surface as forensically compromised.

Si leaned in close and peered at the machine. 'Is that the same one you used around the incinerator?'

'Yeah,' I said, too gruffly.

'What happened to it?'

I sniffed. 'Sat on it, didn't I? It still takes pictures. Don't you worry about that.' I tried not to think about the gecko-shaped bruise that was forming, in unlovely yellow and mustard tones, across my hip and into my stomach.

After I'd taken a few pictures of the security pad I stood back and waved him in to do his work. The photos were hi-rez enough for the tools to lift a few fingerprints. Though prints were a compromised narrative tool for prosecutors these days. Old school. The lawyers preferred something that meant they didn't have to defend all the usual preceding cases in which use of fingerprint evidence had led to outrageous miscarriages of justice.

The door clicked open and we looked inside. It was a vast cupboard. I would've been proud to have it included in my flat. But its three large shelves contained little more than a dusty black cube and a blister pack. The latter held what looked like a playing card in it and a large sticker – alongside the branding – that simply said: 'Press here to start'.

'This it?' I said, heart sinking.

'I'm afraid it is. Sorry. I should've said.'

'Anything missing?'

'No, I mean, this lock looks like–'

'Take a look at the floor,' I said, interrupting him.

He looked down where I was pointing. There was a neat fan scraped into the polymer tiles, where the whole cupboard had been levered away from the wall.

'You shifted this thing recently?'

He shook his head. 'No, I mean, not moved since we started here.'

'That's recent. They tried to scuff it out. Look, there.'

I took a picture of the scuff marks, hoping Bladester could do something with it. Maybe pull it together into a recognisable shoe and grip. 'Have a look at the back,' I said, while doing this.

Si reached out a hand and nudged the back panel of the cupboard. It moved.

'They got into it from behind?'

'Took the screws out,' I said, nodding. 'It's all still here, right?'

'Yes,' he said, staring first at the cupboard and then at the mark on the floor. 'You're really good at this, aren't you?'

I gave him a glance and then looked back at the contents

of the cupboard. The blister pack had some cheesy cartoon drawings of drones carrying grinning cameras. Which had droopy moustaches. 'I'm guessing that's your security package, right?' I said, pointing at it.

'Yeah.'

'Off the shelf. Am I right?'

'Yeah,' said Si, now bristling a little. 'It got all the good reviews. It was cheap. Mr Shin didn't want anything too expensive. Do you know how few people break in here?'

I looked around at all the kit in the shed. 'But you've got some pretty nice tech–'

'Well, it's not many,' Si interrupted, before muttering an apology and backing away a little to give me some space.

'What's this one then?' I asked, pointing at the black cube.

'That the autonomous server; runs this lot,' he said, waving an expansive arm at the loaders, cranes, and other assorted machinery.

'That working OK?'

'Yeah. Seems to be fine. I mean, they're all back-at-base status, so there's not much for them to do.'

I snorted. 'Right. We'll need to check the logs on these as well, OK?'

'Sure,' he said, fishing into the pocket of his hi-viz and pulled out what I assumed was a processor block. It was moulded into the shape of a vintage truck. Si must've noticed my double take. 'Christmas present from my nan.' He took off a glove and waved his hands in front of the device. It sprang into life, projecting a screen onto a nearby wall. Si adjusted the position so he could read between the vertical corrugations in the metal. I noticed the processor had some internal mechanism making the little vehicle rock as it worked. It was the first thing that had made me smile for days.

As he did this, I switched on my bead and fired up the list of local servers. I could see what looked like the autonomous controller, the general wireless network, a few local municipal connections. But nothing that suggested the hilarious drone face for the camera server.

'Did you try changing the batteries?' I asked.

He glanced at me and then back to the scrolling lists of dates in front of him. 'Yeah.'

'Always worth asking.' I reached out and grabbed the blister pack, shoving it into my coat pocket.

'You're not going to analyse it now?' asked Si, not looking at me.

'No. I'm forensics. Not digital.' I'd left another call with Lem, as I'd been driven up here. It was looking increasingly hopeless, though, that he would ever have time or inclination to come and help. How did they get anything digital done around here? Maybe I could call Louie directly and see if he could dust off his old skills? Though, given the state of the man last time I saw him, I didn't think that was likely to work.

'I've just given you access,' said Si. 'You need to authorise this IG contract. It might take a while'

'Eh?' I could see a document icon bobbing on my display.

'This would give you manual control of the entire fleet. That's quite the risk.'

I winced. Then huffed. 'Look, I don't want control of this shit. Can you just check the logs?'

'What are you looking for?' asked Si, turning back to his projected screen.

'Start with the evening of the twelfth. Anything happening then.'

He nodded. A scroll of smaller files swooped across the screen for a moment. He dragged one forward and it opened. The screen was filled with what looked like random code. This was is what digital analysts fucking loved though. Wouldn't catch me digging through that shit.

'What's that?' I asked.

'Log file for machine activity during the twelfth.'

'Looks busy.'

'It was a busy day.'

'Anything odd with it?' I asked.

'I'd need to compare it to other days,' he replied.

'OK, map these codes to the actual machine names. They don't mean much to me like this. Can you do that?'

He turned, with a pained expression. 'I'm not a digital analyst, either. I'm a journeyman recycler.'

'Yeah, I know. Just do what you can, yeah? I'm going to scan this lot while you're on that.'

'OK.' He didn't look any happier about this, or convinced that this would even help.

I cranked up DidNotArrive on my bead and dug out a handheld sniffer from a pocket. The usual polystyrene protector was long lost, so it tended to pick up dust, hair and other muck from my coat. I gave the sensor unit a quick blow. It mucked up the results but then I just extracted my DNA from any results. It was against the rules, but we all fucking did it. No forensics was ever not going to compromise their readings with their own muck.

I set off down the first aisle, passing in front of each machine, waving my sniffer across any extremities. Soon I became lost in the murk of arms and claws and grippers and sliders and trays and boxes and hoppers. All were caked with organic and inorganic matter, all shrieking their own chemical signals, which were fed through the sniffer's default software app, Noseum. It then filtered out the noise and identified the most likely element hitting its membrane – synthesised from a Basset hound's apparently – then presented it in a pretty little keyword display on my screen.

Where I was walking at the moment, I was mainly getting tomato and onions and soy. I moved on, stepping past a toothed machine, which was revealing a significant proportion of European red fox. I shuddered at the thought.

The different set of machines was bewildering. I'd never really considered what went into the business of sorting mess. Each had its own unique function which, together, formed a grand superhuman who could rip and chop and sort anything that came within the walls of its realm.

'How long do we have?'

'Sorry?' said Si, from the other end of the shed. I couldn't see him anymore, as even his tall frame had been obscured by a folded crane arm.

'We've put this place on lockdown. How long before the trucks start to get stacked up at the gate wanting to offload their contents? People are still tucking into squid and pineapple, aren't they?'

'Oh, right. Yeah, well, when a facility goes down, things get rerouted to the others nearby. There's one up north-west of Bradford Levels, that's closest, and another beyond the hill, one at Rochdale. We should have a few days before other sites start complaining about the volume.'

'Good,' I muttered.

'Sorry?'

'Doesn't matter. How're you doing with that comparison?'

'Nearly there.'

The sniffer was feeding the scents back to my display as I wandered up and down between the loaders and other devices. There were some here that squashed , ripped, shredded, sorted, recorded, and many more actions related to recycling, that I never ever wanted to fucking know about. I wasn't bothered by the mechanics, mainly the bio-signatures they were revealing, and these were proper busy. But my nose could have told me that as well. This was the kind of shit the enviro analysts would be getting moist about. But then they loved a bad smell. Especially if it was against regs.

Then I noticed a new signal, among the other lines on the chart, which followed a more familiar path. At least, for somebody in my line of analysis. Not that I wouldn't expect this kind of signal in a recycling facility, but it was strong and fresh. I stopped beside the machine where the signal was strongest. This one looked a bit different to the rest. It had a white plastic protective moulding, and more chrome than expected. The other machines in the shed looked like they should be on a recycling facility a few fields away from a toxic reservoir in the northern regions of England. This one, however, wouldn't have looked out of place in a hospital in any part of the world.

I peered in for a closer look at marks on the surface. There they were: tiny blood droplets.

At that moment, Si joined me. 'I've found something. One of the machines was running on manual in the middle of the night.'

'About one to two in the morning?' I asked, trying to recall.

'Yeah.'

'Which one was it?'

'Didn't recognise it. Not one we usually use. So I had to use the look-ups. All I got was a code, really.'

'Was it code 88-0987?' Stumbling a little, reading the numbers in front of me.

'Yeah,' he said, checking back by flashing the little toy car on the lid of a hopper. 'How did you know that?'

I tapped my nose. 'I'm the fucking forensics, ain't I?' I smiled and nodded towards the white and chrome machine.

'Eh?' he said, not following me.

'Just what the hell does this thing do?' I asked, pointing at a wheeled device. Whatever tools it was supposed to deploy, they were all carefully stored away inside its mouldings.

'Not sure. Mr Shin used that mainly.'

'Sure. Can you make it work?'

'I guess. Why would you want to?'

'It's got blood still on it. Looking at the colour, it's somewhere between five and eight days old.'

'Mr Shin's blood?'

'I'd need to do tests.'

'That's odd, though.'

'Why's that?'

'We don't deal with any organics like that here. I mean, there's some accidental biohazard waste. But that's all bagged up, wrappings and wound–'

'Yeah.' I held up my hand. 'Understood.'

'So I don't know why we'd have a machine like that. To…' He reached forward, flicking a switch on the machine. A small whirring circular blade span out of the depths and whined in the air in front of us. He swore. Despite myself, I stepped back with a sharp intake of breath. I was glad to see Si was also as chicken-shit as me.

'So, what's it doing here?'

'No idea.' He scratched his stubble. 'Maybe it's come over from the Second Facility. Over at Bradford. I mean, they've got a methane fermenter over–'

'What?' I interrupted.

'A fermenter. They've got one over there.'

'What's a methane fermenter do?' I asked, almost not wanting to know.

'It captures gas, you know, via… um, decomposition.'

'Decomposition of meat?'

'That's right.'

I was already dialling up Deborah's number.

CHAPTER NINE

'They wouldn't let me in the front entrance.' Deborah was quite breathless.

'Why's that?'

'Said I was carrying biohazard.'

'Yeah, I get that a lot. Not as much as the environmentals and that, of course. But people can be proper rude.'

'I mean, they bagged it up for me, and all.'

I coughed. 'Just a bag?'

'No,' said Deborah. 'They put it in a polystyrene crate – recycled, of course – and then wrapped that up as well.' There was a pause. 'Still proper stinks, mind.'

'Ah, shit.'

'What's wrong?'

'Do you have a wet-storage facility at the Tower?'

'No, possibly not,' said Deborah. 'To be honest, I've no idea. Do you think we should have one? I'm just a community analyst. Where do you think it might be?'

'Tends to be off site. Where are you at the moment?'

'Just circling Fax Central. Been round twice already.'

'They'll think you're fucking someone.'

'What?'

'The algos … it doesn't matter. Hang on, just let me get hold of Louie.'

I ended the call. I should've added I needed to get dressed, have breakfast, and possibly have a shower, among other things. But I didn't want to show myself up to the new girl. It was about ten am already and, though I made my own working patterns – and anybody who tells me otherwise can fuck off – I didn't really want to have that conversation. Grace had snuck out about two hours earlier, blowing me a kiss from the spare room door and gesticulating in a way that I assumed indicated I could help myself to anything in the kitchen but to not leave a mess.

I tried Louie. It went straight to a recorded message, so I ended the call. Not sure what to do now, I crawled out of bed and into the bathroom. About fifteen minutes later, having cleaned myself up sufficiently and put on some clothes, I suddenly remembered that Deborah would probably have been around the Halifax fly-road about five times now, so I dialled up Louie again.

'Yeah?' he answered, shortly.

'Sorry, Louie,' I said. I explained about the absence of cold storage and what we would use. He seemed nonplussed and dialled off briefly to speak to another colleague, only to come back to confirm.

'There's a meat storage place near to the Tower. Justice've sub-contracted a section. I'll ping you the address.'

'Thanks. You OK?'

'Fine,' came the reply. The tone told something else.

'OK,' I said.

'You?'

'Yeah, I'm alright,' I said.

'Good.' The smallest of pauses. 'Sorry, got to go. Another meeting.'

I was about to ask him about failing to get any form of digital analyst on the job. But then I thought better of it.

'See you.'

'Yeah, ta-ra.'

When the address came into my display, I forwarded it onto Deborah and told her to meet me there. I called for an autocar and fell out of the flat. The old district of Friendly, once a village, had now become encased by the flowing residential blocks and terraces that had filled the Belt over the last few decades. At least it'd avoided sinking into the worst of the Valleys. Only just though, as above me, there swept suspended roads and walkways, even small playing fields set on stilts, connecting the columns of flat and small business offices. This was an affluent area, so the mess was kept to a minimum, but even I could see the smog that hung in the area to the west, above the hills that contained the reservoirs. And the Valleys. And the Dump.

I walked for a while in thought, letting the autocar track down my position, surrounded by the buzz of electric vehicles passing beside me, above me and thrumming in their tunnels beneath. All trying to get from one end of the Belt to the other. All needing to be somewhere. Shifting meat from one space to another.

'Shit.'

I called up some data on transport firms on my bead as I walked. I didn't have the kind of access that a proper digital would have – they'd get this in seconds - but I had delegation. And having delegation meant something. It meant I could drop them a stern email and demand to see their logs. So I fired off a series of messages, demanding data. And fucking fast.

Most of last evening had been spent drinking more synthetic lime cocktails with my sister, then we'd moved on to Danish wine and things had gone bad from that moment on. I'd forgotten most of the case. We talked about her job – making machines talk more like trustworthy humans – and my job – trying to understand what happens when human beings behave like animals. Got angry about our mother. Then she started calling me names from when we were both young, when she found out I was different. She only called me those names when she was really pissed off at me. She pulled out the favourite taunts: Specky Tutu, Tarmy Tuber, even The Runt. And then I got nasty. And then, I forgot exactly at what point she stormed off to bed.

So, all the conversations with Si had been forgotten. I was

supposed to be journaling my thoughts, leads, and evidence. The prosecutors would be on my arse if I didn't have something. So, as I trudged beside a rusting fence that separated me from squealing auto-brakes and probable death, I tried to piece together what had happened so far.

I'd forgotten to follow the basic procedure for how you were supposed to construct the narrative. I was jumping all over the place. This wasn't unusual for me, but I knew I was going to have a hellish twenty-four hours at the end when somebody was going to ask me to put it into something coherent. The problem was twofold. First, I was doing fucking Louie's job here. He was the one who should've been doing all these interviews, journaling all these leads, putting it all together, pruning out the noise, all the false assumptions, prejudices and, unconscious biases. This is what I'd learned during my six-month crash course in 'How To Be A Justice Analyst' in Liverpool, ten years ago.

Second issue was what I had been taught in my course – simple concepts, methodology, and how to apply it – assumed you worked across a team who was following the same. But we'd been issued with these cheap apps – like DidNotArrive, Bladester, or Modlee, for digital – which had their own local methodology. So you were fighting multiple approaches and narratives all the time. Most of us just gave up our training and let the app do the work for us. That was fine. Until it wasn't.

The car creepily pulled up alongside me and there was an insistent beep in my ear.

'I know. I fucking know. Car's here.'

I got into the back seat, leaned back, pulled on the belt, and pulled up my display to full opacity, cutting out the stains on the upholstery.

'Where are we going today?' asked the car.

'Svenson Industrial estate,' I said. I pulled out the code and threw it at the car's wireless receiver.

'Would you like some music today? Or some news? Or

perhaps a story?'

'No,' I said, knowing I had to enunciate clearly for this variant of auto-car. 'I would like silence.'

'Understood,' said the car. A little snippily, I thought.

As we accelerated away, joining the vast Beltway above us, I settled back into the seat and tried to remember what the fuck had happened to me over the past few days. There were definitely some bits I wanted to omit.

The meat storage facility in Svenson Industrial Estate was called TRF Glaciate and had a logo that looked like a sad pork chop inside an ice cube. It was just off the Huddersfield District's southern span of ringway, sat in among other depots and warehouses. This one seemed to have a higher level of security than the surrounding warehouses. It would've been a packing unit for some of the old meat-growers further north, from places like Airedale. Great gobbets of protein slapped down in a machine and sliced into steak, then moved off to places like this for packing and further distribution. Except that business had declined a lot recently, taken over by overseas competitors, so a place like this had to take a bit of public money.

Seemed to be doing all right out of it. The swanky loading area – darkened beneath the criss-crossing lanes of the ringway above us – was lit by ambient reflectors and blue LEDs, and boasted a new paint job. Getting a new paint job round here meant you were feeling flush.

'Morning,' said Deborah, emerging from the other plain autocar parked ahead of me in the bay. She was wearing a surgical mask of some kind with elaborate filters on the side. As she approached, I could immediately catch the pong of rotted meat.

'Yeah, I'd stand back, mate,' she said, as she noticed my recoil and retch. 'Just going to get in the trunk, OK?' The boot lid popped open, and she reached in to retrieve a long polystyrene package. The way she handled it suggested that it was heavier at one end than at the other. I could tell she was struggling with this – but still wanting to make a good impression by doing it herself.

I dug into a pocket and pulled out a couple of menthol sniffs, cracking them quickly and ramming them deep in my nostrils. This was going to be one of those days.

'That car's going to need a deep clean within the next few hours, I reckon,' she said, turning her face away from the package.

'Send it away,' I said. 'We can use mine.'

'Will do,' said Deborah. She shouted over her shoulder at the car, telling it fuck off. It closed its boot and slunk out of the LED-lit loading area.

'Great,' said Deborah, getting her positive vibe back. 'You know where we're going, Carrie?'

'Never been here before,' I said, sticking the sniffs further up my nose. 'You lead the way.'

The stocky receptionist, though unfazed at the smell, still hastily ushered us through a secure door behind his desk and sent us down a long corridor towards the back of the facility. We were met by a couple of young women who seemed to know the drill. We told them we still wanted a moment to check over the evidence before it was stored and so they got us all gowned up and into massive fleece hats and pushed us into a freezing cold room with benches down the side. There they left us, underneath harsh lights, and told us to come and find them when we were ready.

'You going to unwrap it, then?' I asked Deborah, resisting the urge to take a sip of water. I was worried that to do it in here might mean I didn't have long before it froze over.

'Sure.'

It was difficult to watch Deborah hack at the wrapping on the polystyrene crate with her gloved hands, but I was cosy in my mitts and I didn't want them – or any other part of me – stinking.

Eventually, the tape came away, and the lid was lifted up.

'So,' said Deborah, with a flourish. 'What do you think?'

'That's a leg.'

'Right leg.'

'You sure?'

'What … oh, are you joking me?'

'Pulling your leg.'

'Shut up!'

'Here, let me get a reading.' I jammed a probe into the nearest lump. The outer layers were soft from spending a few days in the liquid in the fermenter tank, but were freezing fast. I had to get past a lot of other meat noise before I could get a proper reading.

'Does it match?' asked Deborah, her voice muffled behind her mask.

I waved a hand at her to suggest silence and to wait until I'd done my frigging job. I wasn't about to take my gloves off in this place, so I had to bark commands to my bead. It wasn't that difficult, but it was slow. And I didn't like doing this while I was being watched. It took a few minutes before I got an answer.

'Shit.'

'What?' said Deborah, bouncing a little beside me.

'I think it's got contaminated.'

'Oh, no!'

'Yeah. Here, let me try again.' I stabbed the probe into another part of the leg, the thicker muscle of the calf. Whatever happened in a bio-fermenter – and I took particular pride in knowing sweet fuck all about them – it had turned the skin to a nasty mush. I took the reading and ran it through DidNotArrive again.

Same result. But still not the answer I'd wanted.

'Different DNA,' I said, finally.

'To what?'

'Eh?'

'What were you comparing it to?' said Deborah. 'You had two

readings, you said, from the hospital.'

'Different DNA to the torso,' I said.

'Oh,' said Deborah. 'Shit.'

'Yeah.'

'What does that mean?'

'Fuck I know. Bag it up again and get it into the freezer, will you?'

'You not going to check the … check, the, uh, the wound?'

I laughed. I looked at the top of the thigh. Whatever had taken it off the rest of the body had made a very straight cut, almost perfect right angle to the outer line of the muscle. But any hope of getting a clear pattern from the ragged mess of decomposition on the outer skin and flesh was hopeless.

'Nope,' I said. 'Anyway, I know what they used. Get it bagged up and give it back to Tina or Reina, one of those two in there. I'll tell you about what I found up in the facility.'

On the way back down the long corridor, as we were sprayed by decontaminating mists, I explained the blood specks I'd found on the medical saw device up at the dump.

'I think it's what took his leg off, possibly both,' I said. 'The pathologist thinks how the legs were removed were different situation to the arms and head.'

'Oh,' said Deborah, trying to not wince.

'But I can't find anything on public records for that piece of kit,' I continued. 'Might mean it's military.'

'A military tool, then?'

'Well, more than a tool,' I said, heading for the car. A message had pinged into my display, the first response from the requests I'd sent earlier out to logistics companies. I set it to download the data to my bead as I got into the back of the car, shifting along to let Deborah in. 'It's automated, you see.

It's programmable.'

'Programmed to do what?'

'Where to, please?' said the pleasant voice of the car, interrupting us.

'Back to the bloody Tower,' I snapped.

'Confirmed,' said the car. It had heard members of Justice Division abuse it like this many, many times before. I noted that this one sounded like it came from Cumbria. Clearly, the Halifax accent hadn't reached the Chinese manufacturers just yet.

'Programmed to do what?' asked Deborah.

'Don't know,' I said. Something dropped into my notifications. 'But I've got somebody I can talk to.'

'What about me, because I–'

'Shh,' I said, interrupting her. The little note was telling me the data I'd requested earlier had just downloaded. 'Just got a message. Let me look at this first.'

Deborah blinked but fell silent, slipping into her corner of the car, looking out at the window, her face flickering with intermittent beams of sunlight, as we rose higher out of the lower depths of the city.

I wasn't paying attention to her anymore. Instead, I'd blanked out the background of the car and was struggling my way through voluminous shipping logs. Lists of dates and codes and times and companies. And it was like trying to wade through blood. Fucking Lem! Why was I having to do this? I worked out how to input some rudimentary searches and the key features started to populate. Thankfully, they'd included their lookups, so I wasn't staring at a bunch of code. Some of it was in English. So, I searched for any activity on the night of the twelfth. Getting hundreds of hits. I tried to remember my conversations with Haz, the previous digital analyst who had worked out of Airedale. Fuck knows where he was now. Somewhere in Scotland, supposed to be. Anyway, he'd talked me through this shit before. He knew how to follow his nose.

So I tried to follow mine. Date and location. Date and location.

Then I got something. Or rather, I got a few things. But they still made little sense. There was one name in there I'd spotted, which confused me. It was the right location. But it was a Russian name. I scrolled through my contacts list for Si West. He would know.

'All OK?' asked Deborah, in my ear, freaking me. I'd forgotten she was sitting next to me.

'Just need to speak to Si,' I said. 'He'll know an answer to something … hang on.'

'Right.' But she said it proper distant.

'You OK?' I asked.

'I'm not sure I am,' she said.

'Eh?'

'Feeling a bit rough, you know?'

'Fuck,' I said. 'Car, stop, stop anywhere, alright?'

I pulled myself out of my bead and reached out to grip the door handle, ready for some quick exiting. The car worked its way through traffic and parked itself on a service plinth.

'We are able to remain for approximately two minutes,' said the car. 'Then we will be identified by traffic Enforcement.'

'Yeah, yeah,' I said, heaving myself out of my seat. Deborah was already out of her door.

We were a few storeys above the southern centre of Huddersfield old town. Over to the north was the long raised – and covered – Beltway, the MC05, which ran on an east-west, from Liverpool to York. The lights of cars were just visible, flickering off its translucent roof. Closer to us was the centre of H District, the Justice and Enforcement Divisions' tower clearly defined in and among the other buildings that encircle the centre. The flyover we were standing on was riding on the thinnest of steel legs, which plunged down in an animal fashion in and among the old houses below, maintained a continuous wobble. As you travelled these flyovers, you never really recognised the movement, as you were ensconced within the feedback mechanisms of an autocar, which adjusted for it. But out here, it felt like the entire world was shaking.

Thankfully, the fresh air was helping Deborah. She was gripping the handrails, looking out to the horizon. I noted she wasn't looking down much.

'Better?' I asked.

'Yeah,' she said.

'Ready to go?'

'No.'

'Fine,' I said and walked up the service plinth a short way. I loaded up my bead, found the contact details again, and punched the icon. Despite waiting a full two minutes, I was getting no answer from Si on his bead, on his house number, on his work number. Or on a couple of socials I'd tracked him down to. The man was off grid, for some reason.

'Shit.'

Not sure if I was going to get anywhere, I instead called up Katta Jenkins and tried her. It got through immediately.

'Hi,' she said, confused. 'Who is this?'

'Carrie Tarmell, Justice Commission.'

'Oh,' she said, 'yeah, sorry, I forgot the name. Everything OK? Did you want to interview me now?'

'I've got that booked in for Monday,' I said, guessing. I couldn't be bothered to check my diary.

'Oh,' she said. 'Good. Good. What's this then?'

'Just a quick question,' I said. 'I can't get hold of Si. You spoken to him today?'

'No,' she said. 'We don't talk much outside of work. He not answering?'

'No,' I said. 'Does he usually?'

'Oh, yeah,' said Katta. 'He's very ... oh, I don't know the word.'

'Anyway, doesn't matter,' I said. Though something was making me feel it should. 'Listen, do you take autonomous deliveries... drops-off, pick-ups, that kind of thing?'

'Me, here? Sure, all–'

'No,' I said, sighing, 'I meant at the yard, at the Recycling Facility.'

'Oh, right, sorry. Yeah, we take a few. Mainly it's moving stuff around to other sites. We've got one up in Bradford–'

'Yeah, I know about that one.' I wondered whether I should tell her. But thought I'd better wait. 'I'm talking about third parties. Do businesses come and pick up stuff from the facility?'

'Well, we sell some stuff on. That's part of the model.'

'OK,' I said. 'You ever remember working with an H & H Packing?'

'No,' she said.

I didn't feel like I was getting anywhere. The car was trying to get my attention. 'One last question. Do the deliveries come into the yard?'

'No. We send the loaders out onto the main road. They use the little yard around the back of a place opposite. It's a bakery, I think. Called Sputnik. They do Italian breads.'

'Italian?'

'Yeah.'

'Called Sputnik?'

'What's the problem?'

'Thanks,' I said, laughing. 'Got to go. Speak on Monday, yeah?'

'Yeah, bye.'

Deborah was already back in the car, following some requests for us to move. It had adopted a less pleasant tone.

'Alright, we're going,' I said, closing the door.

I dug back into my data and found the delivery pick-up from Sputnik – the bakery – and tried to trace its meandering journey through the early hours of the thirteenth, as it traversed all the well-known spots in the Belt. It seemed to stop at retailers *en route*. But one name looked very familiar.

'Turn around. Turn the fuck around.'

'Confirmed,' said the car.

'What's wrong?' said Deborah.

'We've got to go back,' I said.

'Forgotten something?'

'No,' I said. Her face was pleading with me to tell her something. I took a breath. 'H&H Packing. They specialise in shipping meat around. They took an automated order early in the morning of the thirteenth. Pick-up was at a bakery, near the entrance to the Fellside. It went to a few boutique shops and the like, but it passed by the freezer depot.'

'Oh,' said Deborah.

It seemed to take twice as long for us to return to the depot. Once we'd come to a stop – and the car deigned to unlock the doors – I jumped out and ran across the docking bay, shouting behind me. 'Don't let that thing leave.'

Deborah caught up with me in reception. Despite having seen us merely minutes earlier, the stocky, suspicious receptionist examined our credentials cautiously on his desk screen before he nodded. This time, we had to be escorted. And we weren't going to the same place as before. As there were few other members of staff about – it was mainly automated loaders and cranes – the receptionist took us through some double doors and into a wide antechamber of benches and chairs and some beverage paraphernalia, where we put on more of the clothing.

Finally, we were allowed into a vast hall stacked to the rafters with pallets and boxes and large bins. Peering inside some of the nearest ones, I could see that all it contained was meat. Acres and acres of meat.

'What are you looking for?' asked the receptionist. He was trying to appear casual, but you could see he was a little excited now. He knew we were following a case.

'We're not sure yet.'

'It's contamination, is it?' he said, wincing. 'I'd have to give Dave a ring, if it were. We had a terrible case last year, crocodile got mixed up with caiman. We had the regulators around for weeks. You're not from environmental, are you?'

'No, we're not from environmental.'

'Oh,' he said. 'Sorry, assumed you were. What are you then?' he directed this last question at Deborah, so she responded immediately.

'Community.'

'Eh?' he said, looking more confused.

'Well, she is,' I said. 'I'm not.'

'Where you from then?'

'Airedale.'

'Nice.'

'Not really.'

'You having some trouble up at the Tower,' he said. 'I was reading about it.'

'Can't comment,' I said.

'Just heard there was an investigation. That's all.'

'See this schedule,' I said, casting him a visual. He picked it up on his small handheld.

'Yes,' he said, peering at it closely.

'Where did this delivery get stored?'

He consulted a couple of different screens and then trotted off, twisting his way among the shelves and freezer units.

'This way.'

We followed, having to jog a little to keep up. My hangover was glad of the cold, but I was more pleased that somebody round here was keen to help.

'Here we are,' he said, reaching a large wooden set of shelves. Each contained a stock of polystyrene boxes. He pulled one down.

'Am I OK to break the seal?'

I shrugged. 'If you need to? I don't know the regs. Just want to see what's inside, yeah?'

He opened the crate and looked in. There was a set of neatly cut steaks.

'Try another,' I muttered. 'How many we got?'

'Only five.

It was on the third that we found it. There, nestled in among the haunches of beef, was the unmistakable shape of something longer, something thinner. I reached down with a gloved hand and pulled it carefully out. Even through the recycled paper - machine-wrapped, they could never tuck in the ends – I could feel the familiar shapes. Shapes I'd felt every day of my life, but mainly on living subjects.

'What is it?'

'Take a fucking guess,' I said, placing the package on the bench. I removed the tags and unrolled the paper.

'Holy shit,' breathed Deborah. 'That's a bloody arm, Carrie.'

CHAPTER TEN

'What do you mean, he's not available?'

'I'm afraid he's ashore at the moment. This is his day off.'

'Not only is he on a fucking cruise, he has a day off as well?'

'I'm afraid you're speaking too fast for me to understand. Could you please repeat the question?'

I noticed the machine had a Halifax accent. I wondered if it was my sister's doing. 'You didn't mean admin Friday, do you?'

'I'm afraid I don't know what that means.'

I was standing outside one of the many side entrances to Calderdale hospital, one hand still resting on the autocar. I'd relented and let Deborah 'work on her admin', which apparently was only on the Friday afternoon here. Something to do with the reduction in staffing they'd suffered. I was supposed to be doing the same – Airedale gave you the whole day – but things had spiralled a little out of control this morning. Thankfully, she'd agreed to catch a different car.

'When's he going to be around again?'

'He is working again on Monday, Ms Tarmell.'

The machine was not only Dr Hausman's personal assistant, it also seemed in charge of unlocking the door. Because I hadn't come with an appointment this time, there was no possible way I was getting inside that building. I was aware of the plastic bag with a rapidly defrosting arm next to me. In hindsight, it would've been much more sensible to have simply walked the fucking limb from one end of the freezer depot to the other and left it alongside the leg. But I'd wanted to get immediate confirmation of the cuts and compare them with the remains of the shoulder of the torso – which was still a little more intact. I hadn't anticipated that the part-timer pathologist was going to off padding around some old ruin.

'Shit,' I muttered, wondering about my options.

'I beg your pardon?' said the machine.

'Nothing,' I said. 'I'll be back on Monday. Can you make an appointment for me then?'

'Of course.' It rattled off a few free slots in Dr Hausman's diary but I told it to shut up and plugged it directly into my appointments app and let them fight it out, between my preferences – nothing before ten – and his time slots and the relative cost of his time to the budget that Louie had granted the case.

I jumped back in the car.

'Where to please?'

I was about to say 'Home,' but I wasn't sure what that meant these days. Instead, I gave the car my sister's address in Friendly. I dropped the arm on the back seat next to me and tried to remember what she did on a Friday afternoon. Technically, like me, she was supposed to be working on her admin, but then she would never not be completely up to date on that shit. So she would use the time for useful and productive ends. I knew she liked to do insane exercises with other insane people from across the globe. That was what was probably happening.

'Stop somewhere for food as well, yeah?' I added.

'Of course,' said the car. 'What would you like to eat?'

It turned out the only thing available – at least, without a long detour – was a sushi dispensing machine alongside the charging ports of an automated service station just of west of Fax Central. I tried to select what looked like the freshest of the packs, while watching the numerous autocars come and go behind me. Nearly all were empty. It was a little eerie to be in a dimly lit subterranean space with so many autonomous machines, all of which could kill me. I remembered a story the Airedale digital analyst, Haz, had once told me. He'd believed the cars were all out to kill him. That the whole place was out to kill him. He'd got too close, he said. It had felt threatened. Like a rat.

The machine behind me beeped, making me jump a little. I retrieved my platter of optimistically-fresh raw fish and vegetables and scurried back to the car.

In between nibbles of salmon and rice, I reached across the back seat and massaged bits of thawed arm. I didn't want the whole thing to defrost and start decomposing, but this temporary softening was useful, because it allowed me to get the probe in. I fished around in my pocket and jabbed the device past the layers of paper and into the outer muscle of the upper arm. It went in a centimetre of so before hitting something solid. Enough to get a reading. I threw another nigiri into my mouth and, as I chewed at the OK-ish tuna substitute, brought up my bead display. It was already downloading data from the probe. I squeezed some of the wasabi directly onto my tongue.

'Fuck,' I said with a grin. I used to play this game with Grace when we were kids. I fucking wiped the floor with her when it came to wasabi. And chilli. And fermented fish sauce.

Eyes watering, I pulled up DidNotArrive and dropped in the code, now streaming across the wireless connection. It took a moment to register and churned through results. The DNA of the arm was registered to a Ratna Manish. I ran a quick further search on the name. He'd not got any form of case file on him, but his medical records – and his business, it seemed – were all in south Manchester. He was still alive. Looking at a recent photo, he was also fully armed, biologically-speaking.

I mulled this all over, still chewing away at stringy seaweed, as the car pulled up outside my sisters' house. By spying up at the front window, I could see that the wall screen of the living room was flashing something — repetitive and bright — so I guessed she was engaged in some form of self-inflicted pain. Probably involving stomping from left to right. That was what it mainly involved. Then too much sweat to deal with.

I sneaked in quietly, slipping along the hallway to the bathroom and silently closed the door. On the bathroom floor, I unwrapped my package. Unlike the leg, this had been nowhere near a fermenter tank. It looked like it'd been frozen very shortly after it'd been severed. I got my gecko to take some hi-def pictures of the wound and set Bladester to analyse these. Then something caught my attention, lower down, on the meat of the forearm: two parallel lines of muck or something. I ran the sniffer over them and came back with a multitude of molecular signals, but mainly general-purpose industrial grease. I guessed this must've been the gripper of the machine that had carried the arm out to the baker's yard. I rolled the arm over and, sure enough, there were similar shaped lines on the other side. I took another reading of each of these, enough to get a strong signature, and dropped that into the case file as well.

I sat back, leaning against the door of the shower, regarding the arm. Bladester alerted me to the results of its analysis: less than fifty percent probability of a match to the torso. I checked a few more readings. Blood thickening on the finger ends confirmed the same date. However, there was still a chance that it was a random find. Not that I believed this, but it was certainly enough uncertainty to fall over in court, not least because the postmortem was taking place on the floor of a relative's bathroom. I didn't have enough to go on here.

Then there was the fact the owner of this arm was still, technically, importing algae crackers from Morocco from an office in Manchester. It seemed the next best place to check out. I filtered for his name. I knew it was Friday afternoon, and I was supposed to be doing my admin. Unofficially, it was the weekend. I could spend some time with Grace. Help her cook something nice.

'Fuck that.'

On my bead display again, I dropped Ratna Manish into my search. It came back cleanly – on the public channels, as well. He wasn't hiding. I pinged him a message. Justice wanted a word. I got an out-of-office – standard for a Friday – so dropped another message. This time telling him I'd found his arm and wondering if he needed it sewing back on.

'See you what you've got to say to that,' I muttered.

'Hello,' said my sister, her voice suddenly echoing at the bathroom door. 'Is that you, Carrie? You back? Talking to yourself?' She must've crept up so silently. Usually I had sharp ears. But she'd grown up a fucking ninja, always scaring me and mum by creeping up on us.

'Yeah,' I said, hastily wrapping the arm in its greased paper again. As it defrosted, it oozed over the floor.

'What are you doing in there? Sounds like paper.'

'You don't want to know,' I said.

'Oh,' she said. 'Is it that bad?'

'Yeah,' I said. 'Be free in a minute.'

'OK,' she said. 'Just putting things away and...'

'Right.'

'I need the shower, though, Carrie.'

'Yeah, yeah,' I said.

I bundled the arm back into its wrapping and mopped up some of the blood from the floor with a piece of her expensive seafibre toilet paper – only the best for my sister. After checking by putting my ear to the door, it sounded as though Grace had wandered back to her room for a moment, so I edged out of the bathroom and slipped into the kitchen. The coast was still clear for a moment, no doors opening. I stepped up over to the freezer and opened the door.

'What are you doing?'

'Just checking if you had... something to eat, really.' I'd half-turned.

'You not had dinner?'

'Grabbed something, yeah,' I said. The arm was hanging by my side, obscured by my leg. But if she came around the side, she'd easily see it.

'I'm making something for tea,' she said. 'Going to have deep fried courgette.'

'Great,' I said.

'You want a walk before then? We could go up the hill?'

'Yeah,' I said. Then a message popped back into my display. It was from Ratna Manish. And the first word was 'OK'.

'Sorry,' I said. 'I've got work this afternoon.'

'Remote?'

'No. Got to… well, interview somebody. Proper Justice work, you know?'

She looked a little crestfallen. 'So, you're heading out again?'

'Yeah,' I said. 'Got to get over… well, to Manchester, actually.'

'Manchester? Today?'

'It won't be that busy.'

'It'll be a mess,' she said. 'You know, you can close my freezer now.'

'Right,' I said. Stepping away and knocking the door shut with my shoulder. This was an error, because I could feel the arm flap about. But thankfully, she didn't notice.

'You're behaving weird,' she said. 'You sure you're OK?'

'Fine.'

'We're going to spend time tomorrow, OK?'

'Alright,' I said.

'I feel bad about what I said last night,' she said. Her eyes didn't mean it though.

'Sure,' I said.

'You said you needed to check out your flat, didn't you? We can go up together and I can help get it tidied up.'

'Sounds like you've got a plan.'

She narrowed her eyes a little, still suspicious. 'I need a shower,' she said, eventually.

'Not stopping you.'

When she'd gone – and I could hear the water starting – I opened the freezer again and took out the cartons and the bags of vegetables. There was just enough space, with a little pressure at the elbow joint, to squeeze the limb into the back of the space.

I called an autocar and refilled my water bottle. I grabbed my coat and made for the door, before remembering what I'd been doing, and running back to the sink to wash my hands, then spotting the light pink puddle on the floor next to the freezer, cleaning that up, and then finally dashing for the stairs.

I was stopped from getting into the car outside by a shriek.

'Carrie!' Grace's head was poked out of a window above me, towel wrapped around her head.

'What?'

'There's a fucking arm in my fucking freezer!'

'I know,' I said, jumping in the car. 'I'll sort it later.'

Although I'd been to the South Manchester sky bridges a few times, the place was particularly impressive on a late February Friday afternoon. A chain of twelve residential and office towers, following the approximate line of the Mersey below them, were linked by vast hawsers of alloy cable, and pinned to the ground at either end. God knows what the cables were made from, but I'd read it had some connection to spiders. Or possibly goats. I knew I should've known – this being my specialist subject – but sometimes the rate of change was so fast, that you had to duck out of some knowledge before it pushed other, more important stuff – like your mother's birthday – out of your head. All I knew was this stuff was strong but light, so it wouldn't bring down the towers. That was also helpful, because the cabling that linked each of the towers also held foot bridges and, slung beneath these, were paper homes. Or, in the case of the one I was just about to enter, a paper office.

Ratna Manish had confirmed the time, as I was about to sink into a welcome snooze on the South Beltline train. I was childishly pleased that the invite had asked me to come direct to his office; I liked the view from the sky bridges. They were so high up, on a clear day you could easily see the estuary snake out into the Irish Sea past Liverpool, the tiny buildings on the seafront, and the mountains of north Wales in the distance. And to the east, the view was equally impressive, showing up the vast half-bowl of hills that surrounded Manchester, and the lights of the ridgeline settlements, of the Fourth Sector creeping over the horizon and joining up the old cities into one, vast conurbation.

I announced my approach to the Manish offices via my bead as I walked through the freezing wind of the bridge. There was a gate set into the handrail, inconspicuous except to those who were expecting it, which clicked as I approached, and a tiny LED flashed green beside a neat plaque. I pushed it open and stepped down a few steps and then underneath the bridge. Far below me, the muck and open fires of pure brownfield opportunity were briefly visible through a passing cloud and I fought a little wave of vertigo. Normally this kind of shit didn't upset me, but there was something unsettling about the speed of those vapour wisps relative to me. I was in the clouds now.

The steps descended and connected to the side of the paper office, swinging on its harness in the breeze. It was about the size of a decent house, so could probably manage a team of six or seven people. From a little searching as I came over, I knew the business was much bigger than this. He also had a depot up north near Formby and one down south somewhere. So this may have been the brains of the operation. But it sure as shit wasn't the full company.

Bastard wanted to keep this conversation quiet.

'Welcome, Ms Tarmell, yes?' I was met by a young man, really a boy, as I stepped through the doors. The reception area was all muted greens and blues and there were photos of lagoons and boats and smiling Moroccans plastered all over the wall.

'That's me,' I said. I gratefully discarded my coat and bobble hat into his arms and strode across to the desk. 'Mr Manish ready for me?'

'He said to go straight in.' The boy waved down a short corridor to the left. 'Would you like a chocolate, or a coffee, or a tea?'

'No,' I said. 'I'll be fine.'

At the end of the corridor was a large room, which must've run nearly an entire side of the building. There were a few comfy chairs scattered around and some low tables. At one end of the room, a man sat, scanning some flexible screens he'd lined up in front of him. He was in his late forties and was wearing subtle but expensive office clothes. A little old-fashioned, a more attentive eye might say, but they still suggested wealth.

He definitely had both arms.

'Ratna Manish?'

'Hi,' said the man, hastily jumping up. He squinted at me, as though surprised by what he saw. I knew my cardigan was a little holey and the black trousers hadn't been changed for a couple of days, but I didn't think I warranted the look he gave me.

'OK if I sit here?' I said, sinking heavily into the chair opposite him.

'Yes,' he said, also sitting. The three screens were loosely rolled up and thrust behind a cushion on the chair next to him. The sway of the office caught me off guard a little.

'Yes,' he repeated, noticing my eyes widen and the firm grip I gave the chair. 'You get used to it after a while. Really, I'm not that happy up here, myself. I might move. It was only for the clients. Now I'm stuck in a long contract and I can't…' He trailed off. 'Still, you're not here to speak about that. Are you here to arrest me?'

I was about to speak, but this stopped the words in my throat, and I changed gears mentally. 'Before all that, why don't you tell me your side of the story, Mr Manish?'

'I've got a lawyer on the call as well,' he said, tapping his breast pocket. I assumed he must have some device in there.

'Oh?'

'Yes.'

'What's their name?' I asked politely.

'Oh, it's a legal service, plugged into a server in Washington, I think. Not a person.'

'Ah,' I said. 'Of course.'

'Do you want me to patch them into your … you have a nose bead, do you?' He had leaned forward, trying to see, but not appear too rude.

'Yeah,' I said. 'Patch them in. I'm going to start recording, right?' Having a legal bot on the call meant I didn't have to offload the IG shit, so I just plugged the flashing icon on my screen into the division's paperwork interface and they sorted it out themselves. Legal bots were usually a pain in the arse – their default was to get their client to shut the fuck up – but they handled the bureaucracy very well.

'You ready?' I said. 'I'm ready, just want your side of the story, OK?'

'No story has been specified.' The legal bot's voice was gently-accented female East Coast, with an absence of stress on any particular word sufficient to set your teeth on edge. I hated it immediately.

'Good point,' said Manish, nodding at me. There was a pause as I could see he was being fed a line. This was followed by: 'What am I being accused of?'

'Nothing,' I said. 'Yet. Your name has come up in an investigation, that's all.'

'Some nonsense about an arm?' he said. Then grimaced, no doubt being reprimanded by his counsel.

'It were mention of the arm that seemed to get me a meeting, Mr Manish,' I said, grinning.

'I was intrigued,' he said. 'I still am.'

'Well,' I said, 'the thing is, we've found your arm, Mr Manish. Your left one.'

'How amusing,' he said. He raised his left arm and wiggled his fingers. 'It's right here. See?'

'I know,' I said. 'This is why I thought it worth popping over to have a chat. We found it stacked between some vat-grown beef rump. In a freezer warehouse off the H District Ringway. It'd just been driven halfway across the Belt in a butcher's van.'

'Huddersfield?' he said. There was genuine surprise in his voice.

'That's not where you'd expect it to be, I take it?'

'My client did not say that,' the bot interjected.

'Like I said,' said Manish, once again wiggling his fingers, 'my left arm is right here.'

'Yeah,' I said, smiling, 'you mentioned that already. Thing is, we've got a DNA match to your medical records–'

'You can do that?' he said, interrupting. Again, there was a raising of the voice.

'I got delegation,' I said. 'It gets me into places, you know? In the data and all. And, like I said, we got a match between your code and this arm.'

'What strength?' said the lawyer.

'I'm sorry,' I said, still smiling directly at Ratna. 'I don't understand what you mean?'

'I will repeat,' said the lawyer. Somebody had clearly programmed it to have an undertone of menace. Even I was slightly on edge. Slightly.

'Good,' I said. 'Do. And explain what you mean?' Two could play at this fucking game.

'Do you have a quantified value demonstrating the match?'

'Fuck yeah,' I said, sitting back. Waving a hand, I threw the DidNotArrive results virtually straight at the lawyer. 'They good enough for you?'

The response was immediate. 'The results need to be verified by our—'

'Sorry,' interrupted Manish. 'Wait up. Can I get a minute with the lawyer alone?'

I shrugged and gave him a friendly thumbs-up.

Manish got up from his chair and walked down the length of the room, whispering. Because of the wind whistling outside the window, and the low tones of his murmurs, meant I couldn't pick up anything of what he was saying. But he was clearly checking something with the legal bot. Of course, there were apps that could have recorded everything, stripped out the window, amplified – even enhanced – and then dropped the full conversation back in my case file. But that shit was way out-of-bounds for a scummy analyst like me. You had to be one of Those-We-Don't-Know-About to play with that shit.

Ratna Manish returned to his seat and sat down carefully.

'They've escalated the service,' he apologised. 'It won't be a minute.'

'Eh?' I said.

'They need to find a human to pick up the case,' he said.

'It's that tricky, is it? So, you have something to say?'

Seemed the legal bot was still squatting on the connection, because it chimed in immediately at this point. 'My client will not answer any further questions until a legal representative is found.'

'How long will that be?' I asked.

'The SLA states all escalations will result in a human representative to be available within two hours.'

'Two hours?' I said. An unkind person, such as my mother, may have described it as a shriek.

'I'm sure it won't be that long,' said Manish. 'Very simple explanation, I'm sure.'

'I'm not waiting here two hours,' I said. 'My DI won't wear that.' I rose from the chair, suddenly rather tired. 'I'll have to come back. But next time with some extra questions and possibly a charge or two.'

'I'm afraid you cannot threaten–'

The soft American accent was cut off and an Irish accent replaced it. 'Does everybody actually work on admin Fridays these days?'

'You the lawyer?'

It turned out he was. That he'd been pulled out of babysitting his – and his neighbours – children, and that he wasn't that happy about it. But we explained the situation and I could ask the simple question: 'Why is there an arm in Huddersfield with the same DNA as yours, Mr Manish?'

To which he was now legally able to give his – checked over – response. With plenty of pauses and extra confirmations, and little walks away from the chair. 'The truth is, I had signed up to a replacement service. Now, yes, I know that kind of business is illegal in this country, but the service is run from China, from somewhere in Shenzhen, where it is legal. And there's nothing illegal in signing up for a service like that, over in a different country, is there?'

'You tell me,' I said.

'There isn't,' said the lawyer in my ear.

'We'll let the court decide that,' I said. But I was only making conversation. He was absolutely correct.

'Let's hurry it along now,' said the lawyer. 'She's talking nonsense. Wasting your time. Finish it up now.'

'So,' said Mr Manish. 'My only thought is that, somehow, one of the… um, one of the replacement items must've accidentally ended up here.' He sat back, clasped his hands together in his lap, and looked expectantly at me.

'*Accidentally?*' I said, trying not to laugh.

'That's what we're going with,' said the lawyer.

Growing replacement limbs and other organs had been medically possible for over a decade now. It had run hand-in-hand through the fields of scientific progress with its best mates, the automated surgical robots and the growing of cow meat in vats. But the national consciousness of some countries had been too overcome by the ickiness of the process, the thought of all those hands and feet in jars everywhere, that they'd legislated furiously and allowed only a few mandated major organs – the heart, liver, kidneys – to be licensed. Even then, it wasn't on a shareholder, profit-driven business model. You couldn't just set up a wet parts service with a bit of credit and a warm warehouse. There had to be universities and courts and legislators and all sorts of shit to go through. I'd actually handled a case a few years ago where a woman had accused her boss of stealing her replacement kidney. Turned out, it was true. The thieving wrong 'un had falsified documents, and everything, even managing to get a replacement kidney, just as her member of staff was going down with renal disease. He was now on the Estuary.

'Any ideas,' I said, adopting my musing face, 'how a fully grown limb, requiring constant attention and specialist transportation, ends up accidentally travelling halfway around the globe? Accidentally?'

Manish was about to answer, but he was cut off by the lawyer again. 'That kind of supposition is exactly your job, isn't it, Ms Carrie Tarmell?' the tone changed. 'Hey, Freya, put that down… put that down now!'

'Trouble with Freya?' I asked, looking out the window.

'Dealt with,' came the succinct response.

'I need to know the details of this company you signed up with,' I said, turning my gaze on Ratna Manish.

'We can provide that,' said the lawyer. He knew I could drop a shit load more delegation on their servers, so this was something of a tactical retreat, to keep me happy.

'You must know how it got in the freezer warehouse, do you?' asked Manish. 'Have you not got some more details on that? Was it a package from China that came direct? Could have been a mix up in a depot somewhere … anywhere, possibly *en route*? Hong Kong? Dhaka?'

'Is that the route they came in on?' I asked.

'I wouldn't know.' Ratna's mouth suddenly clamped shut.

'Maybe you should ask the company yourself?' I said. 'I'd imagine a client of theirs would have rights to ask what they're doing with his money.'

'Well, yes,' said Manish. 'The truth is though, I'm no longer a client. I cancelled my annual subscription … um, years ago.'

'Really?' I said. This was interesting.

'Yes,' he said. 'It was far too expensive.'

The name and address of the company dropped into my display. I pushed it towards the case file. 'So, you're not even a customer anymore. How do you feel about the fact that your arm seems to have gone astray?'

'There are issues that need addressing,' he said. He paused, listening to the lawyer. 'But this is a separate legal matter. A civil matter. Between me and the company.'

'Understood,' I said, standing. 'I'll let you both get back to your Friday.'

CHAPTER ELEVEN

Although Grace was convinced the state of my flat in Shipley was what she'd always remembered it to be like – because I lived, in her words, 'like a feral pig' – the sight of the rotting head in the middle of the floor of the living room was sufficient to convince her otherwise. Even she could see that was a bit much for my low hygiene standards. Although the thing had been decaying for a while now, and had already stunk out the room, I could see that it was only recently deposited onto my blue and cream Guianan rug. Possibly within the last twenty-four hours. I didn't even need to fire up the usual apps to help tell me this; there was only a small amount of water damage in the vicinity. The window through which they'd chucked it was smashed and glass was scattered across the floor. They must've come up the fire escape, threw something heavy in – looked like that loose brick in the corner – and then followed by slinging in the head.

Grace had retired, feeling sick and faint, to my bathroom, leaving me the job of tidying up. But, unfortunately, this was all evidence, so I'd set the gecko to work while I got on the phone to Louie.

'You seeing this, Louie?'

His black eyes, concerned but exhausted, looked back at me from my display. He was sitting in front of a terminal in the coffee shop area of the Shipley offices. Behind him, I could see other members of the Justice team swan about in the background.

'Yeah, I am,' he said.

'This is what happens when they take away my protection.'

'Yeah, I know, I know.'

'Tell you what you can do, Louie. I'm going to zip up all the pics from this situation and drop it into your messages. You can then take these to those Enforcement fuckers and explain why I need that piece-of-crap drone back guarding my place.'

'Yeah, you're right, Carrie. I'm really sorry.' He took a sip of a coffee and glanced up at somebody off camera, giving them a little wave and a wan smile.

'You recognise the face, of course?' I asked.

'Do I?' he said, jumping a little and looking back at the camera.

'Have another look,' I said. I wouldn't let him get away with this. If I was going to withstand the smell of the rotting little bastard, he ought to at least have a look at him. So I waited as Louie scanned through some of my initial photos of the scene.

My sister's voice drifted through the flat. 'You got rid of it yet?'

'Not yet,' I said. 'Still taking evidence.'

There was polite swearing from the direction of the bathroom.

'You have somebody there?' asked Louie.

'Grace,' I said. 'My sister.'

'Oh, right? Give her my love, yeah.'

'Will do,' I said, grimly. 'You found those images?'

'Just looking now … ah, I see who it is. Kai Reed, right?'

'That's right.'

'I see. Bit of statement, is it?'

'Well, helpful of them to give us the missing piece of the case, anyway.'

We'd never found the head. It looked as though they'd dropped it onto some wasteland. It'd been there a while, one cheek imprinted with rocks and grit. The paleness of the flesh around the neck suggested it'd been exposed and frozen a couple of times as well.

'You'll add it to the file, yeah?' said Louie.

'Fuck you, Louie!'

'What?'

I remembered the discussion with Deborah in the autocar on the way up to the Dump, about how things become chaotic when a gang loses its leader. The thought that, maybe, she was correct, made me a little bit furious. 'They broke into my flat! They threw a fucking dismembered human head onto my lounge, Louie! All you can suggest is add it to my file?'

'We're all struggling, Carrie,' he said.

'You've changed, Louie,' I said. 'Whoever's taken over your body, I want the old one back.'

He blinked a couple of times, then nodded. 'Look, I've got to go. Big meeting coming up here.'

'On Saturday?'

'Yeah,' he said, 'things change when you–'

I didn't care. 'Send that shit to Enforcement. Try to help me out.'

'I'll do my best, Carrie. Bye.'

The click of the fingers he made to close down the call was too quick. And too final. I didn't think I was going to get my security drone back in a hurry. Certainly, those news channels I trusted suggested there had been a general widespread rise in incidents occurring all over the Belt and up into the spurs like Airedale. There simply weren't enough of us to cope. This is what happened when the good times ended and those who had the means got up and left.

My thoughts were interrupted by a call from RapidRez down below. I left my broken gecko to finish up taking photos and ordered the house server to let them in on the ground floor. They'd bring all the bags. All the wipes. With a bit of luck, they might also tidy up the flat.

I made my way to the bathroom and banged on the door. 'We're out of here, Grace.'

'So, it were a different head?'

'Yeah,' I said, regretting ever telling her so much about my work.

'But you are looking for a head, aren't you?'

'I work different cases,' I said, as if to a child.

'Oh. I guess I didn't appreciate that.'

'Hmm.'

We walked past the next display. This, also, had nothing in it. But I wasn't sure if that was the point.

'This is nice,' she said. I knew she was lying. 'Did you come here with Mum at all?'

Considering she was only three years younger than me, it was a weird question. 'Yeah, of course. When we lived on St Martins, we used to come here all the time. You were too young to remember. Of course, they had the butterflies then. And the moths.'

'Yeah,' she said, looking round. 'I think I remember.'

The Airedale Butterfly Dome had actually once been a butterfly sanctuary. And also a dome. Now it was a series of renovated and repurposed polythene encased shells purporting to be a visitor attraction. But it was a sad affair. Apart from Grace and myself, there were about four other families meandering their way through the linked tunnels. Around us were the brown remains of flower beds, now holding dead roots and, here and there, the hopeful evidence of somebody actually digging. I'd been here about two years previously with Ronnie and there had been a similar prospect of hopeful futures in the place. But nothing seemed to have progressed. Though I wasn't sure if that was the point. We had both understood it to be possibly an ironic art statement – and the information given to us at the door didn't really answer this question either.

'Why are all the display cases empty?' asked Grace.

'They're not,' I said. 'This one has a note telling us to expect something here soon.'

The space around us was augmented with virtual notices as well, popping up on my bead's display as I moved my head, possibly left over from when this was an operational Dome. Or possibly added at a later date by the artists. To make a statement. The whole thing was a bewildering mess. I wondered how many of these ghost virtual markers there were still out there, telling you all about the thing you were supposed to be looking at but which had, physically, been removed or destroyed years before.

Still, it kept us from the freezing rain outside. This was better than my sister's shit idea of a walk through the haunted farms in the moors.

'You said you came here with Ronnie?' asked Grace, in her way that really meant: 'Have you and Ronnie got back together again?'

A message had dropped into my inbox. It looked like it had come in from Aitch Bee. I was resisting the urge to open it. 'I'm not fucking talking about Ronnie.'

'Just asking,' she said, sniffily. 'Oh look, an actual butterfly. What variety is that?'

'Cabbage white,' I said.

'Well, you're the botanist,' she said, winking at me. 'I'll have to trust you on that.'

'It's a fucking cabbage white,' I said. 'And that's not botany.'

'Like I said,' said Grace, unfazed. She'd lived with me long enough. 'I just did art, so I can't pretend to know all of this. Plus, you don't need to be so rude. Sometimes you can be–'

'Yeah, I know, but everybody knows what a cabbage white...' I gave up. The message on my display pulsed.

'You ever thought about doing summat else?' asked Grace, moving on and staring intently at a line of ants that had made a nest behind one of the old brick walls lining the path.

'What?'

'Things are pretty tough for you at the moment,' she said, glancing back at me with genuine worry in her eyes. 'I mean, you've always been grumpy–'

'I am not grumpy!'

'–but Mum and I always knew that about you. Now you're more distant than ever. Mum says you hardly talk to her anymore–'

'She's a hypocrite. You remember how she used to talk about her mother?'

'Yeah, but she's getting old now. She's getting forgetful.'

'Like I don't know!' I said. 'She still thinks I like unicorns. Gives me no end of grief for it.'

'That's what happens when you get old, Carrie.'

'Well, it's not my fault then, is it? Blame nature. Blame Mum. She's the one who brought us up. She should've brought us up better. Maybe she should've included another parent in the mix, eh? Maybe that would've taken some of the strain off her? Stopped her being such a fucking martyr?'

Grace took a deep intake of breath. 'You know you should never talk about that.'

She had a nerve saying that, especially after what she'd been saying about me the night before last. But I clamped my mouth shut. She wasn't about to talk about specimens. And I wasn't about to remind her that we weren't real sisters.

Grace wouldn't let it go, though. 'You haven't spoken to Mum like that, have you?'

'Haven't spoken to her for weeks now,' I said.

Grace clamped her mouth shut, and we walked on into the next polytunnel. This one simply had flower beds with a neat row of large holes. Like an enterprising wrong 'un had received a message from their fence that a dozen sub-tropical shrubs was going to pay for their pseudo trip for the weekend.

'You been putting up with that kind of thing for a while?' said Grace, after a while. 'I mean, the head in your living room, and that?'

We hadn't spoken much after leaving the flat. As soon as RapidRez had arrived, we'd slipped out and made our way to the station to get on the train to the butterfly dome/art installation. Grace had calmed down a bit. I'd explained that what they'd put on my new Guianan rug was evidence from a case I was working on. I explained the sorry story of little Kai Reed. It sounded like an AI-produced cheapstream when I retold it back to my sister. But she loved the cheapstreams, loved the shonkiness of the acting, the weird hacking jumps in tone that the machine writer introduced. She was an expert in the voices, could hear when they'd got it right. Or got it wrong. Then there was always the unbelievable causal factor in the plot, which made you snort out loud when it was explained in the final act. But then you went onto online archives – the AI's source for all human behaviour – and you found such an event had happened in real life. Usually in Florida. Or Blackpool. Not only that, there was really such a larger-than-life character, such a sorry tale of betrayal, such depressing and tawdry reasons for a death. And you realised that the AI writer knew us better than we knew ourselves. It was at those minutes that I remembered the conversations with Haz, about the digital analyst's app Modlee, and what it knew, and what it created. Then I tended to get a little scared. I really wanted to talk to Haz. I needed to drop him a message.

'That shit in the flat?' I said. 'Nah, only happened in the last few weeks. Normally never get into bother with my work.'

'Is that bother, then? Looks like pretty serious bother?'

'No,' I said. 'I know some people've had worse.' I didn't want to tell her what Gilbie McKenn – our enviro analyst – had had pumped into his letter box.

'You're behaving as if it's serious, though.'

'Am I?' I said and tried to grin.

'You're never normally scared,' said Grace. 'Big sisters don't get scared, do they?'

'I'm not scared of that shit,' I said. 'Just kids throwing rocks around, in't it?'

'You are scared,' said Grace, looking away. 'And it's scaring me. Look... another cabbage white.'

I stopped in the middle of the winding path. 'I've got a call coming.'

Grace stopped as well and shook her head. 'You promised no work today. You'll set off your balance again. Remember last time, Carrie?'

I gave her the look. She shut up and turned back to peer into the holes in the soil, looking for something, anything, that was left. I turned my attention back to the Aitch Bee message and played it. It was from Negussie. Video call. She looked proper pissed off and all.

'My office has been trying to reach you for hours now. I need to talk urgently. If you don't return the calls now, I'm going to escalate to an appropriate officer.'

Good luck with that, I thought.

I scrolled through my contacts and brought up her details. Punched a button and I was through. It took ten seconds before there was a reply.

'Carrie Tarmell?'

'That's me. It's the weekend, you know?'

'I bloody well know that.' The servant was in some drab offices. A stylised painting of the Belt at night hung on the wall behind her. 'I don't want to be working either. But I've got a district to help… to… to serve here! And it's all going to go to shit on Monday.'

'How so?'

'Have you not looked outside? There haven't been any autotruck collections for three days now.'

I jumped, a little guiltily. I'd forgotten about the facility being closed. About all the work that I'd left just getting on with stuff there. 'What about the backups from neighbouring sites? They reroute, don't they?'

'They're full! Been taking in extra over most of last week. I've just had … somebody, can't remember her name, on the phone from H District, the Second Facility, threatening to come up to Aitch Bee and dump the extra waste on our municipal hill gardens.'

'Right.'

'What are you going to do about it?'

'I'll open the site again,' I said. 'I just need to gather in the crawlers–-'

'What?'

'Crawlers,' I said. 'They collect evidence. But it's slow progress with them because they… well, anyway, it's a big site, in't it?'

'I don't care,' said Negussie. 'I don't want the people I serve to find their bins are overflowing come Monday with rivers of slurry outside their front doors. You need to get it working again.'

'What about the team there?' I asked. 'Have you tried them, and all?'

'Our usual contact…' There was a muted chat with somebody else in the room. 'Simon West, I believe, is not available. Maybe you can reach him?'

I could feel a familiar uneasiness. Often came during a case when something didn't feel right. Or soon after I'd eaten a fermented prawn ball. I'd not had a fermented prawn ball for months.

'Got to get back,' I said to Grace.

'Fine,' said Grace, throwing her arms up. 'Another family day out ruined!'

'I'm sorry,' I said. Not meaning it.

'It always ends like this,' she said.

'I can always stay up here,' I said. 'I mean, up in Airedale. They're cleaning up my flat, aren't they?' She seemed to consider it. So I thought I'd better drop in something more. 'I'm sure they won't come back. They won't actually hurt me… I mean, they have. You saw the shockstick marks. But I'm sure they won't do it again.'

She breathed in deeply through her nose and then shook her head. 'No. You need to stay at mine a little longer, don't you?'

'Thanks,' I said. I surprised myself at how much I was relieved. There was no way I was going back to my flat at the moment. It made me feel a little bit shit at myself. A little bit more shit. I needed to find out what had happened to Si West. And Katta. And urgently.

She shrugged and turned back to the exit. Then she stopped and wagged a finger at me. 'And when are you going to remove that bloody arm from my freezer?'

The facility was dark when I got there. I dropped the a-codes into my bead and let myself in. I wasn't happy being alone here at this time. It was Saturday night, so I didn't feel I had any right to call in Deborah. Not that I would've done anyway. There'd been a general comms message out from Enforcement, to all their so-called buddies in Justice, Prevention and Reconciliation, that there was nobody available in their teams for hand-holding, tear-wiping, botty-smacking and shoulder-squeezing. Well, they hadn't written it like that, but I could read sub-text like that from a fucking mile away: *Don't bother us, we're busy.* If bids for more funding were visible with the naked eye, you could have seen that comms from outer space.

I'd repeatedly attempted to reach both Si and Katta on my bead while on the way back from Airedale. In between trying to explain to my sister how it was, I'd been dumped in the Fourth Sector and not my home patch, without giving away too much of the corruption case file. In the end, I'd left messages for both of them. Neither had returned my calls by the time I got to the yard. I had both their addresses. There was a diligent part of me, willing my mouth to read out their addresses to the autocar and to drive across the Fax and H District to find them. But what would I do if I got there? Stand in the street underneath their lit windows and check that they were OK. People don't always respond to messages. Especially those from Justice.

Anyway, Grace had promised she'd be buying a twelve-pack of synthetic lime cartons. My holdall held a bottle of renatured Brazilian ethanol fuel, thanks to the generosity of Airedale's environmental analyst, Gilbie McKenn, who'd found a warehouse of the stuff and was merrily making money selling it to colleagues. Inject a carton of frozen lime juice with sugarcane fuel and synthetic sweetener and you've got yourself an ethanolie. And those ethanolies were calling to me. So I just needed to get in here, get my crawlers and then get the fuck out of it.

The lines of LEDs that ran over the arch above me burst into action as I stepped up to the gate. The RapidRez locks were all intact, and they dutifully flickered across to green as I approached. I'd been given the gate's outer and inner lock codes as well and was relieved when they also clicked back into place. They were old, rusty and dull, and I had little faith that much would work in this place. I pushed at the gate. It was old-school. Needed a human hand to get it moving.

When I got inside, I wasn't sure where to start. My bead was telling me most of the crawlers had returned to their rendezvous location – outside the office in the central yard – but there were a couple still stuck somewhere in the outer ring. On the opposite end to where I was, on the western side of the facility. I looked left. There was a path through the piles of junk and bins and hoppers, which wound itself inside the outer fencing. It looked dark and unenticing. However, ahead of me, there were little pools of light leading my way to the main yard. So I took that instead.

As I walked, I got a strong enough signal to download the data captured from the crawlers. Unlike the gecko, they were low-energy, low-profile, slow beasts. But they picked up a lot. IG meant we weren't able to route their data via the public channels, so a peer-to-peer link was required. And what's more, they actually scraped up evidence as well, not just visuals and audio, so it took a while to manually unpack as well as digitally decode their work.

I found them in the central yard, lined up cutely in a three by four array. Except for a couple of gaps in the middle. Those missing ones must've been the ones that had got stuck in the western end of the compound. The local connection data was now flooding into my bead. Each crawlers' download looked like a slowly-filling bottle of water. It made me need to piss. There was no way I was going to use the Fellside Facility's toilet. Not having seen the state of the place elsewhere. Instead, I tried to ignore the sensation and cracked open the data, dropping it into the case apps, dragging up new project folders, folding it into visualisations, looking for clues, for interesting patterns. It was a sea of data, as expected. The amount of human tissue – skin cells, hair, phlegm, the Dirty Three, as Big Man Vickers had told us in that small room overlooking the Mersey – that the crawlers had recorded across the facility would probably match to most of the population of the Fourth Sector of the Belt. At least, those that made use of the facility. So that was useless. Unless I had something specific I could filter down on. Using timeframe filters produced little else. But the tracks data were producing something here. The yard was built on a mixture of textured concrete, packed earth and recycled matting. It meant the opportunity for visual traces on the ground were thin. But there was still some work done on the relative acuity of angles of treads into the packed earth sections, or the pigmentation levels of the prints on the concrete, which could indicate timings. And the relative distance and similarity of prints could be disentangled and individuals identified. I scanned down for the timeframes involved – ten days previously – but found nothing in the patterns that looked any different from an average day. Perhaps there was too much noise, and the patterns weren't coming out. I focussed on the main route in and out of the yard. There was nothing in that, though there were three sets of distinct prints here, which re-occurred seventy percent more than the noise. There was no way of telling who was who, though it suggested one was a tall man – I guessed Si – and another was a shorter woman. The third could be either male or female, short in either case. Whether this was Mr Shin wasn't clear.

Watching a longitudinal visualisation – a swirling pattern of spiky colours – I could spot that there had been a very recent burst of unique patterns. At least six people, possibly even up to ten, had been tramping around the site. Looked like they'd covered most of it when I checked the map. There was a definite cluster around a western point; a delta shape of prints fanned out from a point in the fence. I recognised it as roughly the similar point at which my missing crawlers had recorded their last data. Timings would suggest it was last night at some point that they, whoever they were, had come onto the site.

'Fuck.' There wasn't much else to say. I started working a little faster. RapidRez may have secured the main gates, but they couldn't secure hundreds of metres of fencing. It meant that the data was now compromised, though at least I'd had clear timings for this.

Though I was working on the bead display — stood in the middle of the yard waving my hands about like a maniac — my ears were now suddenly alert to any odd noises. The wind was covering most sounds, but the rattling of metal and the odd pock-pock of water dripping on polymer pots was now very distinct. My conscious mind was constantly running after one noise to another, providing my unconscious jumps and starts with a reasonable explanation for what it was hearing. It was fucking hard work and all. And distracting.

Hurrying a little, I tried breaking into the bloods. I told myself I'd better do this before I did anything. Before I went to eyeball the fence. This needed doing first. In any normal potential murder situation, these were the primary source. But there was actually much less of this data available than I thought. I'd need to get into the scrapings on each of the crawlers and put them through the hand sniffer. This was a proper tedious job. But the immediate patterns showed a lot of blood – and I mean a lot of blood – in one of the smaller sheds off the main yard. Then a trail of it leading to the front gate. Timings suggested the trail had been a couple of days around the estimated death of Mr Shin.

I closed my bead display and got my head back into reality. Every corner of the yard now threatened violence. I walked, trying to force my heart to stop beating so hard, across to the shed where the high proportion of blood had been found. There was no door. I could see why when I got there. Or, rather, could smell why when I got there. It wasn't quite the time to crack open a pair of menthol sniffs. But it wasn't far short. A couple of metal tables stood on old metal crates in the middle of the shed, and an array of lidded hoppers were lined up against the wall. Each seemed to contain different arrays of organic matter. I looked for the one with the meat. It was towards the middle. It was empty, just containing the odd bit of feather and fur. Must've majored in roadkill.

I went back to bloods data. It suggested that the highest signal was near the table closest to the door. I had a poke around, looking at the floor. It was a thick polymer sheeting, dark green. It could've been my untrained eye, but it looked like it'd been cleaned recently. I ran a sniffer over it to find any evidence. Somebody had used a lot of disinfectant. But the crawlers had found something here. I went back again and followed their path on my bead. It led to the edge of the crate itself. Where the crate met the flooring, I could see a long, black shiny line of something. Something that might be blood. I heaved at the table top and the crate, edging it sideways out of the slight depression it had sat in on the floor. The motion disturbed some built up pressure and a large slick of congealed blood emerged from under the crate. Somebody had cleaned up around the crate. But not underneath it. It was something I could relate to.

I checked the blood with the sniffer and ran it through DidNotArrive. It was a weird mix. Some of it was matching to Ratna Manish, some to the guy, Stan Davi, who'd died a few years ago on his yacht. Some of it was matched to the DNA I'd found on the charred torso. When I ran some against the medical device I'd found in the autoloader shed, it hit a match as well.

'Fuck,' I said, pocketing the sniffer and stretching up. Felt like I was getting somewhere. But I wasn't interested in hanging around here trying to decipher it in detail. I got the gecko to run a series of photos and checked that the crate itself contained nothing. It was clean. There was no other evidence of blood besides the spots which appeared from the door.

I stepped out and pulled up the bloods map data, with my

sniffer in my hand, trying to follow the line of drips. The rain over the past two days have wiped away most of the evidence by now. There was still a vague path towards the main gate. But I knew I couldn't head there yet. I found the flight case in the site office that carried the crawlers and slowly re-stacked them back in.

Then I set off for the western end of the compound. It was at moments like this that I wished the division would issue us with some kind of weapon. But though delegation gave you something, it didn't give you the right to shoot a wrong 'un in the face. That was reserved for Enforcement. So we had to make do with running and hiding. It had served me well in the past. But tonight, when I was tired and needing to sit back and drink something with synthetic lime and sweetener and surplus biofuel ethanol, I was right fucked off.

I could see the damage to the fence from a distance. The track I'd found myself on led me straight to it. Somebody had cut into the chainlink and the compound boards behind – looked like a power tool of some kind, must've been noisy. Then pushed it forward. It was still left there, in the mud of many boots which had run over it.

I found one of the crawlers beneath the section of wall. It was smashed beyond repair. A little further around the path that followed the outer fence, I found the other crawler stuck beneath a pile of metal containers, which must've been knocked over by the raid.

I left the broken the crawler where it was but picked up the other one and went back to damage in the fence. Beyond the gaping hole, now blowing in a freezing wind, was the wilderness of the old moor. Heather and dead bracken, and winding tracks of walkers wound their way into the darkness. In the distance, silhouetted by the orange glow of the western end of the Belt, was the distinctive shape of the hill above Withens Reservoir. Placed around the foot and up the sides of the hill were the flickering lights of open fires. Even in the cold wind now whipping into my face, I could hear the distant noises of music and shouting. The gangs were partying tonight.

I should've probably gone straight up there and demanded some answers. But I didn't want to be doing that alone. I'd got my crawlers back now. Place was ready to go. I dropped a message to Si and Katta to say they could come back in and get the operation up again. Confirmed the same to Negussie. Then turned back towards the front gate. Drinks were waiting.

CHAPTER TWELVE

Not long after breakfast, the argument with Grace grew steadily loud and aggressive and then got worse from there. She was quite precious about the state of her freezer and the issue of the arm being in it wasn't going away. At least in her eyes. For those of us who've had a scientific education – even if it was a cheap and arguably questionable one – we could tell her that nothing much, biologically-speaking, went on at minus eighteen degrees C. Despite patiently telling her, at a volume that would risk permanent damage to my vocal cords, she wasn't having it. So I resumed the elder sister tactic of just folding my arms, cocking an eyebrow and shrugging at every other sentence that came out. Until she brought up how mum must've had a bad day when she lifted my tube from that rack in the clinic, and that she should've dropped it the moment she got it. Then I got proper angry and said some shit I shouldn't. As typically happened, this got her onto a long theme including that we weren't really sisters, that I hated her, that I hated mum, that I didn't really have a real boyfriend, that I had no real friends – at least, none that she'd ever seen – and that I was running away from my cock-ups at work.

I thought of throwing the nearest object to hand at her. But this would've turned out to be the horrible stuffed squirrel she kept by the door, which also doubled as the flat's server, and I knew that to lose management of the flat would have been problematic for us both. There was no need to forego the benefits of a wireless life just because my sister was being a shit. So I threw on my coat instead and stomped out of the house, telling myself – and her – that I was going for a nice walk. Unfortunately, it was now blowing a freezing, wet gale outside, with little stinging flurries of hail here and there. The prospect of a nice walk was low.

When I had arguments with my sister – and my mum – they always found the most sensitive part to prod and then really went for it.

When I got back, Grace had gone out. She'd neatly bagged up the arm in an insulated grocery bag, surrounded by her best freezer blocks, and left it hanging by the door to the block of flats. There was a note attached to it with my name on it. It let me know she was going to spend a day with her friends in Inner Leeds and that she did not expect the limb to still be in her freezer when she got back. I was quite ready to head back up to her flat and dump it right back where I'd put it, but weariness at the shouting business and early signals of hangover were kicking in now. I just wanted a quiet Sunday, not this shit.

I knew I should've been calling somebody about the evidence of the break-in at the facility. But I wasn't sure which category I should use: theft seemed wrong for a recycling facility – surely that was the whole point, to get somebody to reuse this stuff? Was it simply breaking-and-entering? If so, good luck to them. There was something that made me uneasy about it, but I was sure as hell not about to waltz over the hill to Withens camp and start asking questions. That was the kind of shit that got you decapitated.

So, instead, I called up an autocar and got a lift back to the Justice Division storage facility south of the Tower. It was work, so it made me feel better, even if it wasn't a direct lead. By this point in the day, I was ready for anything slightly above shit, so just sitting down in the car was a bonus. It didn't smell as much as others I'd been in. It was heated. I stripped off my soaking coat and tried to dry my trousers and boots a little as we progressed through the grey light of the morning, then turned to my messages. There was another frantic call from Negussie.

She was really pissed off with me now. Plenty of description of what would happen to her Fourth Sector Belt communities, if they didn't get their crap collected. Made it sound like World War Four, just with more bacterial load. Load of bollocks, of course. But I really didn't want to have a live call with her to explain this, so I left her a message instead, letting her know that I'd collected all my evidence now and the place could get going again. Just as soon as I'd reached the team running it. I tried to get through to Si West again, but there was still no answer. Nothing from Katta either.

It was calming to walk into the storage unit on a Sunday. Only a few people were there and I had the place nearly to myself. I saw a new crate had arrived from Calderdale Hospital. Checking the details on my bead, I confirmed what was in it. They'd transferred the torso from the hospital down here. I unpacked it and laid it on a bench. Then carefully laid out the body, leg and arm. It was difficult for me, looking down at these mismatched tones and shapes of limbs, to believe that they had all once been attached to the one person. I'd just got an approximation of a body – even if it was child's composition – when Louie phoned me.

'Hey, Carrie, I just heard.'

'What's that?'

'About the flat, I'm really sorry.'

'No bother.' I said it like I didn't mean it. I still wasn't about to forgive him for this.

'Where're you staying?'

'My sister.'

'Going OK?'

'No. It's shit.'

'Oh, look, I'm so sorry. If you need a…'

'I'm fine.'

'I really appreciate all you're doing for the division.'

'Know that.'

'Just so you know.'

'Like I said.'

'OK.'

Awkward silence. I positioned the arm in place and leaned in close to inspect the join. It wasn't that clear and I was doubting myself now. The whole scenario seemed totally ridiculous. I really needed another chat with the journeymen.

'Oh, Louie. Can you do me a favour? I think there's somebody in trouble. One of my witnesses.'

'I can't get Enforcement to spare anybody at the moment.'

'This is important. Witness could be in danger.'

'What's the risk? What rating?'

'Don't know.'

'You know I need a rating.'

'And you know I don't do that shit. Listen, haven't been able to get hold of him for days.'

'Check him out yourself.'

'You'll authorise that?'

'Sure.' There was a sound in the background. 'Getting the a-codes sent over now. Domestic, right?'

'Yeah. You'll get me a security drone?'

'Listen, Carrie, I'd love to… but I'm really struggling at the moment. Enforcement are stopping all the usual support. They're run ragged at the moment, people dropping like flies. The investigation has reached up here now. It's barely controlled chaos. You know how it is?'

'No.'

'OK.'

'Never been a DI.'

Louie sighed. Rather dramatically, I thought. 'Don't put yourself in danger, Carrie.'

'Trying to protect a witness, that's all. And I've not got enough hands as it is.'

'You got that partner there? That community analyst…

Deborah? I thought you were working together?'

'Yeah,' I said, sighing a little. 'S'pose I could ask her. Felt bad, being a Sunday, and all.'

'Justice doesn't recognise weekends.' I knew he was trying to smile.

'Fuck off.'

'Take care of yourself, Carrie.'

'Don't forget the codes.'

'They're on their way.'

True to his word, I could see the domestic lock-bypass codes drop into my bead a few seconds after I'd cut the call. Hurrying a little now, and suddenly more and more anxious about Si and Katta, I put away the constituent parts of the body – a possible body – and got back into a new autocar. Giving them Si's address, I also put in a call for Deborah. She answered immediately, almost as if she was waiting for the call.

'Of course, not doing anything, Carrie. Where do you need me?'

I gave her Katta's address. 'Go and check on her. See if she's there. She's not answering any of my calls.'

'Will do.'

'Bye.'

Si's place was west of the 'Fax, in a refurbed terrace area. The kind of place they didn't let cars in, unless you were moving house or something. So I had to walk the last section myself. This was a pretty plush area of town. Retro, or vintage, or some old shit. Where they loved to fill their tiny places full of crap, like old speakers and clocks and little display racks full of things which looked like tiny handheld games with a single button. At least it was quiet and nobody was about to fuck me over. It being early afternoon on a wet February Sunday afternoon, every normal person was inside, keeping warm.

Waiting in the street, hammering on the door, I was glad that I wasn't getting too much of an audience. The bell wasn't working either. Or shouting through the cute letterbox. After about two minutes of this bollocks, I let myself in with the codes Louie had given me. This kind of place was exactly where you'd get some shit like an actual mechanical key, but thankfully Simon West hadn't bothered with that.

'Si!' I shouted from the little porch area. There was still no answer. I headed towards the back of the little house, working my way around the plastic paraphernalia. It was a nice place, a really nice place. I was wondering whether I should retrain as a journeyman recycler myself. At the back of the house was a kitchen and small back garden, with some pot plants. There was a small dining room and sitting room. Upstairs was all neat and tidy, with two little bedrooms, one used, one spare, and a bathroom. Nobody was home and there was no obvious sign of a disturbance.

On an instinct, I took out my gecko and handheld sniffer, running it over the surfaces and through the air. The signals it returned were all within tolerances of a small, vintage terrace like this. Except for one spike, especially around one of the chairs in the dining room. It showed a scent, one which didn't come up on the normal commercial databases. Some mix of patchouli and sandalwood. And fuck loads of synthetic mandarin. I couldn't smell shit at the moment – a perennial cold, variant of 4453.2.3, a bastard which I'd had for the past four years – but I could tell that, if I could smell this, I wouldn't like it.

Intrigued, I punched the graph into the broader files in the Justice department. Didn't get a match. I let it wander the data freely. It went wider and wider into the commercial data mountains: East Pennine, national, European. Then I got a match. It even had a name, a ridiculous name, covered by manufacturer's registration: *Breathless Whisper*. Three other cases had recorded a similar spike pattern. All had, with ninety plus authority, confirmed it as a bespoke scent sprayed onto passengers as they passed in and out of the terminal at Abu Dhabi. The signal seemed to be two to three days old now, though that was only by molecules in the seat covering, so it didn't give an estimate of when the scent had been sprayed. I tried asking our only travel database whether any Si Wests had been out of the country. It returned a negative.

Who the hell had sat here a few days ago?

Taking a moment, I perched on another chair at the table and fired up my bead properly. I pulled the strands of what I already knew together. I'd got the name and address of the spare parts business from Ratna Manish now. It was called FFRC BioTechnology. There didn't seem to be much that was secret about it. You could trawl its public-facing immersive and walk through its grim, gurgling tanks of body parts. It was based in a large science park just to the north of Shenzhen. I got a lot of detail of its shitty little saplings growing the length of the entranceway. Young, by the looks of them. But I couldn't get much more information than that. I knew better than to directly approach the company– that would've kicked off an international shitstorm even Ibrahim couldn't resolve – so, instead, I got to work on the data I had to hand. I'd already had the travel database open to check on Si's movements. I went back to this and filtered by dates and location. I pulled up a list of any that had come in from Abu Dhabi over the past week. Only a few hundred thousand.

Fuck. Who did this shit for a job?

I filtered it down again by those with a Chinese passport. Tens of thousands. Still useless. I tried to run a media scan for everything connected to the company. I learned that it'd been going for about ten years now, servicing customers all over the world, and that it was controversial. Then I spotted something about East Pennine. But it wasn't a local news story. It was from a regular channel from Lagos, which seemed to specialise in police stories. It was relatively recent, about two years ago. I watched the droning news presenter for the channel for a few minutes before giving up and demanding a transcript from my vid app. Reading was easier. The story spoke about a decommissioned hulk bound for Hartlepool.

It'd been intercepted in Lagos, *en route* from Bangladesh, about two years ago. The Lagos Federal Inspectorate had found a hidden container on board, refrigerated and full of body parts, and they'd accused FFRC BioTechnology of being the source. But they'd not been able to get the case to court, and the investigation had been shelved. There was a generic mailbox you could use to send any queries.

So, I immediately dropped in a quick message. And sat back for a moment. Regretted it, tried to recall. Failed to recall. Swore aloud.

Then I remembered something from a few days ago. I went back to the files and pulled up the details of the name of the person whose DNA match had been returned for the rotting leg. The name flashed up again: Stan Davi. He'd died off the east coast, near Bridlington. The coroner's report suggested a genuine accident. But then, I doubted even simple accidents these days. Came with the job. The picture of his corpse laid out in the New Hull pathology facilities – very plush, lucky fuckers, wish my town'd got drowned out and had plenty of government bungs thrown at them as well – kept drawing my attention. His leg, perfectly attached to his body.

I tried a little search against Stan Davi. He'd been a highly-paid financial consultant working out of a little start-up in York. I got to see a few photos of him in the wild. Stan had been a little man, with plenty of hair, always grinning. Always fucking playing somewhere. No family to speak of, so nobody I could talk to. But he'd been a sailor for twenty years. Been sailing the east coast for most of his adult life. But then got caught out in a dreadful storm late one winter's night. Certainly seemed suspicious enough for me. If somebody had been caught out in such a way, there may be others.

I stood up. I'd been here too long. Getting worried again, I called up local Enforcement and sent them a message saying I urgently needed to speak to a missing person by the name of Simon West. I dropped in his description and last known whereabouts. Gave a little background, his job, clothes, etc.

They agreed to patch the parameters into their next high-altitude drone pass. See what they found. Agreed to pass onto neighbouring forces as well.

I'd just cut the call when my bead trilled again. It was from Deborah.

'Yeah?'

'Found Katta, Carrie.'

'Good. Nothing from Si at this end. He's missing. Put a call into Enforcement.'

'Oh, yeah?'

'Yeah.'

'Problem though.'

'Yeah? What?'

'She's changed her story.'

'Who? Katta?'

'Yeah.'

'Ah, fuck.'

Of all the shitting annoyances, the one that really pissed me off the most was when a witness changed their story halfway through a case. You relied upon a witness to help build your narrative for a prosecutor. If they went and changed their story, they were next to garbage in the eyes of the lawyer. Not to be trusted. Any words that came out of their mouth treated as the meandering waffle of a pseudo-addict. It was like delicately building a house and then somebody coming in and taking out an entire wall. And then turning the ground underneath that wall into quicksand. You would never re-build that wall as solidly as before. Sometimes, your entire narrative had to be re-constructed from the base up. And, well, if they went and changed it again – back to the original draft, for example – you'd be forgiven if you stuck the fuckers in the eye with one of those plastic stylus they gave you to sign your life away in the Trench.

So I wasn't in the best of moods when I reached Deborah and Katta. They'd taken themselves off to a coffee shop overlooking the 'Fax ringway. Well, underneath it, at least. A small jutting protrusion with a semi-circle of glass, giving you the best views of the spiralling autocar flyovers and flyunders as they descended to the old town, or rose out of the depths and headed off north Airedale and west across the higher moors. Of course, today the view was shit. But at least the lights of the cars and the roads, mixed with the dribbling rivulets of rain down the glass, made the display something like an avant-garde piece of imprez-digi-art. Or something. Wasn't my specialist subject, to be fair.

'What the fuck is going on?' I demanded, plonking myself down opposite Katta.

'Hey, Carrie,' said Deborah.

I ignored her. I'd decided which role I was going to play here. It was the same role I always played.

'I'm sorry?' said Katta, politely.

'Debs here says you've changed your statement?' I said. 'Tell me about it.'

'Simple, really,' said Katta. 'The truth is… well, me and Si, we were just playing a game, you see.'

I checked out her face. She'd been crying. I could see the redness around the edges and the streakiness of her purple eyeshadow.

'What kind of game?' I asked.

'Well, it wasn't a game, really. It was just a little lie. To get us through.'

I turned to Deborah. 'Fuck she talking about?'

Deborah turned to Katta. 'Tell her what you told me. About Mr Shin.'

Katta looked down at her hands and then at the untouched hot chocolate in front of her. When she spoke, it was mumbled and monotone. 'Mr Shin never existed. Never been such a person. That's why you can't find his name on any databases. You've tried looking, haven't you?'

I stared at her, letting my face communicate nothing. 'Go on.'

'Well, it was Si's idea, really. When old Jilly Mangold left for Scotland, about five years ago, we were without a proper master recycler. Spent months looking for one, getting hassle from the commissioners. We weren't about to make it to master for a few more years ourselves. Journeymen tend to keep that way for a decade or more. We were young, for our grade. So we knew the yard needed a master. Also, the contract with the public commissioners specified it. It's very clear, you can't have a facility, without having a master. Black and white. So we knew we were in trouble. But, then there was an election, that new Servant came in – Negosa, or something?'

'Negussie. Bridget Negussie.'

'That's her. Anyway, she wasn't that bothered with the detail. Her office dealt directly with Si. He said we were about to get a new master recycler. Their team were happy to accept that. And, eventually, we agreed just to make somebody up. Mr Shin. Invented a backstory for him, like he was a master recycler who'd worked on the biggest yards in Dhaka, had even spent some time in China…'

'Where in China?'

She breathed in quickly. 'I'm not sure. Does it matter? We were making it up.'

'Did you make up where in China?'

'I don't know… near Shenzhen, I think.'

'Yeah?' I said. Then, without really thinking, I said: 'Odd that?'

'How so?'

'Nothing,' I said. 'Go on.'

Underneath the table, I'd slid out the handheld sniffer. I tried waving it about near the coat crumpled on the floor, seeing if it could pick something up, anything. My bead was passing the information back to my eyes. It was showing the same spike pattern as I'd found on the chair in Si's dining room: *Breathless Whisper.*

'This is all very interesting,' I said. 'But I happen to know everything you've said is grade-A horse shit.'

Katta blinked. But her sullen face wouldn't reveal much. She was terrified of something. 'Oh? Really?'

And I was just about to explain my conversation with Mr Shin, on that night nearly two weeks ago. But then I realised I didn't want to talk about that right now. To her. Or to Deborah. Instead, I leaned forward and simply hissed: 'Yes. It is.'

'I don't understand…'

'We have a body,' I said. 'We found a fucking rack of ribs in your burner, an arm was sent out of your facility and ended up in a meat store, a facility down the road received a load of organic waste which contained a lot of leg. How do you explain that?'

She shrugged. 'We get everything come through on the autotrucks. Everything comes through in the facility. It's what anybody who works there says. Often have body parts coming through. Of course, we're unauthorised to manage that kind of thing. But we get them.'

'And you don't report them?'

She hesitated. I could see that she was now struggling with this. 'We don't look out for them.'

I shook my head. The idea that somebody would just casually toss a full torso into an incinerator was too much to believe.

'We're out of here,' I said, turning to Deborah. 'This one's wasting our time.'

Deborah dutifully rose from the table. But she still looked down, concerned, at Katta. 'Are you sure there isn't anything else you could tell us, mate?'

'Nothing,' said Katta.

'Fine,' I said. Then I leaned in close. 'But you and Mr West are going down to the facility first thing tomorrow. You're going to start work again. Right? Mr Shin or no Mr Shin.'

'OK,' she said. 'It was you that said we had to stop anyhow.'

I'd nothing in response to that, so I just nodded, slowly. Then backed away. 'Anytime you want to tell me you've forgotten something, let us know, yeah?'

'Will do.'

We left her to herself in the cafe and walked back out to the swaying deck, where the autocars buzzed in and out. The weather was clearing a little now, so it was possible to have a hurried chat in the corner, without being heard but also without being soaked to the skin. Still, I wasn't sure I liked the massive fucking drop off my left, down to the 'Fax town hall below me.

'She's been got to by somebody,' I said. 'Tampered.'

'I reckon,' said Deborah, nodding. Like she knew shit.

'I think I know who as well.'

'You do?' said Deborah, eyes widening.

'Well, I got something this morning,' I said. 'Si's place was empty... fuck knows where he's at... But I got a reading on an odour trail. Somebody been sat at his dining table two days ago. Somebody who's breezed through Abu Dhabi.' I explained the details of the scent and the records. 'Same signature just found on from Katta in there.'

Deborah nodded expectantly. 'Yeah? What else?'

I closed my mouth and frowned. 'I mean, that's it, for now.'

'Oh, right.'

'I've checked the transport database and all, trying to filter down possible suspects. But it's all noise. Too many people.'

'Right,' said Deborah. Her excitement had dissipated, to be replaced by a twitchy boredom. 'So, what now? We need to find Si West?'

'Yeah,' I said. Though I didn't mean it. I was tired. I wanted to curl up in bed and spend some time somewhere else. With some real friends. 'He'll turn up. I'm sure about that. He better, or that Servant will have my fucking arse. She's in a right mood.'

'And Katta?'

'What about her?' I asked.

'Don't we need to follow her? Put a drone on her?' asked Deborah.

I laughed. I actually laughed in her face. 'No. We ain't got any of that shit to play with. Follow her if you like. I'm going home though.'

'That the official protocol?' asked Deborah. For the first time, I saw anger rising in her normally breezy eyes. Although I could see it coming, I could smell it on her. A self-destructive part of me was willing it to come out, just so that I could have the shouting match.

'Don't talk to me about fucking protocol!' I said, harshly. 'Don't need that shit right now. Especially from a community analyst.'

She took in a deep breath from her nose and carefully dug out her tablet from her bag. 'I'm going to catch a separate ride home.'

'You do that.'

I was just getting into bed, after a quiet night avoiding Grace, when I got a call back from the Fourth Sector Enforcement team. I'd been trying to watch immersives of old films and my fingers were itching to get back to the project, so anything was a distraction at this point.

Odd thing was, the call was from a human handler, not an algo, and this wasn't the usual drone team. Somebody senior had taken the time to call me direct. I was kind of honoured.

'Hi?'

'Carrie Tarmell? Forensics, right?'

'That's me.'

'This is Enforcement Chief Operative Kal Ghaz. We have news regarding your missing person.'

'Yeah?' I was trying to be as quiet as possible. I didn't want Grace barging in here, letting me know she'd a busy day tomorrow, teaching computers how to drop definite articles.

'We've found him…' There was a pause. 'Simon West, right?'

'Yeah.' The tone of voice already told me what I'd feared.

'Drone boys'd fixed on a match. Pictures align.'

I knew what was coming. I asked the question I didn't want to ask. 'A body?'

A sigh. 'I'm afraid so, yes.'

'You brought the body in?'

'Not been recovered yet.'

'What do you mean? You want me to go out and check it out?'

I was expecting this Kal Ghaz to say: 'Well, you are a forensic analyst'. But I got, instead, a little coughing sigh.

'There's a problem with the recovery.'

'How so?'

'It was found floating in the Withens Clough reservoir.'

Fuck.

'You know we can't just pop up there for a chat, right?' said Kal. 'Not at night, anyway.'

'Yeah,' I said. 'I've been briefed about Withens.'

'The Head will speak to you tomorrow. I think she wants to gather a team. Go in hard and start taking in some of the leaders. Do you agree?'

I wasn't sure why they were asking a forensic analyst about their strategy, but I didn't want to be left out of the action, either.

'Sure. Sounds like a good idea. I'll be at the Tower first thing tomorrow.'

CHAPTER THIRTEEN

'With all due respect, to you Chief, and to you Operative Ghaz – oh, hi Carrie – I think the idea, this idea, this whole thing is a huge, walloping mistake.'

Nobody was sure how Deborah Goolagong-Maloney had managed to get into the room and be part of the discussions. One minute it was just me, Kal Ghaz from the Syndicates Armed Response team, some of his team, and the Chief – Melonnie Franks, and then, as if by magic, Deborah had appeared at the back of the room. Seemed she'd been listening to the whole briefing. Also the plan.

'Oh, hiya Debs,' I said.

'What's the community analyst doing here?' said Kal, ignoring Deborah, and instead looking towards one of his team. 'She's with Reconciliation, isn't she?'

'I'm on the case with Tarmell,' said Deborah, nodding towards me.

'This true?' asked Kal, turning to me.

I shrugged, trying not to grimace.

Kal shook his shaved head and sighed. 'Well, this is out of Justice's hands now. Thanks, Deborah, we won't be needing your input on this one. It's a clear-cut one, this one, int' it?'

'Community analysts are supposed to be involved in all activity relating to the gangs,' said Deborah. 'If you're taking out the BoTies, you need to know what you're dealing with. Because it's not just them up at the reservoir. There's also Grinsers, and some YYs scattered here and there.'

I wasn't sure if she was making this shit up. Sounded like the mumblings of somebody riding a bad phial of black pseudo. Except for the YYs. Even I'd heard of the YYs. They had a nasty rep. Supposed to have originated online, then emerged in multiple places in most of the English-speaking world.

'We know about the Grinsers,' said Kal Ghaz. 'And we know about the YYs.'

'YYs are armed,' said Deborah.

'Yeah,' said Kal, 'we know.'

'With bio,' said Deborah.

This made Kal fall silent. Even the Chief, Franks, stopped tapping at her rolled screen and looked up.

'Bio?' said Franks.

'They breed it up there, in the shallows.'

'But… they live on the water, don't they?' asked Franks, looking up at Kal for confirmation.

Deborah strode forward, heading for the table at the front of the room. 'Yeah, they do, but they don't give a shit. If any of them fall in, they're out of the group. Ostracised. If they die, they just poke 'em out into the middle and leave them. Seems that's what happened to this West fella, am I right?'

'Bio isn't a problem for us,' said Kal. 'We've got protective protocols.'

'You go in hard — like you've been talking about — and you'll kick off a shitstorm. Not just up at Withens, but all along the other encampments. You'll stir up Sutton, North Dereham, Upwick – the whole chain will go.'

'We're just retrieving a body,' I said, quietly.

'That's not how they'll see it,' said Deborah, turning to me. 'They'll see it as provocation.'

'Somebody's been murdered,' said Kal. 'There needs to be justice, right?'

'You don't work for Justice,' said Deborah. 'You're just Enforcement. You're not here for this.'

'Correct,' said Franks. 'But this is an Enforcement meeting.

And your DI has OK-ed the approach, so this interruption is wasting all our time, Deborah.'

She was somebody who took no shit. I liked her.

Deborah continued shaking her head, though. 'It'll unwind years of work we've put into that group. You'll never get the support you had from those people…'

'People?' snorted Kal.

'You don't realize how much they've helped us. Your thugs are about to wade in and… and just fucking ruin everything.' She turned to me, surprisingly. 'Tell them, Carrie. You tell them this is a bad idea.'

'I don't think this is a bad idea,' I said.

'Please leave the room,' said the Chief.

Deborah closed her mouth and breathed heavily through her nose. Just before she turned and headed out the door, she cast me one last look. She looked right pissed off. In fact, I don't think I'd ever seen her look pissed off. I mean, it wasn't the worst I'd ever seen somebody look. But it was dead weird. Like your goldfish flicking you the bird. With both fins.

'Right,' said Franks when the noise of the slammed door had subsided. 'Can you please repeat the tactical sequence once again for our operatives?'

A couple of hours later, I was bouncing along in the backseat of an ATV. Enforcement teams in the Buckle had hardware. We were second in a convoy of four. Beside me sat Kal Ghaz, suited up in his flak jacket and matte black helmet, the Belt's logo emblazoned on its crown alongside a massive 'E' – so you didn't get shot from above. He was watching the feeds coming in from the drones and operatives on the ground, muttering orders to his officers, and swearwords to no one in particular. I'd been given the a-codes to see all this shit, but after Deborah's outburst, the whole escapade was weighing heavy on me now and I didn't want to watch the show unfold in hi-def after the event and not have a chance to make things right. The fact that Si West was now dead had added to the guilt that was fucking me over. Though Katta's story seemed to have been pulled directly from her arse, I was ready to believe it. Perhaps there really had been no Mr Shin? Perhaps that late-night phone call had just been a chatbot, made real as a cocktail-addled and sleep-deprived hallucination? An AI being tested? Perhaps those two journeymen had really made that facility work just by themselves and a load of automated units and a Servant who didn't give a shit.

Still, if there really was evidence that these wrong 'uns, in their semi-autonomous nation within a nation, had dragged Si out of the Fellside Recycling Auxiliary Facility and drowned him in their filthy, noxious lake, then I was happy to let Enforcement do their worst. And I knew what their worst actually meant, and all. I didn't care anymore. I wanted to be free of the Buckle, with all the wasteland and the roads and flyovers; back in Airedale. It was still shit, but it was familiar shit.

I looked out of the window. We'd passed through the outer fencing of wasteland area. The quality of the road deteriorated fast, and the ride wasn't comfortable. This kind of vehicle, designed for rugged countryside and hostile environments, didn't pack as much suspension as I'd have liked.

Kal leaned forward and tapped the driver on the shoulder. 'Find us some high ground.'

'Sir,' barked the driver, and we swerved off the road. If anything, the comfort level of the journey improved when we hit the mud and heather. It was dead steep, though, and I was already feeling quite sick.

'Park us below the ridge. Avoid line-of-sight. Don't want to be a target.'

'Sir.'

A few minutes later, we were parked in a gritty open patch of dirt and Kal hopped out.

'You coming to watch?' he asked, looking back at me.

'I guess I'm here, yeah?' I said.

'Put this on,' he said, pushing the Enforcement helmet my way. Again.

Wrinkling my nose a bit – and trying not to think of dead skin cells and hair samples – I pulled the helmet on. The HUD slid down automatically, but I pushed it back up. Although it was light enough, still early afternoon, I didn't want to trip over and make an arse of myself. They were being generous enough, allowing a justice analyst along for the ride. I guess I was also the one who got blamed if it all went wrong. And if they found nothing.

I followed Kal and a couple of his immediate officers up a narrow path which wound itself through the clumps of heather and gritstone rocks towards a ridgeline of boulders. There was already the distant sound of yelling and the low whump-whump of shockdrones as they passed overhead.

'There are about two hundred of them down there,' said Kal, hunkering down as we approached the boulders. He signalled for me to duck down as well. 'We've already notified them that we need to speak with their leaders. ThreeDave is the primary target, though Hendersons is also useful, as she knows most of what goes on up here.'

'Hendersons?' I asked. I knew about DaveDaveDave. That was a name that got thrown around a lot when talking to colleagues. He was a legend. Or a nightmare. But I'd not heard of this other one.

'Kristy Hendersons,' said Kal. 'She's one of the elders, been there since the beginning. Brought the Grinsers up here from a little enclave deep in the Valleys. Not a violent one, but she's got a nasty streak in her. Got a lot of followers and all. Right, here we go… hey, Naz, get yourself down!'

An operative at the end flattened herself onto the ground. We'd reached the ridgeline. I put my back to a boulder and peered through the cracks. Away from us, I could see the rising Withens hill, with its messy scrawl of buildings and debris on its flanks, some cut into its sides, some perched uncertainly at the kind of angles that wouldn't have passed a structural audit. Down to its right was the clean horizontal line of the dam. The old Victorian stonework had been painted in fluorescent yellows and greens and reds, making elaborate snake and eye patterns. Beyond the line of the dam was the murk of the water itself, a nasty brown. Here was the mass of buildings, old polymer containers perched on reclaimed timber joists and stolen steel posts. A small town of shacks, linked by bridges and walkways, beneath a fluttering of banners and bunting and stuffed animals on string.

Approaching the dam, creeping up the small approach road, was the first of the heavy-armoured assault ATVs. The wind was blowing in the wrong direction to hear clearly, but I could tell there was a loudhailer blaring out some message for the inhabitants. And, already, some of the gang members – I was uncertain as to which denomination – were scarpering over the hill and up the far banks of the reservoir. Some must have had children because they were also bringing them out of the stilt houses, thrusting coats over their shoulders or feet into wellies, and dragging them across the walkways.

I was almost beginning to feel sorry for them.

It depended on the political flavour of your local Servant, but the way these gangs were handled differed all over the country. Some populations liked a bit of colour in their community and were happy to let a little bit of mess and muddle slide for the principle of freedom. So they allowed the gangs and subcultures to get root and grow and act in a way that ran counter to their lifestyles. And, of course, some folk fucking hated it. Hated a blade of grass being out of place, a collar not turned in right, a single light on past midnight, a noise after eleven. The Servants had to give their people what they wanted. So they balanced this shit out. Glad it wasn't me having to worry about it. Seemed the Withens gangs had found a location where they could live out their frontier dream without too much hassle. Bucklers were a forgiving lot, perhaps. I tried to recall conversations with my sister about this place. I don't think she ever mentioned directly; their presence was noted merely in glances and shudders and subtext and omission.

'We're going to give them the warning signal,' said Kal, possibly to me, possibly to his crew. 'Prep up.'

The ATVs, and the hovering array of drones, all released a synchronous bark of noise. It was supposed to be directional, so up here on the ridge it was muffled, and my helmet had compressed my ears for the moment. But even so, it was deafening. This was the intention. Carefully calibrated sonic cannon, designed to stun or, at least, to get your attention.

Some of the children fell to the ground, screaming at the noise, and were comforted by parents. Most were picked straight up and carried on backs and fronts and shoulders for the hills. There were some adults, on their knees at the water's edge, heaving up their guts.

More commands were barked out of loudhailers. Some residents were complying, gathering in the old parking area, now used as a location for a stack of inhabited packing crates. The rest were scarpering. The ATV parked itself in front of the crowd. I could just hear the names of our key suspects being read out.

'I think we can join them,' said Kal. He stood up. 'Let's go in now.'

We got back into our ATV and carried on down the approach track. The other two ATVs were parked up, covering the exits from the settlement. Not that anybody was getting out of there in a vehicle. Most they had were bikes and boats. Plus, what looked like a wrecked flying suit hanging from the end of a packing crate.

The operatives were taking details, scanning faces with flickering lights of their helmets, as we drove up the last stretch of road.

Then the counterattack began.

'Oh, fuck,' said Kal.

The driver ground to a halt as the gunfire erupted. He thrust us into reverse.

'No,' said Kal. 'Let's wait it out. We're protected here.' He turned and spoke to me directly. 'Stay in the vehicle.' He then turned on his display and jumped out.

I dragged down my visor. I could immediately see a multitude of camera views – drone level, ground level from the vehicles and shoulder-cams. The few scarpering members, those who'd run to the hills, had been running not to escape but to retrieve a cache of weapons. The images were grainy, but even I could see that some of these were quite serious. And some were clearly incendiary.

I wondered at what point a Molotov cocktail of illegal hydrocarbon was going to hit the ATV. It felt inevitable. Then at what point I was supposed to evacuate. Brief considerations of whether I preferred to be burned by chemical flames or choke on floating breeder tank pathogen flickered through my mind.

The YYs had bio. That was all I needed to know. I stayed put.

On the screens, I could see an array of the members emerge from foxholes and tents on the hillside, carrying weapons and slinging on what armour they could find. There weren't that many of them. Most of the cameras were focussed on a large man with a yellow hi-viz jacket on, festooned with trinkets and graffiti. At least, he looked huge, fat chested and vast arms, but there was something odd about how puffed out it all seemed. His face was marked with stripes of living paint, which pulsated in a rainbow of colours, and his head was protected by a recycled hard hat. I could recognise the features of DaveDaveDave – David Davis-Davidson. ThreeDave. The king of wrong 'uns.

He was striding down the hill, carrying an enormous hunting rifle, which he cocked and put to his shoulder every now and then, releasing round after round. Usually there was a sorry collection of cast offs and antiques and polymer homemades in these gangs, but he seemed to have got hold of something more up to date. There was already a set of tranq darts peppering his arms and chest, but they didn't seem to be slowing him down.

I struggled to see what he was shooting at. There was nobody writhing on the floor or screaming. Either he was a dreadful shot, or the intention wasn't to take down any of the Enforcement operatives. I peered out the front of the ATV – hoping that the reinforced glass was going to hold against a hunting rifle – and tried to look up towards the dam. Then I saw what he was doing. There was a stack of poly drums running along the top of the dam wall. These ones weren't painted in the lurid colours that they'd splashed elsewhere. They were new, sealed, and carried neat little biohazard signs on them. With every shot, he punched a perfect hole through them and vapour emerged from the newly-minted vents.

When I saw that the cloud released was a sickly green, I laughed. 'You stupid twats,' I muttered.

Kal Ghaz must've already spotted the target of ThreeDave's rifle because I could see him running back to the vehicle, calling into his comms and waving at his crew to retreat. All the Enforcement operatives fell back, clustering around the back of their respective ATVs and clambering in when they had clearance. I peered over my shoulder and tapped on the glass to Kal Ghaz, who was now sitting on a seat in the back, tugging on a white hazmat suit.

'I wouldn't bother,' I said, directing my comms to Kal.

'What?'

'You seen the colour of their poisonous gas?' I said.

'What... there, get the pack there, pull that cord... what are you saying?'

'Bet you there's nothing but food colouring in those drums,' I said.

'We have protocol,' he said, turning back to a tricky angle on his boot. Much swearing followed.

I turned my attention back to the screens. Most of the gang members with weapons had been subdued by tranqs now and were splayed out across the hillside. Even ThreeDave had caught one in the throat, and was floored, laying face to the sky in the middle of the little car park.

I opened the door to the ATV and hopped out.

'Hey, Carrie, get back here,' barked Kal, into my ear.

'This is all dramatics,' I said. And I should know, I said to myself, as I've lived with this shit since I was three years old.

I walked up the gravel track to the car park area, keeping half an eye on the people closest to the smoke, in case they started actually dying. Though I was convinced, it wouldn't do to be a complete idiot. Half of the crowd that had been gathered there were still milling about, unsure as to what they were supposed to do next. Some of them must've remembered the drill and were either donning gas masks or coughing dramatically. One of two were even retching into corners, proper method-like. But others were less interested and, now that the Enforcement operatives had retreated and stopped firing at them, a few had returned to their cabins on the water, shrugging their shoulders. The rest were running up the hillsides, to comfort and look after their tranquilized loved ones.

'What do you want?' screamed a woman, about my age, as I came up to the group.

I took off my Enforcement helmet, placed it on the ground and raised my empty hands. 'I'm just here to retrieve a body. I'm with Justice.'

'Take your pick!' said the woman, waving an arm at the hillside.

'They'll recover,' I said. 'There's one in the water I need.'

'Go get him then.'

'You knew about it?'

'Of course,' said the woman. 'We told you a few hours ago.'

'Right,' I said. 'Didn't know that.' I looked towards the drums. 'I'm guessing that's nowt in there, is it?'

She shut her mouth tight and glared at me.

Kal Ghaz was now puffing up the slope behind me. 'Tarmell, I'll have to report–'

'You picking up anything toxic?' I interrupted.

'That's not the point.'

'This lady here just told me it were nowt in those drums.'

'Never said that,' said the woman.

I grinned. 'Not in words, sunshine.'

'Is that how Justice works now?' spat the woman.

Kal Ghaz was now at my side. He'd given up on the hazmat suit. I ignored her and looked Kal up and down. 'All clear then?'

'Yeah,' he muttered, 'all clear. Nothing on the sensors. Nothing on the dial.'

'That's good, yeah?'

'You didn't know it were safe, though. Bloody stupid move, if you ask me. How did you really know there was nothing?'

I shrugged. 'Educated guess.'

'Bloody fool,' he muttered again.

'We need a boat,' I spoke to the crowd. 'Anybody have a boat?'

'We've got an inflatable,' said Kal. 'No need to ask that lot for one.'

'Just seeing if they want to help?'

He glowered at the crowd. 'They help nobody, this lot, least of all themselves.'

The woman who'd been talking to me turned back from a child she was comforting and looked up at Kal. 'Your lot are the worst,' she said. 'We're just trying to make a life up here and you–'

'This is Kristy Hendersons,' said Kal to me, cutting across her.

I nodded. 'Right. Grinsers, yeah?'

'You realise we phoned you about this?' said Hendersons, to Kal.

'Phoned?' laughed Kal.

'Yes,' said Hendersons. She was bristling. 'We have comms. Not many do have phones, but we do it the old way around here. Check your records and you will see that we phoned in a report on a body. But nobody picked it up, as usual.'

'We'll follow it up,' said Kal.

She narrowed her eyes and stepped back, disappearing into

the crowd.

While the rest of the Enforcement crew took in the sleeping warriors, bundling them into the cages at the side of their ATVs, I walked up the shore a little. I'd already brought up the aerial footage on my bead to locate the corpse. Though it wasn't necessary; against the eerie flatness of the reservoir, it was pretty easy to spot the floating shape, the blues and yellows of his clothing standing out, even under this dim sky.

I released the gecko and the sniffer, to cast their eyes along the bank for data, and looked back towards the little settlement. The polystyrene blocks which held up most of the deep-water placed houses were rocking violently from the activity of being turned over by Enforcement operatives. There was a significant volume of wailing drifting over the water.

Then I saw Kal and a couple of other operatives coming down the shore with the boat.

'You coming out?' asked Kal, as he approached.

I wrinkled my nose. 'Not a fan of deep water, me.'

'No problem,' he said. 'We'll bring him in.'

They pushed off and fired up the quiet outboard, little more than an apple on a stick. I continued to mooch my way along the shore, kicking at stones and mulling over what might have happened. Footage from the sniffer was coming back now but the gecko's data were too much to process. Sniffer had found the odour trail down to the water. It was a little further up the shoreline, not far from the ruined control tower. Once, when this was used as a water source, that's where they would have managed the flow, I guessed. Looked like nobody used it now, as the mesh walkway to it was broken, twisted and hanging from the dam end. All the windows had been smashed by projectiles and half of the roof had fallen in.

I walked further along the shoreline and had a look around. The tracks of something wheeled was clearly evident in the water. Though there were footprints in the mud and sand on the bank, they seemed to be fainter. I got the gecko to take hi-res pics and scanned the area. Squashed into the mud and grit of the shore, I could see the faint shape of something pocket-sized. With my hand wrapped in a protective polymer ziplock, I reached and dug out the object. It was the small car-shaped processor Simon West had used to analyse the bots. Swallowing back some emotion, wasn't sure which one, I stood back up and dropped the package into my bag and logged the find with the gecko. A couple of hard coughs later and I'd recovered, continuing my search of the shore and the shallow water. I thought I could see something silvery in the submerged a little distant out. I was just about to get in when Kal's shouts drew me back.

'We've got him.'

A minute later I was looking down at the corpse. He still had his clothes on but they were ragged from the damage he'd taken to his body. His face was a mess, not only half-eaten away – most likely a crow but could've been a gull – but it looked to have been battered as well. Each of his fingers were splayed out at odd angles, fingernails missing. It looked like a brand had been applied to his neck and cheeks as well.

'We good to get it out the water?' asked Kal.

'Yeah, fuck it,' I said, sniffing. Fuck, this place stank. Not the good, wholesome stench of a decent, recently-rotted body. No, that was the kind of familiar scent I could cut out with a couple of menthol sniffs. This stank of chemical spill and novel pathogen. It stank of things that would worm their way into your system, hide there for decades and then spring something fuckawful on you when you least expected it.

They bagged up the body and put it on one of the ATVs. I wandered back into fray of bodies, of people being bundled into trucks and names being taken and a bit of first aid. I noticed that, despite all the noise of weapons, there had been no serious fatalities. Not even a proper injury to the Enforcement crew. They really had come properly tooled-up.

I located the prone form of ThreeDave, being lifted into the first ATV. The Hendersons woman was also there, haranguing an operative.

'You really taking him in?' asked Hendersons, pointing at ThreeDave. 'You're arresting him? Because somebody used this place as a dump?'

'It is a dump,' said Kal, arriving at her elbow and gently trying to move her away.

Hendersons was about to answer but she seemed to have run out of options. She turned to me. 'And who are you then? You don't look like you're about to thwack me with a shockstick.'

I sighed but played the game. 'I'm Forensic Analyst Carrie Tarmell, seconded into the Fourth Sector Justice team, covering the murder of Simon West, whose body we just retrieved from your reservoir.'

'Seconded in?' she said, interested. 'Your name sounds familiar. Where you from, love?'

'None of your business,' I said.

'Airedale, perhaps?' she said, eyebrows raised slyly.

I stared at her for a moment but didn't respond.

'Get in the vehicle,' said Kal.

Hendersons ignored him. 'So, you've come to Calderdale, have you, Carrie Tarmell?'

I said nothing. There was nothing to say.

'You're welcome to the place,' said Hendersons, then turned away and raised both hands towards Kal. 'Are you going to beat me up now? Or will you be doing it later in the Tower? I'm anxious to clear my diary.'

'Shut up,' snapped Kal, as though Hendersons' very words could cast a spell on him. 'Get in the back.' He indicated where she should go.

'See you back at base, Carrie,' said Hendersons, over her shoulder. 'Hope your bruises have gone down.'

CHAPTER FOURTEEN

'You and I need a long talk, when you get back, OK?'

'Listen, got to go, I'll be late.'

'Not stopping you now, just need to talk later, yeah?'

'OK... about what?'

'I'll tell you later.'

'Grace!'

'OK, OK. About you staying here. That's what I want to talk to you about.'

'Whatever, it'll just be for a few more days, alright?'

'Well... we need to talk, that's all I'll say. Things have... let's talk.'

'What?'

'I'll tell you later.'

This annoying little exchange was still playing in my mind as I pulled out the recycled bamboo chair and slumped in it, nodding to Louie, who was hunched over in the corner of the interrogation room, letting the bead in his glasses play over his eyes. Without moving his head, he waved one hand at me.

'Conference call?' I asked.

'S'right. The commissioners.'

'Well, tell 'em to fuck off from me.'

Sitting up straight and beaming into space, he made the unmute signal – not unlike the crocodile shadow you would make as a child – and introduced himself to the group. It still sounded strange to hear him announce the words 'Detective Inspector'. It really wasn't that long ago that Louie, Haz, and me were working the streets across the Pennines; learning how to get our ugly collection of apps and tools to construct a semblance of truth. Picking through the wrong 'un's business and make sense of the faint signals among the static. To see Louie sat there, feigning seriousness and being all grown-up like he knew what the fuck he was doing, was a little unnerving. Of course, I was glad he was getting on in the world. But I felt like I'd lost another one of my friends to the machine. Haz had escaped to his new life abroad. There was just me now.

'Doesn't matter,' I muttered, annoyed at him for being on a conference call, while I was running the interrogation protocol. But I didn't want to be seen as being childish. He was only here for regs, anyway. Gotta have a DI in the room – whatever they were doing. He could've been sat there with a keg of blackmarket kelp beer and a hat that read: '*I went down on Hull and got wet*' and it would've still been legal. Just needed a DI in the room.

'Sorry, Carrie,' said Louie, closing the crocodile's mouth tight. 'They caught me out there, they were just going around the room.'

'Shouldn't you be there in person?'

'Of course,' he said, shrugging. 'But they know what's going on, don't they? They're not idiots… well, some of them are, but they know I'm covering two jobs at the moment.'

I resisted the urge to ask if he was OK doing these two jobs, and instead I just grunted.

'Where's your partner?' he whispered, as though that meant he couldn't be heard on his conference call. 'The community one? Reconciliation branch?'

'Debs? Fuck I know. She's gone AWOL.'

'Hey? Since when?'

'Since I gave the nod to mess up her game of happy gangs, up at Withens.'

'Saw it on the news. Right military, that one!'

I shook my head. 'No it weren't. It were all smoke and mirrors. Nobody got really hurt.'

'But no Deborah?'

'No,' I said.

'You need a partner?' he asked, as though willing me to say 'no' – because it would be difficult to arrange – but also seemingly worried about the thought of me being by myself. Like a fucking loose cannon.

I turned back to the table. 'No.'

'OK,' he said. 'Just asking. If you...' the crocodile reappeared in his hand and he beamed into space. 'Nothing to report from Justice this week. Numbers are down, but we're on it.'

He'd better not be doing that in the middle of my interrogation. I fired up the InterroGreat app and flowed the metadata in. It was when I'd got the date of Simon West's death, that the door banged open and two heavily-muscled Enforcement operatives pushed ThreeDave through the door and down into the seat opposite me.

'Cheers, fellas,' I said, rubbing my eyes.

After they'd manacled the mountain to his chair – which seemed to stretch the bamboo fibre towards the worst stress test – the two operatives smiled at me, waved at Louie, and made a swift exit.

'Nice place,' said ThreeDave, flexing his arms.

'No it's not,' I said, looking around the grimy room. Interrogation Room 334 wasn't somewhere I'd been in before. And it wasn't somewhere I'd be booking back into in a hurry. The decor looked as though it was forty years' old. Apart from a few cameras, protected by grilles, and the recessed lighting clusters, there was nothing else here. The only interesting piece of decoration was the elaborate mould spores working their way down the wall opposite the door, no doubt sparked into life by a burst pipe, at some point years ago.

'Can I get a nice cup of tea?' He smiled.

I shook my head. 'No. Not during interrogation.'

'Just asking.'

For somebody with such a fearsome reputation, David Davis-Davidson, seemed extremely relaxed. Now that I'd finished prepping up a new file for InterroGreat, I took a moment to contemplate the man lashed to the chair opposite me. He was well over six foot, and as broad as a rhino, or some other extinct megafauna. His face was gentle, though his eyes darted here and there, calm but alert. In his ear, I could make out the small bead, its tiny LEDs flashing in the gloom of the room. So they'd brought him here prepared, at least. That earbud housed his AI lawyer.

'This will take about an hour,' I said, reading through the usual IG preamble and switched on the recording. 'I'm Carrie Tarmell, Forensic Analyst, contracted to Airedale and seconded into the Fourth Sector. That gentleman in the corner is Louie Daine, the Detective Inspector responsible. The case is 444-494, narrative identified as 'Simon West Murder', with supplementary infractions still pending. Does that all make sense to you?'

'Yeah,' said ThreeDave. 'It means you're still trying to work out what you can do me for.'

I ignored this and ploughed on. 'I'm going to ask you a series of questions. You can pause to receive instruction from your lawyer.' I pointed to the device in his ear. 'But you must answer the question, unless it is perceived to contradict protocol. Are you OK with this?'

'No problem.'

'OK.'

I went through the preliminaries, confirming names and dates of birth and the like. Normally this part of an interview was an opportunity for the wrong 'uns to throw in some FUD, give me slightly wrong numbers, subtly different names, introduce chaff to the proceedings, which helped to impact the consistency-algos. But ThreeDave was happy to play by the rules, for which I was thankful. Louie wanted a quick finish and to get me onto other stuff. I knew he had a couple of urgent cases – gang deaths – back up in Airedale that needed wrapping up.

Not only that, the local Enforcement commanders were keen to get this resolved. Kal and the Chief, Mellonie Franks, wanted to justify their little military incursion to the Servants. It was already blowing up in the media reports: 'Enforcement destroy peaceful settlement' and they'd been spending much of the morning placating the politicians.

I switched on the InterroGreat stream. It started feeding me the questions: 'You're accused of the murder of Simon West. The body was retrieved from the Withens Reservoir yesterday, at the time of fifteen thirty-four. What do you know about Simon West's death?'

ThreeDave tilted his head to the side, listening to his lawyer app. 'I'm innocent. I don't know that name.'

'You admit that you were in the vicinity of the reservoir over the weekend?'

'Yes, I confirm. But it's a big place. I don't know everything that's going on.'

'But you're in charge?'

'No, I'm not. We're a *flat-hierarchy collective.*'

This seemed to throw InterroGreat off a little, as there was a pause. Once it had correctly parsed flat-hierarchy collective, it came back swinging.

'If you're not in charge, why did you put yourself as chief representative during negotiations with the Fourth Sector Enforcement team in the winter riots of last year?'

'I was representing,' said ThreeDave. I wasn't even sure if he was relaying the lawyer's words now. 'Representing isn't being in charge.'

'Representation is a form of leadership,' I said, reading out the words on my screen. Then, unable to help myself, I snorted with laughter. This whole thing was too ridiculous. I wasn't sure if I was pleased – or annoyed – but ThreeDave smiled and nodded in sympathy with my position.

'No, representation is the opposite of leadership,' he said, haltingly, waiting for the app to feed him the words.

I frowned and turned back to my own stream. InterroGreat seemed to have given up on this angle of attack, because it totally changed the subject. It quite often took you down surreal conversations. But you had to read out what was appearing in front of you. 'Now, please tell me what you were doing on the night of…' I squinted at my screen, reading out the date carefully. If you messed up this kind of detail, the lawyer app would have you.

ThreeDave answered the question with a carefully-worded alibi. He was used to these scenarios now, having been in H Tower a few times previously. He could probably draw that mould stain from memory.

He was also aware of the quixotic direction the interrogations sometimes took, whether to catch out the wrong 'un on a point of detail, or draw them into a mood of conspiracy, or simply to bamboozle them with ambiguity and points of philosophy. The app had been developed over a few decades now and had been doing quite an effective job at automating the process of banging up criminals with fewer and fewer people needing to get involved. Literally, a well-trained cockatoo with headphones could do my job. Though they probably wouldn't pass IG control. Still, it worked, hence why we used it, however degrading it made you feel. Or, at least, it'd been working, until the more sophisticated lawyer AI services came on board, over the last year or so. These were smarter than the InterroGreat algo and had really put a stinger across the progress of Justice, across most of the world now.

I knew we were only a few decades short of the time when the InterroGreat app and the virtual lawyers would go head-to-head in their own digital world, letting us meat racks sit back and wait until they'd had their algo battle, and then pass judgement on their human kin. Thankfully, we weren't at that stage yet.

'We have all the evidence that points towards the BoTies entering the Fellside Recycling Auxiliary Facility. Trail leads right back over Withens Hill. Got all the prints and pictures and everything. You want to show me the sole of your boots? I bet I can find a match.'

ThreeDave leaned his head over to one side and raised his

shoulder, rubbing his ear vigorously on his upper arm. The small earbud dropped out and onto the floor. I looked over at Louie for some advice at this point but he was looking down at the earbud as well. All I got was a shrug.

'Got an itch?' I asked, turning back to ThreeDave.

'Not really.'

'You want me to pop that thing back in your ear?'

'Nah, it was boring,' he said. 'Are you still recording?'

'Yeah, got to prove I didn't poke your testicles with a shockstick to make you confess.'

'Keep recording and, well, there's no need for that kind of talk.'

'Really?' I said, raising my eyebrows. 'Thought I heard worse up at the Hill.'

'That was just for show,' said ThreeDave, smiling. 'I knew you had me. Had to demonstrate something for the folk up there. We are a collective. But I like to make all the decisions.'

'You and Hendersons?'

He frowned, momentarily, at the question; almost looked scared. 'What's Kristy got to do with it?'

I had no idea why he'd decided to eject his lawyer, but I wouldn't miss this opportunity. 'Seemed that you and her jointly run the scene up there, yeah?'

'No,' he said, smiling. 'It's always been Kristy.'

'Should we be getting her down here then, for a little chat?'

'No,' he said. 'She didn't get a small gang together, she didn't break the perimeter fence of your little recycling facility, she certainly didn't find and torture and finally kill your dump operative, and she didn't carry the remains back to the lake hoping to weigh the body down and hide it among the mud and weeds and toxic waste so that nobody could find it.'.

'Oh, right,' I said, sighing a little. 'You going to tell me who did then?'

'Of course. It was me.'

'That a confession?'

'Yeah. We done?'

I came in through the door to Grace's flat feeling hugely deflated. Though I'd achieved a successful confession – had I really done anything, though? – it still didn't feel like a proper piece of work. I just wasn't sure why though. The narrative was a self-starter, I had all the evidence from the crawlers, we had drone footage from the reservoir, and now the fucking cherry on top was ThreeDave's confession. And I could already see the jiggling icons of three new POs posted to my screen; Louie really wanted me back in Airedale, it seemed.

None of this seemed to smell quite right. We'd had the chat back in our training days from Big Man Vickers, in his room overlooking the Mersey, about the importance of input and throughput and output and turning over the cases and getting something that would fly in court and then moving onto the next. This wasn't a fucking immersive, set in Alabama, where sharp-suited teams of forensic experts spent days on a single scene. This was the modern era: we had an increasing number of killings and decreasing supply of funds and we had to work on productivity above all else. Get your PO; work your case; submit your case file; let the apps do the heavy lifting.

But on this one, I wasn't even sure if the apps had done the heavy lifting. ThreeDave just straight out confessed. I was also kicking myself for not asking him questions – especially when he was lawyer-free – about the missing master recycler. This'd been down to guts rather than memory; I hadn't wanted to show myself up by asking a question about somebody who may or may not have existed and who had no obvious connection to ThreeDave. At least, unless I'd asked him directly.

So I was in a funny mood when I stepped in the door to the

flat. And found somebody else sat on the sofa, with three neat bags sat at her feet.

'Hi, you must be Carrie,' she said, popping her teacup back on the low table and rising at once to come and shake my hand.

'Yeah,' I said. 'You are?'

'Djin,' she said, smiling. 'Djin Dowe.'

She was a few years' younger than me. Or, at least, hadn't fucked up her complexion and body as much as I had. She was dressed in expensive-looking but minimalist sea-fibre baggy trousers and blouse. Long, curly black hair was plaited and arranged in an elaborate and precarious routine on the top of her head. It was impossible to guess from which part of the world her parents may have come from: for every corner and from none. I'd heard somebody describe this as an Earth face, a Terran face. She was a little taller than me and, from what I could see of her arms, was alarmingly muscled. I'd stuck out my hand, out of habit more than anything else, and I was now in quite a bit of pain from the grip I'd just received.

'You still do the hand thing,' she said, stepping back. 'I love that.'

'We do, yeah,' I said. 'Where you from?'

'Dhaka,' she said. 'I'm over here for work. Working with your sister, in fact.'

I could hear the toilet hiss in the background and the door slam.

'Great,' I said. 'Is that her?'

'That's right,' said Djin. 'You want a tea as well? I've brought it with me, as a house gift.'

'House gift?' I said, as if the words were foreign in my mouth, unused.

'That's right,' said Djin, flashing me a bright smile, and heading for the kitchen. She passed my sister coming the other way, who spotted me and forced an unhappy smile, which then turned solemn. It was the face of somebody who relaying news that they thought the recipient would take badly but that she was absolutely loving. She'd last adopted such a face when she told me that Gregory, my pet snake, had died.

'Hiya.'

'Hiya,' I said. I looked at the bags. 'New lodger?'

'Yeah,' said Grace. 'That's right.'

'Moving in now?'

'Yeah.'

'That's lucky,' I said.

'Why's that?' said Grace, carefully.

'Because I've completed the case,' I said, just as Djin returned, bearing a steaming cup of something. I took it from her with a nod. It did smell good.

'Let's all sit down, yes?' said Djin, seating herself near her bags. 'You were saying you've completed a case? Grace was telling me you work in Justice, normally up in Airedale, but that you've come down to help out in the Fourth Sector? The Buckle, you call it? I love that name.'

'That's right,' I said, sitting down opposite her. I looked up at Grace. 'Grace sure likes talking.'

'I know, I love it like that, I'm so lucky that this room has come free,' said Djin. 'Grace has just been telling me all about what she does for work as well, doing all... all the accents, you know?' She said 'accents' with an unrecognisable accent. I dutifully tittered, as I was supposed to.

'Just one accent, really,' said Grace, sitting down next to Djin.

'I love hearing about everybody's work,' said Djin.

I sipped my tea, staring at it, because it was less unnerving than staring at Djin's eyes. I could tell she was wanting me to ask her about her own work. This had been Big Man Vickers' Mersey-lesson second module: basic psychological leading, suggestion and habitual patterning. I was hesitating because I wasn't wanting to be led by the nose so obviously, by somebody I didn't know. But then I was also interested in what she was going to say.

'So,' I said, putting down my cup. 'What is it that you do, Djin?'

'I'm so glad you asked me that.'

'Yeah.'

'Well,' she said, 'I've come over to work at the same company that Grace works at – I mean, different team, different office, but still the same company.'

'How'd you find each other then?' I said, half to her, half to Grace.

'Bulletin board,' said Grace.

'That's right,' said Djin. 'I posted on the company bulletin board that I was looking for a place to stay, that I was over from Bangladesh, that I needed a wonderful new flatmate–' Here she gave an alarming grin towards my sister, who had the good grace to look alarmed in return. '–and that I was ready to move in immediately.' Her voice dropped low now and she looked about the room carefully. 'The hotels here are not good, I'm afraid. Not what I'm used to.'

I nodded. 'Yeah, it's a shit-hole. What do you do?'

She laughed. 'Of course, I forgot. You are very good at your job. You always get people to confess?' My silence as I drank up the rest of my tea spurred her on. 'Well, we're… I mean, the team I'm in, we're working on artificially-generated voices. Much like the machine-training that your sister does, but we're able to create an artificial conversation.'

'What for?' I asked. 'Why?'

'Good question,' she said, pointing a finger at me. 'You are really very good at your job, Carrie. So, the reason we do this is because, well, because of the games, the immersives, you understand? They need to have proper AI-generated conversations so that the player is not jolted from the false, well, the false experience! For example, we have advanced it so much, that… do you want to know something?' She leaned in conspiratorially now.

'What?' I said.

'I've heard from the team that they sometimes test their machines, by phoning up real-world places using their trained algorithms. That they book appointments at salons. That they even order pizza! And other things, besides.'

At that moment she sat back and nodded, staring at me. I stared back, not blinking. I didn't know what the fuck she was doing, but it was freaking me out. I wondered whether I should just straight up tell my sister to get this stranger out of her flat and out of her life. Then Grace cleared her throat to talk.

'Carrie knows all about artificial things.' Grace grinned at Djin. 'After all, she is one of those–'

'I'm going to pack.' I stood up and left the room.

CHAPTER FIFTEEN

I took a bite out of my reheated breakfast burrito and surveyed my flat with disgust. RapidRez may have taken away Kai Reed's head and done a bit of localized clean-up on my rug but the place remained a mess. As well as meat rot, it now smelled of industrial disinfectant. It triggered queasy memories of visiting my grandmother (technically, Grace's grandmother, but I still loved her) in hospital at the age of nine. She died while we'd gone to get chocolate from the kiosk next to maternity and we'd gone back to find an empty bay and a bot buzzing around the floor, spraying out its chemicals, and playing its naff little tune to itself. I'd never liked cleaning bots after that. I did my cleaning by hand. Or not at all.

RapidRez had taken the Guianan rug away with them as well, but it left a gap in the middle of the room, such that the furniture and items that clung to the walls no longer formed a whole, existing in their own little space, alone. It had ceased to be my living room. It felt like an alien place. When Ronnie and I had been together, he once or twice turned up unannounced, when I was out at work, and deep cleaned the place, like a fucking subcontracting ninja. He said it was a kind gesture on his part; I always thought it was because he had issues with germs. We were never going to make it work.

I took another bite of burrito and glanced at my unopened holdall. It had been a busy few hours after the interview with ThreeDave. As soon as I'd left my sister's flat and nodded a weird goodbye to her and her weird new flatmate Dowe, I'd got a car to take me somewhere. I didn't want to go back to the Tower, and I didn't want to go home – just yet – so I got it to go cross-country and park up in a layby. There were some archaeologist and bone-hunter types working their way through a nearby farm, so it was quite busy, but I hid in the back seat of the car, kicked open the door – just to get some fresh air – and set to work on the narrative. In truth, I clicked a virtual 'Go' button on my apps, told them to get their shit together and make me a case and they did their thing. There was little to no human involvement here. Clear cut confession, primary evidence was robust, circumstantial evidence fitted into place. Beyond reading it through to check for inadvertent swears or blasphemy or other, I was dropping in my signature. I spent most of the rest of the day – and a good part of the evening – catching up on stitching new faces onto the project and getting my apps to do my admin.

And I'd not thought of Shin, until in the middle of the night, when I woke up, thinking I could hear footsteps in the hall. And I checked the time, and it was the same time he'd phoned – or something had phoned – and I could hear that worried voice again. And I knew that I owed it to that voice. And it wasn't a fucking AI, no matter what possibilities that scarily-intense woman in Grace's flat had put in my head.

Unable to go back to sleep, I spent the next few hours wandering the flat and checking the windows for any fresh sign of mask-wearing gang members, and I knew I had to seek an alternative place to be for a little while. Also, I had questions about that machine I'd found at the dump, with the blade and the blood. I needed to talk to somebody who knew about that kind of shit and I happened to know one of them, over on the west side of the Belt. If things went well with them, they might even let me stay over and give me some food.

It was too much of a stretch to bag a Justice car. This trip was going to have to be off my own credit and it was going to be alongside other, nasty, mucky people. Much like me, to be fair.

As I'd walked down the hill towards the station, I plugged in my destination and tried to wangle a route via the tops. I'd had the algo explained to me by Haz one time; if you select the right parameters, you can get the journey you want, with the views you want, the passengers you'd rather smell. If you mess it up, the machine will direct you via an optimal mix of the least traffic, highest likelihood of prompt arrival time, more efficient use of power and, most weighted of all, the greatest advertising billboard estate. This tended to mean the Belt. And I didn't want to go through the Belt, because it sent you through tunnels and cut-n-overs, and it blinded you with ads. I wanted a view. I wanted to see trees and grass. It was a grim old day, cold and grey, so all I might be seeing was fog and dead trees. But it was better than just watching flickering images selling you a better life, selling you somebody else's life.

'Bastards,' I muttered, as the result came up on my display and turned the corner. I wasn't get the scenic route.

'Nice hat,' said a voice.

I turned my head and saw a couple of young 'uns sat beneath the cover of a fire escape, both wearing identical chick masks.

'Fuck off,' I muttered, pulling the hood of my duffel over the bobble of my hat.

'Have a nice time,' one of them said, as I turned the corner into the station.

'Call Louie,' I said, into the air, bringing up my bead display.

'Calling Louie Daine,' said the bead. At the time of issuing it, I'd requested the voice to be 'Friendly Calm #6'. According to the wisdom of crowds, this must've actually meant 'Possibly Spanish'. I'd grown to like its ambiguity, as it reminded me of somebody I'd been friends with at school, somebody who had never seemed to be at rest in one place, and it suggested there was something else out there, somewhere, other than the desolation of the old farms and the stink of the Belt. A warmer country. And at least the voice didn't sound like my sister.

'I like your hat,' said Louie.

I was about to snap something obscene at him but resisted.

'Hiya, Louie.'

'You catching a train? Where you off to?'

'Coast.'

'Nice. What can I do for you?'

'Look, Louie, thanks for sending through those two POs. I'll get onto them asap.' They were a couple of tidy-ups. All the data had been gathered by a third-party outfit, a big frigging mess, to be fair, but at least it was rich. Louie just needed me to stitch together the narrative. Both were domestics. Both wrong 'uns banged up by Enforcement. Sad but safe, as we liked to say.

'Well, nothing urgent,' he said. 'Sorry I don't have anything else at the moment.'

'Not a problem,' I said. 'I wanted to talk to you about the Shin case.'

'Hey?' he said. 'You found another piece of the body?'

'Well, no… I mean, I'm not sure. Why, do you know something?' I heaved myself up the steps into the last carriage.

'Oh, you said "shin", that's all.'

'No,' I said. 'That's his fucking name, Louie. Are you paying attention? Excuse me.' I worked my way down to a spare seat.

'Yeah, of course. Good job on the West case, by the way. I always knew you had it in you. Sorry I had to rush off… another meeting, you know?'

'No bother,' I said, pulling off my hat and coat and slumping back into the seat

'What did the pathologist say?'

'Hmm?' I said. I hadn't even read Dr Hausman's report on Simon West's body. It was stuck there in my inbox – marked as read so the apps would trust that I'd done something – but I'd not dived into it. They'd trawled through and lifted the key metadata for the purpose of the report. Everything came up with green flags.

'The pathology report? Did that corroborate with the confession?'

A part of me wanted to have genuinely read it all through before I lied to Louie. But that would've been lying to myself. 'Course.'

'Super,' he said.

'It's all in there… all backs up the confession and the data from the crawlers. 'There were multiple signs of torture to the body, fingers broken, but the doctor thinks he died before it go to the real gruesome stuff. Before it got messy.'

'His blood was found in the facility?'

'That's right. I mean, his and a few others…'

'Eh?'

'Somebody had cleaned up. There was blood from a few other people there as well. But I'm coming onto that.' The man next to me deliberately dropped some mufflers over his ears and settled back to sleep, waking up his dozing minimink. 'Point is, West was murdered onsite, was carried on an automated loader across the moor, and then dropped into the water. Was supposed to have been weighed down by summat – old bricks or breeze blocks and bit of rope – but they must've come off the body. I took some photos of abrasions to the wrists and around the thumb. This one'll post a record time in court, I reckon.'

'Grand,' said Louie, sounding happier than he'd ever been.

'Listen,' I said, taking a breath, 'about that Shin case?'

'Yeah?'

'That's still open, isn't it?'

'I think so, let me see.' He paused. 'Priority's low, you know, for a missing persons… often they get deprioritised further with, newer cases coming in.'

I took a sniff. 'I'd like to follow up still, if that's OK?'

'Whatever,' he said. 'You're on your own time. The case might be open but that PO's expired.'

'What?' I spat. 'You're not trying to save budget up there, Louie. You're supposed to be finding a whole new team. How're you doing with that? Not going to help by expecting your team to work for free.'

'It's supposed to be a disincentive,' said Louie, grinning. 'Make you spend more time on the actual victims.'

'What about somebody to help me?'

'You had Deborah Goolagong, didn't you?'

I stared at him for a moment, saying nothing.

'Ah,' he said, after a pause. 'You lost another one, did you?'

'She were shit.' I'd tried to be restrained but it came out more forceful than I'd hoped; the mini mink woke up, startled, and eyed me for a moment.

'Really? What's your criteria for that? Pretty loose, knowing your standards?'

I ignored him. 'I'll need a digital.'

'I'll give Lem another call.'

'He's useless. Never there.'

Louie sighed, a little dramatically. 'Fine. Because it's you, I'll put in a special call, OK?'

'What?'

He winked. 'I have ways and means, Carrie. That's why they made me the DI.'

'They made you the DI because you were the only one who said yes.'

'Well,' he said, 'there is that.'

'Fine,' I said. 'I'll do it on my own time. But send me the easy shit in the meantime, Louie, OK?'

'Sure,' he said. 'See ya.'

'Bye,' I said, waving my hand and then hiding it quickly; the mini mink had spotted it and was preparing to pounce. I gave it a glare and pulled my bobble hat low over my eyes. I'd no need to stare out the window now. It was just going to be tunnel until the coast.

What I hadn't mentioned was the conversation with that new flatmate of my sister's, that Dowe girl. She'd obviously been planted there in order to relay that elaborate story about AI-generated chatbots phoning Enforcement. I wasn't too worried, because she looked harmless enough, and I didn't want to scare my sister. But none of it made much sense to me when I played it back in my head. Why did somebody want me to think that this conversation with Mr Shin was with a machine alone? Like Katta changing her story, there was somebody who really wanted me to believe that there hadn't been a phone call and that Mr Shin had never existed.

Point was, I wasn't stupid. I could tell when somebody wanted me to drop a case.

I also knew that this could be done under the radar.

'It's nice to see you.'

'It's just a few hours.'

'I know. It's only ever for a few hours.'

'You like it like that.'

'Do I?'

'You said you did the same for your mum.'

We looked out the window together. Mum's house didn't have a nice view, like out to the sea proper, towards Ireland or somewhere like that. No, unfortunately, she had a house that faced south. It was old, she'd hung onto that, but it'd been part of the compulsory purchase, and so she'd had to accept that what'd been a three bedroom semi was now converted into a three-storey monstrosity housing three different families, separated by vegemer boards and almost a whole canister of spray-on insulation. And my mum, on the first floor, was left with her little kitchen and her little bathroom and this, the living room. It'd once been her main bedroom, where I'd crawled, many times, in the middle of the night, crying from nightmares. Even in those times, I'd been able to watch the water come into the estate.

We stared at it now. Formby Island wasn't its official title. It was a joke from the locals. It wasn't even a proper island, as there was still some soggy land connecting it back to the mainland in the north. But it certainly felt surrounded on all sides. It would've been nice to have looked down onto a sandy beach – like where they'd buried all those statues. Instead, we looked out over a sea of some collapsed roofs and some still-standing buildings of the old housing estate. These were all partially submerged in the sea, at least for half the day. When the tides went out, they left the remains of sandy roads and a few sturdy fence posts and even the odd car. I'd heard there were a few people still trying to live in the upper floors of their old houses, punting in and out on homemade rafts. At some point, the supporting walls of their homes were going to be pulled apart and the whole structure would collapse in on them, killing and burying them and their houses beneath the waves.

My mum liked living in the place because she said she could see all the entrances. Her house gave you views of all the landing points. She liked to call it her castle. Though it was turning into more of a ruin every day.

'Number twenty went down yesterday,' said my mum, pointing.

'Yeah?' I said.

'That were Chanel's. You remember Chanel?'

I shook my head. Possibly a buzz cut and slippers and a flatulent beagle. That was all. 'Kinda. She OK?'

'Chanel died ten years ago.'

'Oh.'

She grunted. 'How are you, anyway?'

I drummed my fingers on the windowsill. 'Good. Right good, you know.'

'You look it. You look like you're getting enough sleep and your stress levels are right down.'

Mum'd been a paramedic. She liked to wheel out the old skills now and then.

'Alright,' I said, 'then you look like you're getting younger and taller and dead pretty and that.'

She laughed. 'You do smell of dead bodies, though.'

'Eh?'

'Maybe it's just the sniffs, the menthol ones, maybe it's just on your clothes. You been touching meat recently?'

I sniffed my fingers. Now that she'd mentioned it, it did

remind me of the decomposing thigh.

'You still enjoy it?' she asked.

'Yeah,' I said.

'I wonder,' she said, still staring at the sunken houses, 'whether I'd have enjoyed that more than what I did with my life.'

'Your life?' I said.

'What?' she said, turning to me, willing me to say something mean.

I met the challenge. But I tried to soften it. 'You mean your life spent screwing up two girls and then living in a house overlooking a swamp?'

'Yeah,' she said, her eyes not moving. 'That.'

It felt like the right moment to reach in and give her a squeeze. But I wasn't about to start on that shit. Not now. So I grunted instead.

'How's Grace?' she asked.

'Same,' I said.

'That bad,' she said.

I dutifully sniggered. 'She put me up,' I said. 'Let me sleep in her spare bedroom.'

'Wow. Why?'

'Couldn't go back to my flat.'

'Oh.' For the first time, possibly in a decade, I heard the first quaver of concern in her voice. That one word nearly sent me off but I fought back the tears.

'They'd left a head in it.'

'Course.'

'Didn't fancy staying there.'

'Hence the smell.'

'Eh?'

She looked at me sideways. 'The smell on you. Probably that rotting head.'

'Could be,' I said, shrugging. 'Could've been the arm I left in Grace's freezer.'

'You really left an arm in Grace's freezer?'

'Yeah.'

For the first time in many years I actually heard my mother laugh. 'Did she boot you out?'

'Yeah.'

'I actually know about that,' she said. 'She called me, earlier.'

'She does that,' I said, trying to find the incriminating inflection in my mother's voice. But it had become so nuanced, I had to wonder whether it was me who had projected it.

'Eh?'

'Does she call you up?' I repeated.

'Yeah, she does.'

Even then it was difficult to find. 'What'd she say about me?'

'Nowt. Said she'd got a new flatmate. Lovely girl called Djin. At least, Grace made her sound lovely.' She waved a hand vaguely at her wall screen. 'Even sent me a picture of them two together at that butterfly place. She looks very nice, this Djin.'

A picture of Grace, half-embracing a laughing Djin, appeared on the wall screen. They were standing in the butterfly house up at Shipley.

'Grace likes her,' I said.

'Yeah. Can see why.'

'She were more hygienic than me.'

'That would do it for Grace. You met her?'

'Djin? Yeah, briefly.'

'Got one of them faces,' she said.

'Eh?' I said.

'One of them modern faces. Them Earth faces. All the genes. Probably another, you know like…' Whatever she was going to say died in her mouth. She was avoiding my eyes.

'Like me?' I asked. 'A specimen.'

'Different batch,' she said, shortly.

'Why'd you say that?'

'There were some bred for more than families. You know that. The Nada Set.'

I did know what she was talking about. About a quarter of a

century ago, new specimen farms had been discovered all over the world, where they'd been breeding infants for uniformity and strength, possibly commercial, possibly military. It'd had all been shut down, of course, with huge prison sentences and changes in international law. This'd been the final straw for some folk. At least I was just familial commodity. They were something else, the Nada Set.

'Thought they defrosted them all?' I said.

'Yeah,' she muttered. 'Probably.'

'Don't want to talk about it, anyway.'

'OK.' She sniffed and then cast me an appraising look. Beneath the shaved skull and the deep kohl around her eyes, she looked more and more like a shaman, trying to look into my soul. Never say anything like that to my mum, though. You'd be getting a slap or worse, a three hour lecture on appropriation and wilful misrepresentation of another culture's sacred mores. Or summat.

'What you out here for anyway?' she said, pulling the picture off the wall with a snap of her fingers. 'Don't tell me you were trying to get back together with that Ronnie?'

'No,' I said. I didn't need to say anything more. I'd learned never to talk about boyfriends in front of my mum. She liked to tell both me and my sister that she'd gone through life without needing anybody at her side. At the age of eight, she'd let me know that I wouldn't have a daddy in my life, that I was a specimen embryo, liberated from a commercial lab and that my biological parents meant nothing and that she was my parent and there was nothing that she couldn't give me that another parent might. I'd cried for about three days solid after that. It must've shocked my mother because, when Grace was eight, she was more circumspect, and had addressed the issue with evasions and omissions and let her know the truth through more gradual snippets of data. Of course, at least Grace had some of my mum's DNA in her. Didn't fuck her up any less than me when the truth had come out. But then Grace was the kind of person to make something like that into a lifetime of drama. I learned not to mention it too much.

So, there was never any talk of relationships. That was for the weak.

'I just wanted to drop by and say hi and give you a hug,' I said, straight-faced.

'Fuck you did.'

We had both achieved the right tone of voice for this exchange. I congratulated myself internally.

'Actually, I've got a work question. Can you look at something for me?'

She perked up at this. 'Medical?'

'Kinda,' I said.

'Not rotting corpses again?'

'No,' I said. 'It's some kit I found. I wondered if you'd come across something like it when you were working. I think it's possibly battlefield class.'

I cast the image of the white-polymer encased cutting machine onto her wall screen. It was an old model of screen, not compatible, so there was a pause – and a few swearwords – before I could get it to work. 'You recognise one of these?'

She looked at it for a moment. 'Yeah, that's military.'

'Thought so.'

'They were Japanese-made, possibly Korean. I remember being trained on something similar.'

'Quite old then.'

'Piss off, Carolyn Tarmell. Where'd you find it?'

'It was part of the Fellside Recycling Auxiliary Facility's collection of automated tools.'

'Fellside Recycling Auxiliary Facility?'

'Sorry, that's a facility in the Fourth Sector, the Buckle.'

'Oh, right. That's somewhere in that direction, isn't it?' She grinned, waving her hand.

'Yeah,' I said, sighing, 'that's right.'

'Recycling facility had that? Rather overpowered for a

recycling site, that. Handy, I guess.'

'What's it used for?'

'We used them in the medical corps in Svalbard and northern Greenland, for amputations and stitching.'

'Stitching on replacement limbs?'

'That's right. Legs and hands and the like. They're automated for that… you just click a button and it'll put a new arm on you. Handy for battlefields, especially when you're missing a few nerve specialists.'

'So, even idiots like you could use them?'

'Yeah,' she said, 'even people like you could use them.'

'Were they used for amputations as well?'

'Of course,' she said. 'You can't go around stitching a new arm onto somebody if you've a messy stump there. This thing'd go in and make it all clean, find the nerves, cement the bone, vessels, sinew, the lot, connect it all up.'

'What kind of noise they make?'

'Eh?'

'Can you remember what noise they made?'

She turned to me, frowning. 'No. I really can't. Not sure I ever saw one working.'

'Your lot were too good to get hurt?'

'You got it.'

'Shame,' I said, chewing my lip. 'Really need to know what they sound like.'

'Fire it up,' she said. 'Get yourself a bit of that vile vat-grown and put the saw through that.'

'Pork?'

'Don't even talk about it, though.' My mother didn't believe in meat.

'Yeah, OK. Good suggestion. I'll have a look at it.'

'So, this a murder case then?'

'No,' I said. 'Just tying up some loose ends. Trying to make a case.'

'Speaking of the Buckle, I saw Aitch Bee on the news last night.'

'Oh yeah? Rated source, was it?' I stared at her suspiciously. My mother liked to watch unrated news sources. Even though the news algos had been compromised so many times in the past, the latest batch was doing a fairly good job at approaching what we could all collectively agree was strong truthiness. But the shit my mother immersed herself in was way over the unrated line. There had been too many conversations where I'd had to talk her back from believing that there were alien signals hidden in secure servers in the Zheng-Yan lunar station, or that an ancient race of ammonites had created their own tentacle language, or that Those-Who-We-Can't-Discuss had worked out how to read our minds and were plucking off people who matched the fabled 'Black-Red Parameters'.

'It was. I saw their Enforcement team had attacked an encampment of BoTies. Some YYs in there as well. That connected?'

'Yeah,' I said. 'That were my case. Can't talk about it, though. Not until it's hit the court.'

'Right.' She fell silent. 'You staying a bit longer, then?'

We had a cup of tea – something obscure and fashionable from the Chilean Andes – and she talked about the lectures she'd been giving virtually to her friends across the world. Except she didn't call them 'friends'. To her, they were her 'kind'. I listened, mentally counting down the time before I could take off. Before I'd set off that morning, I'd thought I could grit my teeth and stay the night and spend some more time with her. I was almost ready to suggest that her sofa looked comfortable when she went in and said the kind of shit that I remembered her most for.

'You know,' she said, 'you don't need to worry about being alone.'

'What?' I said, knowing I'd lost my cool a little.

'I can see you're worried.'

'I'm not.'

'There's nothing to worry about being alone.'

'I'm not going to be like you, Mum.'

She snapped her mouth shut. 'I'm trying to think of your mental health, love.'

'Sure you are. Mine, yeah?'

'I'm just saying–'

'I've got work,' I said. 'Some of us still work, you know. To pay for people like you.'

She smiled. 'I only said that once, you know. You keep repeating it.'

'I was there when you said it.' It'd been to my grandparents, my mother's parents. An argument had ensued. 'It sunk in.'

'Well,' she said, looking around her flat. 'Thanks for keeping me in such luxury, Carrie.'

'Yeah, well, bye,' I said, pulling on my hat and tugging up my hood. It was dark outside and sleet was starting to hit the living room window.

'You brought a bag,' she said. 'Thought you were staying?'

'Nowt gets past your beady eye.'

'I'm sorry if what I said upset you, Carrie. It was meant… I don't know what I meant by it. We all live differently, I guess.' The proud eyes, piercing blue behind their black aurora, stared at me, for the first time looking as though they might burst into tears. Doubt was seeping into the certainty. 'Don't follow the rutted path, is all I'm trying to say.'

'That what you say to your kind?'

'It's what they say to me.'

'Not sure I'm following any kind of path,' I said.

'That's my girl,' she said.

She looked like she was about to go in for a hug. There was no way I doing that shit so I gave her a nod and ran for the door.

CHAPTER SIXTEEN

They'd ended up being called an MMS, or a 'man-man', but their full, legal title was 'manual manslaughter' events. It was generally when some idiot decided they knew better than the algorithm and flicked the manual override, striding in and getting their clumsy hands on a control unit. This one was a bad one. It must've been, because Lem Kawinski had decided to turn up as well.

Despite being lanky, he was quite adept at avoiding the eye, shuffling in behind all the paramedics and large med drones, which were coming in from Calderdale. It was only because I'd dropped in a proximity alert the week before that I knew Lem was here at all. You were only able to do that kind of shit with members of the team. It must have felt nice for him to know he had somebody who had his back in a crisis.

'You're in so much shit when I get to you,' I muttered, watching the proximity alert float around my screen, with its over-engineered directional, altitudinal, and velocity readings. Crap which was supposed to be designed for the military or some private army ended up being used by folk such as myself to track down workshy analysts. I gave myself a mental note not to leave the site without backing him into a corner first.

We were at the base of the Fax Central ring, where the subterranean train lines briefly saw a little daylight before disappearing back into the ground. There were about seven ancient lines running across this gap, surrounded by buildings of weeping concrete and blackened stone, abandoned municipal parks and even a dead museum, its primary coloured letters partially stolen, leaving a ghost of pale polymer behind. Nearly every surface was tagged with something luminous and swirling, living paint breathing a little colour into the depths. Above us, the spiralling roads rose up and joined the various MCs as they sped off west and east, the sky a harsh cloud-covered white circle, making you squint and wish you'd brought sunglasses. It also made you wish you'd never got out of bed that morning.

For me, I'd wished I'd never got home. I'd spent another night of being woken up by kids in masks, throwing things at my window and dialling me up orders I didn't need. I was almost glad to have had the call put through. Multiple injuries, some possible death. MMS. Fax Central.

Now I was here, though, I wasn't so sure. Perhaps even low-level aggravation from local gangs would've been better than this: stepping my way through the debris of seventeen autocars and one bike. In among the metal and glass and polymer there were the heads and faces and arms and hands and fingers of those who hadn't made it out on the backs of the paramedics' vehicles. Fifteen people I'd counted and recorded and photographed and even been able to pull up their ID and name and address and let Enforcement know. This was a lot of death from one MMS. Still, they'd had a long way to fall. About five storeys up, there was a piece of polymer-steel crash barrier waving in the breeze, where the cars had come off. We'd been assured by the peacefully-voiced RickyRoads Maintenance liaison unit that they would be removing the barrier in a safe and controlled manner. I'd been up there first, letting the gecko run around to take some evidence. Not that it mattered too much. The flyovers and risers were all covered by three-dimensional sensor footage. It was all going to be immersive fun for a court team soon.

The proximity alert floated into my display, getting in the way of the form I was filling in for the dead teenager in front of me. Lem was nearby. I looked up and scanned past the heads, looking for the blonde hair and dark glasses. I could see him crouched over the ruin of an autocar, trying to extract its temporary storage cache. Letting the form fall away in front of my eyes, I hurriedly tried to make my way past an autovan and across to him.

A call popped up on screen from Louie.

'Yeah?' I said. There was a med drone in my way, waiting for its contents to be picked up by someone. I sighed, dramatically.

'Good morning Carrie,' he said, sounding dead professional, for a fucking change. 'Are you free about now?'

'Not really,' I said, trying to squeeze past the drone and the van on the other side. 'Kinda busy. There's been an accident down here.'

'Oh, you're at the HIA-7773?'

'Yeah.'

'Bad one?'

'Yeah,' I said. I gave up on trying to get past the drone and worked my way via a different route.

'Know what caused it?'

'Yeah. Some dad knew best. He thought the AI on his family car was going screwy. Intervened. Now this.'

'Sorry to see hear that,' said Louie slowly, as though he was focused on something else. 'I'm sending somebody to see you. I think he's… um.'

'What?'

'I think he's quite important, OK,' said Louie. 'So don't show us up, you know?'

'Eh?'

'He's a fed. I mean, he's national, from Nigeria. Lagos inspectorate. The federal one. He said you'd dropped them a message about the *Tafola-3*. He said he wanted to speak to you about it.'

'Never heard of Tafola-3,' I said. 'What is that? Sounds like an immersive.'

'It's a ship,' said Louie. 'He didn't say much else. But make us proud, and that. Show him that we've got our shit together here, yeah?'

I was still trying to work out the Lagos connection, and had remembered sending a message to some generic message box, which was why Louie managed to catch me off guard by saying: 'Oh, and I've got Deborah Goolagong here on the other line. Apparently, she's been trying to reach you. You can explain about the case and that, can't you?'

And with that, Deborah's face appeared on my screen. I had to properly bite my tongue not to swear out loud, as this was the last thing I needed right now. I'd seen the little recorded calls stacking up in the bottom right of my display for the last few days. It wasn't that I was deliberately ignoring them; it was more that I couldn't muster up the energy to have this conversation. That bastard Louie was going to pay for this.

'Hiya, Debs,' I muttered.

'Good morning, Carrie,' said Deborah. 'I'm sorry, did I catch you at a bad time?'

I looked around at the carnage of the crash. 'Nah. 'S fine.'

'Ah, good. Listen, I've been trying to call.'

'Yeah?' I said. 'I didn't realise.'

'Left a few messages.'

'Really? Sorry, been snowed under, you know?'

I could still see Lem's icon on the display, but it was receding. He must've finished with that car. A light rain had was falling through the white circle above, mixing in with the blood and ancient grease of railway tracks. My crawler team completed their sweep of the third set of tracks and needed moving to the fourth, their insistent – borderline needy – beeps distracting me from the call.

'Sorry I stormed off out of that Enforcement meeting with Kal and the team,' said Deborah. 'You know how it is… you must've had times when all your hard work is trashed in one decision, right?'

'Yeah, I've had that.' The first crawler had worked its way through some unidentified matter and I had to pick it up very carefully to avoid getting too much on my hands. A careful wipe of my fingers on my duffel coat followed.

'So, those tanks going into that BoTies camp, that was… well,

I don't often swear, but that was bloody annoying for me.'

'Yeah? Shit.' I resisted the urge to sniff the ends of my fingers.

'So, anyways,' said Deborah, 'I've been busy on the case. I think I've found the last bit of the puzzle.'

'Eh?' I said. I hadn't anticipated that she was still working on the case. 'Missing persons, now. Deprioritised. Didn't you get that PO cancellation? Algorithms have downgraded it. No victim, no murder.'

'I saw that, yeah, but I assumed that was just paperwork, you know? It's still a case, isn't it?'

'No.'

Her face crumpled a little on my screen. It was disturbing. But I was refusing to feel sorry for her. She was a big girl. She didn't need hugs.

'Oh, right,' she said. 'I thought we were doing a good job, don't you think? I mean, it was all—'

'Listen,' I interrupted, 'sorry about the PO and all that, but I really need to speak to Lem. Cheers and that. Good luck with all the Reconciliation work, yeah?'

'Yeah.' It was quiet and distant. 'It wasn't me, was it?'

'What?' I said, having to focus back on the call and tear my attention from looking for Lem. 'No, no, it wasn't owt like that. It were just that we didn't have a… there were no victim, you see? No named victim, nowt on the system, meant the algorithm simply took it off. The algo can't cope if there's no name.'

'They used to.'

'Eh?'

'In the past,' said Deborah, sniffing a little, 'they used to assign a name to the deceased. Something generic, like John… John Dole, I think?'

'Right,' I said. 'That were before DNA data mountains, I guess.'

'So, we could do that, give him a name?'

'We have already,' I said. 'We called him Mr Shin.'

'There you go!'

'But now nobody remembers meeting Mr Shin, and the only person who admitted to knowing him is dead. The algo can't cope with that. And if the algorithm can't cope with it, I sure can't handle shit like that. So, it's over as a case. Possibly summat about use of an illegal replacement service.'

'OK.' There was a pause. 'Right, I'll be seeing... no, hang on, what do I do with this leg?'

'You've got a fucking leg?'

'Damn right.'

'A right leg?'

'What? No, it's a left. But it's the right kind of length.'

'Get me a sample,' I said.

'Does this mean we've got a case again?'

I was distracted by a loud noise approaching from above. Something blotted out the pale light. 'What? No, just send me the results of the sample. Drop me a DNA package, OK?'

'OK,' she said, crestfallen. 'What's that noise?'

'Transporter drone,' I said, craning my neck. 'Expensive one, by the looks of it. Top end taxi, like.'

'What's it doing?'

'No idea. What? No, can't hear you anymore, Debs. Sorry. Bye.'

The gleaming machine, whining like a hornet on amphetamine, descended past the spiralling roads and towards a small park which lay on the other side of the chain link fence. All the various emergency personnel stopped what they were doing to watch its approach. As it came within a metre of the once-grassed surface of the park, downdraughts generated by the hidden blades churned up gravel and dust and peppered the fence and faces of the onlookers. There were a few swearwords and people turned back to their work.

I grunted, anticipating what was about to happen, the awkward call with Deborah and the search for Lem temporarily forgotten. Not wanting to make an idiot of myself, I hung back, watching the transporter out of the corner of my eye. Its motors finally glided to a soft hissing halt and the doors unlocked, releasing a tall, broad-shouldered man. He struggled a little to get out of the small two-seated machine, like it was a child's toy, and stood up, failing to conceal the grimace as his nostrils encountered the scent of the Fax Central's lowest level.

Adjusting his smart suit – even from this distance, it looked like it was the newest micro-feather weave – and scratching at his head, patterned with stylish alternating tessellations, he approached the chain-link fence. As he came nearer, the logo on his small scarf came out clear, showing the Nigerian flag and a smaller symbol.

'Hello there,' he called to nobody in particular. He spoke with the authority of somebody who expected a team of people to shout affirmatives back every time he opened his mouth.

'Hiya, love,' muttered one paramedic, who was unfortunately the nearest, and thereby made to wear the mantle of spokesperson. She didn't look very happy at the prospect.

'I'm looking for a member of the Airedale Justice Commission,' said the man. 'It is very urgent.'

'No Airedale here,' said the paramedic. 'This is the Belt. Fourth Sector, the Buckle, you know? You'll need to head north.'

'I was told she would be here,' said the man. 'Goes by the name of Tarmell, Carrie Tar–'

'It's me he's talking about,' I called out. 'I'm Carrie.' Sighing a little, I left the semi-circle of crawlers in front of me, pocketed the gecko, and hopped my way across towards the chain-link.

The paramedic, glad to be rid of this complicated social interaction, smiled a grateful smile and ducked back to her work.

'Hello,' said the man, waving uncertainly from behind the fence. 'My name is Sunday Sule. I'm an officer in the Federal Investigation of–'

'Yeah,' I said. 'Louie called ahead. Said you'd be dropping in. Said you needed my help.'

'No,' said the man, immediately. 'I need no help from local operatives. I simply have some questions.'

'Right,' I said, shrugging.

'My name is Sunday Sule,' he repeated, 'and I work for the Nigerian Federal Inspectorate, Division of Contraband and Standards. Lagos Branch.'

'Standards?' I said, grinning. 'That's the worst crime, isn't it?'

He glowered at me for a moment before answering. 'I do not understand.'

'Don't matter,' I said. 'Well, I'm Carrie Tarmell, Forensic Analyst for the Airedale Justice Commission, temporarily seconded to work on this Sector.' I looked around at the mess. 'As you can see.'

'I can.'

'Listen, shall I pop round that side?' I said, looking up the fence for some means of escape. 'So we can talk, um, more easily?'

The suggestion that I get closer to him clearly unnerved him a little and he stepped back, frowning. 'This is fine, isn't it?'

'These people are busy and they're on the clock,' I said. 'I don't want to disturb their work, you know?'

'OK.'

I could see his eyes skim the area. Anybody who came in from Lagos to the Belt must've had a bit of a culture shock. He would've left lagoon pods and submarine gardens and cloud stacks, and sunshine and heat, and now ended up in the lowest level of the Buckle, smelling the rust and blood and shit of a stupid car crash that should never have happened. No wonder he was jumpy.

'Don't worry,' I said, moving down the fence. I'd spotted a gate. 'I'm not carrying a blade or owt. I'm not going to stab you.'

'Good,' he called out, bravado making his voice crack a little. He adjusted his scarf a little, neatening up the folds around his thick neck.

Once I'd forced my way through the gate – admittedly locked but still sufficiently flexible for a titch like me – I scuffed my way back along the dead grass and cracked mud of the park towards Sunday and the transporter drone. He'd found himself an old stone monument and was examining it quizzically, as though contemplating whether he should sit on it.

'What is this?'

'That,' I said, squinting at it. 'It's to remember the dead.'

'Which ones?'

'Fuck if I know,' I said. 'It's hard work, finding out.' I smiled, briefly, and then turned back to the crime scene behind me. My crawlers had managed to find a way of following me over the tracks and were now lined up behind the chain-link, their LEDs blinking out of time. Out of the corner of my eye, I was momentarily drawn to the shape of somebody standing under the dark eaves of one of the ruined buildings. As my head turned towards them, they ducked back into the shadows and disappeared.

Sunday hadn't noticed me whirling around but was, instead, busy taking out some invisible glasses from a small chrome tube and placing them on his nose. Of course, they weren't invisible. Everybody could see the bloody things, but we were all supposed to agree that they were invisible. Because that's what the marketing people had told us they were. And marketing people apparently made things real.

'I'm sending you a picture,' said Sunday.

Still distracted by the shape under eaves, I set the gecko to scan the area and to alert me of any high risk hazard concepts. When Sunday's data arrived, I dragged the pulsing file onto my display and clicked it open. The image of a rotting hulk of a ship appeared, being pulled across the high seas by a small flotilla of other ships. Though I wasn't that nautical – famously being sick going out on a pedalo in Scarborough – even I could identify them as tugs. 'This the *Talofa*?'

'*Talofa-3*,' said Sunday, waving his finger.

'Whatever.'

'It's important. The *Talofa-1* is currently traversing the Bosphorus, carrying a cargo of hydroponic wheat strain, and the *Talofa-2* is moored just across the international waters line off the coast of Fiji, housing refugees from seven atolls. Do you confuse Johnny Jones and Jimmy Jones? No, you do not. Ship names are important. Do not confuse them!'

'OK,' I said. Sunday Sule was going to be right fun. 'I get it. Why's this *Talofa-3* important then?'

'This ship – technically, it is now classified as a hulk – is currently coming into dock at your port, Hartlepool. I'm here in the country to visit it.'

'Nice.'

'Where it will undergo recycling and deconstruction. It was en route from Dhaka and paused briefly at Lagos. This was where I attempted to board the hulk but, unfortunately, legalities prevented me. However, we have more promising reciprocal relationships with your East Pennine government, hence me being here.'

'And why've you come to see me?' I asked. My hand had found a lone mint, rolling around in the pocket of my coat. Then it found another.

'You left a message,' said Sunday. 'It was you, wasn't it?'

'I did, yeah,' I said. I pulled out my hand and offered the mints to Sunday. 'You want a mint?'

He leaned in more closely and examined my hand, then his eyes fell upon my fingertips. 'Have you been running forensics at the scene?'

'Yeah.'

'And have you washed?'

I threw a mint in my mouth and stuffed my hand back in my pocket. 'It's your loss.'

'Indeed, it is.' He stepped back, breathing in from the side. 'Does East Pennine not follow the Rio international standards on forensic hygiene?'

'Probably.' I chewed noisily. 'We still put wrong 'uns away, though.'

'Wrong 'uns?' he enquired, a small smile creeping onto his face. 'How quaint.'

I bit down hard on the mint and tried to stop a curse emerging from my lips. 'Like I said, it were me who sent the message in.'

'Good,' said Sunday, flicking his forefinger beside his head. I assumed he'd just done the equivalent of opening a notebook on his screen. 'What can you tell me?'

'Well,' I said, 'I was more interested in what you could tell me.'

This made the smile drop from Sunday's face and a troubled look appeared in his eyes, like a man who had just ordered the sweetbreads and had massively misunderstood the menu.

'I'm sorry?'

'I said that I sent in that message because I was following a case and I needed to know some more information. What can you tell me about the smuggling of replacement parts through Lagos?'

He flicked his fingers beside his head once more. That notebook was now closed. 'Um… well, I can tell you nothing, actually, Ms Tarmell.'

'Eh?'

'I cannot reveal details of federal investigations to anybody domiciled in countries outside of our rigorous IG standards.'

'We got IG standards and all.'

Sunday opened his eyes wider. 'Are they rigorous?'

'Ah, fuck it,' I muttered. 'Listen, I don't really care. I just wanted some more data on a case. Your investigation came up after I searched for FFRC BioTechnology.'

The fingers flickered back again. 'And what do you know of FFRC BioTechnology?'

I sniffed. I wasn't sure how much I was going to get here, but I needed to lay a little trail of bait. 'Fella in Manchester's been partaking of their services.'

'Along with nearly a million others across the world,' said Sunday. 'That's not news.'

'How about this, then?' I said and spoke in a lower voice. 'This man's replacement arm turned up about twelve kilometres from here.'

That got his attention. His nose twitched. 'Really? Verified?'

'Yeah, our apps confirmed.'

'Which app?'

'DidNotArrive, of course.'

He winced. 'I was afraid you were going to say that… these countries! Oh well, it will be sufficient. Within these borders, the actual operationalising of the replacement service would be illegal, yes?'

'Fucking right, it would be!'

'Hm. You have the arm?'

This was enough for me. 'How about you tell me where that boat came from? Who's the contact in Dhaka?'

'I'm afraid I can't, Ms Tarmell,' he said, tightening his scarf. 'Is that all you can tell me?'

'For now.'

'Well, in that case, thank you very much,' said Sunday. 'That's all I need for now. I need to get to Hartlepool.' He turned back towards his drone and strode off. 'Goodbye.'

'You're not taking me with you?'

He stopped. 'I apologise… I don't understand.'

'To see this hulk? This ship? The *Talofa-3*?'

Sunday blinked, surprised. 'I apologise. I mean, you're a forensic analyst for a regional homicide unit… why did you think you were part of this investigation?'

I knew I had one shot at this. 'Because it's part of a murder case.'

He regarded me for a moment and then stepped back towards me. 'Tell me more.'

I took a deep breath. 'A master recycler, Mr Shin, based here in the Fourth Sector, was murdered a little over two weeks' ago. I have multiple leads, of varying strengths, that suggest there's a connection to his death and FFRC BioTechnology.'

'Really? Go on.'

I didn't spot the warning signs. I was too eager. 'The arm's been found.'

'The arm belongs to a man in Manchester, isn't it?'

'Well, yeah,' I said, sweating now. 'But it's connected.'

'And the body?'

'Well, bits of a body and–'

'You see, I had an interesting discussion with your DI, Louie Daine about this very topic. He explained that the likelihood of there being a victim you could legally identify – legally, physically, genetically – was receding and that this case had… I think his word was "evaporated".'

'Bastard,' I said to the air. 'He loves a chat, does Louie.'

'He does indeed,' said Sunday. 'He is an endearing man. And I hope he finds love once more.'

I shook my head in disbelief. 'He told you about that?'

'I know a great deal about the tribulations of his relationships. I could provide some comfort to him. I am skilled in areas such as this.'

'Eh?'

He smiled. 'I, however, am more discreet than he. So I cannot speak more of that.'

'I'm still following up on the Shin case.'

'In your free time, I believe?'

'There's something there. If you take me with you, I can explain.'

'Things fall apart sometimes, Carrie. Investigations, especially.'

'There's summat going on with… with that case, with Shin, with the arms and legs. And somebody else, somebody who worked with Shin, worked up at the recycling yard, they got murdered and all. Found floating in a nearby reservoir.' I started to talk too fast. 'They'd had a story, told me about Shin, sounded like he might've come from Bangladesh originally, hence the Dhaka side. Then they're dead. The other employee's changed her story, said there never was any Shin, said she and the dead one'd made it all up. Why change her story? Somebody's got to her. And somebody's been coming in from Abu Dhabi as well. Come in to talk to the dead one and there're all these arms and legs around from people who are long dead, or are still alive, and…' I trailed off, going a little red.

Sunday was squinting at me, a half-smile on his face. 'OK.'

'What?'

'I said "OK", you can come with me. This is more interesting than what your Detective Inspector told me.'

'And you can tell me what you know?'

'No,' said Sunday. 'But you can come with me.'

'Fine,' I said. 'I just need to get my kit together.'

'You've finished here?'

'Nah, but I've got enough… oh, I just need to catch someone first.' I pulled up my proximity alerts again.

'We don't have long,' said Sunday.

'Ah shit.'

'What is wrong?' asked Sunday.

'I've lost him,' I said. 'The bastard's disappeared.' I clicked my fingers in the air again, trying to get his proximity signal. But Lem was gone.

'A suspect?' Sunday was distracted by a loud creak above our heads. I guessed it was the remains of that crash barrier, swinging in the breeze.

'Worse than that,' I said. 'Our digital analyst. I can never get hold of him. Been trying for a week.'

'Ask another?'

'We don't have another!'

'You do not have another digital analyst?' asked Sunday. There was a further creak. People behind us were starting to shout.

'We don't have another anything,' I said.

Sunday looked around the mess of the lower level of Fax Central. 'Yes. How the mighty have fallen. Broken, really. It is sad, in its way.'

Although I wasn't especially endeared to my home region, the tone he adopted, the sneer and the way he seemed to try to avoid breathing the air, had got me more riled than I should've been. 'This place is perfectly fine, thank you. There's nothing broken about it!'

About four metres distant from where Sunday and I were standing, the long piece of polymer-steel crash barrier that had been swinging from the accident above us, decided to fall and smack into the railway line, sending up a dust maelstrom.

'Fuck!' I shrieked, grabbing Sunday's arm like I was six years old.

'Thankfully that missed the rental,' said Sunday. 'Shall we go?'

CHAPTER SEVENTEEN

'You want a FocXy chew?'

Sunday eyed the small paper bag I offered him with disgust. 'No. I have to watch my… I'm sorry. No.'

'I'll keep asking,' I said, popping one of the sweets into my mouth. I was immediately aware of the scent of blood and worse under my fingernails. I still hadn't cleaned them properly since packing up the crawlers. Normally, this wouldn't bother me, but Sunday's comments from earlier stung a little. I dug into another pocket and picked out a pack of wipes, diligently working out the muck.

Sunday turned his head away and looked out of the window. We were flying east through the maze of towers and spires and arching garden walkways of the Leeds end of the Belt. Cloud was low, so you couldn't see far. Shapes loomed ahead and then clarified into buildings before we banked away from them and left them behind in the gloom. It was a shame, as this part of the Belt got prettier, especially as you moved towards York, but we weren't going to see it today. The English childhood memory of staring out at a rain-stricken grey through condensation streaked glass rose up inside. Sunday had already bored himself with the view and was now snapping his fingers and tapping away at some messages, his invisible specs perched on the end of his nose.

I'd never been a top-end rental like this, so it was a first to see how the other half lived.

'I imagine you all get around via sky in Lagos, right?'

'There are plenty of transporter drones, yes?' said Sunday,

dragging off his glasses with a grunt.

'Pretty swish, I'd imagine.'

'What is?'

'Lagos? It's where it's all happening, right?'

'We have been fortunate,' said Sunday.

'Highest proportion of trillionaires, I heard.'

'Not quite. And there is poverty still, as well. Around the fringes of the city... I mean, the megacity bounds. That's further out, you see. We haven't been able to house everybody who came south, though the northerly forest defences have kept back the dunes effectively. They are rehousing many there.'

'And where do you live?'

He gave me a quick glance, as though checking out my credentials. You needed the proper Sunday Sule a-codes to see that kind of data. 'I live on the lagoon. In an Okon module, interconnected to a quiet but supportive community cluster.'

'Nice,' I said. I'd no idea what an Okon module was, but I was sure it was the bollocks. 'Is it hot?'

'Hotter than here, yes.'

'Too hot?'

'Sometimes, yes. Is it too cold here?'

'No,' I said. 'It's never too cold, just continuously–'

'Yes,' he interrupted, 'that's what many have told me already.'

'You've been here before?'

'A couple of times,' he said. 'I once studied here and–'

We banked hard to avoid a large zeppelin rising from the opened roof of a warehouse unit.

'Shit,' I muttered, grabbing onto the handle above my head. 'That were close.'

'No navigational signature,' said Sunday, peering at the automated display in front of him. 'Must be operating illegally.'

I shrugged and grunted. 'Well, we do try to keep things flexible up here.'

'What do you mean?'

'Politicians think businesses working at the borders of what's legal helps drive innovation. We're not supposed to intervene too much.'

'Unregulated? Like a black market?'

'It's complex,' I said, nodding. I was still feeling a little defensive, though I had no idea why. Place was a fucking dump, didn't need me arguing its case. I looked out of the window. To our left, and a little behind us now, was the thick leg of Airedale, its constellation of blurred lights plunging north-west, into the blackness of economically-dead farmland and statutory wilderness. 'Think of it as a market of many shades, you know?'

'You don't have a black market?'

'Perhaps you can call it a free market?'

'What about standards?' he asked.

'Yeah,' I said, chewing. 'We got some of them, and all.'

'OK,' he said. 'Remind me not to buy street food here.'

'It's alright,' I said. 'Never had any bother.'

'It explains why your country may be a suitable destination for this cargo.'

'Replacement's still illegal here,' I said, swallowing back the last of my FocXy chew.

'But things are flexible?'

'Enforcement, the activity, not the people, well, that's dead hard,' I said. 'We got the rules but we haven't got the willing, if you know what I mean?'

'You lack personnel?'

'Yeah.' I contemplated another sweet but decided to leave them in my pocket. Instead, I removed my gecko and gave it a clean over with the remains of my wipe. 'Just can't get the right people to enforce the law, to deliver justice. That's why you get the crappy ones like me.'

Sunday was uncertain how to respond. 'Yes. Right.'

Ahead of us, a huge array of micro drones were running a three-dimensional display, advertising some obscure financial company. They weaved and flashed through their numerous LED colours, finishing with a large rotating, orange moon. We didn't get this kind of sky display over Airedale. You needed eyes watching with fat credit lines. There was nothing like that where I lived.

I turned my eyes away from the mesmerising show and looked at him. 'I were fucking joking.'

Sunday blinked a little and nodded, smiling in a way that suggested he hadn't understood. 'Anyway, let's leave that. Can you please tell me all you know about FFRC?'

'If you tell me what's happened in Lagos?'

'In time.'

So, as we turned north, heading up the major north-south VOM conduit – dales to our left and moors to our right – I relayed everything I knew. I even told him about the phone call I'd received from a terrified Shin in the middle of the night. All of this he was taking down on his recorder and his notes, barely listening. He didn't seem that bothered by any of the recycling facility stuff, to be honest, though he perked up when we turned over the body parts. And he was very interested in the equipment we found.

'You've got a military stitcher? In a municipal recycling facility?'

'Yeah, that's right,' I said, proudly.

'You know it's military? You've had it certified, have you?'

I remembered the conversation with my mother. 'Fucking right, I have.'

'And you believe this stitcher was used to… I forget, was it used to remove limbs from this Mr Shin?'

'I reckon,' I said. 'I think it was used the night he was murdered.'

'But we don't know there is a Mr Shin?'

'I had a phone call,' I said.

'But this could be artificially generated?'

'True.'

'So, we have no corroborating evidence – beyond this dead employee's possible story – that there was ever a man who lived called Mr Shin?'

'No,' I said. 'At least, I believe it.'

'What do you believe?'

'That there was a man called Mr Shin.' Saying it out loud didn't make me believe it.

'That does not suffice.'

I shrugged. 'Anyways, we got a torso, with signs that limbs from other bodies were attached.'

'That's robust?'

'Yeah,' I said. 'We got a proper doctor to tell us and all.'

'I would be interested in talking to her, if that's possible?' said Sunday.

'It's a him,' I said, 'and he's not really around to speak to, but you can call him.'

Sunday opened his mouth and was about to ask another question, before he thought better of it. 'Fine. You realise that it is possible to attach replacement limbs together into a supporting structure without that broader supporting structure to be a coherent organism?'

'Eh?'

'I mean, they may have been using that torso as a means of keeping the meat alive for longer. A more integrated circulatory system is better for the material.'

'How'd you know that?'

'I did a doctorate in it,' said Sunday.

'Oh.'

'You have not found the head, yet?'

'No, there's no head.'

'Well.'

And I shut up at that point.

CHAPTER EIGHTEEN

The Hartlepool wreckers' pontoon stretched two kilometres into the North Sea, its huge corporate logo in simple sans serif font only visible from the air: Gunnison & Harwick. A vast interconnected string of floating docks, repurposed from dismembered oil rigs and welded together hulks of ships. Further along the coast, the dry docks were just visible from the drone, cut into the land or built directly into the sea, housing the final skeletons of the beasts. These dry docks took the shape of huge pools, formed by an ugly array of corrugated steel platforms, smashed into the muddy foreshore.

Here, they sent the really rusting shit to die. As other yards across the world had gradually tightened regulations on toxic waste and by-products, Hartlepool spotted a gap in the market and some enterprising Durham Servant had pushed through a subtle piece of land legislation; followed by the first of many bids to scrap the remaining fleet of redundant tankers, cruise liners, and fish factory ships. The vast majority of towers in northern England had been constructed using recycled steel from these dead hulks, ripped apart by the yard's lethal flying arc drones.

'That's the one,' said Sunday. We were flying out over the neon lights of a seaside entertainment zone, south of the main pontoon. We could see the *Talofa-3* in the distance, a few hundred metres from the outermost pontoon dock. As midafternoon drew in, blue, green, and red LEDs intermixed with the common white, casting avenues of light out in the brown sea. The lights observed an obscure dockland protocol, or messaging system we didn't understand.

The visitor's landing pad was a repurposed antique clockface spray-painted onto the floor of a larger pontoon, in the middle of the warren, surrounded by a couple of large tankers and further pontoons heading out to the sea.

Automated loaders whined around us, making their way back from the frontline of ship breaking and toward the dock, carrying hoppers of wiring and burnt polymer. Sunday seemed nervous about stepping past them, edging out into their path before jumping back as one neared. Whether it was my benign trust in their sensors, a need to prove my worth, or simply having given up caring altogether, I can't say, but I walked through them, raising a hand to command them to stop. They halted immediately, and we passed through, Sunday begrudgingly nodding thanks at my initiative.

A couple of bored young women approached, both wearing Gunnison & Harwick Security uniforms; a grey-brown hue not dissimilar to the North Sea on a bad day. For the North Sea, this meant every frigging day of the year. I was glad I didn't have their shitty job. They perked up, straightening their jackets and pulling their belts a little tighter, as Sunday neared. They were less interested in my duffel-coated, bobble-hatted presence.

'I'm Mensies and this is Corva,' the one on the left said, her red hair pulled into three girlish bunches around her head. 'We're with corporate security, but we've got national customs delegation. Don't use it often, mind. You must be Mr Sule, yes?'

'That's right,' Sunday agreed. 'Hello.'

'Good afternoon.' Corva's brown eyes gleamed under the brim of her peaked cap. She then looked at me, a little less impressed, though considerably more suspicious. 'Are you also a Nigerian Federal inspector?'

I grinned.

'No,' Sunday interjected. 'She is leading a murder investigation on behalf of the Fourth Sector Justice Division. Normally contracted to the Airedale unit.' He turned to me. 'Is that right?'

'Airedale?' said Mensies. 'That's some place inland, isn't it?' She looked at Corva. 'That's where you're from, isn't it?'

'I wouldn't know.' Corva shrugged off the question. 'Does she have a name?'

'You *would* know,' I said, pointing to her hands. 'You've worked vats already. Most likely in Airedale, I'd say.'

'Yeah, I've worked vats. What does it matter? Am I under investigation?'

'Nah,' I said, deciding I didn't like Corva. You can smell it on some people.

Sunday was more interested in the people who weren't there. 'Where's the rest of the team?'

'Eh?' Mensies gulped.

'I'd requested a full support team,' said Sunday.

'Assumed you'd bring them.'

Although I didn't want to undermine my new partner in front of strangers, I would've loved to step in at that point and ask the same question. Where was Sunday's team?

'We can't move personnel between countries at speed. There are protocols, which is why we expect local support and partnership.' I could tell he was avoiding my eye at this point.

'Here we are,' Mensies jested, spreading her arms.

Sunday grimaced. 'You have power and heat scanners?'

'Of course,' said Mensies, brandishing a large device. To the untrained eye, it looked more like a hairbrush, but I'd seen the brand before, even used them on some cases. They'd do the job.

'And you?' asked Sunday, looking at me.

'Gecko can scan for heat,' I said, nodding.

'You good, then?' asked Mensies.

Sunday looked anything but good. Instead, he turned towards the sea. 'She's nearly docked,' he said, nodding significantly at the distant shape of the *Talofa-3*. The tugs were now dragging the hulk into the dock, and cranes were hauling ropes into the air. 'Are we able to board her?'

Mensies flagged down an empty loader, and we climbed on, hanging onto whatever we could find. For me, this mainly meant Sunday, which was awkward, but he didn't seem to mind. Neither did I, I realised, after a minute of clasping him. I tried to calculate the last time I'd been this close to someone.

'You have a manifest for the crew of those tugs?' he said, shouting above the whine of the loader.

'Yeah,' said Mensies. 'I've already cast it to your glasses.'

'Thank you. Yes, I can see.'

There was a small line of heavily-coated figures leaving the small tugs now docked beside the vast hulk of the *Talofa-3*.

'Where do they go?' I asked, looking up at Sunday.

Corva cut in. 'They go and get wasted in the town and then get back on the last of the tugs. All the way back for the next one.'

'We interested in them?' I asked.

'No,' said Sunday. 'I'll run a digital trace on them later. What we need is on the *Talofa-3* itself, not the tugs. How long do we have?'

'You've been allocated an hour and a half,' said Mensies.

'Ninety minutes? For something that size?'

'That's protocol.'

'Where is it protocol? I've never come across this before.'

Mensies looked at Corva momentarily. 'That's right, isn't it?'

Corva nodded. 'Yes, I checked. Standard policy for this kind of international investigation. Ninety minutes is what you get.'

'I'll have to check this,' said Sunday. 'I'll have to get back to my legal team in Lagos.'

'That's what it is,' said Corva with a shrug. 'Sorry, that's the deal.'

'That does not appear like a reciprocal arrangement to me,' said Sunday.

'Well, we're here to help, if you're pushed for time,' said Corva, yelling a little above the growl of the motor and the battling waves. 'We can cover other decks? The upper ones only, of course. I'm not sloshing about in the bilge.'

The upper decks had been for the high-end cabins and swimming pools. I guessed Sunday was more interested in the catering and lower decks, so it seemed sensible.

'Thank you,' said Sunday. 'That will help.'

The loader stopped a little distance from the ship and we all climbed off. I turned my attention back to the grim sight above me. What had once been a pristine white cruise liner, moving rich people around rich parts of the world at an income-generating slow speed, was now an invalid, carrying scabs of rust and open wounds down its side. I was surprised it'd made it this far. A swell rose up and moved the pontoon we were on violently to the side. The two customs agents were clearly used to the movements and adjusted their posture but both Sunday and I staggered off to the left, like bad extras in a disaster movie.

Corva worked an automated gangplank in place so that we could board the hulk. As we waited, I pulled up some info on my bead. I was trusting my ability to smell out a wrong 'un and there was something I wanted to check. I'd seen the vat stains on her hands.

First off, I dipped into the employment records of the East Pennine Justice Command. I had high level access – just above where IG lawyers started getting jumpy. I knew that we could expand the data by plugging in other sources. So, I scrolled through the other options, looking for a specific acronym. All the while distracted by the whining servos of the dockside machines, as they struggled to keep the liner from drifting away from the dock. This was coupled with the view, now vague behind the lines on my display, and the vast grey-brown hulk towering over us.

Found it. I popped a chew into my mouth and started to work at it.

'Are you OK?' asked Corva, intrigued by my hand motions.

'Just prepping up the case,' I muttered.

'OK. Watch yourself on the gangplank now. It sways.'

I nodded and carried on with my work. I'd noticed that she'd now donned gloves, which handily covered the vat stains. Her name was right there, joined the crew two years' ago. Previous employer was an outfit called Pinho Holdings. I ran a quick search on the founder's name: Robert Pinho. He'd been in Airedale for a while, before moving to the Bradford Borders. He seemed to have inherited a fortune from his parents, plenty of land around Bradford, Airedale, the Buckle, founded a vat business in his twenties. It wasn't going that well, reading the headlines. But then, what vat business was? It'd all gone overseas now. People had to branch out.

I had nothing. But remained suspicious. I prepped up the tracer drone from my top pocket.

We approached the side of the hulk and the relatively miniscule chrome gangplank.

'Is it safe?' I asked, not liking the way the thing moved in the swell. I stared up at the upper decks.

'Enough,' Sunday interrupted. 'This one's in a fairly good order. There may be a few issues with floors and stairs, but the whole thing's not going to collapse around us. You have to have some internal integrity in order to make the journey this far. Nobody wants a cruise liner to disintegrate going through the English Channel, do they?'

'Guess not,' I said.

Sunday stepped onto the gangplank, gripped the metal handrails, and climbed to the small opening on the side. Mensies followed. When it came to my turn, Corva invited me to go first, but I made an anxious face and shooed her onto the plank. While she climbed, I retrieved the chew from my mouth and spat it into my hand. With a little swear, I pretended to stumble and fell into Corva's back, slapping my palm into the space between her shoulder blades. The little chew sat there for a while before slipping down her back and into the sea. It was enough.

'You OK?' said Corva.

'Sorry,' I said. 'This is scary shit, right?'

'Don't worry. We do this every day. Never been a drowning yet.'

'Good to know.'

We clustered in the lobby and agreed on the decks. Sunday would take the lowest levels, I would cover the main lobby and cabins, then Mensies the middle decks, and Corva at the top.

'What we looking for?' asked Mensies.

'Last time, they fitted out a freezer compartments with all the tanks,' said Sunday. 'They had the whole automated ecosystem in there, generators, nutrient dispenser, lights, heating, etc. That's what we're looking for.'

Neither of the two women looked like they were expecting to find anything. But they seemed relaxed about helping out anyway and trotted off, playfully pointing their micro torches into the others' eyes and shouting 'Boo'.

'You OK?' asked Sunday, after they'd headed for the sweeping wreck of the main staircase.

'Fine,' I said, fishing out the kit from my top pocket and unfolding it.

'What's that?'

'Tracer drone.'

'Won't work,' said Sunday, smiling condescendingly. 'I've already tried that. They mask the signals with countermeasures. You need heat and power sources. That's what they need to keep the meat alive.'

'Not looking for meat,' I said, pointing the tracer's sensors at the mess in my palm and sending it off. It buzzed around the lobby for a while before picking up the scent at the bottom of the stairs and then tracking up. I'd set parameters to keep its distance, but to maintain a good record. I dug out another wipe and cleaned my hands.

'Was that one of your pieces of confectionery? You are quite messy, Ms Tarmell.'

'Me?' I said, grinning. 'You don't even want to know.'

With that parting comment, I turned on my heel and headed off along the corridor that led towards the bow.

CHAPTER NINETEEN

It was hard work, trying to cover the allotted area in the time we'd been given, but I quickly got into a rhythm and found myself working through room after room at a steady pace. Before the liner had been sent to Hartlepool, still docked in Dhaka, there'd been an internal recycling team who'd been rigorous at clearing out the fixtures and furniture, so each space was empty of clutter. All the hatches and doors had been unlocked and propped open, so all it took was a quick glance inside before moving on. Whoever they were, they'd been thorough. The inside of the ship actually looked cleaner than my flat.

After half an hour, I checked in with Sunday. 'You found owt yet?'

'Nothing,' said Sunday. 'Look for heat and electronic signatures, yes?'

'Yeah, yeah,' I said. I'd got my gecko to pick up on that shit already and it was doing a grand job of skittering on ahead for me, taking pictures.

In truth, I wasn't paying that much notice to the heat signals. All my attention was on Corva; while I was moving dutifully from empty room to empty room, checking for heat and suspiciously locked doors and the like, I was also tracking the path my tracer was following. It was already dropping in a steady stream of coordinates and timestamps, ready for processing. This meant, when I'd returned to the *Talofa-3*'s lobby area ahead of the rest of them, and was sat down on the stripped floor, back against the cold clammy steel, I was already working on the map of the tracer's journey across the upper floors.

'Nothing?' asked Sunday, as he came up a smaller set of stairs from below decks.

'Nowt from me,' I said, not looking up from my work.

'Hm, I also found little. Nothing substantive, at least.'

'They usually lock down the timings like this? Ninety minutes? Seems tight.'

'I have queried it with my legal team but there is no answer.'

'Oh,' I said, still half listening. Instead, I was trying to analyse the map of my tracer drone's progress. The pattern of the flight path wasn't really making it that obvious. I needed something to compare it to. 'You got any blueprints of this ship?'

'Of course,' said Sunday. There was a few seconds' delay and then he flicked them across to my display.

'Ta.'

I dropped the blueprints across the processed map of the tracer drone's progress. I had to fiddle about with the Z axis and the decks, but I got there in the end. In front of me, I had the greyed lines of the *Talofa-3*'s upper three decks and, across it, the coloured smudges of drone coverage. On the lowest of these, there was a clear gap.

I got to my feet. 'Come on.'

'What have you found?'

'An omission,' I said, trying to keep my voice down.

It didn't work. We'd already been heard.

'What's said.' It was Mensies, coming down the stairwell from the upper decks. She had Corva in tow.

'I've got a feeling, that's all. Just one last place to check.'

I stood up and made for the stairwell, passing Mensies and Corva. Sunday followed.

'Where're they going?'

'You're out of time,' called out Mensies.

'Just need to check on something,' I shouted back.

'We'll have to escalate,' warned Corva, suddenly edgy.

'We've got five minutes,' I said, now running.

I was breathing raggedly by the time we reached the right

floor, but I clung to the handrails and made my way along the outer deck. The sea out to my right was blowing a chilly breeze, which helped keep the sweating to a minimum. I checked the map and dived into the nearest doorway. We were in a corridor of small rooms, each cabin door open, as with other floors of the ship. I worked my way down.

'Check the ones on the right,' I said to Sunday, who had appeared behind me.

'Why are we here?'

'It's a gap,' I said, gathering my breath. 'On the map, the blueprints, when I compared it with the path of the tracer drone. She never checked here. Corva never went down here.'

We hurriedly raced down the length of cabins, my gecko dancing ahead of me. Every cabin I came to contained the same: carpet adhesive strips on the floor, holes left in steel and the ghosts of old fittings left in the dust and grime of the walls. There was nothing obviously wrong. Then I noticed that end of the corridor seemed to go nowhere. There was an odd space at the end, which felt like it should contain a door.

'What's the point of that? It goes nowhere.'

Sunday peered down, getting out of his flashlight. He looked closely at the wall as he approached. A hand was slowly placed on the wall and he gave it a push. Then he grunted.

'What?' I said. There wasn't that much space.

Then he turned around and strode back to me.

'What is it? Anything?' I said, backing up and out of his way.

Expecting Sunday to barge past me and off the boat in a rage at the ridiculous practices of this backwards little island, he instead reached the end of the little corridor, then turned around, facing the mysterious wall and ran towards it. As he neared the end, he put out his shoulder and tucked down his head. The end of corridor exploded into a mess of wood, polymer and polystyrene.

Using the light from my gecko, I ran down the corridor to see what was going on.

'Shit,' I could hear Mensies behind me, who had followed us up.

I reached the opening, as Sunday was getting up and dusting himself off. There was now a clear hum of machinery. Around the walls of the large chamber were sound-proofed panels and large insulating slabs of polystyrene. In the middle of the room was a cluster of large meat-growing tanks, each containing a human limb, some of them small, like hands, some of them tiny with fingers, and larger tanks with whole legs. A ramshackle stack of high-end batteries blinked their LEDs from the corner of the room. I immediately released the gecko to start taking some footage.

'Is there a light?' asked Sunday, sweeping his torch around the room.

I stumbled across a cord hanging from the ceiling and looked up. It connected with some cheap external lighting, which had been glued together along a metal strut. I pulled it and the lights came on.

'Whoah,' said Mensies, at the door.

'Don't touch anything,' I said. 'I need to get the pictures.'

Sunday stepped back from a tank, raising his hands. 'Good point, of course.'

'We should have picked up the power from here,' said Sunday, looking back at Mensies accusingly. 'It's heavy with battery.'

'Yeah,' said Mensies. 'Sorry, looks like you were right.'

'You covered this floor?' Sunday asked.

'No,' said Mensies.

'Corva did,' I said. 'Where is she?'

'Not sure,' said Mensies.

'Get her,' I said, with one hand dancing in the air to bring up my bead display and the other loosening my scarf from my sweaty neck. I pinched my fingers and brought them closer to my eyes. 'And while you're doing that: under paragraphs three and four of section forty-eight of the Justice Bill 2031, I'm hereby declaring this facility – and all known points of access – to be a formal crime scene within the jurisdiction of East Pennine.'

It felt good to be able to do my job.

CHAPTER TWENTY

'No, actually,' said Sunday. 'I have to correct you, Ms Tarmell.'

'What?' I said. He'd better have something sensible to say. I'd just hit the submit button on registering the case. It was a bugger to unsubmit this kind of shit.

'This is not the jurisdiction of the East Pennine.'

'Yes,' I said, 'it is.'

'Under sections five, seventeen, fifty-five and two hundred and three, of the maritime legal charter,' said Sunday, as if he weren't even reading the stuff, like he actually remembered it, 'I hereby declare this site the jurisdiction of the Convened International Array of Shipping Investigators, or CIASI.'

'We're in fucking Hartlepool, Sunday!'

'Neither Fourth Sector, nor Airedale, nor anywhere where you might be contracted, has jurisdiction over this scene.' Sunday clicked his fingers and fired the relevant paragraphs and accompanying links across to my bead.

I didn't look at them. Instead, I glared at him for a full minute. This usually had the desired effect, but Sunday seemed immune. He turned around and pulled out a chrome cylindrical case from his pocket, similar in style to his spectacles. He clicked a button on the side and the top popped open. One by one, white bee drones rose from the depths of the cylinder and started to fly around the room, flashing their incredibly bright lights as they did so. In retaliation, I drew out my gecko and placed it on the floor, setting it off on its default patterns.

'All evidence captured at this site,' said Sunday, watching

my gecko with a light sneer, 'will be subject to analysis by the Federal Inspectorate.'

'Whatever,' I said. 'As long as I get to see it.' I reached into my top pocket and pulled out my meat probe, advancing on the vats.

Sunday immediately stepped in front of me. 'Absolutely no interference with the goods.'

'The what?'

'The goods, the cargo.' His eyes widened. 'The assets.'

'Eh?'

A hand was placed firmly against my shoulder. I was about to punch it viciously away when something caught my attention on my bead. A stationery icon flashed in a miniaturised map. New movement identified by my tracer drone, still following the last scent capture. The FocXy chew was on the move.

'Hey,' I said sharply, turning to Mensies, 'where's Corva?'

Mensies turned around as well. The other dock operative was no longer with us.

'This isn't finished, you know,' I said to Sunday, before loosening my scarf a little bit more and starting to run.

'Where're you going?' said Mensies as I ran past her.

'You'll be next,' I snarled over my shoulder.

I could just hear Sunday barking at Mensies as I turned the corner to the upper deck. 'You need to close the gates. You need to close them now.'

Corva had a good lead on me, but the tracer was now in the air, so I knew exactly where she was going. I legged it the length of the upper foredeck before plunging down a series of stairwells. Some rain had pooled at the bottom of a stairway, causing me to skid and crash into the railings at the side. My head swung over the railings and I stared down at the white lines of waves crashing against the side of the ship. I swore and pushed myself back to safety. A few more staircases and the trail then led back me into the belly of the hulk. I worked my way through the cafeterias and the bars, my breath becoming more and more ragged as I went, until I got back to the lobby.

I took a breather at the top of the gangplank, looking down to the docks. Though it was dark now, I could just make out the shape of the other woman heading down a pontoon towards the exit of the facility. Behind, high in the sky, was my mobile tracer drone, lights blinking furiously.

'Should give us fucking guns,' I muttered and sprinted down the gangplank, narrowly stopping myself from tripping on the rotting rubber cleats. As I stumbled onto the rolling dock, I looked up to the sky and had an idea. I pulled up manual controls and dragged the tracer drone from its holding position above. It whined as it passed high over my head and towards Corva. A small window, showing the drone's camera view, popped up on my display. Not certain whether this was entirely legal, I sent it careering towards the back of the woman's head. It was only an ultralight, so I concluded there would be minor abrasions at best. At worst, I could always blame faulty manufacturing. Nobody was going to check.

As it turned out, there was fuck all to worry about. The machine must've been hard-coded to avoid people, so it swerved off to the left and passed by Corva's ear.

'You piece of shit,' I muttered.

However, it had the effect of unnerving the operative, for she suddenly turned to the right, trying to avoid the drone, now in her eyeline, and ran down a spur of the dock, towards another ship, an oil tanker.

'Wait,' I shouted, unable to be heard above the sound of the wind and the waves. 'Corva!'

The woman continued running, ignoring my cries for her to stop. She turned right again, up another pontoon. But this one was a dead end.

'Wait there,' I called out again.

I sent the drone ahead of her, trying to herd her back. But she was off again, lashing out at the small machine as it buzzed past her head, and charged on. At the end of the pontoon, I spied a small boat with the Hunter and Gunnison logo and colours splashed on its side.

'Shit.'

She reached the boat and jumped down onto its deck, skidding as she landed, then disappeared into the cockpit. I stopped running now, fully expecting to hear the roar of a motor and see the white foam trail of this speedboat disappearing down the coast. Except it didn't happen. Checking on my small camera view of the drone, I could see Corva at the controls, desperately trying to get it started. I picked up pace again, trotting down the last empty stretch of the jetty, until I could look down into the boat. I wasn't sure whether she was going to be armed, so I edged my head carefully into view. She'd untied the painter from the dock and the boat was starting to drift out into the sea.

'Corva,' I called out.

She was weeping, jamming her thumb repeatedly into a sensor.

'Corva,' I said. 'You need to come with us.'

'No way,' she said.

'Yeah, you do,' I said. 'We'll sort it all out.'

'I've seen it. I've seen it all…'

'What've you seen?' I said, gently.

She still didn't stop trying to get the boat to recognise her thumbprint. 'You don't want to know. You really don't want to know.'

'I do,' I said. 'It's my job.'

'I don't want to end up like that.' She could hardly speak now, her voice coming out thickly.

A swell took the boat further out. I considered whether I could swim across the gap. But it looked dark and cold. And I was a shit swimmer.

'We'll get somebody to come and get you,' I said. 'Stay there, yeah?'

'Nobody's coming to get me,' she sobbed.

I heard the whirr of a loader approach. I turned and saw Mensies, and some other agency workers, coming down the dock. Two of them looked to be armed with tranqs. I held out my hand to get them to stop. They were going to make Corva do something really stupid. At least, more stupid than what she was doing at the moment.

'Wait.'

When I turned round towards the boat, I could see – almost too far out to make out – Corva had wrapped herself up in something. It looked like frayed remains of a rope and the accompanying anchor from a much larger ship.

Then she rolled over the side.

'No, there was nothing that unusual about her.'

'How soon did she join the team?'

'Sorry… can't you wait a minute for this? My manager will be here soon, I think.'

We were in a larger office, a prefab module pasted onto the reinforced stumps of the old pier. Outside the windows were the lights of the pontoon docks and the black shadows of ships. A few dozen people were now milling around, both inside and outside the offices, some in the uniform of the agency, some in the overalls of the registered wrecking companies. In front of me, staring at an empty cup on the table, like it was magically going to flood with tea or booze or something, was Mensies. And she was a fucking wreck.

'I know,' I said, putting a hand comfortingly on her arm. I'd seen other people in Justice do this to their interviewees. I wasn't sure what it was supposed to achieve, but I was game for anything about now. And I needed to get the info out of her before Sunday waltzed in.

She smiled gratefully. 'Thanks.'

The touching-the-arm shit seemed to work like a treat. I followed it up with another question. 'Did she live locally?'

'Yeah,' said Mensies, and coughed up some phlegm, then swallowed it back with a grimace. She blinked her black-streaked eyes. 'She lived in town, like. Just down the coast. She was renting a place, she told me.'

'Do you have the address?' I asked. It was almost a whisper.

'Sure,' she said, then shook her head. 'Look, do we have to do this now? My manager, Walt, he'll be along in a minute. He can help you out.'

'Sure, sure,' I murmured.

Mensies nodded. Then looked down at her cup.

'You want something to drink?' I asked, looking down at the cup as well. This was something else you were supposed to do. Keep 'em drinking. Perhaps needing to have a piss helped speed things up.

'What? No, no. Just… not sure what to do now. Have they brought her up yet?'

I'd been there, about twenty minutes previously, when the paramedic team – assisted by some submarine drones, commandeered from the wrecking company – had lifted up the coils of rope and anchor. There was a corpse attached.

'Yeah,' I said, with professional authority.

'Right.'

'Look, I can get out of your way here, if you get me that address, yeah?'

She frowned. 'You're in a hurry, aren't you?'

'Eh?'

'Why the rush?'

The grip on her arm tightened. 'Don't matter.'

'You're…'

'What?' I said.

Mensies eyes were narrowing. 'I was just going to say that… that you, you're look like–'

I smiled. 'You have no idea.'

'I'm not happy doing this.'

'That's fine by me. I just want the information, don't I?'

A large, round man had entered the offices, momentarily blocking out the light. He wore the same uniform as Mensies and scanned the crowd for faces. I guessed he was probably Walt. Mensies hadn't spotted him yet, as he was behind her, but it was only a matter of time.

'And you'll leave me alone?' asked Mensies.

'I'll be all done, yeah.'

'You're a real mercenary.'

The man had spotted Mensies and was approaching. I didn't have long. 'Just give me the address, buddy,' I muttered, half standing.

Then it was on my bead. I was done. Walt called out a greeting to Mensies as I nodded a quick thank you and then I was away, out of the door.

It took a few minutes, but I finally found Sunday barking orders on the main access pontoon. Due to me calling in the crime scene, he'd managed to bring in some subcontractors – looked like a local equivalent of RapidRez – who were now wheeling out a series of slick containers from the *Talofa-3*. Surrounded by the swirl of bodies and loaders, it was quite an effort to reach him.

'Alright, Sunday?' I said.

He turned away from giving instructions to a member of the team. 'Hello Ms Tarmell. Are you OK?'

I pointed at the containers. 'I wanted to get a sample before they went, that's all.'

He smiled. 'I'm afraid not. They cannot be tampered with.'

I was getting quite tired now. It'd been a long day. 'I don't think you understand, Sunday. This is evidence for my case.'

'I know,' he said. 'But also for the Federal Inspectorate, so I'm afraid I take precedence.'

'Where are you taking them?' I asked.

He looked at me as though expecting the question. 'To a secure location.'

'Should never have sent that fucking email, should I?'

'I beg your pardon?'

'Ah, fuck off.' I turned to walk away. I'd been about to offer him the chance to join me on the house call at Corva's place. He'd just blown his chance.

'Do you require transport back to the Belt, Ms Tarmell?'

'No. I'll be fine.'

'It's no effort. I can call for another transporter rental.'

I didn't answer and carried on walking, throwing another FocXy chew into my mouth. When I was out of sight of Sunday, I slapped the side of a container, leaving the sticky mess on its side. 'Take care of these,' I said, nodding and smiling at the surprised operative driving it.

Time to make a house call.

Corva's flat was in one of the few remaining wooden blocks still left standing up this coast. There'd been a wave of Scandi-love about thirty years' previously, resulting in a boom on wood: wooden houses, wooden railings, wooden steps, wooden memorials to the dead, even a frigging bus shelter made of larch went up outside of Ponteland. The story went that they were all treated to be flame-retardant, that they were compressed wood, so they'd only burn an outer layer of carbon, or some shit. Look at the Scandinavian countries, they've got this stuff all over, why can't we?

Because we're English. Most of the buildings didn't make it past five years. In one year, fifty of these wooden apartment blocks went up in flames. The rest were eaten away by some boring mites some comedian had brought in from Borneo and released into an estate of retirement huts somewhere out by Bridlington. Just to see what would happen. That took a lot of work to clean up. Some environmental analysts like Gilbie McKenn still talked about the Brid Bugs, seeing them turn up here and there, new strains resistant to the insecticide they'd deployed across the whole region.

So, it was quite a treat to be walking up the staircase of one of these. They'd painted it, of course, to keep out the Brid Bugs and to ensure it was aesthetically aligned with the surrounding landscape. This meant, naturally, that they'd painted it an off kind of grey. With a bit of green.

Though there were noises of families and the smell of food being prepared elsewhere in the building, I didn't meet anybody as I hauled myself up two floors of stairs. I got into Corva's place with ease. The fact that all it took was for me to wave my hand to open the door was telling in its own way. Professional wrong 'uns would've had that hacked and barred the moment they moved in. This told me that Corva was something else.

The place was sparse inside. It hadn't come furnished and she mustn't have had the money to fill it. There was an inflatable bed – a cheap seaweed job from Indonesia – and some cardboard chairs and table, but other than that, she was living out of suitcases. Once I'd done a human-eye check through each room, I set the gecko and a crawler to work. I also released the tracer drone, letting it hum away out of sight. A quick riffle through personal effects brought up nothing of note. She didn't even have any storage slivers or a home server, clearly working off the block's router. Whoever she'd been, she was travelling light.

It was past teatime now, and I was getting hungry. I wasn't really sure how I was supposed to be getting back home, but Airedale wasn't exactly calling me. When I thought about my own flat, it actually made me feel a little sad and a little sick. The smell of rotting wrong 'un head was never going to fade. And I was never going to be able to feel fully safe there now. Those little shits from the golf course were going to keep coming and coming and ruining my life. I probably wouldn't let my own mum through the door.

So, with the threat of tears running down my face, I wandered through the living area, past the table and chairs, and an inflatable sofa, towards the window. It looked out towards the North Sea. The height of the building and the small rise it was placed on afforded a view over the tops of the beachside retail and entertainment. I stared at the view, the sea now cloaked in darkness, the occasional wave marking the shoreline in a transitory white streak. Lights were coming on along the beachfront. But only half of them. This was off-season, so it was catering for the alcoholics and the problem gamblers and those who couldn't get enough gaming immersive. I liked watching the signage though. It reminded me of childhood.

This was a prime location. There weren't that many people who could afford to spend their evenings watching the silt brown foam of the North Sea. Somebody who'd only recently moved into a job at a dockside security agency, who'd previously been a vat monkey in the dales, shouldn't be able to afford this. If I'd had a digital analyst helping me out, I may have been able to get into some financials. But that tended to be locked down tighter than a GUM clinic in Aitch Bee. We didn't bother too much with the hard stuff. Look out for the easy leads. That was important.

Then something caught my eye. There were a couple of roads I could make out, bisecting the back of the houses and shopfronts along the beach. Standing at the corner of a shop on the end of one of these, just in the shadow of an awning, a figure was weaving their hands in the air. The motions were instantly recognisable. Drone control. My eyes scanned the sky, looking for the tell-tale signature of LEDs and movement. But there was nothing visible. Perhaps they were just a tourist, running some footage of the crowds, feeding credit into the public domain of content.

The gecko had finished its run and was waiting expectantly at my feet. I crouched down and picked it up, placing it carefully on the windowsill. I set it to scan the view outside and to report hazard concepts, hoping it might pick up something more on the figure.

While it did this, I went in and checked what it'd found in the flat.

There was nothing. Nothing that my apps thought worth following up, anyway. The tracer also came back, having completed its run. It did have a couple of things to report, though. The first was the scent signature that I'd picked up in Simon West's flat: *BreathlessWhisper*. It was older, fainter, but still robust enough to stand up in a court narrative. There was something else: a heavy hydrocarbon signature. I ran it through the databases. It wasn't in the recent files. I searched back a bit. There it was. Something proper retro: petrol.

Checking the crawler's progression pattern on the map, I could identify where the signature was strongest. It was around the utility cupboard just outside the kitchen. I'd already searched here, so I opened it with a sigh. Perhaps it was an old boiler or some kind of heating system, but now that I was standing there, I could smell it. This pissed me off, as it was exactly the kind of thing I liked to pride myself on. I was getting lazy.

The shelves of the cupboard had the usual crap you'd expect to find – cleaning materials, battery units, – but nothing that was going to give off hydrocarbon signature like this. I kicked at the back of the cupboard. It was solid beam. I tried the floor.

Found it.

A tile moved, and I shifted it to the side. Underneath was a cavity. Getting on my hands and knees, I found the cache. About six large plastic containers of liquid. The smell down here was incredibly strong. There was enough to run a fucking bus. For quite a while. Assuming you didn't want to end up in prison. Or get a retributor take you out with a bladed drone to the forehead. I took a picture of the canisters with my bead, then returned to the living room, trying to think what all this meant.

The word 'drone' flashed in yellow across my display. The gecko was telling me that it'd spotted a drone. Then it spotted another drone. And a further drone. These were low level hazard. Nothing else worth noting. I pocketed both it and the crawler and turned to the door. However, I froze when I heard something tap against the glass of the front window. It was a light tap, a familiar sound. Sighing a little, I turned back from the door and walked towards the window, trying to peer out into the darkening sky.

'Lights out,' I called to the flat. It complied and everything went dark.

The tapping came again. I still couldn't see what was causing it.

My nerves were telling me to get the hell out of there, but I was getting angry at this flat, at Corva and the whole fucking place, and I wanted an excuse for an argument. So I slammed open the cute wooden door and stepped out onto the small balcony. Freezing wind from the sea hit my face. I looked towards the window. There was a drone, running on black, hovering in the air. It turned around to face me. Running a drone on black was highly illegal. I moved towards it, thinking I might be able to grab it out of the air before the owner reacted.

It worked. The rotors stung my hand a little, but I'd got it.

Then there was a distant noise, like a crack, sharp and still noticeable above the noise of the wind. The window behind me shattered, collapsing like a waterfall into the room and across the balcony.

'Fuck.'

I staggered back, hitting the doorframe and dropping the drone, wondering what'd happened. It took a couple of seconds before I realised there was a new pain in my shoulder. A serious, this-might-need-hospital type of pain. My right hand reached up and clutching at the source of the point. I felt moisture. My hand came away black in the half-light.

Some fucker had shot me.

With my good hand, I scrabbled at the still open door and yanked it open. Everything was slippery now. Adrenalin was pumping through my system. I tried to make the necessary hand signals to bring up the emergency Enforcement commands, drop a locational beacon, get somebody here fast. Somebody with a bigger fucking gun. But it was dark, and the bead couldn't read bloodied fingers in the dark, crooked with pain and fear. I barked commands into my bead instead, using the verbal options.

Halfway through leaving a message on my location and situation, I heard a nearby whirr, and I caught the shadow of the drone pass through the shattered remains of the window, and into the living room itself. It crashed against the far wall, spilling some contents. Then there was a flare and the whole wall went up in flames.

I swore and dived for the door. I had to fight my way through the flames, but I managed to get into the flat's entrance hall. I fought with the door controls for a moment, hearing the roar of the fire behind me, driven wild by the wind now whistling through the front room window. Eventually I managed to make my useless left hand do something with the manual override and I was out into the corridor. I slammed the thing behind me and hurtled down the corridor. As I reached the top of the emergency stairwell, I hammered the fire alarm with my elbow and set off the sirens. Then hastily made my way down the steps.

Around me, across other floors, I could hear residents starting to make their way out of their flats, with plenty of grumbles and queries. Then some nearer the fire must've realised that this wasn't the fault of some pisspoor QA process at the alarm factory, it was an actual face-searing, skin-crackling, lung-choking fire and they had better get the fuck out of there.

The emergency stairs filled up around me, and I could leave the building surrounded by other residents. A few noticed that I was injured and asked if I needed help. Not wanting to draw too much attention, I gave them a tight smile, and told them I was just on my way to the out-of-hours unit.

Slipping into the darkness, my fingers flicking through the detritus in my pockets. I knew I had a strip of painkillers in there somewhere. By feel – and the light of a broken streetlamp – I managed to separate the drugs from the extra strong mints and dry-swallowed a couple as I hurried on. A darting shape in my peripheral vision make me whirl around but it was only my gecko, skittering through a tangle of razor wire atop a nearby wall. Holding out my hands, I stepped up and caught it as it leapt, dropping it back into a pocket.

'Where to now, eh?' I muttered.

I decided to head into the depths of the residential estate, away from the beachfront, and away from whom I assumed had been the person who'd taken a shot at me. However, working my way deeper inland soon proved to be a mistake. I started to come across physical – and virtual – warning signs. Whole streets deserted, houses with smashed in windows and collapsed roofs. Their condemnation orders were plastered across front doors in the lurid pinks of the East Pennine government. These orders were supposed to have been enacted years ago, residents rehoused, or dead, or simply moved away, and their homes still waiting for the final decision.

The occasional head popped up from a window. There was the smell of woodsmoke tinged with the acrid scent of chemical burn in the air, the signature of a piece of laminated flat pack being reduced to its constituent elements.

Then I got shot at a second time. They missed, thankfully, hitting the near wall, making tiny pieces of brickwork and mortar pepper the side of my face.

'Fuck you!' I screamed into the street and turned around, the shambling trot now progressing into a run. The painkillers had not really touched the intensity of the shooting shards coming from my shoulder. I was struggling to keep from yelping with every step.

Another shot. This time it hit the road beside me.

I kept going and rounded a corner. I decided I needed to adopt a different approach, so I headed instead towards the lights of the beachfront. Best to be among other people. My bead was telling me that the services were on their way, that there was a unit at this very moment heading out from Middlesbrough Complex.

In a few minutes, and with no further gunshots, I'd reached the seafront. The lights of the shops and arcades dazzled me, but I felt a lot safer now, weaving in and out of other gratifying broad-shouldered, protective bodies. The sight of a bleeding young woman in their midst didn't seem to faze them that much and they carried on with their entertainment, some in parties, some alone, but all deadly serious about the need to find the fun.

I reasoned that if I kept moving, I would be safer. The approaching beacon of the Enforcement unit wasn't that far away now. So I carried on making my way north along the pavement, making use of kiosks, and signage to cover my presence.

Then the figure I'd seen on the street corner earlier stepped out in front of me. They were a little taller than me and moved lightly, but with purpose. The clothes were plain, black, the kind of thing you'd wear if you were into Whitby and all that shit. They stood out among the bright colours of the party goers around them. But the face was covered in a mask, a red-horned devil. They advanced towards me, their brown eyes not leaving mine. They carried a knife, a simple knife, like you could buy in any online store.

'Ah shit.'

I fell into the nearest arcade. This one specialised in immersive gambling. Poor sods slapping at algo-generated icons in the air in front of them, believing there was a pattern that they could find and, with that knowledge, make it rich. They'd convinced themselves that they could beat the machine at the game it created, and had recreated many times, based upon their own actions.

There wasn't much space. I pushed in deeper. Then my heart jumped into my throat when I felt a hand on my shoulder — my good shoulder.

'You Carrie Tarmell?' said a voice behind me.

'Yeah,' I said, turning.

'We're the Enforcement team from the Complex. You put a call out for us, though it's been a job to find you. Have you sustained an injury?'

I glanced down at my bleeding shoulder. 'Yeah. Somebody shot me, right.'

'We've got a unit ready to take you in.'

'OK,' I said. I glanced around the room. 'There was somebody you need to find. About my height, wearing a black suit.' I gave them more details, starting to feel faint. Space had cleared around me. There was plenty of talk from the Enforcement team. Somebody was trying to talk to me. Trying to tell me something.

I'd worked it out before I blacked out. But whoever it was who'd shot me, they'd gone.

CHAPTER TWENTY-ONE

They woke me up from the general anaesthetic through the unpleasant – and downright primitive – approach of applying direct sunlight to the face. Even when feeling at my best, this was brutal. I guessed it was some medical algorithm electronically tweaking those curtains back, as there weren't any medical staff in the room. They loved it when they hit on some banal solution to complex healthcare, shit like making you eat fruit and veg. I screwed up my eyes and looked around to see where I was. After I saw the state of the man in the next bed, I wished I hadn't. It was a mixed ward of other major trauma patients, most of whom were sedated, with various states of bodily injury, some involving whole limbs. Must've been another firefight in the Complex overnight, involving the fermenters, by the smell. I guessed I was in an interim care unit, the kind of place Justice sent their crew to when there wasn't much budget. Mainly run by poorly paid medics, volunteers and robots. The walls had once been grey, but they'd tried to paint them a winsome blue and then stuck up dynamic wallpaper – which had broken – and now showed an out-of-focus dreamy scene of a beach. All the fucking way around. How anybody worked in this, I didn't know.

'You've got a visitor,' said a voice from a pair of speakers taped to the headboard.

'Thanks,' I said. 'Can I get a drink?'

'Drinks are extra,' said the voice.

'How much?'

It quoted a list of beverages, and the costs associated with them.

'Who's paying?'

'Personal budget.'

'Shit. Who's paying for the care?'

'Not you, don't worry. You want that drink?'

'I'll have nowt.'

'Suit yourself. Visitor's on their way.'

I shifted myself up in bed. I may have been out in the middle of Middlesbrough – I'd surmised this fact from the view of flaring chemworks outside my window – but at least Louie had made the effort to come and see his contractor. That was nice of him, especially as we'd parted on bad terms.

Except it wasn't Louie who meandered his way down the middle of the tightly packed beds. It was Haz. Hasim Edmundson, Digital Analyst for Airedale, who'd had a bad time the previous year and had dumped it all to run off with some woman from Scotland. I was glad to see he hadn't changed that much, though he seemed somehow fuller in the face, and the coat he wore seemed newer than the usual parka.

He wasn't happy about being near all the blood and was trying to avert his eyes.

'Hiya,' he said, giving me a little wave as he approached.

'Hiya,' I said. 'Wasn't expecting you.'

'Yeah,' he said. 'Got a call from Louie, didn't I? Heard you were needing a digital, and all.'

'I guess,' I said. 'Need a fucking medic more than a digital right now. You turned your hand to that?'

He stood awkwardly, peering down at my shoulder, wrapped tight in adhesive strips. 'You were shot, yeah?'

'Always a big asset to our Justice team, Haz. Top end observational skills.'

He grinned and sniggered. 'Yeah. But it were gunshot, right?'

'Dunno,' I said. 'It's kinda tricky getting Bladester to work on my own shoulder. But it sure sounded like it.'

'Well, your notes said gunshot,' said Haz, coming round the

other side of the bed and checking out the relative state of consciousness of my nearest bed neighbour. 'We can talk?'

I tried to shrug, but it hurt too much. 'Yeah, whatever.'

'Good.' He sniffed. 'What's that smell?'

I tried to crane my neck to look out of the window. 'This is Middlesbrough Complex?'

'Yeah, why?'

'Middle of the fermenters, in't it. That's probably genetically-modified seaweed starch that's been brewing up for a few weeks. Smell gets stuck on the clothes. Doesn't come off ever.'

'Oh,' he said, peering at the nearest invalid, 'how'd you know all that?'

'Used to date somebody from Saltburn.'

'Oh. Not anymore?'

'Fuck off.'

He peered out of the window. It was a high cloudy day, the light that hurt your eyes, but didn't make you warm. The Complex wasn't lit up in the daytime, so you see the sprawl of the city beyond, small wisps of smoke rising up and then being drawn out to sea by the wind.

'Nice place by the window.'

'Yeah, must've been good timing, or summat,' I said. 'Wait up, how'd you read my notes?'

He smiled. 'You know.' He tapped the peak of his cap. He'd invested in a new one. This looked nice, like it had come in from Paraguay.

'Oh.'

'I've been busy on the way down here,' he said, sitting on the end of the bed. 'Took an overnight car to Preston and then across to here. Not really slept much. Been talking to quite a few people this morning.'

'That's useful,' I said. 'Knackered analysts are the best, I find.'

He regarded me carefully for a moment. The once edgy, nervous eyes of the Haz I knew had been replaced by something different. He looked older. But in a good way.

'First off,' he said, 'I called up Deborah Goolagong-Maloney.'

'Wouldn't have bothered myself.'

'Yeah?' he said, giving me another odd look. 'Anyway, she got me up to speed on the case.'

'She were useless. You'd best start again.'

'She were pretty good, actually,' said Haz, quietly.

I was beginning to get pissed off with this. I would've jumped out of bed and got cracking on things myself, but I'd the sense that my legs wouldn't carry me that far. At least, not for an hour or so.

'What about Louie?' I said. 'He knows what's going on… at least, when he's not crying about his marriage.'

'Louie's got a lot on his plate,' said Haz. Again, there was that strange look. 'He dropped me a couple of files but couldn't spare much more. I did speak to him. He's the reason I'm here.' He made a face. 'Seemed a bit pissed off, to be fair.'

'He just needs some sex,' I said, grunting.

'He's well… he's not good, is he?' Haz said, looking down at the bed. 'I can appreciate what he's going through.'

Was I really going to have to listen to this shit? 'He's getting paid enough. What did Debs tell you?'

'Summat about plenty of legs and arms and shit turning up all over the Belt.'

'That were it,' I said. 'In a nutshell.'

'So, nowt more than that? There were summat about a lake and a recycling operative being drowned in it.'

'Yeah.'

'Somebody's confessed, some gang leader, being processed as we speak. Job done.'

'Well, he said he did it.' I wrinkled my nose.

'And now you've got Lagos feds crawling over a boat in Hartlepool.'

'Feds? Only one, right?'

Haz shrugged. 'Yeah, that's right.'

'And it's a ship. No, wait, it's a hulk. Yeah, a hulk.'

'Not my area. Anyways, you've got this ship, this hulk, full of bodies, right?'

'Body parts.'

'And then you got shot?'

'Yeah.'

Haz took a deep sniff. 'Why'd you get shot?'

'I were in the flat of a bent security officer.'

'Somebody were compromised at the dock, yeah?'

'Yeah.'

'And you find owt?'

'No, not much… actually, I did. She had the same visitor as the dead recycling operative and the… you know, the other one, who changed her story?'

'Same visitor?'

I told him about the scent that my sniffer had picked up, *BreathlessWhisper*.

'Abu Dhabi?'

'That's right.'

'That's probably *en route* from Dhaka, isn't it?'

'Yeah,' I said, nodding. 'Or Shenzhen.'

'Eh?'

'That's where the parts are coming in from.'

'Legs and arms and that.'

'That's right.'

Haz nodded and blew out through his lips. 'You got a lot of shit happening. When you put it all together, does it make summat you think? Or is it just a lot of shit happening?'

'Fuck I know,' I said, slumping down in the bed. The pain was getting worse. Hope they doped me up proper and fast.

'Well, I'm here to help,' said Haz. 'Promised Louie I'd do what I could.'

'Don't need a partner,' I said.

'Louie said you needed help.'

'I needed a digital analyst. The one they've got down at the Buckle is useless. Never around. So I just need some digital input. But I don't need a partner.'

'I know,' said Haz. 'You've already got one.'

'Eh?'

Haz nodded. 'Louie told me, Deborah summat... that Deborah Goolagong.'

'She were crap.'

'She were your partner,' said Haz. His voice had more authority than I'd heard before.

'Ah, you can fuck off,' I said. 'I want old Haz back. One who listened.'

'You sure you don't want to call her?'

'No. I do not.'

'She should find out who shot you.'

I laughed. 'Doubt anybody will find that out. Nobody even called me yet. I left all the details with that Enforcement team. They said they'd pass it on. Haven't heard shit since then.'

'They're all quite busy.'

'Yeah,' I said. 'And it's getting busier. Not helped by some analysts pissing off to Scotland once things got heavy.'

Haz was silent. He was waiting for me to apologise for what I said. So I kept my mouth shut.

He crumbled first. 'I couldn't do it anymore,' said Haz. 'You know how it ended up.'

'Wish I could do that,' I said with a sneer. 'Jack it all in.'

'You could,' said Haz, his brown eyes regarding me gravely. 'Might be safer.'

'You think I could?'

He smiled. 'Nah, probably not. You couldn't do owt else than this, could you?'

'Perhaps I should find out myself who shot me?'

'Guessing you'll be doing that anyway.'

'That's why I need you, Haz,' I said, leaning up in bed. The pain almost too much to do this. 'You can get access to all the ratios, to all the cameras.'

He shook his head. 'Not really. Not with the a-codes Louie gave me. Owt else you need me to do? I could probably decode some weakly-encrypted messages for you.' He gave me a small smile.

'Well, you're shit,' I said, slumping back in my bed. I'd forgotten mostly what I'd wanted Lem to do for me now. There was something about the security cameras of the Fellside Facility, something about upgrades to that stitcher, possibly something about where those deliveries were going. But it all seemed a distant memory to me now. Like it hadn't really existed.

'Soz,' said Haz.

Then I remembered something. Something that I'd not been able to answer, something that Haz probably wouldn't be able to answer. But he was the only one here right now, so I was going to ask him anyway.

'Could you tell if you were talking to a machine?' I asked.

'What?'

'A machine, an algo, chatbot, whatever… could you tell if you were talking to one?'

'Weird question.'

'Well?'

'Dunno. Is it important?'

I told him about the phone call. Then about the conversation with Djin Dowe in my sister's flat. He pulled something up on his bead; the lights flickering across his eyes.

'Checks out,' he said.

'What?'

'That company, where your sister works, they are designing artificial voices, driven by algorithms. So, this Djin woman, she weren't lying.'

'She were proper dodgy. Why'd she tell me that?'

'That reminds me,' said Haz. 'I spoke to your sister.'

'What for?'

'And your mum, actually. She's dead interesting. We had a proper long chat.'

Surprised, I laughed and then coughed. It hurt. 'You're welcome to her.'

'Just saying.'

'And why were you speaking to them?'

'I were trying to find you,' said Haz. 'Louie gave me the name of your sister – Grace, yeah – who said she hadn't seen you for a few days. She suggested I speak to your mum. So I did. Me and her had a right good chat. Like I said, she's dead interesting. Didn't know she were in the army.'

'She's mental,' I muttered. 'Don't go chatting to my mum. She'll mess you up. She's not interested in what I do. You don't see her here, do you?'

'She don't know you're here,' said Haz. 'Not that I'd tell her, mind.' He looked out the window briefly. 'It's a long way to come, especially over the hills. And I wouldn't come through the Belt.'

We were distracted by the grinding whine of an automated med dispenser. It wheeled itself down the middle of the ward, taking its time, as the room had become too cramped for the size of the machine. It made its way directly towards my bed. I noticed that it was the same design as the military grade stitcher I'd found in the shed in the Fellside Recycling Auxiliary Facility. The one with the blood on it. I kept telling myself that this was perfectly normal. We were in a hospital. Kinda.

'Medication round three,' said the device. 'Please read the supplementary information regarding your medication. It has been dropped into your device.'

I saw a message appear. I'd never read any of this shit before. I wasn't about to now. 'Whatever.'

'Complied,' said the machine.

'Time for your drugs?' said Haz.

'I guess,' I muttered. Though something about the dispenser was making me edgy.

'Excuse me,' said the gentle voice. 'Please make room.'

Haz stood up and allowed the machine to raise its extendable arm towards the pouch containing my intravenous drip.

'Haz,' I murmured, looking at the machine.

'Eh?' said Haz, turning his attention from the machine – which had now inserted a small syringe into the bag and squirted something colourless into the colourless solution – to my face.

'I wasn't awake when they did this last… so I don't…' I felt a burning on the back of my hand. It started to work up my arm.

'You alright?' asked Haz, seeing me twitch.

'Shit!' I quickly ripped out the needle from my hand.

'What's wrong?' said Haz.

'That machine,' I said. I was finding it hard to speak.

'Maybe it was supposed to help you sleep… Carrie? Carrie?'

'I'm not supposed to sleep,' I said through my teeth. 'Get me a doctor…'

Haz was already halfway down the ward. 'Sure.'

'Haz,' I called out after him. 'Forget it.'

'Eh?'

'Let's go.'

'OK.' He came hurrying back.

The machine had finished dispensing its payload and was now trying to get past Haz. 'Please excuse me. Please excuse me.'

'Stop it,' I called out. 'Immobilize it, or summat.'

Haz stood directly in front of the machine, setting its automated collision avoidance systems whirring and beeping. He flicked open a panel on the top of the case and found the emergency shutdown switch.

Around the room, there were a few thankful cries and a little set of whoops.

'What's going on?' A private security operative had entered the room. 'What's that noise?'

'We're just leaving,' I slurred.

The operative noticed Haz and the immobilized dispensing

unit. 'If you've been interfering with property of the estate, you'll be liable for damages.'

As Haz tried to explain the situation, I rolled out of the bed and crashed onto the floor. Other patients, those who were still awake, grumbled at the commotion. My clothes were in a plastic bag near the bed and fumbled to get them on.

'Are there no fucking medics in this place?' I said, loudly, as I stomped past the security operative.

'They're busy,' he said. 'Have you been signed out?'

'Check my beacon, motherfucker!' And I cast him the Airedale Justice icon. Delegation meant something, even in a hospital like this.

Raising his hands apologetically, he stepped back, allowing my bare feet to stride past him and out of the room.

'You alright?' asked Haz. 'How's the arm now?'

We were in his car, speeding away south, past the cloud-topped bulk of the Moors to our left.

'Hmm.'

'You'd passed out for a while back there. We need to get you to a doctor… a different one.'

'Where's nearest?'

'No idea. Don't know this part of East Pennine at all.' He looked out of the window. 'It's all fucking polytunnels round here now.'

I managed to scrunch my eyes enough to focus on what was happening outside. We were, indeed, surrounded by fields and low hills crammed with the coverings seen in most of the lowlands. This place used to produce some award-winning wines. Once. Now half the polytunnels were ripped, exposing their soil and weeds, and the rusting wrecks of the automated machines that once farmed them.

'I know a doctor,' I said, rolling each word around my mouth like a hardboiled sweet.

'Yeah? She near here?'

'They're a he, and he's on a boat in the fucking Mediterranean.'

'OK, take it easy, Carrie. I were only asking. You're making no sense, you know.'

'No,' I said, insistently. 'That's the one I meant. We need to call him.'

I tried to raise my arm to activate my nose bead, but it was too heavy in my lap.

'Fuck.'

'I'm pulling over,' said Haz. 'Car, take the next exit.'

'Where are we going, Hasim?' the car said jauntily. It clearly hadn't read the room.

'Nearest place to stop.'

'There is a village near here called–'

'Anywhere,' said Haz. 'Stop in a field.'

A few minutes later, we were parked up alongside the tattered remnants of a polytunnel, its fingers of white snapping loudly in the breeze. Inside, the gnarled remnants of a line of vines could be seen, disappearing into the distance.

'Can you get me his details?'

'Hausman. Dr Hausman. Works out of a place… a place that doesn't exist. A place they made exist, once, many years ago.'

'Eh?'

'Calderdale. He's in Calderdale.' I started giggling. 'He's in the Med.'

Haz weaved his fingers in the air and linked me into a conference call. My eyes struggled to focus.

Hausman's white-bearded face appeared before us. 'Hello Carrie and… Hasim, is it?'

'That's right,' said Haz.

'You were previously a digital analyst in Airedale, yes?'

'Yeah. Don't remember meeting you.'

'You didn't,' said Dr Hausman, 'but I'd read about your tête-à-tête with our Enforcement colleagues. With great interest.'

'Didn't know I were famous,' said Haz.

Hausman made a face. 'Hey, nobody's saying you were famous, man.'

I groaned.

Hausman took note of this and turned his attention to me. 'Anyway, how can I help?'

'I've been poisoned,' I said.

'Really? How?'

Haz relayed the incident in the hospital.

'So, a med dispenser injected something into you? And you believe it was poison?'

'My arm were burning. And I can't speak properly.'

'You're not slurring. At least as far as I can tell. Perhaps it's this comms app, straightening things out. Are you in further pain?'

'My shoulder knacks,' I said. Now that he'd said it, I could tell my voice was getting better.

'Well, you've been shot, Carrie. You require an ongoing series of analgesics.' He consulted something beside him and took a big slurp of a bright blue cocktail. 'Your visual data – dilation, sweat, eye movements – suggest you are in pain, you have a high level of anxiety, fatigue etcetera, but nothing suggests you have been compromised with anything of high toxicity. In fact, the visuals suggested not much more than somebody who has been partially sedated. Do you know what it was?'

'Eh?' I said.

'The drug,' said the doctor. 'What they injected you with?'

'You've got that message,' said Haz, quietly. 'The machine said it'd dropped it into your bead.'

'Oh, yeah,' I said, remembering. Then I took a deep breath. 'Oh, feeling quite sick now.'

'Ah, nausea,' said the doctor, looking down to his side and finishing his drink.

I took another breath, raised my more able hand and cast the med dispenser's message across to the doctor.

'That's all in order,' he said. 'I mean, it's been a while since I've looked after a trauma patient, but there's nothing in that prescription that I wouldn't expect for somebody like yourself. Possibly a little pedestrian – there are more effective means around these days – but for a facility such as that, it is to be expected.'

'What was it?' I said.

'Painkiller,' said Hausman. 'Quite a strong one, so you would have… where are you going?'

I slammed open the door and fell out of the car into a puddle of ice-cold water. Scrambling to my feet, I jammed my elbow into the door to slam it shut and stumbled into the skeletal, rusted remains of the polytunnel.

The doctor's voice was still in my head. 'Hasim, I believe you may need to follow–' I snapped the comms shut with my hand.

Behind me, I could hear the other car door open and Haz shouting my name, but I carried on. Tears were now streaming down my face, and I was fucked if he was going to see me like this. I worked my way past the overgrown vines. On some of them, there were still grapes, now shrivelled up against the cold. Small, pathetic, sour rejects.

'Wait up, Carrie,' shouted Haz. 'You need to take it easy.'

I stopped. Taking huge breaths, I tried to calm my heart beating. It felt like it was about to smack its way out past my ribs. I tried hanging onto a nearby vine, but I had no strength and I tumbled into it, dead leaves covering my shoulders. The pain hit me much harder now, and I screamed. The screaming seemed to help, so I screamed some more, not from pain, but from everything.

'You're all so useless! You're all so fucking, fucking, fucking useless!'

I didn't care that Haz was now standing above me, trying to help me up.

'Carrie, we gotta–'

'Fuck off!' I roared in his face, Then I screamed again, at him, into my lap, and into the soil beneath my hands.

Haz retreated then, stepping back. A fine rain had started falling, cutting through the gaps in the polytunnel, and he pulled his hood up over his head.

Several minutes passed, of me alternating between screaming and then crying, until I got myself back to an equilibrium of low-grade bitterness and cynicism.

'Carrie,' said Haz, softly.

'Yeah?' I said, sniffing back some snot and spitting it out.

'I think you might need some help?'

'You think?'

'I'm not joking. I don't think this is a joke, you know.'

I looked up at him and wiped the tears from underneath my eyes. The rain had now mixed in with it. I checked my hands and could see eyeliner and mud all over them. I could guess what my face looked like. I couldn't help but laugh.

'Yeah, this isn't a joke,' I said.

'You want to come back to the car?' said Haz. 'Have a sit down?'

I took another deep breath. 'I do need some help, Haz.' I straightened out my shoulder. 'I need a fucking digital analyst.'

Haz stared at me for a moment, but then shook his head. 'I can't work alongside with you on this one,' said Haz. 'I know Louie asked, but I'm not… I can't. I really can't get back into this. But you always helped me in the past, so I made the effort to come down. I'm going to see my mum and dad, actually.' He frowned, looking worried. 'I mean, I wanted to come and see you and all. To see how I can help, of course.'

'But I need a digital, Haz.' I rearranged myself so I could haul myself up. Haz leaned forward to give me a hand.

'I don't do that anymore.'

'Of course, you do. You don't just stop doing this job.'

He grimaced and then smiled. 'Sometimes you do.'

'Don't believe it. Give me the tools, then, give me Modlee.'

'I can't do that,' said Haz. 'But I can talk to Louie, see if Clive can pay you a visit?'

'But you'll not help?' I said.

'I don't do that anymore,' Haz said.

I took a breath. This was all too uncomfortable. 'Well, fuck off then.'

'No,' Haz said. 'I'm not leaving you like this.'

'Don't need you here, if you aren't going to help.'

'Try asking other people for help,' said Haz.

'I am,' I said. 'I'm asking you.'

'I can't, Carrie. But there are others who will. How about that Nigerian fella? That fed?'

I took a deep breath, swallowing back the sharp comment I was about to make. 'Good point. He's got summat I need.'

'Know where to find him?' asked Haz.

'Not yet. But I've got the means of tracking him down.' I sniffed back the last of the snot and reached into my pocket for a FocXy chew. Threw it into my mouth. 'Can you give me a lift somewhere, then?'

'Yeah, sure. Where?'

'Back to the wrecker's yard.' I pulled out the tracer drone from my pocket. 'Let's see where the bastard's gone.'

CHAPTER TWENTY-TWO

'How did you find me?'

I flashed my virtual Justice beacon. 'I got delegation, love. That means summat around here. We're still in East Pennine, you know.'

'What do you want?'

I sniffed. 'I need some help.'

'Oh, yes?' This fact seemed to amaze him, as his eyebrows leaped a good few centimetres up into his forehead.

I held his gaze. 'Yeah.'

'Do you really need my permission? Or are you just going to walk in here?'

'I can just walk in here,' I said, 'cos I got the badge. Like they let me walk into the building and straight up here. But I'd just like it if you asked me how you could help, yeah.'

To be fair, the reception system and the security crew had all taken a little more convincing. It wasn't hard to see why. I was a bit of a mess. Even I, self-trained to a ruggedly-high threshold for general grimness, could see that most normal folk wouldn't let me step through their door, let alone on their rug. There was strata to my muck. Even though I could smell menthol-sniffs in my dreams, I could still detect the underlying rot of leg and head in my clothes and hands. Rolling about in the dirt of a dead vineyard a few kilometres south of Darlo had only added cosmetic sheen to the ragged, blood-soaked bullet hole in my duffel coat. And I was about two days' short of a shower.

So, I was a little ashamed to be standing here at Federal

Inspector Sunday Sule's hotel room doorway, begging to be let in.

'Come in, then,' said Sunday, trying to stand as far from me as possible.

It was a proper nice set of rooms. Looked like there was a big bedroom through one half-opened door, and a bathroom further in. This first room had a low table and a full wall screen and a couple of comfy chairs. There was also a large, curved window, looking out across the late afternoon. Floor fifty-three, which meant we were high above the mist covering the York end of the Belt here. Lights of the coastal settlements were just visible in the distance, and the ribbons of vehicles heading north. Nearby, the red and green LEDs of dozens of passenger drones were flitting in and out of the clouds. Somewhere down there, I thought I could just see the illuminated towers of the minster, half-shrouded in mists.

'Feds get better rooms than us,' I said, looking out the window. I was already sweating under my coat. Sunday seemed to have the heat turned up to WetBulb. As he was prancing about in his shorts and a loose cotton shirt, I guess this made sense. I tried to avoid looking at his thighs too much. Even that act was making me sweat a little more.

He sensed my unease. 'You want me to help you with your coat?'

'I've got it,' I said, trying to shrug it off my busted shoulder, without causing me to weep tears of pain.

'Oh, let me help, for the sake of God,' said Sunday, stepping up and holding me still with his right hand, while his left slowly lifted the weight of the coat.

'Whatever,' I said, trying to look quizzical, while also not screaming out in pain. I felt it unpeel from its damp resting place, grinding my teeth as he did so.

'Just be still, please.'

The coat finally came off.

'What do you carry in here?' said Sunday, lifting the coat a few times. 'It weighs a ton.'

'This and that,' I said. 'I like it because it's got big pockets.'

Sunday peered into one of them.

'I wouldn't,' I said, quickly. 'Not a pretty sight, what you'll find in there.'

With a grunt, he laid it on the back of a comfy chair. Then he hastily grabbed it up again, staring closely at the bullet hole.

'Don't want to stain the fabric?' I said.

'A little,' said Sunday, distracted, casting about for somewhere else to put it.

'I wouldn't worry,' I said, grinning. 'That duffel coat can cope with anything.'

He ignored me and hung it on a hook on the back of the door. 'How'd you find me here?' he asked.

'Well,' I said, watching him go back and readjust the hang of the coat, 'I managed to track the evidence back to a temporary warehouse unit in Middlesbrough.'

'How'd you do that?' he asked, with a professional's interest.

'Slapped a sweet on a crate and used my mobile tracer,' I said.

'You walked from the port? But you were attacked kilometres away from—'

'Shit, no,' I said. 'I set it off and then got an autocar to the place later. Much later. After all this.' I indicated my shoulder. 'It's got a hell of a range. I waited for most of the day, expecting you to turn up, but you never showed. Then I convinced the guy on the front desk that things would go badly for him if he didn't tell me where I could contact you directly. What the hell were you doing?'

'Dealing with lawyers.'

'Oh,' I said. 'Nothing to do with me, I hope.'

Sunday sniffed. 'Look, do you want a… a fresh set of clothes? I could try to get reception to send something up?'

'It would've been a lot easier,' I said, 'if somebody hadn't decided to block my calls.'

Sunday regarded me coldly. 'I was annoyed.'

'Why?'

'You'd just upset my carefully-calibrated interview sequence.'

'Eh?'

'Mensies.'

'Oh. That.'

'Yes,' said Sunday. 'You'd already got her upset at things. Then her manager was there, and then lawyers came into it and I had a terrible time trying to unpick the international protocols. Took me most of the rest of the afternoon, like I said.'

'Sorry,' I said. 'I found Corva's place, mind.'

'I could see that,' said Sunday. He quoted some numbers at me. 'Eh?'

'Your size, isn't it?'

'That's right,' I said. 'You could be forensics with that kind of skill.'

He turned away and spoke quietly into a comms unit beside the door for a moment. When he turned around, he had the look of a man who'd decided to make best use of a bad situation. 'So, I've ordered you some clothes, some food. Am I to understand that you also wish to make use of the spare bed?'

I bristled, about to retort that I was absolutely fine. Then I thought about my flat. And then I remembered the conversation with Haz. If I was truthful, this was the exact reason I was here.

'Yeah,' I said, twisting my face into a smile, 'that would be great. Thank you.'

He nodded, his face betraying nothing. 'Thought so. So what did you find at Corva's house?'

'It were a flat,' I said. 'Dead nice one, and all, overlooking the sea. More expensive that she should've been able to afford. That were one thing.'

'Anything else?' Briskly whipping a spare towel off a pile near the door, he protected the back and seat of a chair and indicated I should sit down.

'Same perfume.' Too tired now to argue, or be rude, I slumped into the chair. It felt good.

'I'm sorry?' he said, sitting opposite me, pulling on a large woollen jersey. He must've turned down the heat, for I noticed

I was sweating less profusely now.

Committing myself, I told him about the Abu Dhabi trail and the perfume signature. I mentioned that Abu Dhabi is *en route* from Dhaka and reminded him of where the *Talofa-3* had started off from. I was expecting him to be incredibly grateful, so much so that he released all the evidence he'd gathered from the limbs recovered from the shit. Instead, he just wrinkled his nose.

'Circumstantial,' he said. 'What can we do with that?'

'I know it's fucking circumstantial,' I said. 'I weren't about to go and draw up a narrative for a lawyer and send in Enforcement!'

'So,' he said, 'how does it help?'

'It demonstrates a link, doesn't it?'

He shrugged. 'We can't use it. Anything else?'

'Nowt else.' I glanced at my shoulder. 'Except I got shot.'

'Yes,' said Sunday, nodding enthusiastically, 'that is more significant. That is a very good start.'

'Fuck off.'

Sunday blinked. 'I mean, for the case, of course. Not for you. For you it was… I'm sure it was…'

'A bit crap?' I offered.

'I'm certain it was, yes. That was what I meant to say.' He curled his legs up and sat cross-legged opposite me. I noticed that his specs were still lying in their case on the table next to him. Whatever it was he wanted to hear, he wasn't about to start making notes. I got the feeling that Sunday liked to make careful notes of each of his shits, so the fact that he just wanted to listen made me feel a little more wanted than I'd been for the past few days.

The door signalled there was somebody present. Sunday called out to the room to let them in and a small wheelie bot trundled in, barked out its delivery contents and deposited them on the floor in front of me. With a little chirrup, it wheeled its way back out of the room and the door closed behind it.

'You want to get dressed in something a little cleaner?' said Sunday, nodding at the pile of clothes. It was wrapped in beautifully-printed seagrass paper. It was too perfect to touch.

'Yeah,' I said. 'In a bit.' I was just getting comfortable on my shoulder and didn't want to start sweating again.

'Fine. It's there.'

'I can see.' I struggled, but managed to make my face smile. 'Thanks.'

'So,' said Sunday, 'who's trying to kill you, do you think?'

It was a question I'd been asking myself. I'd not managed to reach an answer, though. 'Fuck I know. Too many bastards want me dead.'

'Including?'

I listed off the gangs in Airedale and now in Withens, plus whoever it was who was paying off Corva, plus whoever it was who'd killed Simon West.

'I heard about the raid on that reservoir,' said Sunday.

'What, they had that on the news in Lagos?' Even I was impressed.

'No,' said Sunday. 'I was researching. Researching you, in fact.'

'Oh.'

'That level of event would not register with our media algorithms, I'm afraid.'

'Yeah, yeah,' I said. 'I get it. Not bothered with what happens in East Pennine, normally.'

'Some tourists, perhaps,' said Sunday, shrugging. 'You look like you're not fully recovered. Did you seek early release from your care?'

I decided not to tell him about the incident in the Middlesbrough hospital, so I nodded, in a non-committal way.

'I have let your DI know, by the way,' said Sunday. 'I hope that's OK?'

'That I'm here?'

'Yes.'

'You told Louie?' My heart sank a little. I was enjoying the thought that this little encounter was just going to be between Sunday and me.

'That's right. I've let him know that you are safe. In fact, it's going to be…' He trailed off and put his finger to his lips.

'What?' I said, annoyed. The idea that he and Louie were keeping secrets was irritating.

'Listen,' said Sunday, 'you can stay here overnight if you wish. Help you recover, then we can send you on your way tomorrow. OK?'

I suddenly flushed. 'Might need a shower.'

'You may use the shower,' said Sunday.

'Ta.'

'Anything I can do to help somebody in need.' said Sunday.

'Yeah?' I came to the point of why I'd bothered to turn up. 'Well, I need the DNA data from the cargo.'

Sunday winced. 'Provision of that data is delayed in some interesting – if not technically-complicated – legal discussions.'

'Rubbish,' I said. 'Just give me the data.'

'I am afraid that is not possible.'

I'd seen it in the way his eyes flickered. 'You're lying, Federal Inspector Sunday Sule.'

He frowned. 'That's quite an accusation, coming from an Airedale… what are you? Some analyst? Forensics?'

'Don't change the subject.' I nodded my head. 'OK, I'll take back the word "lying". Let's call it bluffing, instead, shall we? You were dead pleased to see me come through your door a minute ago. Although you'd normally be spraying disinfectant wipes around if somebody like me were to sit on your couch, you let me in, you've given me clothes, you've even offered the chance to sleep over–'

'Not together,' he added, hastily.

I was a little disappointed he'd been so quick to state this. But I wasn't about to show it, so I continued. 'Yeah, me neither, buddy. So, you've been asking me questions about what I know – Corva, who shot me, the case up at Withens – all for a particular reason, yeah?'

'I do not understand.'

I'd been thinking about this a lot over the past few hours, especially remembering the way Sunday had behaved at the port. I took a deep breath and started to lay out my analysis.

'Your case back in Lagos got put on ice, didn't it? Everything ran cold. Somebody probably had a word, high up, and somebody else had a word, bit lower down, and then you got a deprioritise notice sent through and suddenly all the years of work you'd done on this got put in a zip file and dropped into a quiet corner of an encrypted shared server and you were told to move on.'

He said nothing.

'So, you did,' I continued. 'You were given other cases – probably smaller, less important cases. You're a dutiful kind of fella so you investigated and interrogated and followed up leads, like everybody should. But you still had half an eye on that old case. You'd set up a generic inbox, just in case somebody gave you summat, gave you owt. And for so many years there was nowt. Until you got my message. That were a new lead. You'd got summat to take to the bosses. So you did. And you've been allowed back on the case. Or have you?'

'What do you mean?' His face remained completely neutral.

'You're bluffing back at base as well, aren't you? What did you tell them? In Lagos, from your swanky lagoon apartment–'

'It's an Okon module.'

'Whatever,' I said. 'You had a little chat with your boss, told 'em you had a dead exciting lead, didn't you? Told 'em you were going to crack open that old case because you had some cast iron evidence.' I paused. 'Or maybe you didn't? Maybe you've just jumped on the next plane and flown all the way to the great Northern Belt just for the chance to make it big. Are you putting this on expenses? Or are you paying for this out of your own pocket? I bet you are, you know. This is one massive fucking gamble for you. You know you've got summat. But you've not got your usual minions here to do your bidding. You're on your own. You need somebody to help tie all the pieces together.'

'You think you are that person?' he said, after a pause.

'Nah, I'm not going to be your skivvy. But I am here offering you the chance to crack that old investigation of yours, to get back on that knackered horse and ride it straight into town. Am I right? You'd give a lot to get the information I have. And I'm willing to share if you just grow the fuck up and give me access to the DNA data of that shipment.'

He stared at me for a long time. I would've said it was like a cat, but the only cats I'd ever shared a room with were the two illegal kittens Ronnie had saved once from a derelict on the end of the Wirral. And they'd not paid me a moment's notice. Except to piss on the hem of my coat once. No, it was more the stare I'd got from my sister, sometimes, especially when we were younger, when I'd called her out on some of her teenage nonsense, and she was trying to work out how to negotiate her way out of the situation. Without losing face, of course. Losing face for Grace was worse than leaving a rotting arm in her freezer.

Sunday cracked first. 'OK.'

'We got a deal?' I said, rising from the chair. It was an effort, but I did it for dramatic effect.

I wasn't certain, but I thought he was also thinking about standing up, to keep on the same level. But he remained seated and nodded. 'What you said makes a lot of sense to me.'

'Good.'

'Very good.'

I shook his hand. 'I think I'll take that shower now.'

The shower was an amazing experience, an all-encompassing drench, massaging, and washing at the same time. Hydro dynamics had certainly come on since the time those cowboys had installed my dribbler. Getting into the bloody thing was harder work, especially the shoulder. But I wasn't about to ask for help again. The gauze they'd used to patch up my wound had had a waterproof finish applied to it, so I could shower without it being affected. I could pull on the blouse and the cotton print trousers. They'd even provided some underwear. It was practical, fresh out of the packet, and slightly the wrong size, but I wasn't complaining. Coming back out from the shower, I'd never felt better. I was even starting to think about my appearance. Checking myself in the mirror of the bathroom had reminded me that I did still have tits and – I liked to think – a surprisingly adequate tummy. Given all the crap I fed myself. Like my mother said, I'd been given a high metabolism. From somebody. She'd said that too: 'from somebody'. Like she didn't know how that made me feel. That's my mum.

When I returned to the living area, there was a tray laid on the small table. Amazing smells of fresh bread and something savoury crept from within. Sunday had been out on the balcony, chatting on his specs to somebody. As soon as he saw I'd returned, the door slid to the side, and he came back in. Freezing cold air followed him, and the burnt metal and chemical scents of the Belt at night.

'I ordered something,' said Sunday. 'You hungry?'

The thought of having to eat here with him suddenly made me super anxious. I couldn't remember the last time I'd actually sat down to have a meal properly. Meals with Ronnie tended to involve his friends, a certain amount of melodrama involving stoves, and lots of issues with watching out for a raid by the fishing authorities. Whenever he'd come around my house, we would sit ourselves in front of an immersive and stuff our faces with something not too awful, while knocking back his illegal brew or my homemade ethanolies. I wasn't sure if I remembered how to do this.

'I guess,' I said. I lifted the lid on the tray. It was a collection of small plates, holding things like cured meats and eggs and potatoes.

'What is this?' I asked.

Sunday shrugged. 'I think they called it a Kozovan meze. Apparently, it is all the rage. I mean, those are the words the lady used.'

'You not had it before?' I asked.

'No.'

'Maybe you won't like it?'

'Sorry?'

'I asked, what if you don't like it?'

'Me? Oh, I'm not eating,' he said.

This was odd. But then I assumed his body clock was all messed up from the flights and that, so I didn't think much of it. 'So, you're going to watch me eat this?'

'Yes,' he said. 'That's fine.'

'Well, I ain't talking and eating,' I said. 'Tell me about summat warmer than fucking East Pennine.'

So, for the next hour or so, while I stuffed my face, Sunday told me about his life in Lagos. He made it sound dead swanky. They had moonlit barge regattas across the lagoon, seagrass harvesting time with huge brewing sessions, and dolphin-watching dives all year round. Then the clubs and bars of uptown, the international stars, the coders splashing their money about. It sounded like he'd been a little outside of all of it, though. Federal inspectors must be a bit too serious for all this.

When I'd finished off as much as I could eat – which was a lot, I was bloody starving – he checked his watch and waltzed off to his room. I assumed he'd gone for a piss but, for some reason, when Sunday strolled back in, he was dressed up as though he was about to go out. I looked over at my coat, thinking that I didn't really have to put that on again tonight. He'd not provided anything to replace that. Before I had a chance to ask him why we were going somewhere, the door alerted us to a visitor.

'Ah,' said Sunday. 'At last.'

'Who's that?' I said, knocking back the last glass of white wine. 'Dessert?'

The door opened and in walked my boss.

'Hiya, Louie.' I said, coldly. 'What the fuck are you doing here?'

'Hiya,' said Louie. He eyed me nervously, like I was about to go off. 'How's your arm?'

I wasn't getting a hug tonight. 'Fine.'

'Looks it.'

'Just a bullet.' I shrugged, mentally.

'Course it is,' said Louie. 'A bullet wouldn't stop Tarmell. Not a hospital, by the sound of it. They told me you did a runner.'

'What you doing here?' I repeated, ignoring his question. I looked from him to Sunday and back again. A dark suspicion was starting to emerge. The wankers.

'Little bit of international liaison,' said Louie.

'Getting over Barry?' I asked, nastily.

Louie glowered at me and glanced anxiously at Sunday. However, this little comment didn't seem to ruffle the features of the Nigerian. He remained standing by the door, smiling.

Louie turned to Sunday. 'Sorry, can you please give us a minute? Just some work-related stuff.'

'Of course,' said Sunday. 'I'll go check my hair.' He ran his fingers lightly over the shaved tessellations running across his scalp and disappeared into the bathroom.'

'What's up?' I asked. 'Am I not going out for dinner with you two, then?'

Louie made a rueful face. 'That wasn't the plan, you see–'

'No, makes sense,' I said, refilling my glass. 'I'd just be getting in the way. Guessing you'll be wanting the big bed when you get back?'

'He said you could stay?' asked Louie, aghast.

'Yeah.' My chin was doing a lot of jutting.

'Out of the question,' said Louie. 'You're gone by ten, OK? I'll send you a car.'

'Directive from the DI?' I asked.

Louie's face crumpled. 'From a friend, Carrie. I really need this, you understand?'

I was about to say 'I really don't understand' but something stopped me. I was about to be left alone again. It was what I liked, after all.

'Eleven,' I said. 'It's a nice room. I want to enjoy it.'

'Half ten,' said Louie,

'Eleven!'

'Fine.'

'And you send me a car?'

'Of course,' said Louie.

I stared at him for a long moment, willing him to say something more, but his dark eyes, though twitchy, remained still.

'You done?' I said.

'I spoke to Haz,' said Louie.

'Oh, yeah. What did Haz have to say?' I was hoping that he'd not relayed too much of my little moment in the vineyard.

'Said he thought you should be given some a-codes. Said you could cover the digital side as well. Get access to Modlee, and that.'

'Handy,' I said. 'Saves you a bit of budget, that, doesn't it?'

Louie shook his head. 'It's not the money, Carrie, it's… There's nobody free, Carrie. It's a bloody wave of… I don't know. I can pay you more.'

'Good,' I said. 'I'll need it.'

'But you'll need to cover those other jobs as well?'

'Yeah, yeah.' I spotted some left-over breadstick, so picked one up and had a chew.

'Here're the codes.'

I saw the icons pulse in my display, before sinking back into my nose bead's storage. 'What about Modlee?'

Sunday returned from the bathroom. He checked his watch impatiently.

'Clive's going to sort that,' said Louie.

'I have to talk to him directly?'

'Afraid so.'

I groaned. 'Fucking hell.'

'Who is Clive?' asked Sunday, coming over.

'He handles our apps, with access and IG and that,' I said. 'He's a fucking nightmare.'

'He's not that bad,' said Louie. 'At least you don't need to find him. He's going to find you. He'll catch up with you when you're back at your flat.'

'Who says I'm going back to my flat?' I asked.

Louie frowned. 'You'll need to go back, eventually.'

'You got that security drone sorted?'

He shook his head. 'No.'

'So, you'll be fine when one of those toerags take me down? Drop a little firebomb through the letterbox?'

'There's not going to be any trouble,' said Louie, too quickly. 'Listen, I really can't spare anybody else. We're so short of people. You as well. This thing you're working on, it's not even a proper case.'

'Missing person is a proper case.'.

'Maybe not even that.'

Sunday cleared this throat. 'We're going to be late if we don't leave now.'

'Sure,' said Louie. He turned back to me. 'Just give yourself a break tonight, OK, Carrie? Haz seemed to think you were…' He trailed when he saw my face. But I could work out what he was trying to say.

'Fuck off,' I said. 'Go out. Have fun. Leave me here so that I can do some work.'

After they'd gone, I simply sat on the sofa and looked out at the view. I flicked my nose bead on for a moment, wondering if I should see if any more faces had been added to my project by DidNotArrive. But somehow, that seemed a little banal tonight. Plus, I didn't have the kit.

I started to open up the probe data from Sunday's files and drop them into the case folder. I hadn't gone that far before I fell asleep on the sofa.

I never even made it to that huge bed.

CHAPTER TWENTY-THREE

A few minutes before eleven o'clock, I was woken by an alarm. It was best described as Caucus pipe symphony mashed up with Chinese opera. When you weren't prepared for it, it entered your dreams with some messed up imagery. I woke snarling a string of swear words, realising I hadn't moved from the sofa I'd curled up on a few hours before.

'What?' I shouted at the room.

'A car has arrived for you, Ms Tarmell,' said the room.

'For me?'

'That is correct.'

'I didn't ask for one.'

'It was a request call from a Mr Daine.'

'Bastard.'

My shoulder reminded me that it wasn't happy and things got gradually worse until I'd managed to find my coat and rummaged through the contents of the pockets for more painkillers. I necked what few I'd found in among sweets and fluff, choking it down with a couple of miniatures of Uruguayan whisky, which were stashed in the chatty minibar.

I threw some water on my face and re-did my eyeliner a bit. I was looking a bit ghoulish by now, but I wasn't bothered that much. It all helped to add to my mystique, I liked to think. The bloody great hole in my duffel coat wasn't great. I took a moment to soak the corner of it in the sink for a bit, getting rid of most of the blood and the dark colour of the felt helped to hide it a little. I regretted not taking the chance to wash my other clothes. I stuffed what I could into my satchel.

Suitably prepared, I grabbed a coffee from the machine, a few more miniatures of spirits from the bar fell into my pockets, and I made my way out of the building. The car was buzzing away on the slipway by the front entrance. A few latecomers were stumbling into the building, laughing and giggling.

'Next client's waiting,' I said, winking at the concierge as he helped me into the car. 'It's been a busy night.'

'This is an Airedale Justice Commission car, ma'am,' he said, not blinking.

'Like I said.' I slammed the door and waved at him as we drove away.

'Where to?' asked the car.

'Just keep driving me around the ring roads,' I said.

'Please be more specific,' said the car.

'Random route,' I said. 'I want to be back here in the morning, OK? Take me via the coast. It's a nice night.'

'That's a significant level of power consumption, Ms Tarmell,' said the car.

'Louie's paying this, right?'

'Yes, Mr Daine is paying.'

'Take me to the fucking coast then and, I don't know, park up in front of the sea, or summat.'

I fell asleep within twenty minutes. When I woke, it was to experience a harsh cold morning overlooking the brown North Sea. We were parked in a small bay on the beachfront of some sleepy town; the waves crashing on the pebbles in front of me. I didn't recognise where we were, but it felt like it wasn't far from Brid. I dug in my pockets and necked one of the spare miniatures for breakfast. I told the car to put the heaters on. There was a little cold coffee left in a cup beside me, so I swallowed that as well.

The whisky took the edge of the pain in my shoulder but also numbed my brain a bit. I hoped the coffee might help.

To the north I could make out the black ridges of the moors and, beyond that, the eternal smoke which concealed the Middlesbrough Complex. Looking at it reminded me of the pain in my shoulder and I touched it involuntarily. Whatever off-retail painkillers I'd taken the day before were fully out of my system now, and I needed to find something more than the cheap shit I'd found in my pockets. I was also worried about having left the ward too early, and about what was happening under that bandage. Were things going to mend all right? I'd seen the effects of untreated wounds on plenty of folk, whether victims or wrong 'uns, and didn't want that to happen to me.

Medical shit could wait, though. First off, I wanted to get into the data files Sunday'd shared the previous night. I fired up the bead and started to work.

There were nineteen limbs and organs in total that'd come in on the *Talofa-3*: four legs, eight arms, two hands, four kidneys and a heart. Interesting that they'd included organs – growing that shit wasn't illegal – but I guessed that some people wanted the whole package. Sunday had tagged the files accordingly, but not added any further metadata to the samples. Seemed he hadn't run them through any of his own records. Perhaps he had staff to do that for him normally. He'd also given me a small text file. I loaded this up and had a quick scroll. It was the access codes to a genetic database. I did a quick search. It was his federal database. I checked a parameter. This had international codes.

'Fuck.'

I fired up my apps. The DNA downloads took a while, but I soon had them dropped into DidNotArrive. I was trying not to think too much about the possibilities of the international database. I just needed to make it talk to DidNotArrive. With a couple of minutes of fiddling with some interface settings, DidNotArrive and the database were exchanging their virtual fluids like teenagers wrecked on pear cider.

Though it was possibly off limits for IG reasons, I knew what

I wanted to do with this. This database access had a lot more potential than any of the limbs on that boat. So I searched through my DidNotArrive case files and found what I was looking for: code from the headless torso. This was the one where I hadn't found a match. Without realising that I was holding my breath, I fired off a search query.

No match. Seemed that Lagos didn't know who Mr Shin was either.

I grunted, disappointed. I realised my heart rate had accelerated, and I needed to calm things down.

Before I went back to the data files for the *Talofa-3*'s cargo, my hand hovered in the air over the federal database search query for a long time. There was another data file I had – a file I'd carried on this bead since I first got it – and which, when things had been darkest and I'd been loneliest in the middle of the night, I dropped into search boxes. I wondered whether I should try it on this one.

'You saddo,' I muttered to myself.

So I left it, hidden away in its layered folders of obscurity. Only I knew the where to find it and what I'd called it and what its obscure contents held.

The nineteen data files for the ship's cargo of body parts slid into DidNotArrive's folder and I ran a general search, against the nationals, against East Pennine's, Airedale's, the Belt's databases, as well as Sunday's international one. I got a one hundred percent success rate on all. They were all local, all on the general database. That meant they were proper citizens, like you and me, not a shady wrong 'un who'd dropped off grid.

Not sure if I was caught up in the moment – or if it was the lingering aftereffects of necking Uruguayan whisky at speed – but I couldn't help whooping at that moment. A herring gull, standing on a small knoll in front of the car, turned its beady eyes on me, momentarily distracted from its ongoing mission to find chips. Having determined that I contained no fried goods, it turned back to the sea.

I started to check through the names and locations, mapping them out. They were spread across the Belt, five people with normal jobs, normal families. But just that little bit richer than normal people. The addresses certainly suggested money. I could tell that without even having to run a comparative analysis.

I stared at the list for a long time. I wasn't sure what to do now. I needed that bastard Haz.

I took a swig of cold coffee. Finished it. Looked at the names again. I ran them through searches on our East Pennine crime database, in multiples, pairs, individually. Nothing. Then I tried to drop them into a public search engine, again in different configurations. Nothing. Then I tried their businesses, and their addresses. And still nothing.

I drew up their images instead of their names, hoping to find a link visually. I laid them out in a line, in a circle. It didn't help. They were bright-cheeked successes, by the look of them. These were people who'd made it big in the Belt, lawyers and entrepreneurs and genetic engineers. They had the skin tones of people who didn't leave hospital too early and had to scrabble in their pockets for painkillers. Neither were they the kind of people who got severed heads heaved through their window. They were people who had proper parents.

I'd hit a bit of a wall by now, though. I was about to start to dial them all up, one by one, when I finally felt the pain in shoulder. I didn't really want to have to schlep around five different houses, hassling security guards to be let in. The thought of all that work made me sweat.

I got out of the car for some fresh air. It was freezing. Got back in. Checking myself in the mirror, I could see that I was pale now, and I'd started sweating quite badly. I stared at my face for a bit. Not enjoying the sight of my bruises, I brought up my bead display instead. The line of faces was still there, beaming at me. Then I had a thought. I turned back to the search on my bead and brought up a window for configuring a public search. Configured a visual search. Five happy faces were fed into the engine with a flick of the fingers.

I got a successful hit. I dragged it up and flicked through the archives. There was a picture. It was a small news item, in a minor business page. There was a crowd of people standing on the lawn of a fancy house. It looked like an orchard, by the spacing of the trees. Must've been midsummer time. Three of the faces from the search were highlighted with red circles, scattered among the whole group. My eyes scanned the rest. I immediately recognised Ratna Manish, grinning in the front row. And I thought I could even recognise the features of Stan Davi, who had died on his yacht down the coast. Sitting in the middle of the group was an older lady, white hair drawn up into a bun, her hands clasped in front of her, smiling gently, like a mother in front of her extended family.

New health insurance conglomerate established by Dr Hillary Godden.

The Godden Institute for Healthcare and Wellbeing.

I checked the address. The Great Northern Belt. York end.

'Car,' I said.

'Yes, Ms Tarmell,' said the car.

'Take me to this address.'

The Institute was tucked away on a quiet residential street in a corner of the eastern end of the Belt, the far side of York Oldtown. I was let in at the reception area by an elderly lady with a dismissive manner and a sleepy, white-maned Alsatian. It looked like it would rip your throat out if you coughed too loudly. She told me to follow the path in towards the house and let me through the door. Beyond reception, things opened out into an orchard. Most of the fruit had been picked, and there were only a few russet, shrivelled orbs hanging in higher branches. Beyond the trees, the path wound through some hedged gravel driveways and then onto an ancient house. This was sandstone, with red creepers working their way up to the small windows and the tiled roof.

There were four other people in the gardens. Most of them must've been other patients, as they were moving with the speed of people in mild pain. I wondered if I could shake them down for drugs. They might have better ones.

As I approached the house, a small light flashed on a discreet comms unit, tastefully tucked into the door jamb.

'Welcome to the Godden Institute.' There was something familiar about the voice. I wasn't sure, but it had a cadence. Then I realised it was Grace. Or an approximation of Grace. She was bloody everywhere. 'You carry no patient beacon. How can I help you?'

'I'm here to see Dr Hillary Godden,' I said. 'I've checked in at reception already. Name's Tarmell, Carrie Tarmell.'

'We apologise for the inconvenience, Ms Tarmell,' said my sister's voice. 'We have sigma-level security at the Institute.'

'Yeah, yeah,' I said. Sigma-level security sounded like total bollocks. I took a guess. 'You need my iris scanned?'

'That would be very helpful,' said the machine.

I made a big show of poking my eye at the machine.

The door clicked open.

'Follow the green lights upstairs. Dr Godden is waiting for you in the room at the top of the stairs, the green door.'

It was all vintage inside. Looked like a fucking museum. It was rare to see this kind of thing these days. My mother's generation had had a brief phase when they decided that anything old was definitely shit and then went through a destructive period. They'd even eyed up Stonehenge for a moment, wondering if they should reconfigure the assets, make those stones into something a bit more useful for their generation. Until somebody told them to grow the fuck up. So, it was rare to catch sight of things like oak-panelled rooms and, well, just so much hardwood all in one place. The retributors would have a panic attack in here. I wasn't even looking at the fox head at the wall. I was sure its eyes followed me as I made my way up the stairs.

Halfway up, I stopped and shrugged my coat off my shoulders, easing it away with my good hand. I folded it in such a way that the two holes were now longer visible and draped it across my arm. This little moment was enough to set off the throbbing pain, and I could feel sweat beading up on my forehead. They kept this house dead warm and all, which didn't help.

The green door was open, and I spied a figure at a desk, bent over a tablet. She must've heard the creaks on the floorboards, or my laboured breathing at the climb, or maybe she just noticed movement and looked up as I approached across the landing.

'Come in, come in.'

It was a brisk, kindly voice. The kind of voice I'd liked to have heard from my mum as I grew up, telling me to do my laces, to wear matching socks, to avoid eating too much chocolate. You felt in good, safe hands with this voice. Wryly, I considered that most of these kinds of conversations with my mother, from the earliest age, would've been along the lines of: 'It's your choice as an individual whether to make.' When I was fucking five, probably.

'Dr Godden?'

'That's right,' said the woman. She stood as I entered and stuck out a hand in greeting.

I carefully shook it. The coat was still draped across my right hand, so it made things a little tricky. 'You are with Airedale Justice, right?'

'Contracted to the Buckle... I mean, Fourth Sector, actually. But, yeah, I've worked for Airedale.'

'I haven't been west for a long time,' said Dr Godden, nodding. 'I do love the hills but... work, you understand?'

'No bother to me,' I said. There was an awkward silence. Then I cleared my throat. 'So, the reason I'm—'

'If you don't mind me saying, you're sweating a little,' said the doctor. 'Are you OK?'

'Fine,' I said. 'I'm fine.'

She looked at my stance, then at my shoulder.

'Are you injured?' asked Godden, still examining my shoulder and then peering at my face. 'You appear to be in pain. And there are recent bruises here.'

'It's fine,' I said. I didn't like the way she was examining my face so closely, almost with professional appraisal. 'I need to ask you some questions.'

'I can help.' She smiled. 'I am a doctor.'

'I don't think I could afford your prices.'

'Nonsense,' she said. 'A doctor heals, whatever the money. You're here now. You need assistance. Sit down here. Let me have a look.'

'I'm here to ask you some questions, Dr Godden–'

'Yes, yes,' said the doctor, pushing me into a chair. 'All in good time, Ms Tarmell. Can I call you Carrie?'

'Yeah,' I muttered, biting my lip. She'd started to press into the flesh all around my arm. I yelped and then swore, instinctively: 'Fuck off.'

Godden seemed to have heard worse. She wasn't fazed. She held up a hand and presented fingers dyed in blood. 'I think you need this looking at, my girl. You need proper attention. And a sling.'

'Leave me be!' To my ears, this didn't sound as authoritative as it was supposed meant to. I stood up from the chair and made to walk to the door. My legs weren't working that well. Some bastard had glued my feet to the floor. I tried moving again. This was a mistake.

'Ah,' I whimpered, as I hit floor.

Godden ran past me to the door and yelled out a couple of names. I didn't really care at this point. All I was worried about was the blazing pain now bursting from my shoulder and rippling across the rest of my body. I couldn't even find the will to drag in my splayed limbs and curl into a comforting ball.

After a few moments of groaning pain, I was joined by a

small bevy of medical types and whisked into any adjoining room – which looked very much like a surgery, but a top-end one, like out of an immersive – where I was made to lay down on an operating table and my blouse was carefully pulled back.

One of the assistants shot me in the right arm with something. Must've been strong, as the pain ebbed away fast and I could get my breath back. I blinked away the tears and, using my good hand, tried to wipe the black streaks from my cheeks. Gotta regain some dignity.

Once I felt I was in a good enough place to demand answers, I turned to Godden, who was fussing over a small table of various medical gauzes. 'Is this going to take long, doctor?' I said. 'Only, I've got a busy day.'

'Back with us?' she asked, not looking up.

'I tripped up,' I said. 'It's nowt.'

'You can't take your health for granted,' said Godden, looking me straight in the eye. I wasn't sure if she meant it as a threat. 'I'm going to remove the previous dressing, OK?'

She stepped around to my wound and started unpicking the adhesive strips. I gasped as the blood-stained rag came away. From the corner of my eye, I could now see the small hole, feathered by black flecks of blood. I realised then I hadn't even put it through Bladester.

'Somebody's been shot,' said Godden, conversationally. Her face betrayed no emotion as she said this. She turned to one of her staff and read a set of instructions. As she turned back, she saw me twitching my right hand in the air. 'Are you OK?'

'Just getting some pictures,' I said, grimacing. The gecko skittered up the wall behind me and started flashing.

'That is rather distracting,' said Godden. She seemed a little annoyed. 'Can you do it afterwards?'

'You'll have messed with the evidence by then,' I said.

She smiled. 'That sounds ominous.'

'I need to see the back as well,' I said.

'You need to lie still,' she said.

'Fine, do it myself,' I said, rolling sideways, so the back of my shoulder was exposed. It wasn't a nice experience. I didn't like the look of what the gecko had found, either. 'Jeez.'

'Lie back down, Ms Tarmell.'

'Nearly there,' I said. The gecko finished its work and returned to my jacket pocket.

'Done?'

'Done.'

'We're going to apply some local anaesthetic,' said Godden, 'then we have a mesh which we can apply to both the entrance and exit wound. It will help the body to heal itself naturally. In addition, we will be issuing you with a targeted cocktail of bespoke analgesic, which I will send as a standard file to your health app now.'

'Don't have a health app,' I said.

'Oh?' said Godden. 'Well, just try to remember the dosage, OK?'

'Uh huh,' I said. I wasn't really listening by this point, instead plugging the footage into Bladester, then adding other criteria, such as clothing, the angle, distance and others. It got a match pretty quickly. Bladester was sixty-percent certain I'd been shot by a lightweight composite hunting rifle, an SHD-55, also known as a Frosty. There were very few in circulation in Europe. They were mainly used by government institutions – and various subcontractors – from the south-east corner of China. Mainly around Shenzhen.

'Shit,' I muttered.

'Are you in much pain?' asked Godden. The others had now left, and it was me and the doctor in the sleek surgery now.

'Just worked out who shot me,' I said.

Godden blinked and looked down at me, smiling. I could tell that she was forcing it. 'Really?'

'Well, what corporation, anyway,' I said, grinning.

'Really?'

'Yeah,' I said. 'We going to be too much longer?'

'We have to let the mesh settle in,' said Godden. She looked across at a monitor screen for a moment. 'Your blood sample tells me you're quite unique.'

'Yeah?' I said.

'You're one of the stolen specimens,' she said, looking back at me. The room, empty now of everybody but us two, seemed too quiet, too intimate.

I frowned. 'Haven't you broken a few fucking hundred IG rules by telling me that?'

She shrugged. 'Not really. It's the law that you are supposed to be informed, ideally by a medical professional.' She paused. 'Did you know?'

'About the law?'

'No. The fact that you're a specimen. One of the stolen ones.'

I didn't answer. I stared at her hand pressing into my shoulder. It didn't hurt any more. 'You know any more... I mean, more like me?'

'I know of one,' said Godden. 'Different batch, though.'

I looked up at her and raised my eyebrows expectantly.

'But to tell you who it is,' said Godden, smiling, 'would break a few… ha, a few hundred IG rules. Now, you can sit up and I'll get you a sling.'

She let me dress myself again while she busied herself at her little table, returning with a small band of spider silk. It was designed to blend in the clothes so nobody could see the material. She started to attach the clasp around the back of my head.

'So,' said the doctor. 'How can I help? You said you had some questions.'

I cleared my throat and thought for a moment. 'Have you heard of the wrecking yards of Hartlepool?'

'Of course. I mean, I disagree with the approach, on environmental grounds, but I appreciate that we have to recycle. It's all about recycling these days, isn't it? There, that's all done. Shall we return to my office?'

I sniffed. If I was in a more alert mood, I would've been more attentive when she said this. As it happened, I'd only reacted to the recycling word a few seconds after she said it. And grunted.

'Yeah. Anyway, a boat… I mean, a ship came in the day before yesterday. It were carrying a hidden compartment–'

'How exciting,' interrupted Dr Godden, holding the door open for me.

I stepped through and walked carefully towards the chair opposite her desk. My legs seemed to be OK. 'Yeah, dead exciting. Compartment contained a nice collection of limbs and that.'

'Limbs?'

'Legs and arms and kidneys and that.'

'So, organs as well?'

I blinked. Whatever it was that she'd given me, it'd certainly fixed the pain in the shoulder, but it was making me struggle with my words. 'Aren't they all organs?'

She tilted her head on one side. 'I was going to suggest, Carrie, that you came back when you're in a healthier state. I'm worried that you should really be recuperating, not working. Can I call a car for you? The Institute will pay, of course.'

'Just need to ask a few more questions.'

'You need to rest that arm,' said Dr Godden. 'I mean, I don't get many of those kinds of trauma injuries to deal with, but I remember my training, and I'm certain that a bullet wound like that needs close attention. Preferably in a specialist care unit.'

I frowned. 'Your training?'

'You must've upset somebody, getting shot like that?' Her face was neutral, but the voice carried with it the gentlest of threats. It reminded me of talking to the old DI, Ibrahim Al-Yahmeni. He could threaten you with a frigging eyebrow.

I took a breath. 'Back to these limbs, Dr Godden.'

'I'm sorry. Which ones?'

'The ones found in the boat. We identified the genetic signatures of all the meat. Turns out it were connected to five people in the area. So, we're guessing, it were a replacement parts business.'

She shrugged. 'I guess that would be a robust assumption.'

'You do any replacements work?' I asked.

The kindly smile disappeared and was replaced with a cold frown. 'Certainly not. That is highly offensive. Is this what you've come here to accuse me of?'

'Just asking questions, me.'

'I can see that. But why ask me? What connection does this Institute have with your cargo of parts?' She leaned in. 'Have you spoken with any of these people?'

'Nah,' I said.

'Oh. Then what was it that brought you here?'

'Because I plugged in the faces of some of these owners into a forensics search.' I coughed a little at this point. Didn't hurt to stretch things a little. 'And I got a hit against an insurance scheme. Connected to this Institute.' I waved out of the window. 'Looks like it was taken out there, actually.'

'So,' said Dr Godden, leaning back now, more relaxed, 'that is your lead, is it? Do you think there is something that links people who are able to afford improved health insurance schemes? I cater for many wealthier members of our community. No doubt, they also invest in some dubious ventures. That's their business. You would need to discuss it with them, of course.'

I was suddenly weary. Possibly it was the drugs, possibly the days of lack of decent sleep. But the points she made were very reasonable.

'Yeah,' I said, bluffing it. 'I will, yeah, of course.'

'You're free to ask me any questions about this clinic, of course,' said Godden. She took a while saying this. 'As I have nothing to hide.'

'OK,' I said, wiping my forehead, 'what is it that you do here at the Institute?'

She smiled. 'Reconstructive surgery. Alterations.'

'Cosmetic?'

She made a face. 'We don't like that label but… yes, I guess you could say that.'

'And that's your speciality?'

'It's what I do now.'

'Oh,' I said, blinking, 'what were you before?'

'I was a battlefield medic. Mainly biohazard, but…' she examined my shoulder. 'A little bit of major trauma as well.'

'Oh right,' I said. 'Fucking hell. Where were you based?'

She winced as I swore. 'Nowhere that dangerous. In various locations across our forward bases: Svalbard, Gibraltar Island, Dhaka borderlines, the South China pontoons, those kinds of places.'

'Been to places, you have,' I said, grinning. 'Wish I could get around like that.' I thought of the lagoons of Lagos.

'I was very lucky,' said Godden.

'My mum did something similar. Not a doctor, but she were out there as well.'

'Very commendable.'

'Yeah,' I said, 'it were dead good.' I was interrupted when an incoming call flashed on my bead. It was Louie. 'Sorry,' I said, 'I got to take this.'

She waved graciously as I stood up and strode for the door. In the corridor, I clicked through the call.

'Yeah,' I said. 'What is it? I'm busy.'

'I am still your boss, Carrie. Bit of respect, yeah?'

I couldn't tell if he was joking. So I laughed at him, just to be sure. 'Course.'

'Where are you? Thought you'd be at home.'

'Following up leads.'

'You need to be back in Airedale. Clive wants to get you tooled up with Modlee. He's on his way to your flat. You miss him, you'll never find him.'

I swore. 'Why do we still give him a contract? Surely you can do something about that?'

'Just get yourself home. Fast.'

'Why are we all scared of this guy?'

'He's good at his job.'

'OK. Where are you, anyway, Louie?'

'Back at the hotel.'

'With Sunday?'

Slight pause. 'Yeah, sure. Why?'

'No reason.'

'Catch you later.'

'Yeah.'

I ended the call. During the conversation, something had occurred to me. Something about the doctor's personal history had sparked a thought. I went back into the room and gave her a smile.

'Problems?' she asked.

'Work, yeah.'

'Your Justice Divisions are terribly stretched at the moment,' she said.

'We are,' I said. 'Look, I don't have time now for a tour, yeah. But I might be back.'

'You make it sound like a threat!'

'Nah,' I said, smiling, 'but I might want to get some work done. If you know what I mean.'

'I see nothing that needs alteration,' she said, smiling and rising.

'Cheers.'

'Can I walk you to reception?'

'I can manage,' I said. 'It's difficult to get lost.' I opened the door and turned to her. 'Actually, I have one last question.'

'There's always a little more, isn't there?' The smile had faded now.

'I wanted to know if you recognised this device?' I found the public interface for her wall screen and cast the image of the blood-stained stitcher at it.

She looked at the device for a moment, before turning back to me and shaking her head. 'I'm sorry. I don't recognise… no, I'm sorry.'

'Thanks,' I said. 'I'll get out of your hair, Dr Godden. Appreciate your time. But you know how we have to follow these things up.'

'I'm afraid I don't, but I appreciate the work you do.'

As I hobbled down the stairs, I nodded to myself. I knew this place wasn't right.

CHAPTER TWENTY-FOUR

It was late in the afternoon when the justice autocar trundled itself off the MC-17 and into the side streets of Shipley. The wintry rain was starting to fall in earnest now, lashing the front windscreen. This was commuter time, for those who still had to get to an office, for those who still had a job, so it was jumbled up with autocars and bikes and loaders and scooters. We were moving slowly through the unexpected traffic, the car's rerouting software unable to find a way around this mess. I could see my block of flats up ahead, tucked underneath the glowing advertising hoardings on the hill. Taking a breath, I realised I was sweating, a knot of anxiety balling up in my stomach. The thought of what I might find through my window, or on the middle of my living room floor was making me ill. I hoped the car took a little longer. I wondered if I should ask it to take a sub-optimal detour.

Still breathing hard, I didn't notice the figure of a man walk out in front of the car, until the vehicle had jammed on its brakes and I was slammed into the restraining clamp of the belts. As I peered through the rain-streaked glass, I could make out the familiar balding head and red hair of Clive beneath a large umbrella. In his other hand he held a child's balloon, emblazoned with the wistful face of a chick, it's helium-filled lightness straining for the sky but being battered by the rain. Clive nodded a greeting to me and indicated with a tilt of his chin that we should rendezvous at a small roadside pie cart.

'We have stopped for a pedestrian,' said the car.

'No shit,' I muttered.

'I do not understand the command,' said the car.

'Run him down,' I said, hoping for the best.

'My controls do not allow that,' said the car.

I stepped out, grabbing my satchel as I went, and pulled up the hood of my coat. 'What the fuck you doing?' I yelled at Clive.

'Good afternoon to you, Carrie,' he said, pleasantly, stepping across the road to join me. 'Do you want a pie?'

I looked at the small cart. It had an awning, at least. 'Sure. I've had a pie from this place before. Not been too sick afterwards.'

'A five-star review!'

Clive bustled into the space, collapsing his umbrella and carefully tying his balloon to the back of a high stool that ran along the counter.

'Airedale Justice Commission discount please, sir,' said Clive, loudly, to the old man serving.

At the sound of this, a good number of the customers who'd also been sheltering under the awning slid off into the darkness, leaving us with the owner and an elderly couple and their pet cat, curled up in a warm ball beneath their chairs.

'Always works effectively,' said Clive, winking at me.

'Not very discreet,' I said, hopping up onto a stool and shaking my hood back.

'This is information freely available,' said Clive. He turned and pointed at the car I'd arrived in, slowly making its lonely way back down the street to the MC-17. 'That is enough for anybody with half a brain to identify you as such. The little logos on the side give it away.'

'Yeah,' I said, 'whatever. Why you got a balloon?'

'Algorithms, my dear.' He turned to the vendor. 'I'll take an Ethiopian wrap with chicken.' He turned back to me. 'What are you having?'

'You treating me?'

'No, I was merely trying to hurry the transaction along. I'm hungry.'

The ball in my stomach wasn't loosening. 'I'll have a water and lime. What do mean by "algorithms"?' I nodded at the balloon.

'What are these cars trained to save, above all else?'

'I don't know,' I said. The man handed me my drink, and I thanked him. 'You're going to tell me, anyway, so why bother trying to guess?'

'Ms Tarmell is performing the feisty forensic analyst this evening.'

I checked my bead and yawned. 'It's not even five. Hardly evening.'

'Number three of the digital analyst trainee's techniques for identifying the data source: ask them the time.' Clive nodded at the old man, preparing his wrap. 'Even this man would've noticed you flapping your hands around your nose. Dead giveaway.'

'Is this a test?'

'You bet it is,' said Clive, suddenly leaning in close. 'I've been told to give you tools, Ms Tarmell, that are significant and that are causal. There is a need for tests.'

'Just let me download Modlee and fuck off, Clive,' I said, yawning again. 'I'm tired.'

'I'm afraid it doesn't work like that... ah, thank you kindly, my good man.' Clive lifted his wrap carefully onto the rain-speckled counter in front of him and regarded it sagely. 'Injera bread. Do you know how they make it?'

'No.'

'It is soured and fermented.' He bit into it and waggled his eyebrows at me. 'Sound familiar?' he said, his mouth full.

'Yeah, very,' I said. I looked down at the cat, curled up under the old woman's seat. Its little harness, made from ersatz emeralds, sparkled in the neon lights of the pie and wrap cart. I was suddenly hugely envious of its life.

'This is very good,' said Clive. 'They also do a great green prawn deep fill.'

'A child,' I said, still staring at the cat and then up at the balloon.

'Hmm?' Bits of wrap dribbled from the corner of his mouth.

'The algorithms are designed to avoid a child. The addition of the balloon makes your ratios appear more like a child.'

'Very good.'

'The first technique for identifying a data source is to scan for it.'

'Excellent.'

'The second is to call the person.'

'We're getting better,' said Clive. 'Now read for me the East Pennine Information Governance code of conduct, from paragraphs three point twelve to fifteen.'

I went into my search for features and found the relevant documents. They were public domain, so there wasn't much of an issue tracking them down. I dutifully read out everything that was required of me. After the IG code, there were a couple more documents to recite and swear by. At least Clive wasn't expecting me to open a vein and cross his pinky finger, or some such shit.

'Is data really this dangerous?' I asked when I'd finished.

'I'm not going to answer that,' said Clive, wiping his mouth with his napkin, 'on the grounds that it is obtuse and deliberately provocative.'

'Obtuse and deliberately provocative is my middle name.'

'Your middle name is…' At this point Clive trailed off, as though he realised he'd overstepped some boundary.

'What?' I said. 'What were you going to say?'

'I was wondering whether you actually knew your middle name?'

The knot in my stomach, which had loosened with lime and water and the general bureaucracy of Clive, now squeezed up tight to my heart and gave it a sharp-toed kick. 'You fu–'

'Carrie.' Clive waved a finger at me. 'Don't start swearing. I haven't given you access yet.'

'Why don't they sack you?'

'I know where all the bodies are buried,' he said, grinning. Then his voice lowered. 'Literally.'

'I bet you do.' I wondered how much he really knew about my background.

'The time has come, Carrie,' he said, standing, 'for us to part. It's been a wonderful evening and I've had a lot of fun, but I'm afraid I cannot come up for a coffee. I have other engagements.'

'I've got it, then? I've got Modlee.'

'You have a time-limited pass. Thirty minutes to download. Then the pass expires and you'll have to arrange another delightful rendezvous.'

'Fine.' I stood up and looked up. 'You not taking your balloon?'

He untied it from the chair and carried it out in the rain. With a small smile, he let it go and it ascended up into the darkness of night.

I followed its progress. When I looked down again, he'd gone.

Modlee had downloaded itself to my bead by the time I'd reached the small flight of steps up to the block of flats. Once I'd presented my face to the security sensor on the front door, the app had automatically interfaced with Bladester and DidNotArrive and was busily sorting its way through my files. Bladester was already complaining – it didn't play nicely with Modlee – but I ignored all the warnings by clicking my fingers repeatedly. Modlee was an advanced app, cutting-edge. It did unexpected things, found surprising links in reality, things you would never see. Bladester was struggling to keep up. Old school.

However, all thoughts of apps faded when I stopped at my front door. This moment had been concerning me for a while. General anger at Clive had distracted me for a while, and trying to get Modlee working had helped, but I was here now and things weren't going well; I couldn't walk those last few metres and let myself into my own flat. I felt very calm, matter-of-fact, about it. This was all completely rational and sane. So, I turned around and headed back to the stairwell, contemplating my next move. When I reached the stairs, I turned right, heading upwards, and made my way to the top of the building instead. Maybe a bit of fresh air would help?

CALDERDALE

The roof of my block had a crappy little garden terrace, with some plants and a couple of rotting gazebos. In summer, it was a nice place to come up and have a few drinks and watch the antics in the dale. Today, though, it was still raining hard and was cold and miserable. I scampered over to the nearest gazebo, which overlooked the main street below, and hunkered down into a corner, pulling some tarp around me, so that I didn't get drips down the back of my neck.

Then I plugged myself in, turning up the contrast to a hundred. The background lights of Shipley faded behind the brighter lines of my display. Modlee pulsed in the bottom-right corner. I popped it open and had a look around. We'd obviously used some of this shit back in Big Man Vickers' college, so I knew the basics. It was all pretty intuitive as well. I started to pull together some of the data, some of the key dates and times and names, mulled over what was available, threw in this and that to see what I could get.

First off, I tried to see what the mash-up of Modlee and Bladester had produced. It wasn't much. In Bladester's visuals, I looked at the murder scene. The multi-bodied shape on the chopping table haunted the screen for a moment before I pulled it down. I'd got more access to data now. All of the faces of the monster were on that image from the media site. Faces circled in red. All except one. The blank face. Modlee had movements of all the potential victims. They were scattered across the country, dots moving on a screen with no discernible pattern. Getting on with their own lives. And being murdered on a table in the Belt's Fellside Recycling Auxiliary Facility.

I gave up on the Bladester connections and went back into Modlee.

There wasn't much. Traffic data confirmed what I already know. I saw the delivery van as a dot moving along a map of the Buckle's wastelands, carrying its cargo of meat. I watched it park up outside the facility. Then I saw it leave, carrying the leg back to H Central. That wasn't interesting. Nothing could tell me about what had happened on that table with the blood.

Checking comms activity didn't produce much. The only data freely available to my access codes was meta, so I could see clusters of activity only, not the content. I plugged this into a map and set the timer scrolling. There was a little activity around the facility. I rolled the time back to the night I'd received the call. There was a comms flash in the area of the Fellside Facility, pinged the local nodes. Most of the Valleys were lit up with continuous light this time. This comms flash was surrounded by blackness: Withens Moor.

So a call had been made. No way to tell to whom, or what it contained. You asked for that shit. They'd send around people with serious law degrees and fat POs, who would threaten to talk to you for three hours about IG legislation. We had to play with the toys we were given. But this was enough. Somebody had made a call.

I rolled the time forward. There was nothing further in the vicinity at the facility until the early hours, when comms flashes started sparking up along the road. Then patterns returned to any normal day. I rolled time forward to the night that Simon West had died. I could see a brief flash of some call happening across the moor. The trajectory was from the Withens Reservoir and heading towards the point on the perimeter fence where the BoTies had broken in. So there was activity. Rolling forward a little, I saw another flash, a trail moving back towards the Withens' hill. I checked the time for both comm flashes. Time moving in was twelve forty-three and returning was six past one. Then I flicked back to the pathologist report and Bladester's work. Time of death was sometime between nine and eleven pm on the previous day.

Well, whoopee-shit.

Simon West was already dead when that comms flash had happened. Whoever it was making that call, moving in from the camp up on Withens, couldn't have killed him. Most likely they'd just come to take the body. I wished I had the bloody camera footage from the site.

'Ah, shit.' I remembered why I'd wanted Lem in the first place. Where was that thing?

My arse had gone to sleep on the hard bench and one of my legs was starting to get pins and needles. I shifted myself, trying to avoid the drips from the gazebo. It was still raining steadily. I rummaged through pockets of the coat. Wasn't there. My satchel was lying at the other end of the bench, so I reached out to grab it, swearing loudly again at the pain from my arm in the sling. Opening the satchel, I flicked past inert crawlers until I found the package. The defective security server in its corporate blister pack. Once I had this lying atop the satchel, I reached into my pockets to find my sniffer and the gecko.

The little device was secure in its AJC-stamped polymer bag, like it was grabbed by a proper forensic analyst. One who knew what they were doing. I ran a quick background check on the air in the gazebo with the sniffer – revealing a surprising level of narcotics – then slid the server out of its protective polymer and onto my satchel, which was acting as a small table. The blister pack looked to be intact. This was normally the way for these things to retain warranty. There was a space for a finger to reset the whole thing. The gecko confirmed West's thumbprint on it. No other prints - except mine - were evident on the thing.

I took a slow, hi-def picture with the gecko and dropped it into Bladester. After a few minutes of watching the progress bar, it alerted me to a descending scale of items of interest. There were the usual data, the points of difference, scratches, smudges, blemishes, failings. None of these seemed very useful. But there was something more much interesting. A miniscule object had snagged on a corner of the blister pack. I zoomed in on the image. Enhanced.

It was a shred of green textile. Not possible to identify with human eyes. I set Bladester to work it out for me, as usual. Internal databases whirred on the app and a little message popped up, telling me it had produced a seventy-strength match. Seventy was enough for a court these days. Natural silk with a common chemical dye.

I tried the handheld sniffer on it. It had salts from sweat, normal background pollutants, the crap from the facility. But there was a hint of something else. The same scent: *Breathless Whisper*.

I turned the server pack over and tried a picture from the back. This time, Bladester screamed out its results. A hole in the plastic, right above the industrial data jack. Something had been inserted into the pack and jammed into the server itself. I wasn't an expert in this, but even I knew that a data jack like that was for manual override of any wireless fail. It could bypass that shit. But they weren't designed for human interaction normally. With a human eye, it wasn't possible to pick it up.

Going back to my files, I looked for the footage from that day I'd been walking the site with West. Footage from the gecko of the cupboard confirmed the thing had been moved. The algo in Bladester identified that the dust marks a little to the right. Of course, that was probably just him trying to get it working. But somebody had messed with it. I dropped the gecko onto my lap and it started to crawl away, looking for a safe, high spot in the gazebo.

I pulled up Modlee and had a scroll to see if it had retail data mountains in there. There wasn't much, just publicly available inventories and catalogues. I checked out green silk gloves. Got a few thousand hits. Swore. I filtered down the hits to those in East Pennine. Then those in the Eastern Belt area. Then I filtered out the rougher end. This left a few sites. But it was still too many for me to follow up on manually. Dead end, yet again. I moved onto the item on my list: which bastard had shot me? I threw in the code for an SHD-55 rifle into the general data selection to see what I could find. There were spikes and nodes of activity across the country, and internationally, but despite trying – and swearing at the app – I wasn't able to get it to filter things down to something significant. It was just noise.

I was distracted when a word appeared on my display. It was

from the gecko. I'd left it running its usual hazard pattern checks.

Watcher.

I pulled myself out of the app and blinked at the rain. I realised I was freezing. I glanced up at the gecko. It'd found itself a perch that afforded it a better angle on the street below the block. I switched on the gecko's live feed, frozen in my seat.

There was a figure down in the street, staring up at the front of the block. They were lurking in the shadow of an adjoining building's awning. Nervously, I zoomed on the image, looking for weapons, a gun rifle, a suspect bulge in a jacket or a hand out of place. But I found nothing, the gecko found nothing. I was about got Bladester onto it, when the figure moved and their face fell into the streetlight. The dark skin tones were instantly recognisable. I hauled myself to my feet, and stepped into the rain, pulling up my hood, and walked a few steps to the railings that surrounded the roof garden. Leaning over the railings, I yelled into the rain.

'You going to stay there all night, Sunday? Or are you coming up?'

The figure looked up towards me.

'Thank you,' he said.

The flat was going to be in a bit of state, but at least I could get into it now.

CHAPTER TWENTY-FIVE

Sunday's face was impassive as it surveyed my living room. However, I could detect the smallest of twitches around the nose.

'This is a nice place,' he said, nodding.

'You're a shit liar, Sunday,' I said, barging past him to get to the kitchen. I wanted to get the conversation well away from the state of the flat. And why I'd not quite made it inside until now. 'You want a drink? I got some… well, I got some fruit juice in here, I think.'

'Just boiled water, please,' said Sunday. Then he hastily corrected himself. 'I mean, hot, just boiled, hot water, yes?'

'No worries,' I said. 'I'd only drink boiled water out of these taps, and all. I'm having a tea.'

I banged about in the kitchen, surreptitiously tidying things up as I made the drinks, and mentally working out the messes he could spy at this very moment. Every now and then, I would step back and check on him. I noticed he'd taken off his coat and found a free hook on the back of the door. A small carrier, not unlike my satchel – but much, much more fashionable – was propped up beside the table.

When I came back, he was staring at my project, draped across the back of the sofa. A hand crept out as if to brush it. When he noticed me standing there, two steaming bamboo beakers before me, the hand retreated.

'This is interesting,' he said. 'I hadn't considered you to be a crafter of vintage. You are skilled.'

'I'm not,' I said. 'That's just summat to stop me from going totally mental at night.'

'Is it a… forgive me, is it a blanket?'

'No,' I said. 'It's just shit for me to do with my hands when I'm bored.'

'And are these faces?'

'What do they look like?'

'All couples?'

I ignored the question and, instead, thrust the beaker at him. 'This is nice, and all, to get visitors, but what are you here for, Sunday?'

He took the drink and walked over to a chair, sitting carefully on the edge. 'I realised quickly, the other night, that your DI was not as well versed in the case as I'd originally thought.'

'No shit,' I said, also sitting. 'Is that why you went out? For a chat?'

Innocent eyes stared at my leer. 'Indeed. Though, well, I could have been clearer at the motive before we moved from the restaurant.' His face creased into a frown.

I sniggered.

'This is not a joke.'

'I know, I know,' I said. I swept a load of textile debris onto the floor and sat at the table. 'So, I take it nowt happened in that swanky hotel room?'

Sunday shook his head, as though shocked. 'Indeed, it didn't.'

'Louie thought it were all on!' I gazed at Sunday's face. He was proper shifty.

Sunday grimaced. 'Yes. I believe that your DI, Louie Daine, is probably a little upset.'

'At you?' I asked.

'At himself.'

I shrugged. 'He'll recover.'

'Anyway,' said Sunday, sipping his drink, 'that's not why I'm here.'

'Uh huh.' I waited.

Sunday gathered his thoughts, cleared his throat, and spoke. 'I was struck by something you said, Ms Tarmell. When we were in that hotel room.'

'Yeah?' I said. 'Was it swearing?'

'No,' said Sunday, smiling, 'but you correctly interpreted the situation I was in, in relation to my organisation, regarding the tenuous hold I have on this case. At first I was irritated that you'd found a weakness in my strategy, but then realised I had to be transparent with you now–'

'Now that Louie didn't turn up with the goods.'

Sunday took a sip of his hot water. 'It wasn't meant quite like that.'

I drummed my fingers on the arm of the chair. 'Wasn't it?'

Sunday shook his head. 'I have new information. If you are still working the case?'

'Why wouldn't I be?'

'Detective Inspector Daine explained it had been downgraded – via some algorithm, it got complicated at that point – from a homicide to a missing identity. And that even that was a weak index.' He took another sip. 'And that you weren't being paid for this anymore. You are a contractor, no?'

I clamped my teeth together and shrugged. 'So?'

'No matter,' he said. 'But I believe that you have multiple priorities. At least, that is what Detective Inspector Daine suggested. There is an ongoing fraud incident still playing out, isn't it?'

I tried not to think about the other work stacking up on my display. I'd been knocking the pulsing icons into the background repeatedly for days.

'So,' continued Sunday, 'you really don't have time for this anymore. But Mr Daine also hinted that, if we were to find a connection between my international federal investigation, and your local matter, that… hmm, well, let us say that the algorithm would produce a different result.'

'It'd be a proper case?' I said.

'That's right.'

'Your case?'

He sniffed and narrowed his eyes. 'As I said earlier, you have correctly identified the issues I have with being here. Though Mr Daine is impressed by the badge, my department is less excited at the thought of me spending time in a region like this, working with a local division, revealing our data, etcetera, etcetera. It's become more difficult.'

I carefully put down my tea. 'You're on your own now?'

'That is one way of putting it, yes.'

'So no more expenses?'

He grimaced. 'Frozen.'

'OK.'

He paused a long time. 'I think what I am trying to say, Ms Tarmell, Carrie, what I'm trying to say is that we could help each other out? How about we work on this… well, work on it jointly?'

'Can we do that?' I asked.

'That was what I considered would be the ideal situation.'

I considered the options. The pain in my shoulder, the shit I'd been wading through, the general state of my life at this moment, helped concentrate the mind and be decisive. I nodded. 'We supposed to shake hands, or summat?'

Sunday solemnly stood and walked across the living room floor and stuck out his hand. 'I think that would be appropriate, yes.'

I stood awkwardly, and shook his hands. 'Righty-ho.' I sniffed. 'Feel like we need summat stronger than just tea and water. You ever injected black-market biofuel into frozen lime juice?'

We'd settled ourselves at the kitchen table. I hadn't used it to eat at since I'd moved in and so it had accumulated broken crawlers, cracked beakers, and leftover felt and material from the project. We shifted the lot to the floor, shouted at the flat to bring more light to this corner, dusted down a couple of chairs. I'd brought a couple of cartons from the freezer, which were defrosting, the crystals forming on the surface glinting under the light.

Opposite me, Sunday took off his jacket and laid out pieces of paper on the surface.

'You're not using your invisible specs?'

He shook his wrist, disturbing a bracelet. 'Of course. But I enjoy working with paper at this stage. It helps me to compose my thoughts more succinctly.'

'Go on, then,' I said. 'What do you have?'

He smiled. 'After you.'

I was about to tell him to fuck off, but I stopped myself before the words came out. I cleared my throat. Then nodded and then cleared my throat again. 'Right, I found a connection in the data you shared with me.' I proceeded to tell him all about the insurance scheme and about visiting Dr Godden. He looked unimpressed.

'There're strong correlations, but it's not enough for a case.'

'I know,' I exclaimed. 'It's summat, though, in't it?'

'It is suggestive of a collective endeavour on health matters, which could include replacement service, I admit.'

'Bits of them came in on your boat!'

'Hulk, please.'

'Whatever.' I took a sip of the half-defrosted drink. It needed a good shake, so gave it one, grinning at Sunday's alarmed features. 'Godden is your next big lead, isn't she?'

'And what do you suggest we do?' asked Sunday. 'You need something more concrete before you march in with a warrant. As you said, it will take time to interview all the members of the group. Plus, what about that security agent on the docks? Corva? She was wholly involved in activities surrounding that shipment. And, as far as I can see, there is no obvious connection between Godden and Corva. Is there?'

I shook my head. 'I've not found anything, no.'

He nodded to himself and looked down at his papers. I let silence fill the room as he took a series of notes. When he'd finished, he looked back up. 'Anything else?'

I hesitated. 'There is something else. But I'm not sure how related it is to the shipment. It's about the death of Simon West.'

'Yes?'

'So, you know we had a suspect who confessed in the H Tower to everything. ThreeDave, we call him.'

'Yes, I remember.'

'Well, I've been given digital access now, and I've been working on the data, and… well, I think I've found evidence that ThreeDave couldn't have murdered West. He weren't around the same place at the same time.'

'But he's confessed?'

'Yeah.'

'I assume this a problem.'

'Yeah,' I said, making a face. 'Confessions are like fucking platinum credit-lines around here – once you've got one, you don't let it go easily. Courts don't like it when a confession-based conviction is challenged. Makes their business look shaky, makes the whole justice chain look shaky.'

'In my country,' said Sunday, primly, 'when we receive a confession, it has to be supported by solid, primary evidence, or the prosecuting team will not take on the work.'

'No shit,' I said. 'Well, in this country, the prosecuting *team* tends to be called Amira or Mandie, and she's fuck-busy most of time, and has to get three or four wrong 'uns behind bars before the end of the day or she can't pay her rent. So, like I said, confessions are proper gold for us.'

He nodded. 'I see.'

'Anyway, I'm not happy about finding this. But I think it's important.'

'I will write it down.'

'Don't be fucking patronising.'

'I don't understand?'

I grunted and took a sip of my drink. 'What've you brought then?'

'Yes.' He grinned. 'It is my turn now.'

'Yeah?'

'Yes. I think I have found out who shot you.'

'Fuck.' He had my attention. 'Who? How? Have you sent in Enforcement?'

'Not so fast,' he said, raising a finger. 'There are complications.'

'Complications?'

'Let me explain from the beginning. Is that OK?' He leaned forward. 'So, after you disappeared to chase that security operative, Corva, I gained access to the Gunnison and Harwick security data files. It took a little persuasion and a lot of diplomatic weight from my team back in Lagos, which I need to repay at some point. I had to withstand a grilling from Gunnison's head of security and another conversation with a member of their board. Anyway, they finally dropped me a link to access their servers. They had a great deal of footage from the night of the arrival of the *Talofa-3*, and afterwards.'

'You've got a vid?' I asked, eagerly. 'You've got the fucker on a file?'

'No,' said Sunday. 'There's nothing.'

'What the–'

'Ahh,' interrupted Sunday, raising a finger. 'What does a proper investigator look for?'

I shrugged. I tried remembering the droning voice of Big Man Vickers. I got nothing. 'Facts?'

'Facts, yes. Or an absence of facts.'

'Eh?'

'I was inspired by how you had found the location of the assets. So I adopted a similar approach. The fact there was nothing of note in relation to the security footage – which is very common nowadays, given the ubiquity of cameras – made me consider things. In fact, I tried to follow this Corva operative throughout her day, and found that there were notable absences from her from the footage. Then I wondered if these replacement parts were to be offloaded and shipped to whatever holding bay they are needed, then there would have to be a clear route from ship to shore, without security footage. I then did something very simple. I took the visual footage and I applied it to a map. Look at this.' He cast an image onto the wall screen. It showed an abstract plan of the docks area, including the various hulks and offices. There were cones of yellow crossing and meeting, which I assumed were the camera views. But, through the middle of these, a dark path was laid out, from one end of the yard to the *Talofa-3*. A path with no visual coverage whatsoever.

'That's how they got in and out?'

'That's right,' said Sunday.

I pointed at the point in the fence where the Gunnison and Harwick yards ended and met up with a public road. 'Would be good to see who's been coming and going here.'

'Indeed,' said Sunday. 'That's what I tried next.'

'How?'

'Finally, I called in some favours. My position allows me to make use of inter-agency assets. Some of these assets include some shared bandwidth on the HighEyes 500.'

'The spy sats?' I hissed through my teeth. 'Fuck!'

'Yes, they are useful.'

'That's some proper shit. That's real Those-Who-Watch-While-You-Sleep level.'

'Hush,' he said, looking around the room. 'Anyway, I got access to that spot in the fence. Looked at those coordinates at one-minute intervals for the previous forty-eight hours. That's all they'd allowed.'

'And?'

'Nothing.'

'Oh.'

'It was around that time that I heard – via Louie, in fact – that you had been shot. He gave me the rough location, and I looked up local news about the fire, made some assumptions, and changed my coordinates. I got the files for that coastal sector, and the timing of when you were shot, and I ran the footage.'

'You can show me?' I asked.

Sunday laughed, long and hard, in my face. 'We may be jointly investigating, Carrie, but you know that I cannot do that.'

'Worth asking. What did you find?'

'Well, we had an agent-node match up between the docks and that sector.'

'Match up?'

'Yes, identified by movement and the like.'

I whistled. 'Shit.'

'Anyway,' said Sunday, 'this agent node displayed anomalous activity, a strange activity profile. An activity profile that stood out from the noise, you understand? Most agent nodes just wander about according to predictable patterns. This one shone out. So I compared it to known profiles. It was activity that matched one of our military profiles, in fact.'

'Oh, yeah? Which profile?'

'Sniper.'

'No shit. You put two-and-two together then, did you?' I was trying to keep my face impassive, but I was massively envious that he had this kind of shit to play around like this. I really, really, really wanted him to display this all on the wall so I could see it with my own eyes. But I had to trust him. It all felt dead weird.

'I did indeed.'

'Where did they shoot me from?'

He read out some coordinates. I plugged them into a map and stared at it on my display. It was down along the waterfront bars east of Corva's flat, near to where I'd spotted the figure under the streetlamp. But there was something about it that seemed wrong. 'Busy place to take a shot at somebody from?'

Sunday blinked. 'It's what the data says. Time and place match up. The application tells me that there is line-of-sight to the balcony.'

'I don't doubt it,' I said. 'But they'd be in among a crowd.

There were plenty of people there, getting pissed and eating churros and shit.'

'What are you saying?'

'It's just that… nah, don't matter, carry on.'

There was a noise from outside on the street, shouting and laughter. Sunday immediately stopped. He went to the windows momentarily and looked out.

'I get noisy neighbours,' I said. 'Carry on.'

He shrugged. 'If you say so.'

'It's not that dead rough round here. Despite appearances. Where did this person go?'

'They returned to this hotel,' he said, returning to the table and casting an image at the wall screen. It looked like it'd been scraped from the RoadEyes service. 'It's not far from the H Tower, which I believe is your HQ?'

'Looks nice,' I said, looking at the hotel entrance. And I meant it. The name was written in such miniscule, obscure font that I was almost unable to read it: C142-H42O-20. 'They need a proper name, mind.'

'You don't recognise it?' said Sunday, surprised.

'What? That place? Never been there before, couldn't afford a place like that. Have you?'

'The name, I meant,' said Sunday. 'That's the molecular code for graphene.'

'Why not fucking call it the Graphene, then?' I said, sighing. I started riffling through my divisional list, trying to track down the hotel's details. I tried both the formula and full name. Found it.

'What are you doing? Can you contact them?'

'Better than that,' I said. 'We can just plug into their external API. We got delegation, so they have to play ball with this. They give us the lot.'

'You get names?' said Sunday, looking a little shocked. 'Customer names?'

'Fuck no,' I said. 'You only get traffic, metadata, that kind of thing. Prior agreement via legislation passed by Durham about ten years ago. You need a proper judge-stamped warrant for names. But it's a good start. Here, look.' I cast an image of the wall. It showed a log of guests, their names anonymised, who'd checked in over the past two days, including those who'd used their passes to gain access to and from the building. I highlighted a row. It matched the timestamp for the bird's-eye image Sunday's friends had provided him with. 'This is the bastard. All we need to do is look through the log for when they've come and gone.' I took a note of the anonymised number and scrolled back up. 'They always use the same unique ID. So we can see when they've arrived and left the building, even when they checked in.'

'That is not the definition of "anonymised",' said Sunday, disapprovingly.

'Who cares?' I said. I kept scrolling up. 'Here, this is the first instance of that ID. They checked in on twenty-ninth January, so that would be about four days before the estimated time of death of Shin.'

'So, we go in and question them, yes?' said Sunday.

'We could,' I said. 'But what if we spook them? Send them packing?'

'What do you mean?'

'They're in a hotel, Sunday. What does that tell you?'

He thought for a moment. 'They're from out of town?'

I noticed, once again, that his eyes had flickered to the window, as though he'd heard something there.

'Yeah, they're either from out of town, or they've got money to burn and want to… I don't know, that's too complicated. Let's assume they're from out of town. If we go in there with warrants and questions, then they could return to wherever they came from and we've lost them.'

Sunday nodded. 'We should monitor the place, at least?'

'I guess,' I said. 'But that needs bodies. And we ain't got bodies.'

'We have you,' said Sunday.

'I'm not doing surveillance. You do surveillance. Plus, I need to talk to ThreeDave.'

'You mentioned him before. That's a real name?' said Sunday, raising his eyebrows.

I looked at him. 'Please. Don't be disrespectful.'

'Of course, I'm sorry.'

'Yeah, it's a real name. There's no way he killed West that night. He's covering for somebody and I need to find that out. He's not going anywhere, so we can safely interview him.'

'Where is he?'

'The Estuary.'

Sunday looked at me and nodded. 'Yes? Where is that?'

'Artificial island in the Humber estuary. It's a prison, love. High secure. Nice place.'

'I don't doubt it.'

'You want to come with me? It'll be after I've done some paid work, mind. Louie's on my back about the other POs, so it'll be later on.'

Sunday smiled. 'I see little interest in this DaveDave character. I would rather identify the individual currently placed in this hotel.'

'Yeah, somebody's got to be watching. That'll be you then.'

Then I realised something. It was something my nose had been trying to tell me for most of the evening. I leaned in close and gave a big sniff of his hair.

He recoiled in horror. 'What on earth are you–'

'Didn't come in a drone taxi, then?' I said.

'What? I mean, pardon? I do not understand.' It was the first time I'd seen him flustered.

'I recognise that smell,' I said. 'That's the smell of a Nefes Type II air-conditioned carriage, after about five years in service, I reckon. I could get out my sniffer if you want me to check.'

'I still have no idea what you are talking about.'

'It's familiar because I was sitting in one of them earlier today. It's used on the carriages of the main East-West line connecting the York end of the Belt to Central.'

He fell silent at this point. I reached across the table and prodded two fingers into his shoulders.

'Hey, that is my personal space, Ms Tarmell and I would like.'

I sat back down. 'Hurts, doesn't it?' I said, smiling. Then I nodded down at his hands. 'As do your fingers. You've never carried your bags that far before, have you?'

'What do you know about my fingers?'

'I'm making a guess, that's all,' I said. 'But I can check.' I rose from the table and went to the window. I looked down to where he'd been standing in the street and called up the gecko to my shoulder. It took a few pictures, and I pulled them up onto the wall screen, zooming in on a specific feature. Tucked into a corner of the alley, just behind a big autobin, was a sheet of polymer, draped over a neat stack of flight bags. All were in the same plain, high-end patterning and quality mock textile finish of his carrier. Sat atop was the winking light of a proximity beacon.

'Worried it might get nicked?' I said to Sunday, pointing at the image on the wall.

'I didn't want to clutter up your home, that's all,' said Sunday.

'No shit.' We stared at each other for what felt like a long time. Until I relented. 'Bring it all inside. But don't let that fucker go off near me, or I'll shove it up your arse.'

I walked back to the table with a massive smile of satisfaction on my face. I wasn't usually this pleased at having done some proper detective shit – and, in all honesty, most of it was luck and guesswork – but there was something about getting one over Federal Inspector Sunday Sule that'd made my night.

'Your expenses account been properly switched off then?' I asked, as he brought the first two bags in. 'You weren't shitting me when you said you'd been frozen out?'

'That is correct,' he muttered.

'How you paying for all of this, then?' I called out to his retreating form.

He only answered when he returned, lugging the last of the

suitcases, and shaking off the rain from his patterned hair. 'I am paying for this out of my personal account.'

There was a long, painful pause. I was building up to it. I'd been wanting to ask him this question all evening. Though, for different reasons than in the hotel room.

'You want to stay here?' I asked. 'I have a spare bed... I mean, I don't know where it is. It's under so much crap, but I have one somewhere.'

Sunday nodded and smiled. 'That would be fantastic. Thank you so much.' He looked at my injured arm. 'And let me sort that out for myself. I think you need to rest your shoulder.'

'Yeah,' I said. He was right, but I still sighed a little inside.

Chapter Twenty-Six

The Estuary wasn't its proper name, of course. Technically, legally, it was called the North Humber High Secure Unit (TS-200). But nobody could turn that into a snappy acronym – at least, one that didn't sound like a sneeze – so we all called it the Estuary instead. It had a history, one you got taught at school, usually part of a geography module, or politics. Then there were the stories you got told by our mates, your elder siblings, about what would happen on the Estuary, about what would happen to you if you ended up there.

So we all knew about the Estuary.

Back when they'd moved all the remaining inhabitants of an annually-flooding Hull back inland and uphill, and called it New Hull – because they were imaginative back then – there was a shitload of mess left behind: semi-submerged buildings, streets rotting away, rusting skeletons of old warehouse units. However, some entrepreneurial types had recycled the remaining buildings and abandoned shipping containers, building their little settlement out into the middle of the river, surrounded on all sides by water. They called it Wyke, or Little Wyke, or New Wyke, and lived a fairly independent existence there for a few decades, until the authorities decided they didn't like the separatist ideology coming out of the place and sent in the troops. Of course, what was left was prime brownfield opportunity. There was space enough to house tens of thousands of people, across multiple buildings and bridges and containers, so it was decided that this could solve a new problem: the rising prison population. A good few additional members had been added to this demographic since they'd stormed Wyke itself. Why not live in the same place? A flashy new algorithm could keep tabs on everybody who came and went, watch for any dangerous conglomeration of the worst categories, monitor patterns that might spell trouble, and send in the heavy weaponry when needed. So, it ran itself. But nobody left.

The outer ring of the prison was water: flooded canals on the north, the river to the south. This was the only way I was going to reach the place. It was a dark, late afternoon, when I was brought into the site, sat in an armoured RIB, with three other visitors (all lawyers) and five security personnel, armed to the teeth. I knew the old DI, Ibrahim Al-Yahmeni, had been here in the past, because he loved to tell us all about it in gory detail, but this was my first time on the Estuary. I was shitting myself, in all honesty. I'd hoped that I would be a figure of disdainful authority, striding in and demanding to see ThreeDave immediately. But this business with the boat and the searching – disturbingly intimate – and the significant calibre on the guns, had all made me a little fearful. It'd been a long time since anybody had actually been murdered in the place. That is, a long time since a visitor had been murdered. The number of bodies which ended up floating out in the tide to the North Sea quite often reached double figures by the end of the month. But that particular grisly fact was so common even the media had stopped reporting on it. More noise amid the darkness, where nobody cared.

'First timers?' shouted the sergeant from the front of the RIB.

The surrounding lawyers shook their heads. I noticed they were wearing the shittest clothes they could find. They looked as though they'd crawled in off the street, having hawked their last remaining shred of dignity in some carnal way for a shot of black pseudo. Guess it didn't pay to turn up to the Estuary in your best gear. I was going to be OK.

'Yeah,' I put my hand up, in the half-hearted way that meant

I knew I had to, but I really didn't want to.

'OK,' said the sergeant. 'You stick with your assigned guard at all times. You don't go for a shit without them being beside you. You'll have two security drones posted to you–' She tapped a metallic crate next to her. '– which will keep eyes on the whole time. One to watch. One for spare. The boat will stay in the dock area the whole time and occasionally make random journeys. You a lawyer?'

'Justice,' I shouted.

The lawyers closest me glanced across. One of them twitched.

'Try not to tell too many people about that,' said the sergeant, grinning. 'But I'm sure you'll be fine.'

I sighed. This was on my own time now, as well. It'd already been a long day, clearing Louie's urgent POs, and I wasn't feeling the energy tonight. Being stuck here in this boat, about to rub shoulders with the kind of folk who like to stick things in between shoulders, well, that wasn't helping things much.

'Happy to say nowt about that,' I shouted back at the sergeant.

The RIB had been approaching the Estuary from a point upriver and was now weaving its way through the ruins of old Hull, along the canals. Most of this could be destroyed by the waves, so was already cleared. Some of the more resilient buildings had been blasted away from the inside, which gave the place the look of a warzone. We came to an open patch of water, an old basin in the dock area, and approached a vast fence, razor-wire coils running along its top and partway up its sides. A small, automated gate had been set into it and the RIB slowed as we approached. The gate swung open, and we passed on through. Ahead of us was the Estuary: dimly lit shapes of shipping containers on steel piles, stacked into the sky, and floodlights scanning the ground, lighting up the fog which had rolled in with the tide.

A small pontoon was set out into the water, where a couple of other RIBs were moored up. It housed a small shack and there were about a dozen other heavily armed guards lounging about under the lights, watching the long gangplank that led up to the structure. This was protected by three more automated gates. As the engines were cut, another noise pierced the night air: the angry buzzing of a hundred security drones moving through their deliberately erratic pattern around the structure. Then, in the distance, I heard the thud of music and the constant hiss of waves washing against brickwork and mortar, grinding it down to sand.

'This is Gregor,' said the sergeant, pointing to a security guard. 'He's assigned to you. He's got level six clearance, so you can say anything you like in front of him, and he's not going to tell anybody about it, even in his sleep. That right, Gregor?'

Gregor, blond and huge and impassive, turned his eyes on the sergeant and nodded, slowly. I hoped I wouldn't have to share a tight space with Gregor. I knew who was going to come off worse in that situation.

The sergeant reeled off a series of other names for the lawyers and people were coupled up and led onto the pontoon dock area. The place stank of seaweed and rust and something else, something you didn't smell as much these days but reminded me of Corva's flat, the undercurrent of hydrocarbons, illegal electrical generation from oil.

Gregor led me up the ramp, following a strict process of stopping and searching, producing ID for various sensors and attaching the odd beacon to my person. Eventually, we were allowed to enter the warren of underpasses and tunnels and into the Estuary. The areas immediately around the basin were relatively quiet. We saw the occasional inmate stood in the shade, having a smoke, or a piss, or just staring out at the fog-bound river. However, as we approached the centre, it got busier. There were a lot of stairs to climb, as Gregor's route must've been designed to keep us out of the more subterranean sections. Above us, the small, expensive security drone – sleek and black, so almost invisible against the sky – made a mosquito buzz. Beyond it, at a higher altitude, larger security drones hovered and weaved.

We came across a large contingent of wrong 'uns as we passed over a square, walking across a long, mesh-encased bridge. They looked up from their game of football, and the jeers and shouts started.

'We ignore them,' said Gregor, keeping his hand gripped to his weapon. 'They know we don't react to words.'

'Right,' I said, trying not to look down. 'Um… and when do we react?'

'If it happens,' said Gregor, 'you'll know. But you need do nothing.' He turned briefly and tapped his pump-action.

As we stepped off the bridge, there was a thump and rattle behind us. I turned to see the football fall back down to the square and bounce, in ever decreasing heights, at the feet of the threatening, cold stares of the players.

'DaveDaveDave, right?' said Gregor. 'That's who we need to find?'

'That's right,' I said, hurriedly bringing my attention back to him.

Gregor checked his cap bead, light flickering into his eyes. 'He's still at the club. We need to move north now.'

We progressed through more open areas and around the sides of stacked residential blocks, keeping to the western side. Occasionally, it was possible to make out the blackened wastes of sunken Hull to our north. Here and there were the fires of a few stubborn inhabitants, trying to survive in areas that escaped the rising waters.

A call icon flashed on my bead. I was about to kill it when I noticed it was from Sunday. I hit the reply button.

'Now's not a good time to call,' I muttered.

Gregor half-turned at the voice, but then turned back and continued on, waving me forward.

Sunday's face appeared on my screen. 'I understand. I was calling to confirm the target has left the hotel.'

'Now?'

'That's right.'

'Shit. You've been waiting there all this time?'

'That is correct.' There was a small suggestion of being deeply pissed-off in Sunday's clipped voice.

'Keep on him,' I said. 'Keep me updated.'

'This is a joint exercise, isn't it?'

'Sorry,' I said, 'gotta go.' I clicked my fingers and ended the call.

'You busy this time of night?' asked Gregor.

'Justice doesn't sleep,' I said.

Gregor nodded. He understood.

The club turned out to be an old warehouse unit, fitted with lights and a thumping sound system. We had to approach it by descending a series of stairs, attached to the outer edge of the entire structure, and running alongside a north-facing, mesh-encased block. We were let through by a couple of heavies on the double doors. Tuvan bass was making the whole building shake. Gregor had kindly passed me some earbuds as I entered the building, which I hastily stuffed into my ears. Clearly, noise reduction standards weren't enforced on the Estuary.

The place wasn't exactly heaving. I guessed it was early in the evening. A few couples were slow-dancing to the music. Mostly people were just sat on chairs around the outer edge. Quite a few wrong 'uns were busy trying to clear up a mess of blood up near the bar. There were some stony glances as we entered, but little surprise. Word of our destination must've been passed around.

ThreeDave was sitting on a large sofa, towards the back of the room, surrounded by a retinue of BoTies. He had a large drink in his hand and was surveying the scene with some appreciation.

'Can we go somewhere quieter to talk?' I shouted.

He smiled and shook his head. 'You don't like the music?'

'I like having eardrums.'

'What?' he shouted, grinning.

Gregor tapped his weapon and raised his eyebrows at ThreeDave.

'Oh, alright,' said ThreeDave, grandly rising from his seat. I'd forgotten what a monstrous size he was, making even Gregor look puny. 'Let's take a walk around the perimeter.'

'He's coming as well,' I shouted, indicating Gregor.

'Yeah, I'd assumed he'd be there,' said ThreeDave, into my ear. He stank of alcohol and vat-grown beef. 'I know how this works.'

So we stepped out of the double doors onto a small dock area and walked along the waterfront, only a few metres from the mesh that descended from the sky into water.

'It's nice that the tide's in,' said ThreeDave, nodding downwards. 'At low tide, that's all mud. And it stinks like crabs and shit.'

'You settled in here, then? Getting to appreciate the views?'

'I have,' intoned ThreeDave. He walked on and I hurried to keep up, matching his strides. Behind us, keeping a few metres' distance, was Gregor.

'Feel you deserve to be here?'

'We're not going to have this discussion, are we?' said ThreeDave, spitting into the muddy waters. 'I can call my lawyer bot back, if you'd like?'

'I'd rather not have this conversation either, but I've got new evidence that means we ought to chat about it.'

'Do I need my lawyer?'

'Up to you.'

ThreeDave grunted. 'What's this new evidence?' He folded his arms. 'Whatever it is, it's not going to change my confession.'

'I only want to get to the truth.'

'Do you Justice types ever get bored with saying that shit? You know truth is a flexible abstraction, right?'

I ploughed on. 'I know you couldn't have killed Simon West.'

'Oh, yeah?' said ThreeDave. Though he was feigning disinterest, I could tell he wanted me to tell him more. Perhaps he wanted to report back to whoever was paying him. 'I've confessed. I'm on the Estuary. It's over. Why're you even talking to me?'

'I've got access to a new set of comms metadata.'

'Fuck is that?'

'Doesn't matter. But it's telling me somebody made two calls from outside the fences of that recycling facility, at about a twenty-minute interval. My guess it was you telling somebody "I'm on my way in" and then again "I'm on my way out". Would I be right?'

He was cautious now, contemplating the news. Eventually, he spoke: 'So what?'

'Did you make those calls?'

'I'm not saying anything more without my lawyer.' He turned to the security guard behind us. 'Take her back now, unless you have a phone I can borrow? I need a lawyer.'

'Those calls were made after Simon West was dead,' I called after him, letting my voice becoming too loud, too shrill. I swore at myself. This wasn't going as I'd wanted it to. I was tired. I was fucking it up.

'You have a right to demand a lawyer,' said Gregor. He turned to me. 'The inmate has requested a lawyer.'

'I can fucking hear him, yeah.'

Gregor's eyes widened a little, but his mouth remained still. 'Abuse of staff can result in criminal charges. Please apologise for your abuse.'

'I'm sorry. I'm really sorry. It just comes out like that sometimes.' I realised I was babbling now. 'I've got a problem with my… Look, I just need a couple more minutes. I just need…'

ThreeDave had already wandered back down the docks area towards the club. I scurried after him, followed closely by Gregor.

'We know you can't have done it, ThreeDave. You need to retract that confession. We can find the actual murderer. You can get out of here.'

'Not interested. Interview is over.'

I felt Gregor's substantial hand grab my arm, stopping me.

'Ah, shit,' I muttered. Then some words from a conversation with Deborah popped back into my head. It was worth a try. 'You love your people, don't you?'

I was nearly sick saying it. But it made him stop. After he'd stopped, he looked at the ground and then turned to face me.

'Of course. What of it?'

I pressed on. 'You'd do anything to help them, to protect them, yeah?'

'They look up to me,' he said.

'That's what you do,' I said, softly.

'Of course.'

'And, because you love your people, you took a bullet for them, didn't you? You've cut a deal with someone.' I shook myself free of Gregor's grip and walked up to ThreeDave.

He took a deep breath and snorted back some phlegm. 'I'm not saying anything more.'

'You've said enough. I feel like I'm a little closer to the truth now.'

'You want to know what's true?' he hissed, spinning towards me and leaning down into my face. 'There're some things too horrible, too terrible, in this world. And I've seen some of them.'

'What have you seen?' I said, lowering my voice. 'Where?'

'It was always closer than you thought,' he said. He shuddered. 'The things I've seen. Horror, pure horror.' The last word was delivered in a whisper.

We stood in silence, surveying the fires of the swamped city, listening to the slop of water beneath our feet and the distant thump of music change tempo as the DJ switched to a new tune.

I was about to ask him what he meant when I got a call through from Sunday again.

'What?' I snapped, stepped away from ThreeDave for a moment.

'He's made his way into the Valleys, by car. I am following.'

'Where's he heading?' I tried to wave at Gregor, to stop ThreeDave from returning to the club. His frown simply deepened.

'Towards that recycling facility. The Fellside, isn't it?'

'Yes. Shit. What's he doing there?' I watched, in vain, as ThreeDave wandered back down the docks, his head hunched into his chest.

'There's something else.'

'Yeah?'

'He's had training, professional training.'

'Eh?' I said, confused.

'The way he is moving, his use of the autocars, stopping and swapping,' said Sunday. 'He is operating to procedures used by agencies such as my own.'

'He's an agent?' I asked.

'Not sure, but he is a professional.'

My heart sank a little. 'So, he knows you're there?'

Sunday's eyes widened on my display. 'I am a little insulted.'

'Don't get precious. I'm just checking.'

'He has arrived at the facility,' said Sunday, more softly.

'Is he going inside?'

'Yes. He appears to have the access codes to… ah, there, he's gone.'

'He's got access codes to the gates?'

'It appears to be so, yes.'

'Fucking amateurs.' They hadn't changed them. 'He must've known Shin. This is our suspect. We need to make sure he doesn't get away. Nobody's working there, are they?'

'No. It's all quiet.'

'Katta will be there in the morning.'

'Who?'

'Katta Jenkins. She's the other key witness. We put her under protection, at least, until ThreeDave was out of the picture. But she's potentially in danger now. We need to get this target neutralised before they arrive in the morning.'

'You want me to go in?'

I laughed in his face. 'What the fuck kind of jurisdiction do you think you have in here? In that place? This isn't international waters, Sunday. This is the Belt. You piss about in there and Aitch Bee will be on your back, pronto. And they don't fuck about diplomacy or nothing.'

'Right,' said Sunday, a little chastened. 'It's just… I have a high level of adrenaline in my system at present. I am possibly making excitable decisions.'

'No shit. Listen, you keep an eye on the gate, see if he makes a move and follow him, if he does.'

'Right.'

Gregor was signalling for me to end the call. 'I gotta go. Speak to you later. Oh... good work, Sunday!'

His eyes lit up for a moment before he disappeared from my screen.

'What's up?' I asked Gregor.

'Threat patterns have been detected,' said the guard. His normally docile face was creased into one of concern. At least, his eyes had narrowed a little.

'Fuck.' I looked around the docks. I could see there were groups of inmates clustering in the corners. Though the music was still thumping in the background, it'd got a lot quieter.

'Follow me,' barked Gregor. He set off, at a half-trot, back along the dock side.

'Where're we going?' I asked.

'Our route in has been compromised,' said Gregor, tilting his head to listen to a voice in his ear. 'There is unexpected patterning along the gangways on the north-west side.'

'Meaning?'

'Meaning we need a different exit point.'

'Oh.' I didn't really have anything else to say. Inmates emerged from the shadows now, edging out into the floodlights around the front doors of the club. Some of them carried homemade weapons.

'Extraction, now!' barked Gregor into his comms, reeling off a complicated code.

'You know what?' I said, edging closer to Gregor and watching the gathering crowds. 'I'm very relaxed about swimming about now.'

'Not advised,' said Gregor. He turned back to his comms. 'ETA?'

'Can't we get the security drones to bring a few of these wrong 'uns down?' I asked.

'Prior data patterns indicate this will trigger a worse–' He was interrupted. 'OK, received.'

'What's going on now?'

'Move closer to edge of the dock,' he said. 'Extraction imminent.'

I could hear the approaching roar of an outboard motor. The crowd could hear it too and some were breaking into a trot, approaching us.

'They're getting quite close now,' I said, a little higher-pitched.

Gregor took my arm and pulled me over the edge of the dock. I screamed – which I wasn't proud about. We fell into the arms of two other guards, stood in a RIB below. The motors were gunned.

Taking a few deep breaths, I got back on my bead and started making urgent calls. I needed to get to Enforcement.

The nasty little algo answered. 'This is Fourth Sector Enforcement offices. There is nobody here at present. Please call emergency handler for an emergency.'

'Enforcement Chief Operative Kal Ghaz, please.'

'Is this an emergency?'

'Just patch me through to Kal.'

'I'm afraid I cannot do that.'

'Fucking machines,' I muttered. 'Get me a human handler.'

'Are you requesting a human handler?'

'Yes.'

'It may take longer to respond to your emergency.'

'Get me a human handler.'

'I'm afraid there is background noise on the call. Are you able to find somewhere quieter?'

'No, not without swimming, I can't.'

'I'm afraid that I cannot respond to that category of abuse.'

'Just get me a human handler.'

The boat accelerated around the base of an ancient, rotting redbrick building and into a canal.

'Hi, how can I help?' said an unfamiliar voice. It sounded like it had its mouth full of biscuit.

'This is forensic analyst Carrie Tarmell, seconded to Central from Airedale. We have an emergency. I need Kal.'

'Carrie Tarmell? Kal Ghaz?' said the now gratifyingly frightened voice. Perhaps my reputation had got around.

'Yeah, fucking Kal Ghaz. Who else would it be?'

'Well, there is a Kal Balil, but he's more of the facilities…' The voice trailed off. 'Yeah, yeah. You don't want that Kal. Let me call the chief.'

'Well done.'

A tired but recognisable voice spoke. 'Yeah? Is that Tarmell?'

'That's right.'

'Where are you? Sounds like you're watching an immersive, or summat?'

'Long story. Basically, I'm in a boat, OK. There's a situation. It's all under control.'

'OK.' Kal laughed. 'What are you after?'

I clung to the side of the boat as it swerved past a steel pile. 'You need to arrest somebody for me.'

'I need to?'

'Yeah. A key witness is about to be placed in danger. So you fucking do.'

Kal sighed. 'You know, you have a most disagreeable tone, Ms Tarmell.'

'Yeah. People tell me that.'

'Perhaps you should've stayed in Airedale?'

'Perhaps, yeah.' We had come out of the cover of the buildings and were in the open basin. A few projectiles landed in the surrounding water. 'The target's at the Fellside Recycling Auxiliary Facility.'

'I know the place. Anything I should know about the target?'

I thought about telling him about Sunday. Then scratched the idea: too complicated.

'Target's been trained in evasion. Possibly overseas.'

Kal laughed. 'Fuck. Do I need the ATVs this time?'

'No, but remember to bring the nastiest shocksticks you can find. This one deserves it.' I rubbed my shoulder.

'If it's overseas,' said Kal, 'this'll need escalation.'

'Escalate the fucker. I don't care. Aitch Bee's a nice place to be, this time of year, even if you're getting shouted at. Better than the Estuary, anyway.'

Our boat reached the outer gate, and it swung open to let us pass through.

CHAPTER TWENTY-SEVEN

'So, I'm involved in an international incident now?' One of Negussie's aides leaned in and whispered in her ear. 'OK, apparently, it's not a formal incident yet. But it's got the...' She looked up at her aide. 'The potential, right?' He nodded.

Unable to stifle a huge yawn. 'I don't know, sorry. You tell me.'

We were in the Servant's offices on the Cliffside. Aitch Bee old town was at the bottom of a confluence of three valleys, surrounded by sharply plunging, forested slopes. Somebody had decided this was the place to put the Great Northern Belt headquarters, so had built a vast, criss-crossing structure of bridges and stacked terraces that covered the valleys below, most of which had become slums of industry or transitory places you passed through in covered subways. The real business was done in the clouds, above the noise and smell of actual work. And the place where the Belt liked to house its Servants was the Cliffside. The outer curve of this beautiful building overlooked the old town below, but also held views to the east, where the Leeds outer ring shone out, a series of huge glass towers, reflecting the morning sun, and to the south-west where the towers and gantries of Manchester hub. Nearby, the rolling hills housed blocks and factories and steam, valleys filled with mist and smoke. From up here, it looked beautiful. It was the only point you really got to see some light.

Negussie was picking her way through some breakfast, a set of freshly baked goods. The Servants probably had a whole fucking patisserie onsite to ensure they were fed well at every hour. It was making my stomach grumble, but I wasn't about to go asking for handouts. Asking for crumbs from a Servant was a DI's job.

'I'm not sure what I can reveal, just yet,' said Negussie, biting down on a small bun.

'Then I'm not sure I can help much.'

Negussie chewed thoughtfully. 'Not only that, but I'm told you've shut down the operation again.'

'Eh? I mean, pardon?'

'Up at the Fellside. That little recycling site, the auxiliary. God knows why we kept that one operational.'

'Oh, yeah. I had to.'

'Why?'

'Fresh evidence,' I said, nodding, and then looking hard at her plate of pastries. Maybe she'd get the hint.

Negussie ignored the hint. She was looking at my shoulder. 'You mean, whoever it was who shot at you?'

'It's related, yeah.'

'Is this about who shot you? Or who killed Simon West?'

'They're related,' I muttered.

'Because,' said Negussie, selecting another mini pastry, 'I thought the Simon West business was all complete.'

'Not really.'

'But you've got the suspect – that DaveDave nightmare, right? He's on the Estuary, right?'

'ThreeDave is locked away, yeah,' I said, nodding. 'Saw him yesterday.'

'On the Estuary?' said Negussie.

'Yeah.'

'Then what the hell is going on?' said Negussie. 'Why is your gunshot wound anything to do with my recycling plant? I've got trucks backing up all the way to the coast by now. Bradford can't cope with the extra demand. I mean, it's not much extra, and they're a big site, but we're coming into winter now. People are getting sick.'

'This is a new threat. A threat to a witness.'

'That's what they told me. That woman at Enforcement, the Chief, Franks, isn't it? Melonie? Lovely name. Terrifying woman.' She took another bite of her *pain au chocolat*, delicately wiping a drip of melted chocolate up with her thumb. 'Guessing Kal will tell us more.'

'When's he getting here?' I wondered if I could ask for some coffee. 'Shortly.'

'OK,' I said, looking out of the window. The light was just beginning to break over the serration of towers to the east. I stood up and walked over to the window. Down below me, just visible in the early morning light, was the twinkle of the old town stone houses, the museum of ancient Yorkshire life, kept immaculate with its brightly dressed automata and fake snow. 'There's just one thing… before this gets too heavy.'

'Yes, what?' said Negussie, distracted by another assistant leaning in to speak in her ear.

'Can I get a coffee?'

'Get her some coffee,' yelled Negussie, to one of her minions standing by the door spitting out some crumbs. I could see she was actually loving being at the centre of something that wasn't about recycling. 'In fact, bring some more in for everybody.'

'Thanks.'

'Where's your boss?' she asked, brushing down her blouse. 'Dale? Daine? I thought he was going to be here as well?'

'He's on his way,' I said. Louie and I'd arrived at the same time, but it'd been a frosty and silent meeting. He detoured via the toilet. I wasn't about to ask why. 'Who else did you call?'

'That Enforcement man… Kal, is it?'

'Yeah,' I said, returning to my chair. 'I know Kal's coming. You said that.'

'And the division also said there was going to be another analyst coming along?'

'Another analyst? From the Fourth Sector team?'

'Yes,' said Negussie. She turned as the door swished open

behind her. 'Ah, are we all here? Oh no, no, it's just your coffee, I'm afraid.'

'Did they say which one?' I asked, standing up to grab the coffee from the minion. 'Ta.' He nodded and returned to his position by the door.

'Hmm?' said Negussie.

'The analyst? Which one? Was it Lem Kawinski? We need a proper digital.'

'No,' said Negussie. 'I can't remember… but it was a woman. Community analyst, I think.'

I frowned. Then I groaned and then, to confirm my worst fears, Deborah Goolagong-Maloney walked in through the door. She was wrapped up well against the cold and carrying a large, insulated mug of something hot.

'Her?' I said, pointing at the newcomer. 'That's the analyst?'

'Good morning to you as well,' said Deborah, giving me a glare.

She was swiftly followed by Louie, who was looking paler than ever, and then by Kal Ghaz, in full tactical uniform. He was followed, in turn, by somebody I'd not met before. She was dressed smartly, not in uniform, though her close-shaved hair matched Kal's in length.

Kal immediately strode up to Negussie and gave her a solid handshake. Louie waved a vague greeting and went to sit over near the window. Deborah pulled up a chair but tried to position it so that she wasn't in my eyeline and was as far away as it was possible to be.

'I'm intrigued to know why I'm here?' said Deborah. Without turning in my direction, she added, 'As I'm sure others will be as well.'

'You were jointly on the case concerning the murder of Simon West and the protection orders for Katta Jenkins,' said Negussie, immediately on the detail. Her ring was already sending flickering signals to her eye. It must've been an expensive one, as was doing its job while also bringing more food into her mouth.

'I'll take one of those,' said Kal, reaching across the table and grabbing a croissant. A drone taxi floated up past the window outside and accelerated off south, descending into the cloud of one of the valleys. 'Are we good to start?'

'Of course,' said Negussie. 'I need to chair an immersive call in about ten minutes, so we need to be quick.'

'OK,' said Kal. 'I'll start in that case. The suspect we apprehended at the recycling facility – on the guidance of Forensic Analyst Carrie Tarmell – is currently in a temporary holding cell in the H Tower.'

'Good work, Enforcement,' said Negussie, her voice on autopilot.

Kal smiled. 'We're professionals.' His smile dropped. 'Despite the cuts.'

'I'll have a word with my fellow Servants,' said Negussie, nodding. 'Don't you worry. Go on. Explain the issue.'

'The issue,' said Kal, 'is why I've asked Izo Laining to join us today.' He waved a hand grandly toward the newcomer. She smiled and nodded at us all in turn. 'Ms Laining is a partner in this month's contracted legal service. It appears we have a potentially-developing international incident on our hands, if we don't resolve things quickly. Durham may get involved, even London.'

'And we don't want that,' said Negussie, crossing her arms, her smile dropping. For the first time, I saw why she'd got to the position she'd got to. I didn't want to mess with Negussie.

'The suspect goes by the name of Chen, Chen Lei,' said Kal. 'He has papers to indicate he is a Chinese citizen, visiting on a work visa. Beyond that, he wouldn't reveal any further details – claiming commercial sensitivity – but he's flown in from Shenzhen.'

'Did he give a date?' I asked.

Kal turned to me. 'No. He didn't.'

'Did you ask him?'

'I don't work for justice.'

'It's just asking for a date.'

'Carrie,' said Louie, warningly.

'I don't know what the issue is,' I said to Louie and then to Kal. 'This man's a suspect. We've got enough evidence to place him at a crime scene. Just because he's from Shenzhen, doesn't make him immune from the Belt's justice system. Does it?'

All eyes in the room turned to me in silence.

The person who spoke first was the lawyer, Izo Laining. 'There are reciprocal arrangements in place regarding the arrest of certain citizens, specifically in business and industry. The authorities in the consulate have already contacted us and alerted us to the relevant clauses.'

'Reciprocal?' I asked, raising an eyebrow. 'Really?'

'They are imbalanced, true,' said Izo, 'but we still have to follow them.'

'What arrangements?' I asked.

'We find primary evidence sufficient to satisfy their hand-picked diplomatic team, or we release the suspect to them and he leaves the country.'

'How long do we have?' asked Louie from the window.

'The diplomatic team are, thankfully, on their way from Shenzhen itself,' said Izo, 'so we have a little more time than normal. I would say approximately forty-eight hours.'

'I mean, do we even wait? Can't we just release him now?' asked Negussie. I saw her checking her watch. She looked at me. 'What evidence do you have at the moment?'

'Footage linking the suspect to the attack on me.'

'Indeed,' said Negussie. 'But, as per my earlier conversation, I still don't see what's that got to do with the West case?'

'They're connected.'

'How?'

All eyes were now on me. I realised that nobody was coming to help me out of this hole now. 'I believe I was attacked because I'm following up on this case.'

'Reasons to believe won't cut it with international law,' said

Negussie, winking at Ivo Laining as she said it.

'Look, we have satellite footage of the suspect…' I stopped. Kal, Louie, and Deborah stared at me. 'I mean, we have footage, evidence, that the suspect travelled from their hotel room to the location from where I was shot – south of the Hartlepool wrecking yards – and shortly afterwards, they also travelled to the Fellside Recycling Auxiliary Facility. That was strong enough in my book to call in Kal and his team.'

Negussie nodded her head slowly. 'Can we see this footage?'

I grunted. 'Not yet.'

'Then I can't do anything,' she said. 'I won't have our Enforcement colleagues facing lawyers with this level of evidence. I mean, I'm not even sure your DI really wants to be here.'

I looked across at Louie. He turned away and looked out the window again. The morning commute of drone taxis was getting busier. Seeing them reminded me of something. Out of sight of the others, below the level of the table, I scrolled through recent contacts and started typing out a message on my knee, tilting my head forward so my nose bead could pick it up. I fired it off and leaned back in my seat. Negussie called one of her assistants forward and started talking to them quietly.

'If we release him now,' I said, interrupting Negussie's discussion, 'then we are potentially increasing risk of harm to a protected witness in the West case.'

'I agree,' said Deborah, for the first time. She nodded slowly. I gave her a small nod. It wasn't gratitude, but it was somewhere in that direction.

'This witness? This is Katta, right? Jenkins?' asked Negussie. She bowed her head and thought for a moment. 'This is how it plays out. Take Katta out of the way. Let this man, this Chen, go. We can't see the footage. He's got to go free. I won't risk our reputation on the say-so of this forensic analyst.' She waved in my direction. 'Send the lawyer's home. All good.'

She stood up from the table. Kal stood also, ready for action.

I could feel myself flushing red. I wouldn't give up this easily. I'd got a message back.

'You can't do that.'

Negussie frowned. 'I can't?'

'This is bigger than you think. It's already an international incident.'

'Not yet, it isn't,' said Negussie.

'If I can request a few seconds of your time. I need to call somebody up.'

'What's she doing?' said Negussie, to Louie.

Louie shook his head, looking at me.

'I'm going to bring in somebody else.' I put in the call. It was answered, and I threw the visuals to the nearest public node.

A wall screen lit up with a flickering image of Sunday Sule. He'd got himself a new suit from somewhere, done up his hair again, and had positioned himself in front of a crisp, white wall. He'd made it look very corporate, with a carefully positioned, ornate frame, just out of shot. There was a faint background noise of voices and laughter. I thought I also recognised a chink of cups and the hiss of a coffee machine.

'This is Federal Inspector Sunday Sule, of the Lagos Inspectorate of Nigeria,' I said. 'He and I are jointly working on this case now.'

There was an audible intake of breath from the room.

'Why didn't you tell me this before?' asked Negussie.

'IG,' I said, shortly.

I could hear Louie snort behind me, but I ignored him.

'You are Servant Negussie, is that correct?' asked Sunday. 'How should one be addressing a Servant of the People in your country? Your honour? Ma'am?'

'Bridget, Bridget is fine,' said Negussie, smiling. 'Federal Inspector Sule.'

'Thank you, Bridget,' said Sunday. 'Please call me Sunday. I am now sending you my credential package via this comms message. I'm sure your team can receive and verify.' He waved a hand grandly towards the screen. He was patched into a local camera, not his normal spectacles. I was still intrigued to know where. As he moved, the camera followed him fractionally. It revealed the contents of the frame momentarily before swinging back to his face. I thought I recognised the Belt Food Hygiene insignia in the top right corner. I immediately started sweating.

'Thank you, Sunday,' said Negussie.

There was a pause as hushed voices near the door to the conference room debated. The assistants nodded their confirmation to Negussie.

'Your credentials have been verified, Sunday,' said Negussie. 'Thank you for giving us some of your time this morning. And, I must say, we're honoured to welcome you to our country and for you to be jointly working on this case.' She turned towards the window. 'Did you know about this collaboration, DI Daine?'

I could feel Louie's eyes boring into the back of my head. There was already a message icon hovering in my peripheral vision in my display, with his initials on top.

'Mr Sule and I had met,' said Louie. 'Indirectly.'

'Why didn't you say?'

'I… to be fair, it wasn't a–'

Sunday interrupted smoothly. 'The Detective Inspector and I agreed that this needed to be outside of public channels.'

'Is that normal?'

'In matters of international crime,' said Sunday, 'we have to adapt our protocols.'

'I'm a politician,' said Negussie, smiling, 'so I recognise that language for what it is. I'd rather the lawyer in the room didn't listen at this point, but I think we can all understand when we need to be flexible.'

'Of course,' said Sunday. He didn't even blink.

'Now,' said Negussie. 'How is it that a dead recycling operative is linked to the Federal Inspectorate of Nigeria?'

'Via the work of Forensic Analyst Carrie Tarmell, who has–'

'Yes, yes,' said Negussie. 'She's explained all that. Are you able to share the evidence? There was mention of footage?'

Sunday smiled. He raised one finger and moved it subtly. The screen changed to satellite view. There was an immediate hush in the room. Sunday talked through the same connections and data points as he'd done with me, linking my attack to the docks.

When he'd finished, he switched the camera back to himself. I thought I could just catch the glimpse of the top of somebody else's head cutting across the view. It looked like they had a chef's hat on.

'I proceeded to surveil the target, to ascertain their movements.'

'Just you?' said Negussie.

'The team,' I said, firmly, cutting across Sunday, as he took a breath.

'Right, great,' said Negussie. 'There's a team.' She nodded, satisfied.

Sunday's eyes had widened a little at my interruption, but he ploughed on anyway. 'So, there was a manual surveillance operation initiated at this location? The operation identified when the target progressed up the valleys, towards the Fellside Recycling Auxiliary Facility and entered the site.'

'It was at this point I called up Kal,' I said, nodding in the Head of Enforcement's direction. I didn't like the look on his face.

'I see,' said Negussie. She placed her hands together and sat back. 'Well, what do you need of us?'

'Ms Tarmell and I just need time,' said Sunday. 'That is all.'

'That's lucky,' said Louie, a little snappily. 'Because that's all we can offer.' He looked at Negussie. 'We don't have any capacity for this, you realise? My team is stretched enough, as it is. We can't take on more...'

Negussie raised a hand from the table to quieten him. She turned back to the screen. 'We can give you time, Sunday. Forty-eight hours, right?' She turned to her side to confirm with Izo.

The lawyer nodded. 'Forty-eight hours.'

'That will be sufficient,' said Sunday.

'Thank you, again, Sunday,' said Negussie, waving at the screen. 'Goodbye.'

'Goodbye,' said Sunday, ending the call.

When the screen went blank, Negussie nodded happily to herself and rose from her seat. Then she cleared her throat. 'Well,' she said, 'I think I can say that I'm considerably more comforted by this news. I'm sure that the forensic analyst seconded to our patch–' Here she turned to look at Louie again, ignoring me. '–knows exactly what she is doing, in her own field, but the addition of a federal agent, international federal agent, gives this work a different weight.'

'It does,' said Louie. I wasn't sure if he'd made it a question.

'Apologies to all,' said Negussie, 'I need to get to my next meeting. A very informative morning. Freddie here will help see you out through security.'

She swept from the room, gathering a couple of her assistants as she did so.

All eyes turned to me. The first to move was Kal. He stood up from his seat, dusting off the crumbs from his uniform, and looked coldly in my direction.

'There were Nigerian feds working the case as well?' he asked. 'Last night, perhaps?'

'Yeah. Had to keep them quiet.'

'But you sent us in anyway?' He was seething. 'You called me direct to get me to send my team in? To engage with a potential threat? When you already had people on the ground?'

'We needed Enforcement,' I said. Then I added. 'We couldn't have done it without you, Kal.'

Kal nodded to himself, then to the rest of the room. 'I've got work to do.' He headed for the door.

'I think you've lost Enforcement,' said Louie, as the door closed. 'But I'm sure your *team* from Lagos can support, where necessary, yes?' He made his way around the large table to the door as well, his hands already twitching up new messages to read.

Izo Laining also stood up at this point and looked at me. 'If you need me, here are my contact details.' A new icon pulsed on my screen. 'The clock is ticking, though.'

'I've got to go too,' said Louie, hand on the door. 'I've got other work this morning. This seems to be all in hand.'

He didn't say goodbye or look back as the door closed behind him.

Deborah also rose from her seat at this point, picking up her insulated cup and pulling on her coat. She walked past my chair, giving my shoulders a little squeeze as she did so.

'Glad you've got a new partner, Cazza,' she said. 'You deserve it.'

Chapter Twenty-Eight

Having Negussie sign off on the work meant I had access to an autocar now. It picked me up from a stacked slipway to the west of Cliffside. Louie and Deborah had both disappeared into the warren of offices and meeting rooms. I wasn't that bothered, to be fair. Though it would've been handy to have Louie to hand to give me access when I needed it, there wasn't much else he could do for me now. Something about Deborah's final comment stung a little, but I wasn't sure why.

As soon as I'd settled down into the seat, I called Sunday up on my bead. By the background noise, he sounded like he was in the same place.

'I am waiting to hear some news,' he said.

'You did well. Got her attention and all.'

'Of course,' said Sunday.

'Now we need to get summat on this fella, fast.'

'Yes. I take it you're interviewing him?'

'That's right. I'm on my way to the Tower now.'

'You want me to join?' asked Sunday. He sounded as though he would really like that. Guess he didn't like the Valleys much. Then again, who does?

'Don't think we've got time for that. We got delegation to check out his room. How about you get across to the Graphene and see what he's hiding in there?'

'Yes,' said Sunday. He hesitated. 'There's just the matter of how…'

'Eh?'

'I'm running a little low on personal funds now.'

'I'll send for a car. Keep me updated.'

There were no more messages from Sunday after I'd fired across some credit. I parked a few POs. Didn't have time for that. Didn't have time for much, as the autocar got down to the Tower in quick time. On the way up from the carport, I stopped off and grabbed a coffee and two slices of Singapore toast from the little man that wandered the ground floor with his trolley. I didn't bother with the egg. Nobody wants an egg in an interview room.

Kal had already arranged for the suspect to be brought up to the interrogation area, so I found my way there, presented my face and voice to the room's control unit, and barged my way in, using my good shoulder. Still fucking hurt, mind, and I couldn't help but swear. After the bustle of the Tower at the start of a new day, it was almost pleasant to be in this dimly lit space. It was a different room to the one I'd interviewed ThreeDave in, but the layout was the same. Multiple cameras. Secure chair for him, a couple of plastic chairs for us. Except it was just me. Again. And this one wasn't as intimidating as ThreeDave.

'Good morning,' the suspect said, pleasantly, as I let the door click behind me.

'Hiya,' I said.

The man kept staring at the door, as though expecting more to come through. 'Are we starting?' he said. He looked relaxed, being in the secure bindings in the chair, like he was used to them. Though he wasn't tall, or overly muscled, he looked like he could handle himself if he was cornered.

'What's your name?' I asked, as I slipped into the chair opposite him and plonked my toast on the table in front of me.

'Chen Lei. But you would know that already.' He stared at the toast, a frown on his face.

'Yeah,' I said, pulling up additional information on my bead. I licked the coconut jam off my fingers in order to click them better.

'Before we proceed,' said Chen, still staring at the toast, 'I would like a lawyer to help parse the conversation.'

'A real one?' I said, with a sinking feeling. 'They're on their way, I was told.'

'Not the government lawyers,' said Chen, smiling apologetically, 'though it is helpful to realise that they are coming.'

I grunted. 'You want a generic?'

'No,' said Chen. 'I have no need for a local stand-in. I have virtual cover. It's a service provided by my company. I'm sorry, but do you require a plate?'

I sighed, shook my head, and then yelled out. 'Interview room thirty-five.'

'Yo,' said the room. 'How can I help?'

'We need a legalbot in here.'

'Of course,' said the voice. 'Which service please?'

Chen then reeled a brief list of service names and usernames and presented his face and his eyes to various cameras until we had another voice in the room. This one sounded male and metallic and a little American. And, if it was possible, it'd been programmed to sound remarkably tired. It made me yawn just to listen to it. I took a moment to gobble down the first of my Singapore slices.

'Please, may I know your name?' it said.

'Who, me?' I asked through crumbs.

'Yes, the name of the interviewer.'

'Forensic Analyst Carrie Tarmell. What's your name? Do I call you Bot?'

'You can call me Ali,' said the device. 'Have you asked my client any questions, Ms Tarmell?'

'His name.'

'Fine,' said the lawyer. 'Anything else?'

I raised my eyebrows at Chen, my mouth now full again.

He helped me out. 'She asked me if I wanted a generic legal protection.'

'Fine.'

'Am I good to start?'

'OK with me,' said the legalbot.

'Then I am also content,' said Chen.

I checked my messages. There was nothing through from Sunday just yet. So I carried on to see what I could find. I thought I'd go in hard with the first one: 'Where's the weapon, Mr Chen?'

'I don't understand,' said Chen.

'Please be more specific, Ms Tarmell,' said the bot.

I pointed to my injured shoulder. 'We have the evidence to prove that you shot me.' I gave him the date and time. 'We have satellite evidence placing you at the location. So, what I'm asking is where have you stashed the weapon?'

Chen seemed interested in my shoulder, leaning forward. 'I carry no weapon,' he said. 'That would be illegal.'

'Which company do you work for?' I asked.

'Jinku Group,' said Chen, without hesitation. 'But you know that already, as well.'

'What sector is that?' I asked, while simultaneously plugging that information into my bead. I didn't know that information, or if I had, it wasn't recorded anywhere. Enforcement not doing their notes again. Wouldn't surprise me. They never liked a form.

'Security,' said Chen. 'We're in corporate security.'

'Sub-contracted?'

'Of course.'

'Who owns your contract for this job?'

Chen waited, as if expecting the legalbot to intervene. 'Do I need to answer?' There was a silence. 'Ali?'

'Signatories to contractual vehicles are not considered protected metadata,' said the bot. 'Meaning, you have to answer.'

Chen seemed slightly peeved at his virtual assistant and huffed for a moment. 'Perhaps I need to procure a new legal service?'

I stepped in. 'I think I can answer for you. FFRC BioTechnology, right?'

There was still no rebuttal from the bot, so he had to nod. 'Yes, that's correct.'

'And you were at the Hartlepool Wreckers yard on the same night, yes?'

'There's no harm being somewhere.'

'What were you doing there?'

'Observing,' said Mr Chen.

'Observing what?'

'Carrying out observation duties on behalf of my client,' said Mr Chen.

'What were you fucking observing?'

'First obscenity noted,' said the bot. 'That's your first strike.'

'How many do I get?'

'Three.'

'Then what?'

'We can raise a complaint,' said the bot. 'This interview room complies with the Green Standard on language and behaviour.'

I laughed. 'You got a lot to learn, Ali.'

'Are we done?' asked Mr Chen.

'No,' I yelled. 'We are not done. On the night of the twenty-sixth, I was in the Gunnison and Harwick Wreckers yards. You were at the same location, same time. I travelled south to investigate a suspect's accommodation, placed…' I took a pause to look up and then read up the coordinates. 'You were there as well, same place, same time. Next thing that happens, somebody shoots me. I was shot from the direction of the beachfront entertainment district. That's where we've placed you as well.' I fell silent for a moment. There was that niggle again. Some instinct telling me things weren't right.

'I was in both places,' said Chen. 'But I have no weapon. Tell me, what were you doing in that apartment?'

'I'm asking the questions.'

'Perhaps we can come to an arrangement?' said Chen.

I raised a finger to stop him. Sunday was calling me.

'Yeah?' I said, rising from my seat and grabbing my coat and my coffee.

'Is the interview complete?' asked the legalbot.

'Paused. Timeout, whatever the fuck you want to call it.'

'That's a second strike,' said the bot.

'That was directed at you.' I slammed the door behind me and strode down the corridor to the viewing booth. I didn't need to watch Mr Chen strapped to a chair, but wanted to be somewhere quiet.

'What've you found?' I said, closing the booth door behind me. On the wall screen before me was a huge image of Chen's face, surrounded by data, name and time. It even had the name of the lawyer's service he'd called up. Mic in there was so keen I could hear him breathing.

'Nothing much,' said Sunday.

My heart sank a little. 'I was hoping to hear you say you'd found a Chinese polymer light rifle, with his fingerprints all over it and a bit of ammo we could plug into Bladester.'

'No weapon,' said Sunday.

'Any clue what he's here for?'

'Not really.'

'Well, what did you find?'

'There's a comms unit, pretty basic. Designed for encryption. Don't think we'll get much off that. Nothing like a proper bead, though.'

'Makes sense,' I said. He would travel anonymously. Enforcement hadn't picked up anything on him when they'd found him. He was paying with anonymous credit chips. Nothing we could hack.

'Something old school, though,' said Sunday.

'Oh, yeah?'

'Ticket. In his bin. He's been to Manchester.'

'Paper? A paper ticket?'

'Well,' said Sunday, 'it looks like cardboard to me. Your country loves vintage, doesn't it? Or perhaps he wanted to be off-grid?'

A thought occurred to me. 'Sweep his clothes. Clothes that he's used.'

'Why?' said Sunday.

'You got a sniffer?'

'Of course,' said Sunday. 'But why?'

'I want to see where he's been?' I started at Chen's taciturn face. 'I think I can guess, though.'

There was a moment's pause. I downed the rest of my coffee. 'Well?'

'Sending you the data now.'

I plugged the package into the locational databases. It had a strong match almost immediately: post-industrial smog of the upper levels of the Manchester circle.

I crashed back out of the door and down the corridor to the interview room.

'You've been to see Ratna Manish, right?' I asked.

'Has the interview recommenced?' asked the legalbot.

'Yes, we've got evidence of you in Manchester, upper levels. That's where Ratna Manish keeps his offices, right?'

Chen didn't answer. 'Should I know this?'

I tried something different. 'If I called up Ratna Manish now, would he confirm that you've been to see him?'

Chen took a breath. 'Yes, he would.'

'Why'd you see Manish?'

'He was a previous customer of my client.'

'Previous?' I asked.

'That's right. They lost him.'

I sniffed. 'That's a big old journey to take to speak to one lost customer, in't it?'

'My client doesn't like losing customers.'

'Customers?' I asked, stressing the final sibilant.

Chen fell silent again. His passive face was now creased up. If you caught him at the right angle, in shadow, and timed it right, it was possible that he looked worried.

'So, how many've you seen?' I asked. As this got little response, I tried another tack. 'How about I drag up a list of names and see if we can place you in their vicinity?'

'You could try that,' said Chen.

'How about you answer the question now?'

'I've got time,' he said.

'How about I drop a message to FFRC and ask them why their man's over here and checking up on a load of citizens across the Great Northern Belt?'

Chen shook his head. 'They would ignore you.'

'How many have you seen?' I asked.

'Is this a question I need to answer?' said Chen, to the room.

'I think he's talking to you, Ali.'

'The questions pose no issue.'

'You are a piece of junk,' shouted Chen, wrenching his wrists in their constraints.

'Don't blame the app,' I said, pleasantly. 'It doesn't know the full picture. Not like me. FFRC have been operating an illegal business in this country for a while now. So I can see why'd you not want to talk about customers too much.'

'Can't you stop her asking these questions?' said Chen, furious.

Things were coming together in my head now. 'You're here because FFRC has lost a customer? Possibly lost many customers?'

'I didn't say many.'

'I'm gonna assume.'

'That should be formally noted,' said the bot.

'Yeah, you note that, buddy. So, why would FFRC lose a load of customers?'

'Is that what I'm being accused of?' asked Chen.

'You're accused of this,' I said, slapping my shoulder. This made me bend over in pain, hissing through my teeth. But it also made me realise something: I hadn't implemented a full model in Bladester yet. My own bloody injury and I'd not analysed it. The niggle in my mind came through again.

'We're not covering that again, are we?'

I raised my finger, deep in thought, then grabbed my coat

again and headed for the door.

'Seriously,' said Chen, 'how much longer is this going to take?'

As I walked down the corridor, I called up Sunday.

'Hello,' he said. 'Have you obtained a confession?'

'Was that a joke?'

'I don't know how things operate in the Belt.'

'Your satellite footage. Can you convert it to a coordinate array?'

'Of what?'

'Chen's movements?'

'Of course,' said Sunday. 'It's a simple export.'

'Thanks. You on your way back?'

While talking, I'd already dug out the gecko's footage of the moment I'd been shot. It was quick work to get a still of the precise moment the bullet hit. I tried not to look at my idiot face in the footage. You're never at your best when receiving a small-calibre round to the shoulder. The grimace wasn't dissimilar to a family photo taken by my mother of when Grace jumped out at as a surprise for my fifteenth birthday. Bitch.

I added the still image to Bladester's input folder, and I ran the usual processes to implement a full model. It would tell me where, when and how I'd been shot. It churned out a coordinate and a time.

'You done?' I asked Sunday.

'On its way.'

I saw the semi-translucent icon appear on my bead's display. I watched the progress counter click through its points on the clock.

'Where you now?'

'On my way back., Passing through Leeds.'

'Pretty, isn't it?'

'I'm in a tunnel.'

'That's what I meant.'

The icon pinged and pulsed. Transfer complete. I opened it and linked the data to Bladester, which compared the two files automatically, but it was just as easy to eyeball it. I scanned down the list of coordinates and timestamps. I found the right timestamp. Checked it against the coordinates from Bladester.

'Fuck!'

There was a long silence. Then Sunday spoke: 'I surmise that you were not shot by Mr Chen?'

'You'd surmise right.'

'Ah.'

I continued to swear for a few minutes. Sunday let me continue without interruption. Maybe he'd turned off the audio for a bit. When I'd finished, I took a deep breath.

'You still there?' I asked.

'Yes.'

'Sorry about that.'

'Shall I come back to the Tower?' asked Sunday.

I didn't answer. I didn't have any answer. 'I don't know.'

'What did you learn so far?'

'FFRC were losing customers. Or, at least, lost one customer.'

'So they send a professional agent?' asked Sunday.

'Perhaps they have an aggressive marketing strategy?'

'They do,' said Sunday. 'Very.'

'Oh.'

'They wouldn't send somebody like Chen unless there was a significant loss in their income. I'm guessing that there must have been more than one customer. Also, they had a shipment to worry about.'

'But why send a boatload of body parts?' I asked. 'That's a lot of expense if you've got no customers at the end.'

'Exactly.'

'How long was that boat on the sea?'

'About five months, in total.'

'Shit.

'They must have had somebody at this end who managed it for them?'

'Corva?'

'Possibly?'

'Somebody who used to take trips up to Hartlepool?'

'Shit!' I slapped the wall. It made my shoulder hurt again. 'Mr Shin!'

'Shin took trips up to the coast?'

'That's what Simon and Katta told me.'

'He stopped working for FFRC?' said Sunday, slowly. 'Do you think that's what happened?'

'Could be. Maybe he wanted out?'

'And that's why they had him killed?' said Sunday. 'But what about Corva? Surely she was their contact on the ground?'

'What if she wasn't? What if she was there to deal with a specific problem? The problem of a long-delayed shipment from FFRC. Something they had to cover up. That's why she had the petrol.'

'The what?' said Sunday.

'The fuel I found in the flat. That was intended for the *Talofa-3*, I'm guessing. Corva was going to head back in the middle of the night and torch the place. Make it look like a natural accident. It's an old wreck. Nobody's going to worry about a little fire like that.'

'Who was she working for?'

'No idea. Gunnison and Harwick. Before that, she was a vat monkey, working up in the dales.'

'A vat monkey?' said Sunday, his face now alert. 'You mean the meat business?'

I frowned and then laughed. 'You don't mean… I mean, they're completely different…'

'Who was her previous employer?'

'I can't remember. Let me see.' I scanned my project files. Then I found the details. 'Pinho. Some operation under the name of Pinho Holdings. They've got some old sheds down in the Valleys.'

'Well, I believe it's worth investigating that connection. Meat is meat..'

'What about Chen?'

'What do you mean?' said Sunday.

'I mean, what do we do with him now? We can't keep him. We've got nothing on him at all now. What else have you got?'

'Just what I've scanned or found.'

'Everything?'

'I've sent you all the files,' said Sunday. 'There's no significant DNA or odour trail, as far as I could see.'

'Odour trail,' I muttered to myself.

'Yes,' said Sunday.

I hit my forehead with my palm. 'You twat.'

'Pardon?' said Sunday.

I was already out of the door of the booth, almost tripping over a cleaning bot as I went.

'Abu Dhabi!' I yelled, at Sunday or possibly nobody in particular, and ran down the corridor, digging into my pocket until I found the sniffer.

'Hello again,' said Chen, as I crashed into the room.

'Recommence interview?' asked the bot.

'Evidence collection,' I said, scanning the sniffer over Chen's clothes and hair.

'What are you doing?' said Chen.

'Yes, what are you doing?' asked Sunday, via my bead.

The sniffer did its scan and automatically dropped its output into my bead. There was a pause before the results. I wasn't breathing. Both DidNotArrive and Bladester gave me their results at the same time.

I grunted. Confirmed.

'What were you expecting?' said Sunday.

'I don't know.' I dropped the sniffer back in my pocket. 'But there's definitely no *BreathlessWhisper*.' I raised my head and raised my voice. 'Room! Room thirty-five.'

'Yo,' said the room.

'Arrange for Mr Chen to return to his secure area.'

'Confirmed,' said the room.

'Is the interview concluded?' said the bot.

'Yeah, yeah, it's over,' I said, pulling on my coat. I ignored Chen's smirk. Then I remembered something. 'No, it's not over. Room, cancel that last order. Ali, we're recommencing the interview.'

'Do you need to keep some notes?' asked Chen, smiling. 'Perhaps a checklist?'

'It's all in here,' I said, tapping my head.

'That's what I was worried about.'

I laughed. I didn't care what this shit thought about me. He may've been correct that I was a mess, but this was all going to come together. I knew it. It always came together. I just needed to trust my nose. Like I trusted that there had been somebody at the end of that call that night.

'What do you know about a Mr Shin?'

Chen's smile dropped. 'There are many Mr Shins.'

'I'm interested in one who used to live here in the Buckle, here in the Fourth Sector.'

'Moved away, did he?' asked Chen.

'Who's interview is this?'

'It was only a question. You said he used to live here?'

'Perhaps he has moved away? Perhaps you know where? It looks like you know about a Mr Shin.'

'My client confirmed neither,' said the legalbot. 'Please do not put words in his mouth.'

'Do you know about a Mr Shin, who used to live here, in the Fourth Sector of the Great Northern Belt?' I asked again. On my screen, Sunday was watching.

'You don't have a full name?' said Chen. 'If not, well, it's not much to go on for me, is it?'

I kicked my chair away from the table. It clattered into a

distant wall. I was too tired for this shit. 'Were you sent here by FFRC to make contact with a Mr Shin?'

'Please do not attempt to intimate my client with threats of violence,' said the bot.

'You can fuck off!' I shouted at the speakers in the corners of the room.

'That's three strikes,' said the legalbot. 'Interview is over.'

'Carrie,' whispered Sunday. 'Take a breath.'

I took a breath. 'A piece of maladjusted code does not get to dictate whether or not an interview is over. Pennine law does not recognise your ridiculous objections.'

Chen looked up at the silent speakers.

'Looks like I've bust your lawyer,' I said, rubbing my sore hand under the table.

'I've answered your questions,' said Chen.

'What if I went to FFRC direct? Asked them about Mr Shin? What if I told them you blabbed all about Mr Shin, that you told me all about his little operation?'

'They would deny it,' said Chen.

'I believe that,' I said. 'I also note that you haven't said it weren't true.'

Chen kept his mouth closed.

'I also believe that your contract wouldn't be renewed. That they wouldn't need to follow up on the truth, because you'd be out on your ear. Just because I'd mentioned the name Shin.' My voice fell. 'Out on your ear, Mr Chen. Possibly worse.'

'Supposition,' said Chen.

'That's a long word, buddy,' I said, grinning. 'I don't really know what it means. But what I think it means is "I'm scared and I'll help this justice analyst if she doesn't talk to my client about too much of this".'

'Ali,' said Chen, looking up again.

'You were supposed to make contact with Shin, weren't you?'

Chen looked down at me. He was sweating now. There was

a long pause, then he slowly nodded. 'That's correct. He was an employee of my client.'

'So you know his full name?'

'Mr Shin. Denpo Shin.'

'That's not a Korean name, is it? I'd always thought…'

'Not Korean, no,' said Chen. 'He grew up in Dhaka. But he'd come across the border as a child.'

'I see. You didn't find him, did you? At the recycling facility.'

'No. There were only a couple of younger employees. That's all I could see.'

'You didn't pop in and say hello?' I sneered.

He ignored me. He looked worried, though. 'You know where he is?'

My sneer fell away. 'He's dead. Mr Shin is dead.'

Chen's eyes widened. 'Dead?'

'Yeah. But you knew that already, didn't you? What do you want to say about it?'

Chen shuffled in his seat. 'Nothing.'

'Nothing?'

'When did he die?' asked Chen.

'You knew he was dead and you know when he died. Because, not only did you kill him yourself, but went to his colleagues and put the frighteners on them.'

'I've not had contact with anybody from the–'

'Then you went and murdered one of them and all.'

'Ali,' shouted Chen into the air.

'It's not coming back. Doesn't matter. We're done here.'

I swept out, ignoring Chen, and pulled on my coat. 'Sunday, when you get here, meet me downstairs.' I was trying not to cry. 'Shin was real. Not made up. Katta Jenkins was telling lies. Somebody got to her.'

'We're going to talk to her?' asked Sunday.

'S right.'

'What about this Pinho gentleman? The Corva link?'

'Later. Jenkins, first.'

'Right. Goodbye.'

'Ta ra.'

When I got near the lifts, I could see Deborah striding down the corridor towards me. This was the last thing I needed right now.

'Yeah? Can I help?'

'I've been looking all over the building for you,' said Deborah. She sounded out of breath and her eyes, though worried, were excited.

'Yeah?'

'You been blocking calls?'

'Been in an interview, in't it?' I nodded my head at the door behind me, avoiding her eye.

'Any luck?'

I shook my head, trying not to give too much away. 'What's the problem?'

'You haven't heard?' said Deborah.

'Hear what?' I snapped.

'No need for that attitude, Carrie,' said Deborah. Her eyes creased up a little at the corner.

'I've not much time, Debs. What is it?'

'I just got a call from the recycling division.'

'And?'

Deborah's face was grim. 'Katta Jenkins didn't turn up for work today.'

'Eh?'

'Like I said, she didn't turn up.'

'She's sick?'

'They thought of that. Tried to contact her. No answer.'

'Anybody been round her place?'

'Not yet, they said,' asked Deborah. Then she added. 'Do you want me to go with you?' She looked closely at my face. 'Are you crying, Carrie?

'No,' I said, immediately. 'And no! I'll check it out myself.'

'I'm always here if you want to talk. About anything.'

'No.'

'OK.'

I continued on my way, leaving her stranded in the middle of the corridor. As I walked, a metallic voice rang out on my bead. 'Yo! Forensic Analyst Carrie Tarmell, this is room thirty-five. Suspect left unattended.'

'Ah, shit. Forgot about him.'

'You wish to continue the interview?'

'No, send him back to his cell.'

CHAPTER TWENTY-NINE

The door opened on my command. Even Sunday looked impressed.

'Hello?' I yelled, stepping back in case something nasty emerged. Like a bullet.

There was no answer.

'Do we go in?' asked Sunday.

'You tell me,' I said, tilting my head, trying to listen for movement inside. 'Aren't these raids kinda your thing?'

'Normally,' said Sunday, grimacing from the other side of the door, 'we would have an armed tactical team, remote support and eyes-on from above.'

'Sounds right nice. Today you've got me.'

I was waiting for him to say something like: 'that's much more effective' or 'I wouldn't switch you out for a tactical team, Carrie Tarmell.' But he said nothing.

I slung the gecko onto the floor and pulled up my bead. Although I would've been sorry to see the little machine, get its head blown off by a crude, hard-polymer home build, it was more preferable than me getting it in the face.

'Anything?' asked Sunday.

'Nowt,' I said and stepped around the door and into the flat.

The place looked immaculate except for a pile of coats spilling out from a cupboard in one corner. I followed the gecko's progress through the flat, seeing the same picture: somebody had hastily grabbed some things and scarpered.

Like Simon West's place, this one was dead nice as well, though different, with views east across the skyline of the

Fax Central, the gleaming spires and towers of Bradford to the north-east and, further off, the vague silhouette of Leeds. People paid good money for views like this, to be up and away from the stink of the Valleys.

'She's gone,' said Sunday, coming back from the bathroom.

'No shit,' I said, still staring at the view.

'Do you know where your Enforcement colleagues sent her before?'

'Eh?'

'She was under protection, wasn't she?'

'Yeah,' I said, turning back. 'No idea where. But I'm guessing she'd not go back to the same place.'

'Do you think we could call them, anyway?'

I remembered Kal Ghaz's face back in Aitch Bee. And the response I'd got when I'd tried calling from the Tower. 'Nah. Wouldn't bother.'

'We're on our own?'

'That's how I like it,' I said, sitting at one of the dining room chairs. I pulled out my handheld sniffer and scanned the seat beside me. Although the reading was very faint – not enough to warrant evidence in court – there was an indication of *BreathlessWhisper*. I'd been expecting it. I dropped the note into my project file with a silent sigh.

'She could be halfway to Scotland by now,' said Sunday.

I nodded. The gecko scampered across the ceiling above our heads, its hi-def camera clicking away and the blinding light catching me in the eye.

'I think we should concentrate on the Pinho holdings lead,' said Sunday.

'And leave Jenkins to fend for herself?' I asked.

'I don't like it,' said Sunday. 'But she has brought this upon herself.'

I remembered the grey face of Simon West as he was pulled in from the reservoir. I didn't want to have to do that a second time. Words kept swirling around in my head. It wasn't my fault. It wasn't my fault.

'Pinho's head office isn't far from here, just on the west side of Bradford. We could be up there in a few minutes and—'

'I'm not leaving her. You go.'

The data from the gecko was streaming into my bead and the little machine pulled itself up my coat sleeve and settled into a fold of my coat, tucking into my neck.

'You sure?' asked Sunday.

'Go, I'll be fine.' I dropped the data into Bladester and created a new project. My brain was fried enough without having to think about this too much. I let the app do its thing. I'd been up too early for any normal day. Any more coffee and I'd be getting the jitters. I needed to get some proper sleep.

'You're going to try to find her? You don't have access to any support.'

'I have some digital files now. Go.'

Sunday gave a quick nod and left.

Bladester ran some scenarios of the situation in the flat, based on the evidence it'd gathered so far, position of clothes, open drawers and the like. Fuck knows who'd fed its algorithm, but some of the low-grade assumptions were proper nuts, all the way from lost keys and through to forced abduction. I moved up to the more believable scenarios. There was one that told me the inhabitant of the flat looked like they had packed quickly and fled. I selected this and ran the second layer of assumption. The gecko had identified fibres, stains and carpet creases and other miniscule detail, all sufficient to pull together a picture. The app churned out its little vid, plastering Katta's face over an artificially-generated body, moving from room to room, showing me the sequence of actions, what she took, where, and when she left. It was always weird to watch this kind of made-up crap play out. Not as weird as watching your face – or a friend's face – pasted into RandoPorno, but there was something spooky about the whole thing.

I noted the details. She was carrying a wheeled, black case, wearing a black coat and blue scarf and seemed to have taken a felt hat that was either brown or a muddy red. Time to bring in Modlee. I started wandering the room, hands weaving in the air. It was quick work to drop in the parameters and I bashed the search icon. Publicly-available data, and the next level of Justice data, were hit, and the timer churned and I waited. They kicked out footage of a woman, wearing the black coat, the blue scarf, the red hat. She'd entered an old building, unlit, some windows knocked out. Looked like it was somewhere in the Valleys. I checked the location of the camera. It was an old municipal one left in the subterranean levels before they'd built over with this section of the Belt. It was about five kilometres from here. Walkable.

I moved to the window again and looked out, trying to peer around the corner of the block. The direction she'd gone in was north-west, so I couldn't really see it from here. As I leaned over, the gecko on my shoulder adjusted its grip for the journey. It was still feeding in data, a stream of conceptual assumptions spilling across my bead's display. Two words popped up that were unexpected. They were coloured red. Their locational proximity had triggered a hazard warning.

Gun barrel.

Scope.

I turned and fell away from the window, hitting the floor hard. I landed on my injured shoulder and sent the gecko rolling into a corner. Swearing loudly, I heaved myself up, keeping my head low relative to the window.

'Piece of shit.'

I fully expected the window behind me to shatter into pieces. But it remained intact. As I waited, recovering my breathing, the gecko scampered back onto my shoulder. I dug down into the temporary store of visual data feed and got it to highlight where it had identified the objects. The gecko's files showed a black clad figure, placed between a fire escape access and heating ducts on a building opposite. The form blended well into the shadow of the pipes, so it was almost impossible to see with a human eye. Although I zoomed in sufficiently, it was difficult to make out any features. I sent the gecko back up to the windowsill to take more pictures. But the figure had gone.

I dialled up Sunday.

'What is it?'

'They're back.'

'Who?'

I crawled back into the hallway of the flat. 'Whoever's trying to kill me.'

'What?'

I gave him a quick summary of the situation. I wasn't sure how I was going to get out of here now.

'Where's Katta?' asked Sunday.

'Somewhere near here. Gone to an old warehouse, looks like. I was just about to grab an elevator down and find her.'

'How soon can you reach her?'

'About twenty minutes. But it's slow progress down there. The Valleys, right? You have to be careful. They're dead rough… I mean, most places are rough, but they're summat else.'

'You want me to come back?'

'Where are you?'

Sunday didn't answer for a minute. 'I don't know. But the next stop isn't for about fifteen minutes.'

'Shit.'

'You've got it covered,' said Sunday, grinning. 'I trust you, Carrie Tarmell.'

I didn't believe him, but I grunted, anyway. Memories of hazy calls in the night came back to me. 'Yeah.'

'If you want,' said Sunday, 'I can get off at the next stop and start to head back to meet you there. We can talk to this Pinho gentleman any time, right?'

I ground my teeth. This was painful to say, but I said it anyway. 'Yeah. Do that. But be careful, OK? They had a fucking scope and all on that thing.'

No frigging way I was going to sit things out until he got here. I gathered my coat and satchel and made for the door, dragging up the gecko's camera on my bead display and dialling up the hazard signals to max.

'You might have to take one for the team, fella,' I muttered and opened the door. 'Off you trot.'

The machine dutifully scurried around the doorjamb and climbed its way to the ceiling. It set off towards the lifts, and I watched it for a few seconds as it made neat semicircles around the light fittings suspended from the ceiling. Once it had reached the corner and, having confirmed no other movement in the further corridor, I set off after it. I turned the corner, trotted down past three other apartments, and finally reached the lifts.

I dialled a justice autocar to meet me at the door of the block. Looked like the allocation algo was going to give me grief about time and expense so I punched in the analyst delegate amber escalation, telling it there were lives in immediate risk. This was guaranteed to get a ride fast. It was also guaranteed to get some creep like Clive knocking on your door at night, demanding to see some evidence. However, I was past caring about that now. I told it to meet me at the front door in five minutes.

The lift arrived fast, with an antique ping, and scared the shit of out me. I'd already clocked that it'd come from two floors below so I wasn't too bothered to hide, but the sight and sound of the doors crashing back into their casings made be burst into a small sweat.

'Bastard.'

The gecko swung into the lift and pressed the hold button with its nose. I called the other lift, currently a few floors above. This one, unfortunately, contained a friendly man with a big basket of assorted exotic fruit.

'Hiya,' I said, hoping my perennial scowl would stop any chat.

I was wrong.

'Well, hello. How are you today, young lady?'

'Pretty shit,' I said, clocking the old-fashioned buttons beside the door. Ground wasn't highlighted. Looked this joker was going to the third. 'Not going to ground?' I asked, just to make sure.

'Not me,' he said, patting the basket. 'I have customers to serve. Would you like my ecard?'

'No,' I said, pressing second. Over in the other lift, I set the gecko to select ground with its nose – which took an effort in overriding the automatic movement and some weird hand movements on my part – and then sent it to watch and wait from the ceiling.

'That's absolutely fine,' said the man, trying not to stare at my gesticulations.

As our lift descended, I called up a local private car firm, looking for the nearest asset. I punched in an order, wincing at the amount they were going to charge. Still, I wasn't going far.

'Marvellous weather for a February,' said the man.

'Yeah,' I muttered. The gecko's camera was still showing an empty lift, but the numbers descended now. Looked like it was about one floor behind us.

'Would you like a lychee?'

'No,' I said. The other lift had come to a stop. An old couple stepped in. Thankfully, they didn't clock the gecko stuck in an upper corner, watching them.

'I can offer a free banana,' said the man. 'Very rare.'

'Look, I don't want any fucking fruit,' I said. The old man in the other lift must've sensed something because he turned his head around and stared straight at the gecko. He was still staring at when our lift came to a juddering halt on the third.

'Good day to you,' said the fruit seller, stepping out of the lift, less ebullient than at the start of his journey.

A woman a few years older than me was about to get into the lift when I held up my hand. 'I should warn you, I'm currently shedding BA.12221-3 and it's a fucking nightmare.'

The fruit seller gave me a backward glance of deep betrayal and legged it out of sight down the corridor. The woman stepped back, shrugging. 'No worries, I'll catch the next.'

She was about to call the other lift when I lurched forward, coughing, forcing her back against the opposite wall. I retained a sustained wheeze until I could hear the other lift pass, at which point I stepped back, hit the 'Close' button and gave her an apologetic shrug as the doors slid shut.

Then I punched the basement, using my Justice codes to get access, and turned my attention back to the couple in the other lift. The man must've told his partner now, as they were both looking up at the gecko. He was about to reach up to grab the machine when they were interrupted by the lift doors opening. I could see the main lobby area behind them. No hazards identified. The man lowered his hand, thinking better of it, and stepped out, looking for somebody in authority. I set the gecko to make for a high, safe place in the lobby. As soon as it started moving, the old woman shrieked, backing out of the lift, and started hollering.

I was passing the ground floor now in my lift and could hear her cries in the distant, muffled through the doors. As I came to a halt in the basement, I sent the gecko to the front windows of the lobby. Still nothing identified. The Justice autocar was just pulling up.

My lift doors crashed out, and I looked up at the gleaming chrome and lurid colours of a sports autocar, coming down a slipway into a nearby loading bay. I sprinted across to it and fell into the back seat, barking at it to get going. The thing took off at speed, back up the slipway.

Meanwhile, the gecko, now with a large audience of residents and a couple of reception staff, had located the door sensor, triggered it with a fat paw and was scampering around the outside of the building. It turned two corners, made a small leap and fell in through the window of my private hire, just as we sped away.

No shots fired. Perhaps I was safe?

'Listen Louie. I just need a drone or something similar. Anything that can protect me, OK?'

'We've got nothing, Carrie. I've been trying with Enforcement for the past week on this. There's nothing to be had. Did you just put in a delegate escalation right now? You've got to stop doing that.'

'I've shown you the vid, Louie. Whoever it was had a light rifle, a polymer handmade. They've taken a shot at me already.'

'Yeah, I know, Carrie,' said Louie, sadly. 'Look, there's nothing I can do right now. I've escalated it. I've added the new data, that rifle thingy, so all we can do is wait now.'

'Is that the truth? Or are you still pissed at me over the Sunday thing?'

'Carrie, honestly, we've got–'

I ended the call with an angry swipe of my hand. I'm sure that any other agency across the world would be tooled up by this point. The so-called DI wasn't playing because it wasn't his game. He could've raised it with Ibrahim, got something moving at that level. We can't have been stretched this thin already? Riots up in Airedale had eased off recently. Prevention had got their algorithms in good working order. Just the gangs now.

I'd grabbed a short rail ride west of Fax Central and had got out to a blistering cold elevated station. It wasn't far from my sisters, up here, but I wasn't about to drop by and say hello. Stretching up the hillsides to the west were rank upon rank of industrial unit and warehousing zones. LEDs of drones and loaders twinkled in the fast-moving mist. Looking east, I could see the serrated shapes of vast buildings stepping their way across the country towards the North Sea. The view to the north was obstructed by more buildings, so I couldn't see my home. Not that it really counted as one these days. Specimen

255. No real family. No real friends.

Oh, well, fuck them.

I caught a public elevator down to the Valley levels, just a few gantries' walk away from the station. I chose a larger one, the kind they used for vehicles and shipments, standing alongside small autocars and low loaders jostling for space, and with the prostitutes and pseudo junkies working the drivers for money. There were smaller pedestrian elevators you could catch, but I wasn't about to get into a confined space with anybody around here. Not when I was going down to the Valleys.

Problem was, I kept getting propositioned by creepy drivers, like I looked like somebody who needed the money or something. Maybe they had a thing for girls in bobble hats and bullet wounds? 'Fuck off, or I'll cut you,' was enough to dissuade some of the more enthusiastic ones, but I was losing my temper.

I stepped out into a dark vaulted space, shaking off the clutches of an old man, his hands knobbled with puncture scars. Around me, the autocars whizzed away into the black tunnels and archways. Representatives of the few businesses which had survived in this subterranean realm stepped out and met their cargo on the low loaders, escorting them off to their various destinations.

Down here, you didn't advertise you were with Justice. In fact, you didn't advertise you were anybody. It paid to be inconspicuous. Looking at the people passing by, jostling their way onto the platform, I noted that my choice of clothing was, at least, not too out-of-place down here. I didn't know whether that was a good or a bad thing.

In a short space of time, things went very quiet. The elevator platform creaked its way back up the side of the valley, taking its permanent crew of addicts and sex workers with it, and the vehicles had disappeared into whichever tunnel or warehouse they wanted to go. Though the Belt was excruciatingly loud up on the Fax Central ring, or around H Tower, down here the buzz and whine and wind was all but extinguished, to be replaced by unnerving creaks and the drip of moisture. Somewhere far off was the continuous hum of passing cars and trains on the various Main Conduit lines which ran east-west across the Belt.

The dark recess of an abandoned petrol station's kiosk allowed me to pause for a moment, keeping an eye on the other elevators. The passengers from these followed the same pattern, emerging quickly and dispersing to their own paths. They all looked as worn down as me, hunched shoulders and messy clothing. Nobody appeared to be carrying a suspiciously long bag. I directed the gecko to my shoulder and asked it to scan for hazard and then, setting my bead display to low light, I pulled up the map of the twisting turns of this section of the Valleys. The warehouse Katta had walked up the steps to was off to the north-west, though the way to get to it followed the valley bottom, and took a meandering route through some of the worst that the Valleys had to offer.

I set off.

As I walked, I maintained a continuous check on my surroundings. Vast alloy girders spanned the air above me, their feet planted in the bedrock of the valley sides, holding up the levels and buildings above. There were a few artificial lights still operational, which was surprising. I guessed it wasn't Aitch Bee that made this happen. More through a bit of local wiring, possibly patching into somebody else's supply. There was a community of sorts, which clung to life down here. But they didn't advertise their presence more than was necessary.

I found myself on an old tarmac road, the holes partially covered in a mixture of gravel and whatever shit somebody had found in their bin. Its length disappeared into the gloom, so I hunched my shoulder and shuffled on. I passed over what must have once been a river, stopping on the bridge to look over the side. I didn't lean too hard, in case the old stones – already wobbly – gave way totally. Below me, ancient green and black boulders butted up against litter and rusting cans and chunks of concrete, with rotting vat meat plugs, and little compacted dams of polymer waste. Through it still flowed a small trickle of black. I guessed you could still call it water. My map display told me this used to be a major river, but I couldn't find the name.

An old woman, pulling a manual loader piled up with what appeared to be an old mattress and some clothes, turned a corner ahead of me and approached.

'Hiya, love,' she yelled, as she approached.

'Hiya.'

'What you in for?' she said, pausing on the bridge, keeping her distance.

'I'm looking for someone, that's all.'

'That's what they all say down here,' she said. 'But I know who they're all looking for, inside their bottles and their hypos and their spore packs.'

'What's that?' I said. Even from this distance, the smell coming from her – possibly her bed – was incredible. But I thought it would be rude to crack open a couple of menthol sniffs.

'You know,' she said. 'You know, like they all do, in't it?'

'Right,' I said, nodding. I turned back to the river.

'Having a peep at the Calder?' she said, continuing.

'The what?'

'That's the river there. The Calder. This all used to be Calderdale, you know?'

'Yeah,' I nodded, 'I know.'

'Few people do,' she said. 'Once they started re-arranging all the parts, they changed the name.' She turned another corner in the distance. 'I wouldn't go swimming in it now, love. It's rotten.'

'Ta.' I looked at the black trickle for one last time and then carried on, over the bridge and along the road on the other side.

This part of the valley had once been densely packed, ancient housing. Terraces of stone built, two-up, two-downs rolled up the slopes beside me. Most were broken-windowed, but a few still had the flickers of fires in them. Some even had electricity, for there were steady glows. These tended to be boarded up with extra grilles on the windows and solid metal doors. Probably where the right-hard wrong 'uns lived. Or possibly people who refused to believe that their old lives had been boarded over and they'd been left stranded.

As I passed an alley, something drew my gaze. Something out of place. I turned and glimpsed a heavily coated figure, with furs around their neck, duck behind the cover of a large compressor bin. Though they moved fast, I could make out their face: they wore the mask of an owl.

I pressed on. At the next corner, I spotted another, this time with the face of a badger. They looked too tall, too broad to be the kids who'd harassed me in my flat in Shipley. There was the fur again, which seemed to indicate a different allegiance.

For the briefest of moments, I considered calling Deborah. Just to see if she recognised the gear. But I squashed the thought quickly. There was no fucking way I'd let that mess march in here.

Instead, I hurried on and past the residential areas, through what would once have been the middle of the town. Blackened holes where shop fronts had once been leered at me from all sides. I felt quite exposed here, like hundreds of eyes were watching me. A few cars passed, approaching at speed, weaving their way through the mess of the road. Every time one came near, I cowered under the eaves of a shop, expecting to be mown down, but they carried on, intent on their own business.

Leaving the old high street, glancing back behind me, I could see four of the masked watchers. They were marching abreast down the street towards me, their shapes silhouetted against a beam of ambient light which had winnowed its way down from the cold day above.

With a quicker step, I turned around and re-orientated myself, checking the map. It wasn't far now. I ducked under cover of an old awning and scurried along by the wall, turning a corner at the end and leaving the centre of the old town. This area comprised of old warehouses, mainly rusting metal affairs, with collapsed roofs. Then, in the distance, I could see the building from the footage with Katta. It was stone built, probably a proper old factory, back in the day, when they made shit around here.

Assuming that I was still being followed – or at least watched – I casually walked past the front entrance to the building and took a turn into a side street, which allowed me to double-back and approach the factory from behind. There were no suspicious masked figures here, so I broke out into a trot and headed directly for the gates at the back. These were locked, surprisingly, with a modern electronic device. But the gates themselves were old and twisted and I could pull them apart and scrape my way between without a problem. Inside was a small yard containing a series of bins, overlooked by some windows and a couple of doors to the building itself. As I crept towards them, I could make out the logo of the Fourth Sector Recycling Service pasted into the side.

Choosing the nearest of the doors, I edged it open and stepped inside. There was a dark corridor with a few doors. Using my gecko, I pulled up a little light and set off down the corridor. I also released the drone tracer and set it searching for trails. There had been recent activity at one junction I came to, so I turned and headed off across a large vestibule area to a stairwell at one end. Though the place was dusty and smelt old, it wasn't as rotten as the other buildings in the area. I guessed it was still being used, in some form, as a facility for the recycling team.

The stairwell was large, built for hundreds of people, and my footsteps were loud in my ears as I crept upstairs, following the scent trail.

It was at the third flight of steps, as I stepped around a corner, that I felt a faint breath behind my head and then heard a crunch of something impacting. It was when I'd fallen halfway down the flight, bouncing off the fifth step, that the pain reached my senses.

I came to rest in a corner of the stairwell, feeling blood seep into the collar of my duffel coat, and looked up. The gecko was skittering around, trying to reorientate itself, so the light was going everywhere, but I could see the figure, half concealed in the corner. It held a large lump of wood, possibly an old chair leg. But it wore a red hat.

'Katta,' I said, raising a hand. 'It's me. Carrie Tarmell.'

'I realised,' she said, 'after I'd... Are you… are you OK?'

'Fine,' I said, standing up. 'I'm fine. Nowt worse than I've already got.' A hand had to be placed carefully on the stone wall of the stairwell to steady myself. The lights were still swimming, and the shoulder wasn't in a right good place, either. But even I was surprised at how calm I was feeling.

'Can't you turn off that machine?' said Katta, pointing at the gecko. 'It's going to give us away.'

'Yeah,' I muttered, clicking my fingers in the gecko controls. 'Good plan.' It switched off its light and climbed back onto my shoulder.

'Can I help… Oh, God, what have I done?' said Katta, coming down the stairs. She put an arm under my shoulder and tried to help lift me up.

I shook off her help. 'I'm fine, yeah. I've got a bullet hole in the shoulder; I can cope with a crack to the head. Leave me be, yeah?'

Katta stepped back, apologising again, in a whisper.

'Shall we get off the stairs? You know anywhere with a view of the street?'

'Of course,' she said. 'Follow me.'

So, staggering a little and clinging to the handrail, I followed her back up two more flights of stairs and then through a wooden door into a huge, low-ceilinged room. It had multiple pillars and beams to support the floor above. But it was entirely empty, except for the tracks in the dust where Katta had clearly been pacing.

'Why did you run?' I asked, following her down the length of the room. 'You didn't turn up at work.'

'Why'd you think?' she said. 'Here, this is the window where

I saw you.'

I looked carefully through the window, trying to keep back from the light from outside. 'You saw me?'

'Yes,' said Katta. 'That's how I knew where you were going to be, so that I could…'

'Yeah, yeah. But surely you could've seen it were me?'

Katta shook her head. 'I thought… I thought it was her.'

'Who?'

Katta shut her mouth tight and looked back outside.

'Who?' I asked again.

Katta's mouth remained firmly shut. 'Nobody.'

'Why did you run?' I said. Another silence. 'Fine. Be like that. Meanwhile, I will try to get us out of here.' I found Sunday's contact details and hit the dial icon. It went straight through to voice mail. I swore and tried again. Same result. I turned back to Katta. 'OK. Looks, we're on our own, for now. So, I'll ask you again – what's the big problem? Why'd you have to run?'

Katta was silent again, but eventually cleared her throat and murmured. 'I was scared.'

'Of this person?' I asked. 'This person you can't talk about?'

Katta looked at me. She nodded. There was a long pause, as many emotions passed across her face. Eventually, she let her eyes drop, and she mumbled something.

'What?'

Katta cleared her throat. 'She showed me pictures.'

'What kind of pictures?'

'Of what they did to him.'

'To Simon?'

Katta's face was streaming with tears. 'No. Not Simon. But they must… Oh, God.'

I gave her a minute. She'd become incoherent. 'You mean Mr Shin?' I whispered.

She nodded. 'She showed me pictures.'

'Who showed you pictures?'

'The woman who came to my flat.'

'This was after I'd come to the yard.'

'That's right, she came round about… I don't know, it was a couple of days afterwards, I think.'

'And what did she say?'

'She showed me pictures of what she'd done to Mr Shin… it was like, something like an immersive, a horror, you know?' Katta stared at the floor, her hands held out in front of her, shivering.

'And what did she look like?'

Katta looked up at me and frowned. 'You know something? I really couldn't tell. She wasn't from… from anywhere, really.'

'How old?' I said, frowning. Something was nagging at my memory.

'Young,' Katta said. 'About student age, really.'

'Long black hair?'

'Yes,' said Katta.

Fuck. I scrolled through my list of contacts. Where was it? There. Found it. Dialled it.

'Who're you calling?' asked Katta.

Fuck. 'My sister.'

The first of the missiles crashed through a window further down the room. Glass shattered everywhere, and the stone bounced into a far corner of the room.

'She not answering?'

'No. Shit.'

'Can we call anybody else?'

I sighed and pulled up a different name. Hit the dial icon. It rang. I got an answer.

'Hello, Carrie. How're things going, mate?'

'Hiya, Debs. Um. Are you free today at all?'

Chapter Thirty

Five minutes after putting in the call to Deborah, and after a few more stones, the first of the homemade incendiaries crashed through a window, only a few metres away from us. Thankfully, the floor of the factory was mainly dust and dirt, so there was little to catch fire and spread. But others were thrown and there were soon small ovals of flame all down the length of the room, burning with a dark black smoke, which quickly filled the low-ceilinged space.

'What are they going to do with us?' yelled Katta, still standing looking out of a window.

'Get back,' I shouted. 'Out of sight.'

Outside I could see there were about a hundred of them now, all wearing masks. These weren't kids. They were fully grown, most of them carrying a weapon of some kind. It looked like they'd come well kitted out for a siege, as crates with more bottles appeared, ready to be filled with the fuel mix and stuffed with a rag. I could see the logo of the Belt's recycling commission on the crates.

'This place got a lot of bottles?' I asked. 'Those bins around the back?'

'A few thousand,' said Katta. 'We were decommissioning it.'

'Yeah?' I said, ducking as another missile hit the side of the building and burst into a huge, dripping flame. 'Well, I think they've got a supply for a while.'

'Do we try to get to the roof?' asked Katta. 'Or make a run for it?'

'I don't think we can run,' I said. 'We've just got to hold out for a while longer. Somebody is on their way.' To be honest, I wasn't that hopeful that Deborah was going to be able to do much. But perhaps she could soak up some of the anger.

'Why're they doing this?' asked Katta. 'Is it because I'm talking to you?'

'Dunno,' I said. 'Don't care, either. Come on, let's find a different floor.'

'Up?'

'Why not? That's further away from them, in't it?'

I took a final glance out of the window. A low loader stacked with fresh fuel had arrived, and the gang were taking the canisters off to fill the bottles.

Although the light was dim, and I was a little distracted by imminent death by burning, I noted that the fuel containers were the same design, possibly the same age, as those in Corva's flat. I sent the gecko up to the windows to take a picture. It flashed away for a few seconds but must've been spotted, because a bottle smashed it from its perch, and sent it spinning into the room, aflame. I ripped off my coat and bundled the machine in it, quelling the flames for a moment.

'What are you doing?' shouted Katta.

'Evidence,' I said. 'I'm getting evidence.'

An unfamiliar noise emerged, above the rustle of flame and the occasional crash of glass. It was a high-pitched hum. Drones.

'Fire brigade're here,' I said, examining the gecko. It didn't look too damaged, so I tucked it into a pocket.

'What?'

I looked out the nearest window. There were a few LEDs flashing in the sky. Then a medium-sized drone flew through a broken window. It sped towards the nearest spot of burning fuel and blasted a shot of retardant powder. The flames died down for a moment. Then burst back. The drone, having done its bit, disappeared back out of the window.

'Fucking useless,' I muttered.

'Is that it?' said Katta.

'That's all they'd spare down here,' I said. 'If it got too dangerous for the levels above, they might let a storm drain open.'

'Really?'

'More likely,' I said, 'they'd just collapse the place with explosive charge and hope that puts out the fire.'

'They would?'

I sniffed. 'Yeah. We wouldn't want to be inside when that happens.'

Katta watched another fire brigade drone drift in and deliver its paltry payload.

'Come on,' I shouted, heading for the stairwell.

Katta followed me close, as another missile crashed into the dust in front of us, sending little islands of flame skittering across the floor, like a burning archipelago.

We reached the stairs and climbed, two steps at a time. I needed somebody who could help me with the fuel canisters and there was someone on the team who might know. I rang Gilbie McKenn.

'Yo, Carrie. You're out of breath, love.'

'Yeah, ta. You got a minute?'

'Course, you after some more Brazilian rocket fuel? Still got some left.'

I cut across his cackling. 'Nah. Summat else, this time.'

'Oh,' he said, more seriously. 'You OK? Where are you?'

'Buckle. Valleys.'

'Shit,' Gilbie whistled. 'No wonder you're running. You in trouble then? Enforcement on its way?'

'Nah, Enforcement's not coming.'

'Oh. You pissed 'em off again?'

'Summat like that.'

'You want me to put in a call?'

'You could try. That's not why I'm calling, though?'

'You wanna wait until you've stopped running, Carrie? I can't make out what you're saying.'

I grabbed Katta's arm and stilled our progress for a moment, taking a breather in a landing between flights. 'Listen, you got a database of petrol stores? Illegal ones, most like.'

Gilbie chuckled. 'Which petrol stores aren't illegal, Carrie?'

'I don't know,' I said. He was the fucking environmental analyst. I didn't mind Gilbie too much, but he liked to make a tit of himself sometimes, just for the jokes.

'You got a picture?'

I sent him the images the gecko had taken from the window, plus the ones I'd found under the floorboards in Corva's flat.

Katta stepped quietly up to the railings in the middle of the stairwell and looked down. 'Um, I think they're in the building now.'

'Yeah, yeah,' I muttered, taking a deep breath and preparing myself for more stairs. 'Gilbie, you got 'em?'

'Yo, they're through. Just dropping them in now.'

'Ta.' I looked at Katta. 'We ready to run again?'

'No.'

'Wrong answer. Come on!' I grabbed her arm and set off back up the stairs.

'We got a hit,' said Gilbie, in my ear, as I made the next flight.

'Yeah?'

'I mean, they're a pretty generic design, but the polymer readings are the same as this one I'm looking at.'

'Just tell me the source, Gilbie!'

'Fine,' said Gilbie, huffily. 'It was found in an old warehouse, west of Bradford Centre. Belonged to... hang on, let me see, yeah, belonged to Pinho Holdings.'

'Shit.'

'Mean something?'

'Yeah, it does,' I said. 'Ta, Gilbie.'

'You sure you don't want some help?'

'Why not?' I said. 'Give our DI a ring a for a start. He's blocking my calls now.'

'Will do! See ya.'

I ended the call and drew in some ragged breaths. The smoke from the fires was now making it into the stairwell. Inhaling was becoming difficult. Could've been my shit health.

'Nearly at the top,' said Katta.

A couple more flights and we were at a steel-reinforced door. I tried the handle. 'Locked. Fuck!'

'Here, let me try,' said Katta, reaching past me and waving her rings at the lock. It clicked open. 'This is a recycling facility, still.'

I ushered her through with a nod. 'Lock it after us and all.'

I was grateful to be out of the building, but now felt fully exposed. Above us were the joists holding up the floor of the Belt, much nearer than before. They threatened an immense weight pushing down from above. The red lick of flames was evident from the front of the building and we could still see one or two fire brigade drones coming and going. There was no siren alerting us to a new Enforcement tactical team on its way.

'What do we do now?' asked Katta.

'Keep an eye out,' I muttered. 'Just give me a minute.'

I called up various apps on my bead, trying some basic searches against Pinho. Seemed to be a standard meat-growing business, like we had all the way up Airedale. Clinging onto the last of its custom, as most of the work had gone to Brazil now. I came across a few pictures of the current owner, Arthur Pinho, short and balding, hitting late middle age. He had kindly eyes but looked scared in most of the photos. There was nothing that gave much away.

Then I pulled up Modlee and opened the project file. Not really sure how this shit worked, I just dropped the Arthur Pinho person metafile into the folder. Then waited.

It got a match within seconds.

'Shit.'

I started calling up Sunday again.

'Hello,' he said. 'You OK?'

'No,' I said. 'I'm on the top of a burning building with about a hundred gang members trying to murder me. How about you?'

'I'm stuck on a slow line to Fax Central. Sorry. Bad coverage. Sorry. I'm not much help.'

'I've just found summat.'

'Yes?'

'Pinho Holdings, you were heading there. We need to talk to this Arthur Pinho.'

'What? I've just turned around–'

'Yeah, I know. Turn around again. We need to speak to the wrong 'un.'

'Wrong 'un?' said Sunday, haltingly.

'Yeah, I'm just looking at a vid from a corporate news site… God knows what it is, a gala evening, awards ceremony, summat, anyway, he's sat right next to Deborah Godden. We've got a connection!'

'Very good. This is building towards something coherent.' Another pause. 'You sure you don't need me there to…' He trailed off.

'Need you here to save little old me?' I sneered.

'You sounded like you needed some help,' said Sunday. He'd gone and put the face on again. 'That's all I meant.'

'I am quite capable,' I shouted into my bead, 'of doing my fucking job without people feeling like they need to help me!'

A furious banging came from the access door behind us. It sounded like metal on metal. They'd be through in a minute.

'Katta,' I said, turning towards to the door.

'What?'

'Any other way off this roof?'

'Don't think so.' She glanced over the edge of the building. But something else caught her eye. 'Oh.'

'What's happening?' asked Sunday, in my ear.

'What you found?' I said to Katta.

'Somebody's coming.'

I looked over as well. There was a single figure weaving its way through the crowd milling around the front of the building. As it passed, there seemed to be a small force-field of space around them, creating a natural gap.

'Sorry, Sunday,' I muttered. 'What I meant was… Look, just turn around and get to Pinho, OK? If I get out of here, I'm needed somewhere else. You're on Pinho. I'm sending details now.'

'Yes,' said Sunday, stiffly. 'Bye.'

I ended the call and looked down to the scene below. The figure had now reached the knot of gang members clustered around the front door of the building. There was a small discussion and then a few whistles and shouts. The gang dispersed into the neighbouring streets, some streaming back out of the doors of the building.

The furious hammering on the door behind us ceased and we could hear steps pounding back down the stairs.

The figure below looked up at us on the roof.

'Carrie? Are you there?'

'Debs? Is that you?' I called back.

'Yeah, it's me. I reckon you can come down now.'

There was very little chatter as we made our way, as quickly as possible, back to the nearest elevator cluster. Though the gang had dispersed, Deborah's furtive glances into every corner we passed – and the occasional look at her old tablet she pulled from her rucksack, showing a stream of messages – gave me a big hint that this was a time-limited deal and we weren't to piss about with congratulatory hugs and toasts.

'Where's this drop us off?' I asked once we'd got into the lift. We'd taken a smaller, pedestrian service, and had bagged an empty one.

'Exit thirty of the MC-3,' said Deborah. 'I'm calling a pool car now. Should be there when we arrive.'

'Why weren't Enforcement coming?' asked Katta. She turned to Deborah. 'Do you know?'

Deborah looked at me, her face expressionless. 'I don't know.

They're busy people. Especially these days.'

'That's why we need people like you,' said Katta.

'I guess,' said Deborah, flushing a little and looking down.

'What did you do back there?' asked Katta. 'You got them to just… I mean, they simply disappeared, didn't they?'

'That was the Flixhead,' said Deborah. 'The lot of them, as far as I could tell.'

'You knew them?' asked Katta.

'Been working with Flixhead for a few years now,' said Deborah. 'Been building a lot of credit with them.'

'So you're friends with them?'

'Just blew all that credit now,' muttered Deborah, fishing out her tablet and ignoring Katta. 'I mean, I have to check the algos later, but… look at these. I can't show my face down there for a bit.'

I cleared my throat and spoke: 'Ta, like.'

Deborah beamed in my direction. 'You're welcome, Carrie. Glad to be of help.'

The lift slowed to a halt, and the doors opened to a bleak, snowy day. For a brief moment, I almost wished we'd stayed down in the relative warmth of the Valleys. But I was enjoying the light.

'Car's over there,' said Deborah. 'Come on.'

'Am I coming too?' asked Katta.

'You're not leaving my… I mean, our side,' I said, pushing her into the back seat and squeezing in beside her.

Deborah jumped into the driver's seat and turned around. 'Where're we going again?'

I gave her the address, and we set off, accelerating up the slipway into the rest of the traffic. As we sped down the MC-3, I tried calling the house again, but there was no answer. I even phoned my mother – who tried to get me into a discussion about whether they'd ever breed grey whales again – but she hadn't seen her either.

'Where're we going?' asked Katta.

'Trying to find the woman you spoke to,' I said. 'I think.'

'You think?' said Katta.

'We've not much to go on,' I said. 'Just your description.'

'Where is she?'

'My sister's.'

Deborah whistled. 'Oh. Right. Bad, yeah? You tried speaking to her?'

I nodded. 'No answer.'

'We going to your sister's now?'

'Yeah.'

'You were staying there, weren't you?' asked Deborah.

I nodded. We all fell silent for a long time, watching the cars outside, trying to find another person, another group of people, where things weren't so fucked up. Leading their own little lives, getting through their own winters.

'What were Mr Shin like?' I asked after a while.

'He was very polite,' said Katta. 'Quite quiet. But he wasn't well, either.'

'No?'

'No, he had some kind of disease,' said Katta. 'At least, that's what Si and me thought. He sometimes couldn't move his fingers and he shuffled around a lot. Like he wasn't well. He was always wearing gloves, so we thought maybe'd got caught something. Off the waste, perhaps.'

'You get a lot of that?'

'Oh, yes,' said Katta. 'There are all sorts of unpleasant things you can catch. We learned about them all during training.'

'Where did Mr Shin train?'

Katta smiled, briefly. 'He trained in the best place in the world. Dhaka. They've got the university there. All the best people.'

I nodded. There wasn't much I could say. We fell into our own thoughts, silent for the rest of the journey to Grace's block of flats. As we pulled up to the building, I considered suggesting the two of them should stay in the car, but concluded that was about as dangerous as going inside.

'Wait a minute,' I muttered, digging out the gecko. 'And keep your heads down.'

There were no lights on or movement in the flat, but I got the gecko to do a scan of the area anyway, letting it skitter around the dashboard and across the car's ceiling to each window, including the back. As it did, I ran it through the generic concept finder on my bead. But there was nothing that came up as amber – or worse – except for multiple chimneys venting something toxic away to the south. I could live with that shit.

'Right, stay close to behind me,' I said. 'Debs, you're at the back, Katta in the middle.'

'Human shield, right?' said Deborah.

I looked at her, readying an angry retort. However, when I saw her solemn face, I knew she wasn't pissing around. She meant it. An aerial view of a single figure walking through a hundred gang members came back to my mind.

'Protect the witness, yeah,' I said. Then I smiled.

We rushed out of the car and into the lobby and up then the convoluted stair-and-corridor mess that led to my sister's flat. I was using the gecko to check each corner, and every window, as we progressed. My shoulder was throbbing; a memory of what could happen if I wasn't careful.

The door was closed and locked when we arrived. I considered hammering on it and demanding entry, but then thought better of it. Indicating that the other two should hang back and keep quiet, I pulled my delegation privileges and unlocked it with my a-codes. This was the first time I'd ever pulled this trick on a relative. At least she hadn't overridden it.

The door swung open, and I sent in the gecko, expecting to hear an explosion of gunfire, or worse, a sad little pop and then see my machine blown into pieces. Instead, there was a deep silence in the place.

I set it to check the whole flat. It gave its report.

'Nothing here,' I said over my shoulder. 'We'll go in, but don't touch anything, right?'

Katta and Deborah nodded. We stepped through and into the flat. Nothing much had changed. Djin Dowe had clearly no interest in overriding my sister's abysmal taste in interior furnishings.

I went through to the spare room, where I'd been sleeping only recently.

'This her room?' asked Deborah. 'The one we're looking for?'

'I guess,' I said. 'At least, it was.'

There was nothing there now. The bed had been freshly made, obviously, and the pillows were plumped. The floor looked spotless. If there was somebody a forensic analyst didn't want at a crime scene before they got there, it was my frigging sister. I wouldn't find anything of note here.

The gecko and the handheld sniffer struggled to find much, but I did get a reading on the curtains. Odour trail was stronger here, like she'd been standing here looking out of the window. I ran it through the database. It came back with an eighty-percent reading: *Breathless Whisper*.

For no particular reason, I started to cry. I knelt down by the bed and checked underneath it. As expected, there was nothing there. Not so long ago, my own holdall had been kicked under there by my tired boot. More recently, was there a case here containing the rifle that'd shot me?

The gecko pinged in something on its hi-def, matching up to data in the project files. Some fibres caught in a screw on the door handle. I stood up, wiping the tears, and checked the image. It was the same green as found caught in the recycling facility's security server. I dropped it into the folder. More evidence. Didn't make me feel any better though.

Then Deborah was beside me in the room, pushing a tissue into my hand. She didn't say anything.

'Cheers,' I muttered.

'Found anything incriminating?'

'Enough,' I said.

We surveyed the room for a moment.

'We good, Carrie?' asked Deborah, checking my face.

'Good,' I said.

'You need a bit of space?'

'Yeah.'

'You've got blood all down your neck. Did you know that?' she asked.

I checked with my hand and then looked down at the mess on my fingertips. I'd forgotten about being smacked by Katta earlier. 'Yeah. I need to get myself cleaned up.' I used the tissue she'd given me to wipe up most of the blood.

'That's better,' said Deborah. Before she went back to join Katta, she gave me a quick squeeze on my good shoulder. I didn't slap her hand away. I had other things to think about.

'You shit,' I said to nobody in particular, and threw the tissue in the bin.

Back in the lounge, Deborah was standing just aside of the window and Katta was sitting in the middle of the room. They both looked at me as I entered.

'She been here?' asked Katta, eyes wide.

'Yeah,' I said.

'What do we do now?' asked Katta.

'Find her,' said Deborah.

'And your sister?' whispered Katta, looking at me.

Deborah looked at me as well. I was finding it difficult to speak.

'I reckon that's best,' Deborah said.

'Why are both you looking at me like that?' I snapped.

'What are we doing, Carrie?' asked Deborah. 'What's the next move?'

I took a breath, about to swear at her. Then I blinked back the start of new tears, turned away and coughed. 'No idea.'

'You need more time?' asked Deborah. 'We can give you more time?'

'I don't have the time anymore,' I muttered. Then I had a thought. 'Perhaps you could help, though?' I asked, looking up at Deborah. 'Put your question out to your people?'

'My people?' asked Deborah.

'You know,' I said, 'the gangs, and that?'

'It doesn't work like that, Carrie,' said Deborah.

'Well, if you're doing nowt, help me think it through then,' I said. I paced into the kitchen, turned around, and then back to the sitting room. I noticed Deborah was looking out of the window. 'Keep down! Out of sight.'

With a nod, Deborah stepped back into cover. I'd got the gecko to keep a constant watch on comings and goings outside, a secondary form of protection, but it was still identifying boring shit like 'car' and 'bin' and 'pigeon'. Despite all that, I still expected Djin to burst out of nowhere, brandishing a high-calibre ballistic weapon.

'You said you'd got some access, some a-codes, to get you some ratio footage?' said Deborah. 'Have you tried that?'

'Yeah,' I said. It was the first thing I'd done, run the picture of Djin that Mum had shared with me through a ratio-generator and plugged that into the public stacks. There were a few hits around Fax Central, but nothing recent. They seemed to be deliberately sparked to suggest she'd been visiting the offices of where my sister worked. If you know how, it was easy to avoid the public cameras. I couldn't go on a general beyond the public ones. I would never get the IG clearance for that kind of shit.

'Any ideas where she might've gone?' asked Deborah.

I shook my head. 'No.'

'Well, what do we know about her so far?' asked Deborah.

I was about to snap back something rude, but took a moment to collect my thoughts, before barking out the facts, pacing as I did so. 'Right. We think Dowe came in through Abu Dhabi, about three to four weeks ago, picking up a heavy load of bespoke ventilator scent known in the industry as *BreathlessWhisper*.

Using that molecular signature, we know she visited Simon West, because I found that scent in his dining room up at the Fax. Either before or after West, I'm guessing she went to see Katta–' Katta narrowed her eyes at me at this point and looked away. '–and then to... well, I'm guessing she came here. We know Dowe threatened Katta over there with summat pretty horrible, unless she changed her story. Hang on, Katta, did you both come up with that story together, or did she hand you a script or summat?'

'She told me exactly what to say,' said Katta.

'But she knew that nobody in Aitch-Bee knew Mr Shin directly?'

Katta frowned. 'Yes, I suppose that follows... she knew about the contract and all the details.'

I clicked my fingers. 'Which means she knew Shin. She knew about Shin's arrangement, about the business.'

'Shit,' said Deborah. 'They were in business together?'

'Must be part of the same operation. Or Dowe is working for someone who's part of the same operation.' I rubbed my eyes. 'What else?'

'We know somebody killed Si... I mean, we've a new victim, haven't we?' said Deborah, stuttering to a halt and trying not to look at Katta.

'Yeah,' I said. 'And that ThreeDave's been fitted up for that murder, which he can't have committed. But somebody convinced him to confess.'

'How'd you know?' asked Deborah.

'I spoke to him,' I replied.

Her eyes widened. 'You went to the Estuary?'

I grinned. 'Yeah. Spoke to ThreeDave. He's no wrong 'un... at least, he didn't kill West. Got the evidence to prove that or, at least, to blow a big fucking hole in a prosecution narrative. And when I spoke to him, he pretty much admitted to being forced to confess, for the good of his people, or summat. He weren't about to dob in whoever spoke to him, mind.'

'He's always been honourable, has ThreeDave,' said Deborah,

nodding with a smile.

I shook my head. 'It's not helpful, though, is it? He needs to talk. If anybody knows what's going on, it's him.'

'Not necessarily.'

'I mean, he's in charge of that place, in't he?' I said. 'He's the king of the lake up there.'

Deborah laughed. 'Is that what he told you?'

'No,' I said, 'but everybody knows it, don't they? I mean, everybody knows ThreeDave. He's the proper boss.'

Deborah shook her head. 'You should've asked your local community analyst, first, Carrie.'

'Eh?'

'There're BoTies up there, plenty of them,' said Deborah, 'but they're only there because they're allowed to be there. Because the real power let 'em.'

'The real power?'

'Yeah,' said Deborah. 'You know who's in charge up there at Withens? It's the Grinsers, not the BoTies.'

'Kristy? Kristy Henderson?' I said, trying to recall the name.

'That's the one. Real nasty piece of work, that Kristy. Never been able to get close to her, but I know all the guys and girls up there are shit-scared of that one. She rules the show.'

'She could get ThreeDave to confess to summat he didn't do?'

'Definitely.'

'So, question is, what's she doing it for?' I said, rubbing my shoulder.

'What'd they threaten him with?' asked Deborah. 'What'd he say about that?'

'Not much,' I replied. 'Summat about there being "horrors" somewhere.'

At this, Katta looked up from her place on the floor. Deborah also noticed this start.

'That's what she showed you as well, isn't it?' I said to Katta, quietly.

The girl shook her head, blinking, before looking down again. Deborah and I exchanged looks, and I nodded meaningfully towards the space next to Katta. Deborah took the hint and moved to sit down next to her.

'You want to talk about it?' asked Deborah.

'Talk about what?' snapped Katta.

'You seen it too?'

'Never saw anything,' said Katta.

'They won't get you here,' said Deborah. 'You're safe with us.'

'Like Si?' said Katta

'What did she show you, Katta?'

There was a long silence.

'Katta? What did you see?'

'Pics,' whispered Katta. 'Pictures of bodies, cut up. Pictures of severed hands, feet. I mean, I work in recycling, I've seen it all, but these were horrific.'

'Where were they?' I asked, sitting down opposite her. 'What were in the background? Lab? Factory? Warehouse?'

Deborah rolled her eyes at me, like I should back the fuck up, but I wasn't going anywhere.

'Don't remember,' mumbled Katta, eyes to the floor.

'All this will help,' said Deborah.

'Don't remember,' repeated Katta.

'For fuck's sake!' I said, losing my patience and standing back up, walking back into the kitchen. 'Fucking useless.'

Deborah followed me. 'Don't give up, Carrie. Keep thinking. What about Hartlepool?'

'It's useless!'

'What happened at Hartlepool?'

I took another breath. 'Shipment of replacement parts came into their Gunnison wrecker's yard. Hidden compartment. Lots of legs and shit. Bent security guard. Went to her flat in south Hartlepool. Found some petrol procured by Pinho Holdings. Got shot by high-calibre weapon. Ended up in some

Middlesbrough hospital. The usual crap. Nothing connects.'

Deborah thought for a moment. 'Did you say Pinho?'

'That's right,' I said.

'Why'd you say Pinho? Why'd you mention Pinho?'

'It was same petrol that the gang were using to torch the building down in the Valleys just now. You've probably still got the fumes on you. Sunday's checking them out now. Why? You know the name?'

Deborah started bouncing on her feet, holding back what could've easily turned into a shriek of excitement. 'You know who owns the whole site up there? The reservoir and the land?'

'Aitch Bee, I assumed. It's public land, in't it? Water supply and that.'

'No,' said Deborah. 'When the microbes came, they flogged it off. Guess who they flogged it to?'

'No idea,' I said.

'Arthur Pinho,' said Deborah.

'Shit,' I said. 'Pinho owns Withens and that land?'

'And I was told the Grinsers cut a deal with the landowner. Kristy must've made an arrangement with this Pinho guy. Perhaps to let them live there in peace. Pinho's got the ear of a load of Servants, hasn't he?'

I rang Sunday on my bead, waving at Deborah, to indicate she comfort Katta or something.

'Hello,' said Sunday.

'Hiya. You found Pinho yet?'

'Not here, no. They say he's gone off somewhere, in one of his transporter drones.'

'Shit,' I said. 'Any idea where?'

'His people aren't saying,' said Sunday. 'But I'm calling in one last favour with my people. See if they can follow flightpaths in the local areas.'

'Cheers,' I said. 'Appreciate it.'

'Where are you now?' he asked.

'Friendly.'

'I beg your pardon?'

'It's a place. My sister's flat.'

'How is she?'

'She's not here,' I said.

'And Dowe?'

'No sign either,' I said. 'We've got nowt here. No suspect. *BreathlessWhisper* everywhere, though. So, it's definitely her.'

'Hell,' said Sunday.

'Yeah.'

'Listen,' I said, 'I've just been told by Deborah that Pinho actually owns—'

'Hang on,' said Sunday, interrupting me. 'I'm just getting the vector data from this building. Looks like something took off about an hour ago, heading east.'

'The east end of the Belt?' I asked.

'Yes,' said Sunday. 'Towards the York end.'

'Godden,' I muttered. I gave him a location. 'Meet me there in an hour.'

'You're leaving the witness?' asked Sunday.

'Ah, shit,' I said. I thought for a long moment, glancing at some pictures on the wall. 'Don't worry. Got a plan.'

'Are you certain?' asked Sunday

I ended the call and strode through to the living room. Deborah looked up at me expectantly.

'What's the plan, partner?' she asked.

I narrowed my lips. 'I got to find my sister. But we also need to get you to somewhere safe,' I said, turning to Katta.

'You could try Kal again?' said Deborah.

'Can't I just stay with you both?' asked Katta.

'Not safe,' I said, scrolling through to find Kal's number. Punched it. No answer.

'He still being a dick?' asked Deborah, reading my face.

I nodded. There were a few other names on my list. None of

them seemed right. Then one popped up. A recent one. She'd help. She'd have to help. It was like an obligation.

'You're going to my mum's,' I said, finding the details on my contacts.

'Your mum?' asked Deborah, eyebrows now hidden in the bird's nest of her hair.

'She loves this kind of shit,' I said. 'She used to be in the fucking army.'

It took about a minute to convince my mother that she needed to help me out on this one. The mention of possible sniper action whetted her interest more than I'd have liked normally, but I wasn't here to be precious about anything.

'Only question is,' I said, 'how we get you all there safely.'

'I've got some people,' said Deborah.

So I waited, pacing the flat, while Deborah made her calls. I could've just trusted her, and just left then and there but I still wasn't feeling right about things. There was still nothing to give me a clue where to find Grace or Dowe. It was clear Godden and Pinho were working together and he was heading towards her clinic. So, it made sense to head there. But was I going to find Dowe? And Grace?

A great roar of old-fashioned combustion startled me from my thoughts. I looked out the window. A vast vehicle, with numerous supplementary appendages, had just pulled up. It was a mixture of matt black and lurid yellow, which gave the impression of a mutant wasp. Two women, faces just visible under hats with long peaks, stepped out and started to approach the building.

'I think your ride's here.'

'Ah, great. They're always punctual, these guys.' She looked over my shoulder and gave them a wave. The two women saw her and returned to the vehicle, with a short nod from each. 'Pleasant ride, isn't it?'

'Subtle,' I said.

'Well, it stands out. But then, very few people bother 'em

when they're driving this.' She turned to me, now more serious. 'Do you trust me, Carrie?'

I regarded her for a moment. 'Yeah.' Then I turned to Katta. 'You're going to take a ride with some nice people Debs here knows.'

'OK.'

'Be polite to them,' I said. 'Oh, and be polite to my mum, and all.'

CHAPTER THIRTY-ONE

Louie wasn't picking up his calls. I left a message for him, explaining what I needed.

While I waited for a response, I nervously checked the carriage. It was a busy ride today, and I was having to stand up against a door. I'd paid for a ticket out of my own money. The expenses team must have had word to dump my privileges, especially after I pulled that delegate escalation trick at Katta's place. It was probably all Louie's doing. The bastard was going to get it between the eyes when I finally spoke to him. I stared out of the window at the flickering adverts that followed us along their continuous wall screen. It was a disconcerting experience, as some screen units had gone down over the years, so the pictures seemed to jump the blackness of the tunnel walls. The advert that was chasing me was trying to get me to get in touch with my inner goddess, seemingly, via spending money on a naff bath. I was frankly insulted. Is that what the algorithms thought I wanted?

A message popped back from Louie. *Sorry. Too busy to talk. Escalating this one.*

Wanker. Who'd he bothered to escalate this one to? I didn't think Negussie was going to get involved again.

A call came in. It was a familiar name.

'Hiya, Carrie,' said the relaxing voice of Ibrahim Al-Yahmeni. I'd not spoken to our Chief Inspector at all since his promotion. Guess he didn't need to chat to ants like me anymore. Still, I always felt he'd got my back. If only to use as a human shield.

'Hiya, Chief,' I said.

'Sounds weird, right?'

'What's that?'

'Calling me Chief.'

'Is it?'

'Call me Ibrahim,' said the Chief. 'Like old times, you know, Carrie.'

'Right, thanks, Chi… I mean, Ibrahim.'

'That's better,' said Ibrahim. He still had the long, jet black curls encasing his face like an ancient painting. 'Now, what can I do for my favourite analyst?'

The fuck was I his favourite. 'Louie didn't tell you?'

'I just received an escalation notice, Carrie,' said Ibrahim. 'I was about to bounce it all the way back down to Mr Daine again when I noticed your name. Then I got interested. What do you need? Talk to me.'

'Arrest warrant,' I said, defiantly ignoring the other passengers near me.

'Exciting. For whom?'

'Not in the best place for that information.'

'OK,' said Ibrahim. 'And can I ask why our colleagues in Enforcement aren't supporting you in this?'

I came out with the truth. It was easier. 'I pissed them off.'

Ibrahim nodded, understanding immediately. But he didn't smile. 'That's unfortunate. But happens.'

'You're gonna say it happens to me the most?' I asked.

'I wasn't,' said Ibrahim. Lying bastard. 'Let me have the form, OK?'

'Yeah.' I sent him the details of Godden and Pinho. I included the batched up data from Sunday as well. Ibrahim was the kind to only read a summary. It didn't take him long.

'I see you've been working with Lagos,' said Ibrahim. 'They're a serious operation.'

'They are,' I said.

'Except,' said Ibrahim, 'they've already been in touch with

me directly. They've confirmed that Mr Sule is operating outside of his jurisdiction here. On a case that has no current agency authorisation. They also had something to say about inappropriate access of data assets.'

We suddenly burst from the tunnel and ascended to a flyover rail, running through the middle of Leeds, momentarily lit by the weak winter sun, before the vast towers darkened the carriage in shadows again. I was glad I could stop looking at folk in frigging baths, though.

'So?' I said, raising my chin.

'Normally,' said Ibrahim, 'I would congratulate your initiative and generally pushing the envelope–'

'Yeah, yeah,' I interrupted, not wishing to listen to him do his usual. 'But this time? It's different?'

'They're a whole different agency, Carrie. They're the Nigerian Feds. You don't mess with the protocols and business of that particular agency.'

'Tell that to Louie,' I blurted.

'Indeed,' said Ibrahim, face serene.

'Sorry, can't you do anything? I just need authorisation to go in and do the… you know, I don't have any Enforcement now. It's just me. I need the package sending.'

'You need the package sending?' asked Ibrahim, as if I'd just asked to marry his first born, or something.

'Yeah. You just need to give the word.'

Ibrahim shook his disembodied head. 'No can do, Carrie.'

'Why?'

'I need something more than what you've sent me,' said Ibrahim.

'What do you need?' I pleaded. This was my last fucking chance. I started babbling. 'Listen, Ibrahim, they've got my… I mean, they've got my sister. I don't know. But she's not there anymore. The primary suspect, they were in my sister's flat. Stayed there, possibly a night. They've both gone. Disappeared. I need to find them. This is my only way… I need the fucking package!'

'Staying there, did you say?' asked Ibrahim.

'Yeah,' I said. The fuck was I going to crying in a public space like this. 'I think she was casing the place. It's a long story. Don't make me tell it.'

'I'm sorry, Carrie,' said Ibrahim. 'If there's risk involved, it's Enforcement, not us. We don't go chasing down the wrong 'uns ourselves.'

'Enforcement aren't helping,' I said, too loudly. 'I already told you.'

'You did,' said Ibrahim. He looked genuinely pained.

'I just need your help on this one, Ibrahim.'

'Make friends with Enforcement again, Carrie,' he said. 'That's the right thing to do.'

I was about to slap down the call when I thought of something.

'Speak to Servant Negussie,' I said. 'She's down here in Aitch-Bee. She'll vouch for me. Negussie. Speak to her.'

'Bridget?' asked Ibrahim.

'That's right. Bridget Negussie. You know her?'

'Carrie,' said Ibrahim, smiling. 'I know many people.'

'Course.'

'How's she involved? She's not a Justice commissioner.'

'Covering during the investigation.'

'Of course, bless her. She would.'

'She knows all about it.'

Ibrahim grinned. 'Well, if I know Bridget, I doubt she would know all about it.'

'Eh?'

'But she would still know if it was the right thing to do.'

'You going to talk to her?'

'Let me call her.' He paused. 'That's what you were suggesting, wasn't it?'

I hesitated. Then nodded. 'Yeah, sure. She'll explain it all.'

'She's a good judge, is Bridget,' said Ibrahim. 'Speak to you soon.'

I sat back in my seat. Conversations with Ibrahim, although

relaxed on the surface, always felt like you were a few seconds away from feeling teeth around your ankle and being pulled under the waves.

A message came back into my display: *Take the next stop. Wait on platform.*

So I waited until the service rolled to its juddering halt at the next station. It was a small stop, above an industrial estate, so would've been packed in the morning and evening, but now it was relatively empty, just a small group of workers in thick coats huddled in a shelter down the way, waiting for a connecting service.

There was no way I was going to join them in the shelter, so I walked over to the barrier at the other end of the platform and looked over the edge. In order to evade planning permission nightmares – and the cost of digging up some prime real estate – this part of the line had been raised above the old skyline of the city. We were about twenty metres up. Not in the clouds, but enough to make it hard when the lifts broke. And if you had vertigo, you could get stuffed. An edifice of light alloys and novel textiles, swinging in the wind: a design feature, not a fault. I tried not to look down too much, keeping my eyes on the horizon, guessing the direction.

After about five minutes of freezing my tits off, I could hear it. A high whine. Then I saw it, a black dot, approaching from the north. It came closer at speed, a medium-sized drone carrying payload. It did a small circuit of the station, turning as it did so, checking us all out, then descended level with my face.

'Carrie Tarmell?' the machine blurted out.

'That's me,' I said.

'Please release your AJC verification a-codes,' said the machine.

I dug around on my bead display for the relevant files and threw them at the machine.

'Thank you, Ms Tarmell,' said the drone. 'Please indicate on the ground where you wish to receive the package?'

'Just give it here,' I said, stepping forward and offering my hands.

'Very good,' said the machine and released its cargo. A small cardboard box dropped from the innards of the machine and fell into my palm. It was much heavier than I'd remembered. I'd only done this about three or four times before. This was Enforcement's job, normally, but if they were busy – and if DI were busy and all – then they could delegate to an analyst. If they thought you were special.

'Confirm receipt,' the machine said shortly.

'Confirmed.'

The machine beeped and immediately accelerated vertically into the sky and then flew off to the north. I watched it go, then noticed I was being watched by the group of workers from the shelter. Some of them must've realised what was happening, for they shrank back into the corners of the cramped space. I gave them a massive grin and dropped the package into the pocket of my duffel coat.

Some wrong 'un was about to get arrested. I'd been given the cuffs.

CHAPTER THIRTY-TWO

I met Sunday Sule at the station, where a car was waiting for us. If this was what a partner was supposed to do, I could get used to it. People with money.

'Ready?'

'Fuck, yeah.' I tapped my pocket. 'Got the package.'

'I beg your pardon?' he said, hopping into the car on the other side.

'Doesn't matter. Means we can arrest somebody.'

In a few minutes, we arrived at the clinic and rolled into the reception. There was no sign of a carrier-drone or helicopter, but that didn't confirm much.

The front desk staff put up some resistance, but eventually gave in when I brandished the cuffs and dropped them the necessary a-codes. Told them to keep quiet and that we would proceed to Godden directly. We strolled past the gate and into the inner garden. A few staff were moving about smoothly but nobody paid us mind. There was no movement at Godden's office window, but I knew that was where we'd start.

We were stopped at the entrance to the house by a smart suited woman brandishing a large tablet. Looked like she could handle it in a brawl, and all. But I wasn't bothered and we strode on past her to the door.

'Excuse me, you can't just–'

'Shut up and let us in,' I said, waving my a-codes towards the electronic locks. When all the locks sprung open, she stepped back, startled. We all entered the wax-scented, wood-lined hallway of the house. She followed us in, still spluttering.

'You… you have no right!'

'This is Federal Agent Sunday Sule,' I said, indicating the figure beside me, 'and I'm from the Airedale Justice Commission. We have a warrant to search the building. I'm just broadcasting it local, right? Check your messages again.' I nodded with a grin. 'And when you're done, tell us where Dr Godden is.'

There was a short pause as the woman scanned her tablet, before eventually nodding and composing herself.

'Very well, everything seems to be in order. How may I help, Ms Tarmell?'

'Where's the fucking doctor?'

'I'm afraid she's not at work today,' the woman said, looking furtively up the staircase.

I barged past and marched up the steps, closely followed by Sunday. Remembering where her office was, I walked straight up to the closed door, waved my delegated authorisation and stepped inside.

The room was empty.

'She not here?' asked Sunday.

I grunted and checked the door into the adjoining surgery room. Also empty.

'Fuck.' I returned to the top of the stairs. The woman below was looking up, frozen in position. 'You still there? Where's Dr Godden?'

'I don't know. She said she was taking a day off… to see a relative, I think.'

I dug the sniffer out of my pocket and returned to the office, sweeping around the space. I wasn't getting much but *BreathlessWhisper* was there. Not at the kind of levels that would excite the prosecution, though. Besides, I was starting to wonder whether more than one person had been through Abu Dhabi. The thought didn't please me.

'Fuck.'

'Anything?' asked Sunday.

'What d'you think?' I said, digging into my satchel. I pulled the gecko out and sent it scurrying around the room to find something else, anything else.

It did.

'Freeze,' I said to Sunday, who was looking through drawers at the desk.

'What? What have you found?'

I pointed to the floor near the gecko and crouched for a closer look. It was almost wholly indistinct but, at the right angle, it was clearly a footprint. Looked like the owner had been in a bit of mud lately. I let the gecko pick up the trail, and it found another, out in the middle of the office. It followed another and then another, leading us into the surgery.

'What is it?' Sunday repeated, following me.

'Shh,' I said. The gecko had stopped at the base of a wall, camera flashing all over the surface. Something banal, but unexpected, had appeared in the conceptual stream: door.

'No shit,' I said to the machine. I walked up to the wall for a closer look. Sure enough, there was a hairline crack running across one of the panels. I tried pushing and it swung open. Beyond was a dusty corridor with some antique twentieth-century stairs at the end. It looked like part of the original house, but without any of the modernist renovations. It smelt of plaster and old wood. There were many footprints coming and going along the corridor

'Oh,' said Sunday.

'Shh. Can you hear that?'

Distant sound of movement from the stairs. I quickly scooped up the gecko, before it gave us away, and stepped carefully down the corridor with Sunday following. We were quiet, if we stepped on the outside of the floorboards. We got to the stairs and descended before reaching another corridor. At the end, another modern door panel was ajar. As we approached,

Sunday's foot hit a creaky floorboard, and a voice immediately called out from beyond the door.

It was a man's voice, stressed. 'Is that you, Deidre?'

'She's on her way,' I called out, beckoning Sunday to follow, and broke into a trot.

'Who is that?' came the now frightened response.

I pushed the door open, half expecting to meet a sawn-off or a homemade pointed at my head. But instead, I saw a man crouching by a cabinet at the end of the room. He had a stack of small boxes opened on the floor in front of him.

The room was another surgery, except this had more equipment. There were about a dozen glass containers stacked around the wall. All seemingly empty, save for one containing a single lower leg and foot, the ball socket for the knee glowed eerily in the flashlight. 'Who are you?' he said, standing. Digital storage slivers scattering from is hands. 'You're not Deidre's staff? How did get in here?'

He was old, looked like he should've retired a while back, but still seemed lively. His thinning hair was dyed retro blue, and a pair of spectacles hung around his neck. I guessed they were a bead or processor of some kind, though you never could tell with some folk. Some just didn't like being messed with medically.

It didn't really matter. I recognised the face.

'Arthur Pinho?' I asked.

'And you are?' said the man.

'I'm asking the questions. Are you Arthur Pinho?'

He stuck out his chin a little. 'I would like to know who is asking the question.'

'Carrie Tarmell, forensic analyst from the Airedale Justice Commission. The gentleman over there is Sunday Sule from the Nigerian Federal Investigation Agency. He specialises in international smuggling.'

'What do you want with me?' asked the man.

'He is Arthur Pinho,' said Sunday. 'I've cross-referenced the public database. Nine-nine point seven match.'

'That's a strong match.'

'What does it matter?' said Pinho.

'Question is: why not admit it?'

'What if I am? Why are you poking around in here?'

'I was going to ask you the same thing.'

'I have business with Dr Godden,' said Pinho. 'And you?'

I smiled. 'I got a fucking search warrant, sunshine.'

'I see,' he said.

'But now that we've found you here, we were interested in having a little chat.'

'Not without my lawyers.'

'You seem interested in getting your hands on Godden's files,' I said, nodding at the slivers on the ground in front of him.

'It's my property.'

'Is it?' I asked. 'Interesting. And where is she? You seen her?'

'No, I was wondering where she was as well.'

'Oh, right. So tell me, are you friends, then?'

His eyes narrowed. 'Is this an interrogation?'

'Do you want it to be?'

He tried to sweep past me. 'I've got places to be, Ms Tarmell.'

'Oh, yeah,' I said, stepping in front of him. 'Where's that? Cos if it's with Dr Godden, I'd be interested in joining you.'

'If you attempt to restrain me, I will be calling my lawyers.'

I reached into my pocket and withdrew the cardboard package. I opened the lid and pulled out a small piece of glittering metal. It resembled a heavy, metal ring, with a thick attachment on the side. I held the device up and clicked my fingers. 'This a Swiss-made Hecle Thumbcuff, Mr Pinho,' I said. 'If I jam it onto your thumb, it will begin to read your rights. When it's finished, it will arm itself. You'll be visible on all law enforcement databases, surveillance systems, beads, whatever. If somebody believes you're running, we can apply measures. It will inject one milligram of Trezcoptim – that's a tranquilliser – and you'll get… well, about three metres before you fall on your face. If you tamper with the device, it will alert us to the fact and administer the tranq. If you decide to do summat clever with a hacksaw and your thumb, don't bother. You will be sprayed with a marker serum that'll show up at all security locations, such as an airport.'

'What?' he said incredulously, backing away. 'You're going to arrest me?'

'I've been given the cuffs, haven't I?'

He knew what that meant, because his eyes darted for the exits.

'We've got a lot on you. You supplied petrol to an arsonist, petrol to a bunch of thugs up in the Valleys, you supplied people to intercept—'

'It was all her doing,' he said, frantically.

'*She* being..?'

'Dr Godden, of course.'

'Of course,' I muttered.

'She approached me,' said Pinho. 'It was always her idea.'

'What was?'

'This,' said Pinho, waving at the surgery around us. He pointed at the leg in the jar. 'That.'

'Replacement service?'

'That's right. She needed a vat business, said it would be good for me. Lucrative even.'

I nodded. He was talking freely now, so I didn't want to mess this shit up. 'Go on.'

'So, we went into business together. But it's gone wrong. I didn't want it to be like this.'

'Like this?'

'It's all gone wrong,' he repeated.

'We need to find Godden. You and I. Do you know where she's gone?'

He blinked and thought for a moment, before shaking his head. Even without the usual interrogation algo, I could tell a lie when I smelt one.

'No idea,' he said.

Pinho was backing into the corner of the room now, hand twitching towards his spectacles.

'Go ahead, phone your lawyers. I'm sure they'd be interested in taking part in this conversation.'

'I might just do that,' he said.

'Cuffs come out then or we can keep talking?'

He hand dropped. 'I've told you everything…'

'When did you go into business with Godden?'

'About seventeen months ago.'

'Sunday,' I said, 'I've got a feeling that there would've been some interesting goings on about seventeen months ago in Pinho's life. Can you give me owt from your revenue data, Sunday?'

'I will try,' said replied. 'What are you looking for?'

'Well,' I said, quietly, 'did you know Mr Pinho, here, owns Withens? The reservoir and the hill and all that land.'

'No,' said Sunday. 'I didn't.'

'Found this out earlier from our community analyst. She knows all the gangs in that part of the Belt.'

'Why is this important?' Pinho asked.

'I'm interested in knowing what Mr Pinho purchased on Godden's behalf. Like I said, got a feeling it'll be interesting.'

Pinho looked from me to Sunday and back again. 'What are you talking about?'

'Let's wait and see,' I said.

Sunday grunted. 'Got it. What do you want to look for?'

'Show us purchases from October to November year before last.'

'Right,' said Sunday and a long list appeared in my display.

'Can we filter it anymore?'

'Filter for what?' asked Sunday, sounding increasingly impatient.

'Forget it,' I said, taking a screenshot of the data before dropping it straight into Modlee. This had probably broken a few dozen IG rules, but I didn't care anymore. Clive could kiss my arse.

'What are you doing with it?'

'Using Modlee,' I said. 'This'll find summat, it always finds the spiky nodes.'

And sure enough, it had. Highlighting one row in particular. I dragged the section highlighted – *Green Dye (SFX)* – out and threw it at Sunday.

'What's that?' asked Sunday.

'Funny purchase, that, in't it?'

'I don't understand,' said Sunday. 'Why did it pick that row out?'

'Because everything else is containers and fluids and feedstock and pipes and fucking control units. Why is a vat merchant buying a novelty dye? Because he needs to create a bit of theatre. Look here, three rows above, polymer barrels. That's what I found up at Withens. They were shooting at barrels of something that came out green. It was nowt. Summat to scare off locals, Enforcement and the like. Pinho, here, bought it for them.'

'Right,' said Sunday.

I looked back up at Pinho. 'Now, Mr Pinho, are you ready to tell me what else we might find up at Withens Reservoir?'

'Can we use your car?' I said, as we hurried back through the front gate.

'Of course,' said Sunday. 'But it's a little slow, isn't it?'

'You can get summat faster?' I asked, excitedly. 'Agency give you summat?'

Sunday shook his head. 'Not the agency, no.'

'How then?'

He smiled. 'I've got a little saved.'

'You'll do that?' I asked, about to give a little squeeze on the arm, but thought both of us would probably regret it.

He put on his glasses and nodded. 'Just give me a minute.'

It was a quick response service and a few minutes later, we

were in the air in a sleek two-person drone, swooping up into the civilian altitude above the eastern end of the Belt. Ahead of us were the skyscrapers of Leeds and, beyond, the industrial smoke amid the hills of the Buckle.

'How far to Withens?' asked Sunday.

'Which Withens, sir?' asked the drone.

'Withens Reservoir.'

'That would be—'

'We're not going to Withens yet.' I interrupted.

'We're not? But your sister…'

'I know, I know,' I said, trying not to think about it. 'But we can't just waltz in by ourselves. We need a proper plan.'

'You are beginning to sound a little like me,' said Sunday, smiling. 'So, tell me, where are we going?'

I dialled in new instructions and the drone banked south. I looked up a number and made a call.

'Debs,' I said.

'Yo,' said Deborah.

'All good?'

'Installed at your mum's,' said Deborah. 'It was a good call, Carrie. You'd need a navy to storm this place.'

'I know. Your friends going to stay there?'

'Yeah. Good. Can you help me out now?'

'Sure, what do you need?'

'You said you'd never been to the Estuary?'

'That's right,' said Deborah.

'Well, it's your lucky day.'

The shape of H Tower appeared from the mists ahead of us. I was going to enjoy arriving like this.

CHAPTER THIRTY-THREE

I edged into position along the ridgeline, a strangely familiar feeling. I wasn't sure if this was the same location we'd waited out with the Enforcement attack team with Kal Ghaz. All clumps of heather looked the same to me, but I got a view of the full length of the reservoir, the dam, and the approach road. As I waited, I munched on a packet of lentil biscuits, and rechecked Modlee. I'd set up the ratios for Dowe, Godden, and my sister, and was supposed to get an alert if they were picked up on any public camera. The only hit I received was Godden, her white face staring out of the back of an autocar, when stuck in traffic in the MC-3. Still, it was west-moving traffic, at about the right time – early this morning – so I took that as good evidence for what I'd called into action. It was all on me, this one, now that Louie and Ibrahim had washed their hands of it.

I crunched on a biscuit. 'Fuck 'em,' I muttered.

It'd gone from midafternoon murk to evening darkness. The fires and braziers were lit around the edges of the lake and along the length of the dam. Members of the three gangs were mingling and going about their business. I checked my watch. Things were about to start. I stashed the lentil biscuits in my pocket and looked back down the road. Sure enough, the lights of about five vehicles were making their way up the twisting and winding road to the reservoir, through the stumps of felled trees and abandoned shanties.

A few of the gang members on the dam had spotted the lights and a shout went up, calling people to take up defensive positions. There were a few of the old antiques and homemades handed round, which I'd expected, but still had me on edge. I didn't want anybody to get properly hurt during any of this. Well, except for a couple, of course.

'Come on,' I whispered.

I'd been checking the skyline of the hill on the other side of the reservoir every now and then. Beyond that black ridgeline a slope led down to the Fellside Recycling Auxiliary Facility and the rest of built-up Fourth Sector residential districts. The glow of orange was bright in the sky in that direction, and I was worried that any figures silhouetted against that would be instantly picked up. But they were being professional and there was no hint of movement yet.

The first of the shots were fired. I turned my attention back to the dam, using the nightsight on my scope to bring up the detail. There were a few figures around the top of the road, where it came to the parking area. They were stood with a couple of polymer handmades, shooting them off into the sky. The vehicles, now a few hundred metres short of the top, had stopped. I could see what they were: a ramshackle collection of old commercial vehicles, repurposed for their new use, with spraypainted images of woodland animal faces on the side.

Peaceful hands waved out of the passenger window of the first vehicle, and somebody shouted towards the crowd. The passenger stepped out and even from this distance, I could see the vast bulk of ThreeDave. The moment he emerged a good half of the crowd along the dam burst into a huge cheer. More guns were fired off, but I guessed in celebration rather than anger. A huge surge of people rushed down the road to embrace their returning leader.

Out of the vehicles behind, numerous others emerged. Though most came open-faced, a few still maintained their mark of affiliation in the form of plastic woodland creature masks. It was disturbing to see so many of them here and me all exposed a few hundred metres away up on a hillside, but at least I knew they were being put to good use now and not wasting their time trying to ruin my rug.

Another familiar figure emerged, jostling herself in alongside the bulk of ThreeDave. She'd already managed to procure herself something to eat and was happily chatting to some of the BoTies, without a care in the world.

'Well done, Debs,' I muttered to myself.

A call came in on my bead from Sunday.

'Are we on schedule?' he asked.

'Yeah, ThreeDave's back. All seems OK so far... ah, no, here we go.'

I could see a small circle had opened up around ThreeDave. Deborah had stepped back into the crowd. It looked like the newcomers and the BoTies were all clustering behind ThreeDave, but the ones I'd taken to be Grinsers were clustering on the other side of the circle. A new figure stepped into the ring. I took out the scope and tried to see the face: Kristy Henderson. She was gesticulating wildly, looking proper pissed off.

'It's starting. Where are you?'

'We're at the shore now. Just getting the craft in the water.'

'OK, I'll keep you updated.'

The argument down on the approach road was escalating. ThreeDave was now shouting in response, riling up his followers. Then a gunshot and fighting commenced; BoTies and Beasties against the Grinsers and XYs.

'Do we go in?' Sunday asked.

'Not yet. Wait.'

Over the next five minutes, the fighting spread out along the width of the dam and into the shanties on the slopes of the hill even onto the water. It was clear the BoTies and Beasties had the edge over the Grinsers. Kristy Henderson's people were holding out for a while, being physically pulled back into action by the woman herself. After about twenty minutes of fighting, they had to admit defeat, and scattered in all directions.

'Now,' I said.

First part of the plan complete.

I rose from my hiding place on the ridge and descended to the dam. The going was rough, and I kept stumbling, but there was sufficient ambient light – from the fires and the distant towers of the Belt – to light my way.

As I went, I spied the scene playing out below me and to the placid darkness of the lake beyond. Then I saw it; the small inflatable was now visible in the water. Making sure to select a particularly bright one, to show up on a security camera. I was hoping Sunday had managed to get the armour he'd promised to secure. They were going to be like frigging extras in a historical immersive out there otherwise.

There was complete chaos around the gang encampment. I reached into my pocket and retrieved something light and plastic, a tawny owl mask. Placing it over my face, I drew my hood over my head and passed through the heaving bodies, still brawling in the mud, or celebrating by raiding the tents and lean-tos of their former brethren.

Down the dam, I could see Kristy Henderson being held by two of ThreeDave's henchmen while he and Deborah spoke to her. There was much shouting and argument, but I could finally see the Community analyst reach out a hand and slip something over Henderson's thumb. A little icon popped up on my bead, showing locational markers and status: first arrest made.

I grunted in satisfaction and edged my way around a couple fighting in the gravel, walking briskly down the length of the dam. The control tower was dark in the distance with no sign of anything happening around it.

'Come on,' I muttered.

The small inflatable approached the end of a small metal ladder. Their presence triggered a security light and the water around the base of the tower immediately illuminated.

'Gotta see them now, you bastards,' I said to myself.

'You were correct,' said Sunday, in my ear. 'This tower is still operational. Are you going to join us?'

'Yeah,' I said.

Under the stark white light, I could clearly see the two shapes of Sunday and Chen in the inflatable. The Chinese operative seemed to be heavily tooled-up, dressed in black. Sunday hadn't changed, still dressed in his suit and scarf.

I slowed my pace. Struggling to see properly through the mask, I slipped it onto the top of my head, and pulled back my hood. I raised the scope to see the top of the tower. There was a set of broken windows around the top with a balcony, which must've once been the viewing station. The flickering of flashlights appeared from within.

'You've got company,' I reported to Sunday.

'Yes,' said Sunday, quietly. 'We are aware. They are very loud.'

The gang members were all armed and piled out onto the small balcony that encircled the platform. Clustering around the top of the ladder which lead down to the water, they trained their various weapons on the newcomers, and one started firing down the gap.

Second phase of the plan complete.

I bit my tongue and swore, but one of the figures below – probably Chen – pointed something up the gap and a gang member staggered back. I didn't know what he'd got hold of – tranq or shocksticks or illegal ballistics – but I wasn't about to find out.

One more gang member collapsed and the remaining put their hands up in surrender.

'OK,' I said to Sunday. 'I'm coming in now.'

Then there was a shout from behind me, somebody calling my name. Without thinking, I turned to see who'd shouted. A short distance back down the dam, towards the main bustle of the fighting, I could see a short figure facing me. It was a Beastie, one of the kids who had been tormenting me. It raised its rabbit mask and peered at me in the gloom. It was a young woman, possibly still a girl. She squinted, struggling to see. I gave her a grin and a thumbs up before pulling down the owl mask again and turning back to trot towards the tower. I could hear the distant scream of recognition and rage. I broke into a run.

As I refocused on the control tower, I could see Sunday returning to the boat. They seemed to have things in order, ready for my arrival.

I reached the end of the dam and turned to check behind me. There was a small group of the Beasties making their way towards me, backlit by the settlement's fires. I vaulted the dam wall and dropped onto the gravel and sand of the shore. Sunday was rowing the small inflatable over to me. I checked the tower and saw Chen slowly climbing the ladder, weapon locked on the two gang members.

'You need a ride?' asked Sunday, breathing heavily as he pushed the nose of the inflatable up the beach.

'Ta,' I said, hopping in. I now had soaking feet but I didn't care 'You alright?'

'Fine,' muttered Sunday.

He was a shit liar. 'You hit?'

'A little.'

'Fucking give me those,' I said, grabbing the oars from him. 'Where?'

'Here,' he said, pointing to his ribs on his left side.

'You want to get out here?'

Sunday looked at the crowd of Beasties who'd now reached this end of the dam and were looking over the wall at us. 'Not really.'

'Come with me then. Just don't bleed on owt, yeah?'

He grimaced and nodded. I wasn't in the mood for small talk, so I put my head down and rowed towards the tower. The Beasties behind were piling over the wall and running down to the beach, screaming insults at us. Sunday gave them a wave.

But they weren't pissed off enough to get their precious feet wet, or maybe they still believed the stories of biohazard, as they milled around the shoreline, throwing rocks.

We were presently at the base of the tower and I climbed up to the ladder.

'You need a hand?' I asked.

'I'll manage. You go ahead.'

I nodded and began to climb. The balcony was tiny and Chen had forced the gang members back into the control room itself, making them drag their fallen comrades with them. I couldn't see any obvious wounds on the two prone bodies, so I assumed they'd be OK; conscious that I was the only one with delegation here.

'Where next?' I asked Chen.

'Where's the Fed?'

'Been shot by these bastards,' I said, waving vaguely outside. 'Here.' I pressed my side.

'On his chest?' asked Chen. 'He has protection, you know?'

'He does.' I said. I called out. 'Sunday, get up here.'

In the middle of the control room was a balustraded stairwell. The stink of rotting ponds and rust and pigeon shit emerged from its depths.

I turned back to the gang members. 'Anybody want to tell me what's down there?'

Hard silence followed in return. One of them even shook his head, as if warding off ill thoughts. I sighed, stuck the gecko on my shoulder and made my way down the stairs.

'You coming, Sunday?' I shouted again.

'I'm trying,' came the response.

'Take some painkillers,' I called through the door. I nodded to Chen, 'I'm heading down there.'

'You remember the deal?' he said. 'I need access.'

'Yeah, yeah,' I said and dipped into my pocket. I pulled out a couple of cuffs and threw them at him. 'Put these on their thumbs. If they move, it'll knock 'em out.'

I headed for the stairs and descended.

It went down a long way, into the darkness. Thankfully, I had the gecko to light my way and scan for any human shapes hiding in the shadows, but it told me there were just stairs and lights and rust, all the way down.

I passed a few airlocks and viewing ports into the reservoir but there was no further sign of activity. A series of newer pipes and hoses were wound around the stairs, gently gurgling with the sound of chugging water, some of which snaked off to the edge of the tower and attached themselves to valves and outlets. Above the sound of the liquid, there was a distant hum, like an engine.

Stepping off the last of the steps into a shallow puddle of water, the thrum grew louder. A section wall in the chamber had been crudely removed by an arc weld, roughly the size of a standard door. Beyond, a short tunnel of rusting metal ran. Peering through, I carefully crept forward into what appeared to be the interior of a shipping container. I must've been beneath the reservoir itself now, able to feel the weight of the water overhead. There were a few wheeled office chairs here, their stuffing ripped out and their rotting covers. Somebody had been using an old polymer barrel in the corner to piss in and throw out old food wrappers. At the far end of the container, the full-length doors were welded shut. but a smaller integrated door looked to be in use. A hole in the corner of this door had been cut out, allowing the cluster of tubing and pipes to run through. The door was closed. I approached cautiously, stepping around the puddles and the coiling pipes.

The door was unlocked and I opened it a fraction. Crouching down to peer around, so that my head wasn't at easy striking height. They didn't teach this kind of shit in the college room overlooking the Mersey. But I liked to watch a few immersives.

The door opened directly into another shipping container. The noise grew suddenly louder. A stark single bulb hung from a hook on the ceiling. Along the long chamber walls of the chamber, four generators were running pumps for the hoses that snaked through the container. Stacks of familiar-looking petrol canisters were stacked in one corner. The door at the far end of the room was propped open. The pipes continued in, but it became harder to see beyond as the far container remained unlit.

I dropped the gecko onto the floor and sent it skittering ahead into the unlit chamber, pulling up my display to receive the feed. The machine's LEDs illuminated stacks of shelves, all containing various sized meat-growing vats. The kind of kit I'd seen up in Airedale, where a few places still grew the beef, lamb, and pork I'd eat for my supper. A few were still emblazoned with the Pinho logo.

I brought the gecko in for a closer look at the contents.

'Fuck.'

A half-grown pair of human eyes were bubbling away in the liquid. Another tank was growing a hand. There was even a neat little penis and testicles balanced on the end of the shelf.

As with the earlier chambers, there was no-one present in the room, but this time there were three other exits, all leading to further dimly lit rooms of tanks and shelves. Coils of hoses snaked all over the floor, disappearing off in different directions.

I carefully stepped through the door and joined the gecko in the chamber. I wasn't bothered by the meat in jars – I'd seen worse, to be fair – but I wasn't keen on the number of maze-like chambers. Which made it all too easy for anybody I found to escape or slip around behind me.

'Fuck this,' I muttered, clearing my throat and trying a more direct approach. 'Dr Godden!'

There was no answer.

'I've got an arrest warrant for you… for you, and Djin Dowe. I know Dowe's here somewhere as well.'

There was no response, only the inert bubbling and gurgling of the tanks around me.

Instructing the gecko to remain in this chamber to cover the exits, I randomly selected the left-hand door, and stepped through into the next container. Another door lead to the right and I could see beyond into a further chamber. Peering into the murk, an obvious figure stepped into the shadows, disappearing from view.

'Dr Godden?' I shouted. 'Djin, is that you?'

No answer came. I checked the gecko feed, but nothing was happening there.

So I proceeded into the next chamber where another door opened to the right.

In the distance, came the sound of plastic smashing. The feed from the gecko crackled to black.

'Shit,' I whispered.

I wondered whether I should return to the first chamber. Whoever or whatever had destroyed the gecko could've made a run for it by now. Whatever happened, I needed to find Grace, so decided to carry on.

Stepping through to the next chamber, I felt a light breath of air pass by my face, immediately followed by a deafening explosion.

Knocked to the ground, but avoiding injury, I scrabbled under the nearest set of shelves. Reservoir water spurted in through a newly rendered hole in the wall behind me.

'You wanna fucking drown us?' I screamed.

There was a long silence. I could hear nothing but the gushing water. Swearing in whispers, I rose to my feet and ran through to another chamber. There was nobody there and I was furious now. I stopped in the middle, not really caring whether I was shot. I noticed what seemed like a near complete body growing in a larger tank, headless and without feet. Whoever was responsible for this laboratory was going down for serious time.

'This is Forensic Analyst Carrie Tarmell of the Airedale Justice Commission. I have a warrant for your arrest and a whole fucking Enforcement Division up top.'

Sounds came from the next chamber and I cautiously opened the door. Tanks and shelves filled the room like all the others, but at the centre, tied back-to-back to a pair of chairs, were the recognisable shapes of Dr Godden and Grace; both gagged. Godden's face was bloodied, as if struck by a blunt instrument. She groggily raised her head, noticing movement and blinked at me. Grace's back was to me, slumped forward, so I couldn't see her face, but I could still hear her breathing. There was nobody else there.

I stepped through the door, towards them, causing Godden's eyebrows to raise and she started to mumble behind her gag, which sharply rose to a shriek. I stopped dead in my tracks.

Movement in my peripheral vision caught my attention and I half-turned. A figure hurled themselves at me, hooked a foot around my ankle, and shoved me to the ground. My head struck the steel floor with a light splash into rapidly pooling water. I was thankful for the bobble hat, which took the brunt of the blow.

'Fuck.'

The figure had disappeared, and despite twisting my head around, I was unable to see them. I tried to stand but my feet slid on the floor, failing to get a grip, and my now sodden coat a huge weight in my back. Disorientated, I wasn't ready for when the figure re-appeared, but I could see who it was now: Djin Dowe, all in black with her hair tied into a braided bun. She leaped from the corner, twisting in the air, and elbowed me savagely in my injured shoulder. I screamed and fell back, bashing my head on the side of a nearby shelf, before landing face down in a puddle. I felt a hand firmly pushing my face into the water and another thump landed in the wound in my shoulder. I screamed and choked in the water, but managed to lash out with my legs, and bring Dowe crashing to the floor. I rolled away, swearing.

'I got delegation,' I screamed at her. 'You know how much shit you're in?'

Dowe's eyes were wide, breathing heavily, but she didn't answer. Instead, she leaped at me again. I fell under her blows, as she continued to pummel my face and shoulder.

I noticed my satchel beside me, with possibly a few crawlers left in. I swung it around and it smacked Dowe on the side of the head. It didn't seem to hurt her but distracted her enough to get an elbow out and jam it into her throat. She rolled back, gasping and I scrabbled back to my feet. Using the momentum, I grabbed the nearest vat – I think it must've contained a leg – and wrenched it hard onto her head. Knocked clean off her feet, she collapsed into the mess at the bottom of the container. I leapt onto her, with her hand feeling for my throat, finding it and then tightening. I couldn't breathe, but had my good hand free, and I dug into my coat pocket, found the package and retrieved a cuff. I pulled it out and reached up to her hands around my throat, trying to slip it on. She realised what I was doing and pushed me away. I rolled to my side, almost knocking a whole shelf of vats onto myself. The cuff clinked loudly on the floor on the container, then rolled away underneath a shelf.

As I was scrabbling in the water, her foot connected with my head, rocking me back like an upturned turtle. She was on me again, hands at my throat. The pain receded under the adrenalin rush. I stuck my hand back in my pocket. But the package wasn't there anymore. My hand felt around me on the floor, looking for something I could use. It bumped up against the slipperiness of a cold disembodied ankle. I grabbed the half-grown limb and brought it hard into Dowe's face. I whacked her again and tried a third time, but it slipped out of my fingers and out of reach. She swore at me, tightening her grip, but she'd been distracted enough to lose her balance a little, so I could shunt her over to one side. She crashed into a shelf and managed to dislodge a vat, which fell, painfully slowly, and cracked her viciously on the side of the head. Woozily, she released her hold on my neck, and I could push myself back and out of her way.

My hand met the soggy cardboard package with the cuffs. I

grabbed it and pulled out a cuff, then lunged forward, wrestling her wrist with my right hand and – whimpering at the pain – slammed the cuff onto her thumb with my bad hand.

'What is this?' she muttered, staring at the cuff. Dowe attempted to hoist herself up from the floor, but I kicked her joyously in the chest and she collapsed back down.

'You move more than three metres,' I gasped, clawing back a breath, 'and that ring'll dump enough tranq into your bloodstream to knock you out in under five seconds. Less, probably, given you're a little 'un, like me. Or I can hit the command to bring you down right now. Your choice.'

With one lithe movement, Dowe reached under a nearby shelf and brought out a thin hunting rifle. I immediately recognised it. Dowe pointed the barrel at Grace's head, standing up as she did so.

'Guessing I'll have time to pull a trigger before you hit that button?' she said. 'You want to kill your sister?'

I'd assumed Grace had been unconscious the whole time, but it seemed she'd just been acting, like a professional, as she spoke now. 'That won't work. Carrie's not actually my sister.'

'What?' said Dowe.

'Shoot me if you like,' said Grace, 'doesn't matter.'

'Grace,' I growled.

'She's not my sister,' repeated Grace. 'So, I wouldn't try that angle. She'll not listen to you. She fights dirty. Always has done.'

Dowe looked up at me.

'She's right. I don't give a shit if you shoot Grace. She's always been piss irritating my whole life. Go on.'

'Like I said,' Grace said. 'She doesn't care.'

Dowe looked from me to Grace and then back again, confused. 'Fine,' she said and pointed the gun at me. 'I kill you first. How about that?'

Grace's mouth clamped up at this point.

'This is fun and all, Djin,' I said. 'But it's probably time you put down that little toy. Let yourself get arrested nice and quiet, yeah?'

'Why on earth would I do that?'

'Cos I've worked out, like a proper forensic analyst, that that particular weapon, an SHD55, sometimes called a Frosty – due to its coolant mechanism – can take up to a maximum of four rounds. I'm guessing this was inherited from the time when you and the good Doctor Godden were working for the Shenzhen-based corporation, FFRC. And that you don't have the ammo to keep it going. Am I right?'

'You been counting my shots?' laughed Dowe.

'No, it's simpler than that. I'm working on the fact you didn't shoot me dead when I stepped in here.' I hit record on my bead. 'Djin Dowe, you're under arrest for the murder of Denpo Shin.' I paused. 'That's it. You've been arrested. Now listen to the little voice as it reads you your rights.' I got the little cuff to reel out the rest. During the entire speech, she kept staring at the device and then up at me. When it finished, she carefully put down the rifle on a nearby shelf, shaking her head.

'Murder?' she said.

'Yeah.'

'Mr Shin?'

'Yeah.'

Dowe laughed. 'It's not murder if he's not dead.'

'What do you mean?' I asked, unnerved.

'He's not dead.'

'He fucking is. You burned his body.'

Dowe looked across at Godden. 'If you let her go, she's going to kill him.'

I heaved myself over to the two chairs, every step sending jagged waves of pain up into my shoulder. First, I pulled the gag from Godden's mouth and then I gave Grace a little squeeze on the shoulder. She grunted.

'What's she talking about?' I asked Godden. The doctor refused to answer and looked away.

'She wanted me to kill him,' said Dowe. 'Made me take him apart.'

'Djin,' said Godden, warningly. 'Just stop–'

'She wanted me to take back what he'd stolen from her, from the business.'

'Don't listen to her,' Godden cried.

'He was all I had left,' said Djin, rising.

'You had me,' Godden bargained. 'You always had me.'

'Don't let her go,' said Dowe, looking at me. 'Don't let her go.'

Godden looked up at me. 'Well, aren't you going to untie me?'

I felt suddenly weary. I tried to shrug the duffel coat off my shoulder. It wasn't coming easily.

'Do you want me to help you?' asked Godden.

'Nah, I'm alright,' I muttered. I wasn't. The pain was making beads of sweat form under the rim of my bobble hat.

'You're not going to untie me?' asked an anxious Godden.

'Not yet,' I muttered. The coat had come off and was now on the floor.

'Are you going to arrest me as well?'

'Yeah,' I said, wondering whether she'd any painkillers on her; being a doctor, and all.

'Everything OK in here?'

I turned around and saw Chen, poking his head around the door.

'Yeah, we're fine,' I said.

'Very good,' he said, tapping on a small bead and processor to the side of his temple. I'd seen them before on military immersives. This was some top-end hardware. This was going to record the scene and sweep up any data available in any nearby storage.

'You going to follow East Pennine IG regulations, with that?' I asked, nodding at Chen.

He just laughed and continued scanning the room. As he entered, I could see Godden and Dowe both shrink away from him. But he ignored them and, instead, moved and slowly gather data from the tanks' inbuilt storage.

'How's Sunday?' I asked.

'He's fine,' said Chen. 'Your friend… Deborah, is it? She's with him.'

'Good. You'll not be back, I assume?'

'I doubt it,' he said, finishing his log of the room's contents before giving me a solemn nod as he stood in the doorway. 'I'm done now.'

'Grand.'

He finally turned to look at Dowe. Face neutral but I thought I could see a little blink of the eye, possibly a tear. 'So, you decided to betray the company, as well?'

Dowe was silent.

'They spent a lot of money on you,' he said.

'They betrayed me,' Dowe cursed. 'They were going to let me die.'

'Did she look after you better?' said Chen, indicating Godden.

Dowe remained tight-lipped.

'She was never your mother, and Denpo was never your father.'

'Don't talk about him,' Dowe hissed, voice breaking. 'I know he wasn't my father.'

'Well,' said Chen, 'I don't speak for the company, and I hold no responsibility, but I will say I am sorry for the situation you found yourself.' He cast his eye briefly to Godden.

'I never asked him to bring me up,' said Dowe, starting to cry. 'I never wanted any of this.'

Chen nodded and then was gone.

'Who on earth was that?' asked Godden, eyes wide.

I was unable to control a snort of laugh. 'Right.'

'Are you going to let me go?' Godden demanded. 'I can help you with that shoulder again?'

'Sure,' I said. 'But you'll be getting a cuff as well.'

'What for?' she asked, eyes stark. 'You've got a confession, haven't you?'

'You're under arrest for provision of a human limb replacement service,' I said.

Godden shrugged and presented her thumb with a sigh. 'You'll be speaking to my lawyers.'

Cuff went on smoothly and I nodded as it started to recite the rights. As it droned away, I rummaged around and found a knife on the shelves and cut away the cable ties around both Godden and Grace. Grace stood up, giving me a half smile. When I got to Godden, the doctor stood, and rubbed her wrists.

'Thanks,' said Grace.

'No bother. Sorry about…' I looked around at the mess.

Grace shrugged. 'I didn't mean what I said, you know.'

Before I could respond, I noticed Godden had stepped slowly down towards the far end of the shipping container.

'Hey, no wandering off.'

'Stop her,' screamed Dowe, scrabbling to her feet. She got a couple of steps before the cuff did its business and she fell onto her knees. 'Stop her,' she repeated, her voice trailing off. She fell forward into a shallow puddle of water.

I stumbled after Godden, trying desperately to get my hands to work so I could call up the required instructions on her cuff.

'She's going to kill him,' mumbled Dowe, behind me, the final word slurred into a dribbling silence.

Godden had reached the end of the shelving unit and was reaching up to get to a vat right on the top shelf. On my display, I'd got to the menu for her cuff. I hit the tranq button. Godden cried out and fell back.

I reached her and caught her slumping form, protecting her head from crashing into the shelves behind. Then I looked up. Floating in a vat, on the top of the shelf, pushed back and out of sight, was the head of an old man with scraggly greying hair and a small mouth, widening into a scream.

CHAPTER THIRTY-FOUR

'Well, the digital package is there,' said Sunday, face hovering on my bead display, 'if you wish to make use of it.'

'You're giving it to me?' I asked, eyes flickering across my display to the little icon pulsing in the bottom corner.

'Not give,' said Sunday. 'It is a loan, a time-limited gift. And strictly outside of protocol.'

'They're the best gifts.'

'You haven't got long to decide. And the other question — what about that? Have you decided?'

I watched a young girl expertly steering a powered wheelchair past me and into the building. 'Can I think about it?'

'Yes. Only, I've got about ten minutes before I board. *I'll take that one, please.*'

'Where are you?'

'In a shop, attempting to buy a gift… thank you, I'll take that one.'

'What're you buying?'

'A sheep,' said Sunday.

'A sheep?'

'A toy, for my niece. *Thank you.*'

'Oh, right,' I said, listening to him complete whatever transaction he was struggling with. When he'd finished, and the background noise had dissipated, I asked him another question. One that had been troubling me a little. 'Have you had any contact from Chen's people?'

'Not me directly, no.'

'Your agency then? In Lagos? Have they had trouble?'

'No. When did you last see him?'

'Yesterday. Escorted him off the premises with his squad of lawyers.'

'They'd sent a few?'

'Seven.'

Sunday laughed. 'Just making sure. I would not want to be in his shoes right now.'

'No,' I said, wanting to get off the call and into the building, but I found myself enjoying this one last chat. 'So, is it snowing there?'

'Yes, a little.'

'Bet you're glad to see the back of that? Get back to your… whatever it is you live in? That Oko pod, or summat?'

'It is an Okon module,' said Sunday. 'And, yes, I will welcome the heat. But, on reflection, I will also miss this place. And the people, especially.'

'Well, we won't miss you,' I said.

'I understand that,' said Sunday, sounding as though he actually did.

I took a breath. 'Look, ta for all your help.'

'I am not sure I did much.'

'I reckon you did.'

'Well, thank you, as well.'

'No bother.' I felt suddenly tired and a little cold. Dreading going inside.

'And where are you?'

I waved my hand at the automatic sensor. 'Calderdale.'

'The hospital?'

'Yeah, that's right.'

'The pathology department?'

'I'm not sure.' I didn't want to let on what I was hoping to see.

'Sorry to interrupt. I think they're calling out…'

I could hear some announcement in the background. 'Yeah. You go fly somewhere hotter, yeah?'

'I'll let you go now, Carrie Tarmell,' he said. 'But let me know your answer.'

'I will, Sunday Sule. I will. Bye and have a good flight.'

I stood in the middle of the low-ceiled lobby in the hospital's entrance. A large queue of patients waiting for today's free treatments were snaking around columns and seats. I tried to step around them, as I waited to be taken up by the doctor. But he was already waiting for me, deeply tanned beneath wild white hair, about a foot shorter than I'd imagined from seeing him on screen.

'Carrie!'

'That's me.'

'You ready?' Dr Hausman asked, clapping me on the shoulder. But I didn't mind.

'Yeah. It's going to be gross?'

'You're forensics, aren't you?' he said, striding off.

'So?'

He smiled. 'Follow me, Carrie.'

We made our way through the entrance before going deeper into the warren of buildings and basements. Dr Hausman was surprisingly fast for somebody of his age, while I was puffing a little after a few minutes. We passed through various security areas, and past the pathology departments, and the morgue I'd previously visited. Then into other areas of the hospital where the crowds thinned. Until just the doctor and I were rising in a pristine lift to the top of a corner of the main building.

'Where're we going?'

'Transplants,' said Dr Hausman. 'Specialist transplants.'

'Oh.'

'It's all rather exciting. You know? I'd not been to this part of the building before. Until our new arrival.'

The lift doors opened, and we stepped out into a corridor. The doctor hopped away to his left, and I followed. A few clinicians were walking the corridors, some talking quietly at a reception area ahead of us. We passed through without a nod, finally entering a darkened room at the end, its walls taken up with multiple jars, all bubbling away. The room's smell was like nothing I'd smelled before; like a newborn baby and freshly dead corpse, chemical and organic, all rolled into one. Most of all, it was cold.

Each of the jars contained something meaty. A piece of human being. All organs. Most I recognised, having seen the inner workings of people on the outside every now and again. The difference between what I'd seen in the daily routine of work and what I witnessed here were that these body parts and human musculature, were still alive. Kind of.

'Where is he?' I asked.

'Down here,' said Dr Hausman, standing before a large cupboard. He gently opened the doors to reveal a deep, red-lit shelf. Inside, a glass bowl with multiple cables snaked in and out in a bubbling exchange of liquids.

'He can't hear us, can he?' I whispered.

Dr Hausman laughed. 'He has no conscious senses at the moment. He's been given a continuous cocktail of drugs to keep him in that state. If he awoke, you could imagine what the experience would be like. He would be driven instantly insane and would most likely die.'

'Is he already… I mean, have they damaged him too much?' I whispered.

'Let's talk outside.'

Dr Hausman carefully closed the door and stepped back out of the darkened room to the corridor. There was a full-length glass window which opened out over the Buckle. It looked west, towards the hills which climbed to the slopes of the Pennine ridge. Just visible, if you knew what you were looking for, was the meandering line of the Calder River itself, as it came down from its valley in the hills, evidenced by the low buildings which betrayed its presence below. Somewhere up there, possibly visible, possibly in my imagination, I thought I could see the top of the Withens hill, and the edge of the

Fellside Recycling Auxiliary Facility nestled at its foot.

'How long has he got?'

'It's possibly already too late.' The doctor leaned on the window and looked out. 'These things need to be done fast, if they're done at all. God alone knows what that Godden woman was thinking she could do by keeping him.'

'I don't think it was her,' I said, remembering the look on Djin's face. 'At least, I think she liked the thought of him being there, out of action. She wasn't in a hurry to do anything about it. She'd plenty of opportunity to do summat.' I remembered the Bladester images of Simon West on the table with the blood beneath its feet.

'You ever worked out what he was doing?' asked the doctor.

'Who? Mr Shin?'

'Yes. With all the additions, the new legs and arms and the like.'

I shook my head. 'No idea. Katta Jenkins, you know, the one he worked with, said that he had issues with his walking and his back. But I don't know if that was before or after he started playing with that military stitcher.'

'There are always improvements one can make,' said Dr Hausman, glancing down at his paunch sadly.

I turned back from the view and looked at the closed door. 'So, he's still stuck in there?'

'I beg your pardon?'

'Mr Shin. They're not trying to find him a body? Sew him back together?'

Dr Hausman made a face that suggested he'd really wanted Mr Shin to be given a new body, but that it was massively out of his control.

'He's not getting one, is he?' I asked. 'I mean, if it's about a donor, I can rustle up something, every day on my rounds, I've–'

He stopped me with a raised hand. 'It's not about a donor, Carrie.'

'You could've done it, couldn't you? I mean, it were possible?'

'Well, not me,' he said quickly. 'This is not my area at all.'

'But somebody could've. That's why we're here, in the transplants.

'It's been done before,' said the doctor. 'But it's expensive. Very expensive.'

'Too expensive for a publicly funded service in the Fourth Sector of the Belt?'

The doctor nodded. 'Of course.'

'So, he doesn't get to live?'

He regarded me through thinned lips. 'You understand the psychological risks involved with an operation like this?'

'Like I said, I can get a suitable donor.'

'Be that as it may,' said Dr Hausman. 'But it would be in the wrong place.'

'What do you mean?'

'We can't do that kind of thing here,' said Dr Hausman. 'We don't have the facilities. He'd need to be in Beijing or Berlin, or somewhere like that. Not in the Belt.'

'Chose the wrong place to die, didn't he?' I said, trying to laugh, but failing.

'He's not dead yet, Carrie,' said Dr Hausman.

Images of the bubbling tank and the closed eyes and scraggly hair, of an old man who had wanted to be something different. 'Is that why you wanted me to be here? To give you… I don't know, permission, or summat?'

'Something like that. I mean, not officially. Officially, that's done elsewhere.'

'Then they get to decide. Not me. It's not like I'm family or owt.'

'I wanted to give you the opportunity, though,' said Dr Hausman.

I felt tears well up in my eyes. 'You're a fucking bastard.'

'I know. And I'm too fat. And I go on too many cruises as well.'

I snorted. 'You do.' Dr Hausman waited for me to continue and I blew my nose. 'You're not going to make me do this.'

'I wanted you to have the chance. At least to see him one last time.'

'Done that then,' I said, turning away and heading down the corridor to the lift.

'So?' called out the doctor.

'Pull the fucking plug and pay for a proper fucking funeral.'

I sat in a cubicle in the toilets, while around me the chatter of various voices covered the ragged and hot breaths of my weeping. I didn't enjoy using the public loos; normally because somebody like Jizzi Rey would come and do one of his horrific shits less than a metre from your nose. My mum'd told me, apparently, you used to have completely separate men's and women's toilets in the past. Sounded weird, but then they were like that back then. And when Jizzi heaved himself into a cubicle next to you, you'd sign up to any legislation sufficient to condemn him to a different room. Different country, if you could.

But right now, I needed the space and so, when I'd controlled the tears sufficiently, I plugged in some music, pulled up my bead, and tried to cut out the noises from around me. The icon with the database Sunday had loaned me was sitting there, pulsing subtly in the corner of my display. I dragged it to the centre and tapped it open. DidNotArrive had already found the connectors, and a message emerged from the background with fresh data. I opened the app and it generated a new space for me. The project, the Me Project, was there, in the recent files folder. I pulled it open and viewed the outputs. There were close to a thousand different faces now. The possible faces of who'd made me. I'd managed to stitch at least half of them onto the blanket now. There were still many to go. Because the app couldn't access to the full data mountains, so it would never achieve a true match, and yet it had managed to generate possibilities. Every possible combination leading to me. Too many possible parents.

However, Sunday had just given me the keys to the final chamber. The place where I didn't need to rely on possibility, where I'd find certainty and answers. I unlocked the fucker and let the data speak.

In milliseconds, it spat out two names: Mary Klang, *Missouri*; Kris Lopes, *Sao Paulo*.

That was it. I hit the "More Info" button and could see their faces alongside their names. She was smiling in her picture, beneath an unruly stack of strawberry-blonde curls, in front of some kind of shrub. It looked hot there, sweaty. He was in a city centre, trying to smile, but seemed a combination of troubled, nervous, and shy by having his picture taken.

I hit the database again and searched for more history about them. Seemed they were both still alive, though much older now. He'd set up and run a business replacing the gears in automated loaders and was now retired, with a family of children and grandchildren. She was still working as an estate agent, had tried running for local government. I kept scrolling through, more and more info, anything I could find. The dates they'd donated their respective cellular gifts to the world, again and again and again.

Then I saw the number of offspring they had, possibly unknowingly, brought into the world: forty-five of us specimens were still alive. A whole cast of sisters and brothers.

Something cleared in my head, the nagging worry had gone, the mental biting of the inside lip, the uncertainty. Now it was clear. It was also bleak, like a freezing cold morning in February, when the wind is chill from the east. But the sun is shining, and the world is clear.

I gently swiped the images from my display.

Instructions from Sunday Sule popped onto my screen. The bastard had given me a timed reminder. It was probably going to keep popping up there every five minutes until I died. But he knew what he was doing, and I didn't want to get him in trouble.

I deleted the data links and results, running a deepwipe app.

My fingers hovered in the air before I deleted the project file itself, but then I squeezed, and dropped with my fingers to confirm. And the thousand faces disappeared. I'd not finished the blanket. But it didn't really matter anymore.

Wiping tears from eyes, I stood up, and walked straight out of the building.

Returning to the H Tower was odd. It felt busier on the Justice Division floors today. There were the same number of uniformed Enforcement types marching in step around the place, but there were more people like me, hanging about in their grubby clothes, looking perplexed or bored or just plain pissed off. Justice analysts.

'Carrie,' yelled a familiar voice from behind me.

I turned to see Louie at the other end of the floor, coming out of the kitchen area, grasping a beaker of something hot. I waved back and meandered my way around the elaborately curved hotdesk areas to join him. We both grabbed a seat in a secure – but disconcertingly transparent – cubicle and stared at the new faces milling around outside.

'So, they were all clean, after all?' I asked.

Louie grimaced. 'Well, they're all back. I don't know what that means. Possibly means they were clean. Possibly means the Servants couldn't hack the backlog. Read it as you will.'

'Possibly means somebody paid somebody else a lot of money?'

'I'm a DI, so I can't expect to comment on that kind of supposition, Carrie.'

I was at once pleased to see that he'd got back his sense of being Louie. And also irritated, because Louie being Louie was immensely irritating.

'Guess an analyst can say what they want.'

'You sent in your primary?' he asked, sipping his tea. It smelt of something exotic, like it was from somewhere hot. Where I was supposed to be.

'Finishing it off.'

'Can't call it murder, I saw.'

'That's right,' I said. 'Lawyers're just working out what it is they can call it. It's as good as murder, in my book. But not in theirs. So, we'll see what they come up with.'

'Something serious, I hope?' said Louie.

'Is dismemberment a criminal offence?'

'Guessing so.'

'You could write the primary for me?' I suggested, looking at him. 'You are the DI, after all. You're supposed to be doing summat.'

'I've got other shit to deal with,' he said, staring at his tea.

'Is that what being a DI's like then?'

'Pretty much,' he said, looking up at me. The old Louie was still there.

'I mean, for what it's worth, coming from somebody like me, I think you're doing a cracking job, Louie.'

There was something in the smile he gave me that suggested he'd been waiting for somebody to say that for most of his life. Or, at least, at some point in the past month.

'Cheers,' he said.

'Don't let it go to your head. Don't want you swanning around Shipley thinking you're all that. Assuming you're heading back?'

'Yeah.'

'Thought so.'

'You hanging around for a while, then?' asked Louie.

'Yeah, I was going to stay at my sister's for a bit. Help her tidy up, get her place in order. Then we were thinking about taking a holiday over at Mum's place. Perhaps try to encourage her to shift off the bloody island.'

'Really?'

'Probably not.'

'And work?'

'Might help out down here and all. Got a few cases to finish. So, yeah, a bit of time.'

'Enough time for them to do a proper deep clean your flat?' asked Louie, grinning.

I turned to him, a little concerned. 'Why? What's happened at my flat?'

'I meant, if it's in current state, it'll need it, yeah?'

'Ah, shut up. My flat's plenty clean enough.'

'It isn't.'

'You're too precious. Anyway, are you heading back today?'

Louie pointed subtly at a thin woman setting out some pictures of her children on her desk, across the other side of the room. 'That's Carmel Rindi, over there. She's the one I replaced on a temporary basis. So, not really needed down here anymore.'

'Back to Airedale then.'

'Kinda,' said Louie, sipping his tea. But he had that face on; the one that wants you to ask him a follow-up.

'What?' I said.

He smiled gratefully. 'Ask me where I'm going to live?'

'Where are you going to live?'

'Well,' said Louie, drawing it out, 'mainly Manchester, from now on.'

'Really? You and Barry?'

'That's right. Seemed I apologised enough. Back on. Back in.'

'Well done. See, I always said, it pays to grovel and apologise.'

'You've never said shit all like that,' said Louie.

'Whatever.'

Louie looked up from his drink and took a sip. He cleared his throat. 'Oh, I forgot. Sunday Sule called me earlier today. Said he wanted to offer you a position.'

'I know.'

'Oh, right.' He looked dead nervous.

'He told me at the airport, just before he left.'

'A position in Lagos?'

I smiled. 'Yeah. Working the lagoon. He said there were an opening in the feds. Is that what he told you?'

Louie nodded. 'Said he could get you a job doing forensics across the narco networks. Working the high-end pods.'

'High end pods?'

'Yeah. That's what he said. Made it sound dead nice.'

I thought of heat and lagoons and sea grass farms and swimming with turtles and coming back to my Okon module. It looked amazing in my head.

'Nah.' I finished my drink as well and stood. 'Not for me. What we got?'

'I don't know,' said Louie. 'You'll need to check your messages from Carmel from now on.'

I pulled up my display and had a look at some POs.

'You got some?' he asked.

I grunted. 'Freddie Hilam's been found, most of his face missing, in the quiet end of the Bradford canals.'

'That'll be Grinsers then.'

'Yeah.'

'Can I have a look?' asked Louie.

'Analysts never stop being analysts. Even when they're a bloody DI.' I shared my screen briefly.

'Cheers.' Then Louie grunted. 'I see that Deborah Goolagong-Maloney's leading on it?'

I nodded. 'Only fair.'

Louie nodded as well. 'Yeah, she knows the area. Knows the people. Could probably tell you right now who did it.'

'Right,' I said, grimacing. 'I'll be on my way then.' I grabbed my satchel, pulled on my coat, and headed for the door. Thought I'd grab some breakfast as well, maybe some porridge. I was pretty sure I knew which one Deborah liked.

NORTHODOX PRESS

SUBMISSIONS

CONTEMPORARY
CRIME & THRILLER
FANTASY
LGBTQ+
ROMANCE
YOUNG ADULT
SCI-FI & HORROR
HISTORICAL
LITERARY

SUBMISSIONS@NORTHODOX.CO.UK

NORTHODOX PRESS

SUBMISSIONS

← → C Q *Northodox.co.uk*

CALLING ALL
NORTHERN AUTHORS!

DO YOU LIVE IN OR COME FROM NORTHERN ENGLAND?

DO YOU HAVE AN INTERESTING STORY TO TELL?

Email *submissions@northodox.co.uk*

☐ The first 3 chapters OR 5,000 words

☐ *1 page synopsis*

☐ *Author bio (tell us where you're based)*

* No non-fiction, poetry, or memoirs

SUBMISSIONS@NORTHODOX.CO.UK

FIND US ON SOCIAL MEDIA

www.northodox.co.uk

@northodoxpress

@northodoxpressofficial

@northodoxpress

@northodoxpress

www.northodox.co.uk

VALERIYA SALT

DIVE BEYOND ETERNITY

A SCI-FI THRILLER

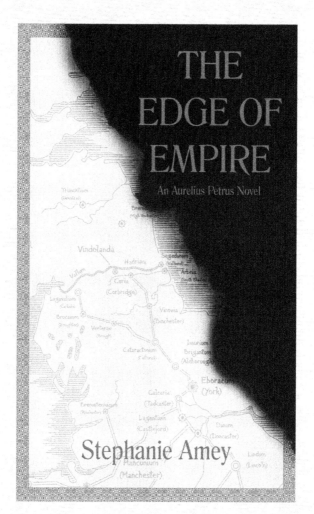

THE
EDGE OF
EMPIRE

An Aurelius Petrus Novel

Stephanie Amey

Printed in Great Britain
by Amazon